"For fans of Brit Bennett's *The Vanishing Half* and Charmaine Wilkerson's *Black Cake*, Charlene Carr's latest is both a charged emotional epic and a gentle exploration of the nuances of love. Motherhood, autonomy, race, politics, grief—every brushstroke works to paint a complex and important picture of the world as it is, and as it could be. This novel is sure to inspire book club discussion and personal reflection, and to stay on your mind long after the final page is turned. Truly a can't-miss read!" —MARISSA STAPLEY, *New York Times* bestselling author of *Lucky*

"Charlene Carr's eye for examining life's most complicated spaces is at its sharpest in this frank, fearless reflection on race, identity, and parenthood. Spanning generations and brimming with family secrets, *We Rip the World Apart* is page-turning and propulsive, heartbreaking and hopeful in turn. An important and necessary book that will stay with me for a long time." —SHELBY VAN PELT, *New York Times* bestselling author of *Remarkably Bright Creatures*

"Intimate and epic. Charlene Carr crafts a sweeping portrait of motherhood and a woman's right to choose across three generations of a Jamaican-Canadian family overcoming generational trauma. *We Rip the World Apart* explores the experiences of interracial couples and their biracial children, telling a nuanced tale of hurt and hope, all about finding yourself and your community." —WILLIAM PING, author of *Hollow Bamboo*

"Charlene Carr's deep dive into the complexities of race and belonging force, in the gentlest of ways, all of us to confront our own role in making the world a safer place. Carr's exploration of unresolved grief and the impact on family is one we need to hear; one we need to understand. A story of family and the decisions we make, *We Rip the World Apart* is a truly human exploration full of doubt, regret, and most importantly, love. A remarkable story from a remarkable storyteller."
—AMANDA PETERS, bestselling author of *The Berry Pickers*

"The novel has the raw feel of a protest, while retaining the heart that sees a family keep trying to connect despite generations of trauma. Moving, intelligent, and complex, it deftly explores our struggle to understand even those who are closest to us, the different types of violence we perpetrate on one another, the identities we fight against and the ones we choose to project, and the different ways in which we cope and respond, despite our uncertainty that any of our choices are the correct ones. The novel is at times a raised fist, at others a much-needed embrace." —CRAIG SHREVE, author of *The African Samurai*

WE RIP

the

WORLD APART

ALSO BY

Charlene Carr

A NEW START SERIES

When Comes the Joy

Where There Is Life

By What We Love

Forever in My Heart

Whispers of Hope

BEHIND OUR LIVES TRILOGY

Behind Our Lives

What We See

The Stories We Tell

STANDALONES

Beneath the Silence

Before I Knew You: A Novella

Hold My Girl

WE RIP
the
WORLD
APART

Charlene Carr

MLP

Copyright © Charlene Carr, 2024

The right of Charlene Carr to be identified as the Author of the
Work has been asserted by them in accordance with the
Copyright, Designs and Patents Act 1988.

First published in Great Britain in 2024 by
Mountain Leopard Press
An imprint of HEADLINE PUBLISHING GROUP

1

Apart from any use permitted under UK copyright law, this publication may
only be reproduced, stored, or transmitted, in any form, or by any means, with prior
permission in writing of the publishers or, in the case of reprographic production,
in accordance with the terms of licences issued by the Copyright Licensing Agency.

All characters in this publication are fictitious and any resemblance
to real persons, living or dead, is purely coincidental.

Cataloguing in Publication Data is available from the British Library

Trade paperback ISBN: 978 1 80279 545 5

Offset in 12.5/18 pt Adobe Garamond Pro by Jouve (UK), Milton Keynes

Printed and bound in Great Britain by Clays Ltd, Elcograf S.p.A.

Headline's policy is to use papers that are natural, renewable and recyclable
products and made from wood grown in well-managed forests and other
controlled sources. The logging and manufacturing processes are expected
to conform to the environmental regulations of the country of origin.

HEADLINE PUBLISHING GROUP
An Hachette UK Company
Carmelite House
50 Victoria Embankment
London EC4Y 0DZ

www.headline.co.uk
www.hachette.co.uk

For my grandmother Violet, who died before I was even a thought. It was wondering about your life, who you may have been and what my parents' and family's lives may have been like if you were with us, that led to the first inklings of this story.

And for my father: you lost your mother when you were so young you have no stories to tell, only a few scant memories, along with the sense, at times, that seeing me gives you glimpses of her.

This novel portrays scenarios that are deeply disturbing and highlight some of the worst beliefs and behaviours of our society, particularly in relation to racial and physical violence. Please be kind to yourself as you read. Set the book aside or speak with someone you trust if you need time or help to process your emotions.

NOTE: When Kareela refers to "Brown" people in the novel, the word denotes not physical colour, but origin: people of African descent who more recently have emigrated from the Caribbean (or "West Indies"), and who, in the community I grew up in, which would be similar to that of my characters, thought of that term as an acknowledgement of cultural connection and a natural way to differentiate themselves from Black people not from the Caribbean.

Kareela

A small wave undulates in the depths of my abdomen as I sink to the edge of the tub. Phone in hand, I stare at the lighted screen, at numbers in little boxes that seem like they can't be true but are. The wave, almost imperceptible, ripples again—not nausea, but something else. Expansion. The body making room. I'd read about this during a scare six or seven years ago. My first year in uni, weeks after a night I'd drunk to excess, gone home with a stranger, then felt the sheer relief when the twenty-five-dollar test stick revealed a single bright line.

I scroll back through the calendar in front of me, my breath quickening, the sickness that brought me to the bathroom taking on a terrifying meaning. Phone still in hand, pressing against my brow, I lower my other palm to my abdomen, hold it there. The body making room—whether I want it to or not.

I stand and hurry through the bathroom door, then sink to the couch, pulling my already open laptop toward me, searching for another explanation. For symptoms that could confirm or deny what I already know. I scan the first page, then another, everything I see

I

making the fear mount. I turn to my phone again and stare. Fourteen days.

The screen buzzes. A message from Jasmine—*Girl, where are you? That belly bug doing better yet? 'Cause it's time to MARCH!* 👊 👊

The rally.

I look to the clock on my phone, see I'm already late. But my eyes draw back to the calendar. Fourteen days from the last day I would have guessed I'd have my period, which is so irregular, I never really know when it'll show. Fourteen days, which would make me at least six weeks along. Yet as pressing as this feels, I don't have to make a decision this minute. I have time. I can go to the rally. I will—despite the promise I made all those years ago. Despite the fear that creeps at the thought of it.

The door to the apartment opens and I slam the laptop shut, then slide it onto the coffee table. Thomas grins at me, his blue eyes lit with something between happiness and relief, the blond wave of his hair falling across the side of his forehead as he shakes it back, uselessly. "So glad I didn't miss you. You ready to head out?" He gestures toward the door.

"Huh?"

"To the rally." He laughs. "Didn't you say we were going?"

I stand. Realization and unease twist inside me like a rag between nervous hands. A lump of something seems to stick in my throat. "I said *I* was going."

"Yeah, so let's—" Thomas stops, something in my voice or expression cluing him in. "You don't want me to come?"

"It's just—" I take a step toward him, uncertain how to express this resistance to his presence. Not wanting to hurt him. "I mean, I'm meeting my colleagues."

"Uh-huh." He steps inside. Closes the door. And I imagine, like me, feels the problem, though he can't quite make sense of it. The way I felt it the first time we were together in their presence, my colleagues' tight smiles at him—the only white face in the crowd—putting a rancid taste in the back of my throat. How seeing their surprise made me wonder at the politics of race in choosing a partner, something I'd never wondered much about before. As I smiled back, made introductions, saw the discomfort from both sides and realized what it stemmed from, it wasn't embarrassment that filled me, it wasn't shame, but something uncomfortably similar to both.

"And there's that plan for Black people to arrive early. To be alone. To . . ." My voice trails off, but not before cracking. I can't risk that feeling again today. That awkwardness and uncertainty about whether— if this is the life I am leaning toward, with this community—he can be a part of it.

He nods. "I just thought I'd wait nearby. Meet up with you after."

I open my mouth, then close it, my own insecurity forefront. *I don't even know if I have a right to be there*, I think, but can't say. *Not quite Black. Not white. Both and neither.*

"And with my brother . . ."

"All the more reason—" He stops, catching himself. About Antony, he never pushes. "Okay." His smile looks genuine, but hurt rests in his eyes. "If that's what you want."

"It is." I smile back, my thoughts shifting from us to the rally—the promise I'm about to break—but also to what's growing inside me, whether the hurt in his eyes will multiply, fester, if I decide to stop that growth. I reach for my bag and clench my fingers over the strap as it falls across my chest. My mouth opens again. *Thomas*, I should say, then let the rest come out. But my mouth closes. I lean forward and rest a hand on his chest, then place a chaste kiss on his lips, too chickenshit to speak.

ɔ

BREATHLESS, THE LIBERATED curls I'm still learning how to take care of frizzing in the heat, I arrive at Spring Garden Road, just between the entrance to the Public Gardens and Victoria Park. My heart pounds from the exertion, but also from the fact that I'm here at last, doing what my father wanted to do in his final days.

I'm fifteen minutes late—two years and fifteen minutes—having missed the time for racial solitude, to sit and memorialize not just the loss of a life that's brought us here today, but all the losses before and after, and the crowd is growing by the minute. Hundreds. Maybe thousands. A sea of Black and Brown faces. Other faces, too. Every colour, every ethnicity. But it's the Black and Brown that strike me. More than I've ever seen congregated in the city, more than I knew existed. The streets are blocked off, with only police cruisers any-where in sight on the road ahead. I manoeuvre my way toward the front of the massive crowd, knowing that's where Jasmine will be, but with her nowhere in sight, I pull out my phone. Before I have a chance to dial, a hand lands on my shoulder. I'm spun and embraced. I step back to the sight of her in a T-shirt displaying a fist similar to the ones in her text.

"You better?" Jasmine looks at me, head cocked to the side, hands on my shoulders.

When I nod, fighting to conceal the fear and uncertainty welling within me, she nods back, then grabs my hand, drawing us through the crush of bodies. Before we've reached the front, the march begins. Hands still clamped together, our arms raise in the air. Our voices, too, in unison, not just with each other, but with all the voices around us. Chanting words that are more than chants. More than a plea. A battle cry erupting through our throats: not just our voices, but the voices of our parents, our grandparents. Our grandparents' grandparents' grandparents.

NO JUSTICE, NO PEACE.

BLACK LIVES MATTER.

NO JUSTICE, NO PEACE.

BLACK LIVES MATTER.

As we pass one block, then another and another, and turn onto Barrington Street, the thrum in my chest syncing with the rhythm of our voices is like nothing I've ever felt. The whole experience like nothing I imagined. The tears. The joy. Connection. I thought I'd feel guilt—shame that this is my first time. I thought I'd feel like an imposter.

Instead, I feel known.

We turn into Grand Parade, where a stage, the type usually used for concerts, is set up. I'm uncertain if everyone will fit but, almost as if it's been scripted, it's the Black and Brown bodies that enter the space, the others waiting, allowing us room. As I move forward, Jasmine still beside me, all that fear that kept me away until now, the things I'd seen on television—rubber bullets, tear gas, barricades—and the things I knew of more intimately, seem a world away. There is none of it. Instead, peace. Camaraderie.

Mostly.

As we find a spot in the crowd, my gaze falls upon the officers lining the sides—there to ensure the protest remains peaceful—and the eyes of at least three of them hold what I dreaded: the desire to step out of line, to attack. These officers, one young, one old, one middle-aged, gaze at us as if they itch to pull out their clubs, bash them against us. See the blood flow.

Yet they stay still.

I tear my gaze away, telling myself I'm seeing things, that my mind's recreating the look I imagined on the faces of three other officers. With the thrust of the crowd, I move forward, until they're out of sight and—the people around me still chanting, singing, gyrating— almost out of mind.

A man steps onto the stage, others behind him. He comes to the centre, and a hush settles. The others, five on each side, flank out in a motion that feels choreographed, imitating the motion of birds in flight. The man takes a knee, and two by two, so do the others. So do we. A screen I've only just noticed blinks to life. A countdown. Eight minutes and forty-six seconds.

Sobs, choking breaths, stifled gasps fill the air, mixing with the distant whir of cars in the unblocked streets. My chest shakes, my eyes burn, as the minutes, then seconds, count down. Then we stand—all of us—refusing to be held down any longer, feeling empowered, feeling as if we've taken something back.

And yet . . .

My throat is closing, pushing away that joy, that connection that existed just minutes ago. I came. I marched. But nothing tangible has changed.

The man on the stage speaks, though I only catch snippets—the way the city painted "Black Lives Matter" on the street without involving the Black community, how these decisions need to be in our hands. How words are great, but action, systemic change, is what's needed. I try to focus, but the thought that nothing tangible has changed pulsates, drowning out his words. And then the question: *Will it ever?*

Antony marched. Antony spoke on a podium. But still we're here. Because of another death. Because of so many. There are more words, more speakers, but all I hear is my own mind's refrain. *Will it ever? Will it ever?* As the rally comes to a close, the joyous energy around me clashes with the sudden defeat and anger that crushes through me.

I'm bumped and jostled, as all these bodies attempt to clear the space, and I lose sight of Jasmine, who I suddenly want desperately. Another one of my coworkers grabs my hand. "Why weren't you up there?" She's grinning, her expression euphoric. Like this is fun. Like we've accomplished something. "You should have been up there!"

Not noticing the way my body goes rigid, she raises a fist before being swept away in the dispersing crowd. "Challenge the state! Challenge the system!"

I stare blankly. My heart pounds.

Antony stood tall before a crowd.

"Kareela."

I swallow, a blast of fear coursing through me as I picture those eyes. Feel the hate. Know that despite our protest, this rally, truly nothing has changed. Because we can't refuse. Not when it counts. That, after all, is the reason we gathered. When they decide to hold us down, they hold us down. When they decide to shoot, the bullets fly.

"Earth to—"

A hand grasps my arm and I whip my head around to see Jasmine, a question on her face. "You okay?"

"Yeah. Yes."

She's silent, her hand still on my arm. She squeezes. "Okay. Well, we're heading to our spot. The one on Quinpool. You coming?"

I nod, then shake my head. "Soon." My voice squeaks. "Just going to find a bathroom."

"Your stomach again?" Her expression crinkles with concern. "I can wait."

"No, no." I wave a hand, as if it's nothing. "You go."

She's reluctant. But a woman I vaguely recognize grasps Jasmine's arm, and she shrugs, waves, and lets herself get pulled along.

As the crowd thins, I stand alone—bits of paper, posters, and plastic

peeled off water bottles all tumbling past, like leaves in autumn—
and the emptiness of the square seems to seep inside of me. A bright
red reach-extender darts out, snatching up errant trash, and I snap
my gaze to meet the eye of the smiling man collecting litter. He tilts
his chin, the way we do, and continues on. I step back as volunteers
do their all to make it look like nothing has happened, nothing has
changed, and the emptiness grows. A crinkled bottle rolls past me and
I pick it up, walk to the nearest bin. One more sign of this gathering
tossed away.

A vibration presses against my bottom and I pull my phone out of
my pocket to see Thomas's smiling face, reminding me of what I can
hardly believe slipped from my mind this past hour. But I can't speak
to him. Not right now. I swipe to decline the call, then slide the device
back into my pocket, surveying, once more, this littered square.

By the time I'm standing in front of the restaurant, my phone is
vibrating again, in sync with that slight, almost undetectable undulation of my womb. A wave of guilt floods me, that I didn't tell him the
moment I realized. That I'm not happy. I pull the phone out of my
pocket once more, decline the call again, but swipe to my messages.

Just heading into a restaurant with some friends from the rally, I text.
Will come home once we're done. XOXO.

I put the phone away and push open the restaurant door to a burst
of laughter, to another, smaller sea of Black and Brown faces. They've
brought tables together, taking up long sections of space. It still feels
odd, stepping into a restaurant, knowing we can eat here, talk without
masks and sanitizer and six feet of distance, without people looking at
us as if we're even more suspect than before, because for some inexpli-
cable reason, even to them, the colour of our skin makes us seem more
prone to infection, to passing it along.

It feels odd, too, to be part of this group, but also like the realization of something I've always wanted. They are loud. Boisterous. Joyful and serious in the same breath, and as I cross the restaurant, I witness Jasmine's face light up at the sight of mine, and a blast of that oneness I felt in the early minutes of the march bubbles through me.

"Kareela, over here." Jasmine stands and waves me to the centre of the largest row of tables, motioning for people to make room on the wooden bench. She clasps her hand on my shoulder, gestures for me to sit, then turns to the man beside her, the one onstage at the protest. "Kareela's who I was telling you about. Her bro—"

"Antony. Antony Jackson." His gaze locks with mine. "I know. Say their names."

"Say their names," half a dozen voices echo.

"I was thinking," says Jasmine, "maybe Kareela could—"

His gaze still on mine, he smiles slightly. "We won't talk about that today." He stops—"I'm Carson, by the way"—then reaches for a menu, passes it to me. "Hungry?"

I nod, thankful for the opportunity to avert my gaze, focus on something other than the eyes now focused on me. They think I'm one of them. Think this is something I've been doing my entire life. Think I'm here for Antony. And I am. But mainly, I'm here for my father. Because when he stared at his tablet, replaying those eight minutes and forty-six seconds over and over again, eyes bloodshot, drink in hand, irate when I told him to stop, he turned his body away from me. Because when he hunched over the screen as I pleaded it made no difference, watching it, trying to understand, that it wouldn't bring him back—neither of us knowing which him I was referring to— clearly, I should have said something else.

I'm here because when I saw him standing, hair combed, dressed for the first time in months, ready to travel to a protest and raise his fist, I was afraid. Upon seeing a glimpse of the father I hadn't seen since childhood—who'd been strong and solid when he wrapped his arms around me, pushing away all fears—I wanted to say yes. But the fears the world held were bigger, stronger, than both of us. So I told him no, and as he fell back onto the couch, that glimpse of the father I once knew disappeared.

"There's a drink menu, too," says Carson as I raise my head, witness the look of concern crossing his features.

I'm here because, as I stared at my father's shrunken form, I told him it was too dangerous. *We don't even have masks yet*, I said, though that was the least of my worries. *We can watch it on TV.*

I'm here because that was the last time I saw him properly dressed. And despite the promise to my mother, I owe something to my father, too.

Evelyn

Evelyn Jackson tramped through the snow: the bottom layer a thick slush from the heat of the black asphalt, the middle a mix of salt and dirt and all manner of detritus from the city, the top attempting to be fresh and pure but dulled by the haze of pollution it had pressed through on its way down.

She stifled a sigh at the way the grey slush dampened her pants—new, pulled from her closet to mark this special occasion. She raised her gaze and yelled, "Don't eat it!" Antony was stopped in front of her, face to the sky, arms and tongue out. At her words, his look of glee transformed to one of despair and obstinacy. He withdrew his tongue, crossed his arms, then stuck his tongue out again tentatively, staring at her instead of the clouds, waiting for a reaction.

She wanted to grab his arm, chastise him for this attempt at defiance. She wanted to wrap her arms around him, hold him close, kiss his cheeks, his forehead, to make up for not having the heart to explain that snow was now dirty, rain dangerous. Acid, falling from the sky.

His brown and only slightly rosy cheeks crept upward into an almost-there smile too cute for words. She smiled back, deciding she'd let him do what he wanted. He *should* be able to stick his tongue out, let the flakes fall and tingle and melt. Be a child. She knew all too well that childhood could be ripped away faster than a Band-Aid torn from tender flesh.

Antony's grin blossomed, his tongue out all the way now. She reached for his hand. "Come on. We don't want to miss our trolley." She squeezed, smiling, remembering her own rare joy at catching the falling snow—a girl in a field, spinning, letting her cares melt along with those flakes on her tongue, able, for a few minutes, to forget what waited at home.

It was easier to smile now, to focus on the good times. Everything easier than it had been when she'd fled Nova Scotia, and then, years later, when they'd fled Jamaica, Antony still a babe in arms and fear for everyone they'd left in Kingston making her perpetually on edge.

Back then, trying to push the dread aside, she'd pushed her baby through the slush in a rickety stroller or carried him in a makeshift sling—the way the women on the island had shown her but that seemed foreign to the women here. The white women, at least, who'd lean their heads in to see—*Is that a baby you've got in there?*—then pull back, their smiles twitching or faltering or vanishing altogether.

Antony tugged at her. "Can I surf?"

Evelyn laughed. "Yes, sweetie. If there's space. Now, come on!" She tugged, but gently, eager to race the trolley gaining on them. It pulled to a stop just seconds after they did, the doors opening to blast them with a gush of hot, stale air. Antony skipped up the steps, waving at the conductor as Evelyn dropped their tokens into the receptacle, the sound clanging over the voices of the other passengers. Antony strode to the back, walking tall, proud, just the way his papa did, and spread his arms in front of a seat—reserved just for her. Evelyn sat, nodded primly, as if he were a porter and she a fine lady. Just the way he liked it. "I can surf?" he asked again, his gap-toothed smile making it hard to hold back her grin.

"If you're careful."

Antony positioned his feet and arms, a look of pure determination crossing his features. Evelyn kept an eye out for the people crowding in, conscious of assuring that no one was getting too close or giving looks that might turn into a complaint. Then she looked at Antony— riding the trolley, exuberance flowing from him as if he really were out in the ocean, conquering a massive wave. He'd been asking to surf the streetcars and trolleys almost since before he could string together a coherent sentence. When you're six, she'd told him, again and again and again, thinking by then she'd feel ready, thinking six was ages away. It had come so fast.

As the gentle sway of the bus took them deeper into the city, joy bubbled up in Evelyn. The look of her son's face, the sun glinting off the snow on the awnings of buildings, which, from this far away, looked almost as white as the snow of her childhood.

Life had been hard, with only patches of good times. Those first years after she'd moved to Jamaica were the golden standard, before fear crept into every day, reminding her of what she'd tried to escape in Juniper Cove. But the fear in Kingston was different; unrest, politics on everyone's tongue, war in the streets. And since returning to Canada, it'd been a different fear again, a different struggle—adjusting to city life, to the stares, to never knowing whether she and her family would be accepted or judged or worse. Here, life was full of so many little disappointments and frustrations: regarding Kingsley's education and then job search, always trying to make ends meet, all of it taking years longer than they'd intended; regarding the slights and injustices they could never quite prove. It'd been exhausting. Not at all what she expected. But they were, at last, on track. And she wanted to believe this wouldn't simply be a "good patch," as transient as the snow, but their life now.

Except situations popped up, every day, that made it hard to believe.

Her joy fizzled when she saw the newspaper in the hands of a man across the aisle. Words in bold black letters. A war. But not the kind that sent soldiers to faraway lands. The man stood up at the next stop, leaving the paper on the seat beside him. Evelyn crossed the aisle and held it in her hands, reading beyond the headline. A war against drugs, Mulroney's sanctioned message said. But everything else pointed to no, not really. She'd heard chatter on the streets and on radio shows, seen signs of the discontent brewing, the outrage toward the "Uzi-toting Jamaican thugs," who spread through the city in "murderous posses."

And now here it was, in black and white: a war against Kingsley. Against Antony. Even though they had nothing to do with it. A war against Caribbean men—Jamaicans, specifically—demonizing them. As if they were all derelicts. As if it were a part of their genetic makeup.

She pulled the cord for their stop, trying to force the article out of her mind—the fear it prompted. They were on their way to Dulcie's Fresh and Tasty Authentic Jamaican Cuisine. Not Evelyn's first choice, nor Kingsley's. It was food they could make at home, though didn't often, but Antony had begged, his interest in all things Jamaican seeming to increase by the day, so they'd agreed, because today was meant to be a celebration—Kingsley, at long last Assistant Professor at City University—but the words on that newspaper robbed her of any sense of festivity. Evelyn knew more than most what headlines could do to a city. How articles and talk shows on politics transformed into fighting in the street, guns, violence, bloodshed.

Like the slogan that had covered Kingston's newspapers in the early days, Prime Minister Manley shouting it from podiums, making sure it was in every newspaper: "Better must come!" And the tongue-in-cheek truth that followed on whispered lips: "Dem say better must come, but fe sure, bitter did come."

Evelyn looked again to the article, a sense of foreboding working its way through her bones. They'd fled to Canada to get away from that unrest. To give them all, and Antony specifically, a better life. To keep him safe. Yet the words, discarded on the trolley seat, swam before Evelyn's eyes. She stood, gripped her son's hand, and walked away from the paper, the fear it prompted. She was ready to walk into this next phase of their life. Their good, solid, finally-where-they-wanted-it life. However, as she watched her skipping boy, dread and frustration seeped through her at the realization that danger seemed to follow them always, that despite how much she tried, she'd never be able to keep the ones she loved safe.

Evelyn

Over a decade later, Kingsley embraced Evelyn, tilted her head back, then pressed his lips to hers, long and full of feeling— the way he used to when they were two kids standing in the island sun, warm breezes dancing around them, her dress flowing in a way that made that scrawny-legged girl from Nova Scotia seem like another person entirely.

Kingsley released her and clapped a hand on Antony's shoulder. At seventeen, he was still a scrawny kid, with shoulders that were starting to broaden, a chin that was losing its baby-faced softness as it morphed into the defined lines she'd fallen in love with on his father.

"Full professor." Evelyn took Kingsley's hand. "A new house." After three apartments, and in Scarborough Junction, the type of neighbourhood they'd dreamed of.

"We've made it." He squeezed her hand back as they headed toward Dulcie's yet again, his easy island gait, which was never as easy in him as in other men, nearly a thing of the past.

"We've made it," echoed Evelyn. Except that "it" should have happened at least five years ago. They should have been celebrating tenure by now. The men who started alongside Kingsley had been tenured for two, three, one as long as five, years. *Twice as hard for half as much,* Evelyn had heard people say. But with his drive, his determination, she'd somehow thought Kingsley would escape that. She somehow thought—despite the derision she'd heard from time to time in her childhood, despite having never even seen a Black person until, at eighteen, she'd moved to Jamaica—that here, in Toronto, a place with culture and diversity, the saying wouldn't apply.

But it had. Just as they'd quickly learned she needed to be the one to show up at apartment viewings or meetings at the bank. That if she wasn't the one behind the wheel, they were exponentially less likely to get where they were going without being stopped. She hated it, but it was the way things were.

Lately, Antony had been pushing for his licence, and they'd been pushing back, saying it was an unnecessary luxury. Which was true, of course. Transit would take him anywhere he wanted to go. But so many other things were true, too.

"What'll it be?" Kingsley pulled up a chair in the small restaurant, looking somewhat out of place in his dress shirt and tie, suit jacket, hair perfectly combed and cropped close. But the venue was used to that, and used to her, the only white woman in this long-standing hole-in-the-wall.

Only Antony looked like he belonged, with clothing that adhered to what she'd learned was "hip-hop culture" and short, poky dreads Kingsley despised but had given up arguing about. Because when it came to Antony, it was pointless to argue.

"Ackee, for sure," said Antony, scanning the menu with the excitement of that six-year-old he once was. "Rice and peas. Oxtail. Curry goat. Ma, you in the mood for jerk today?"

"Whatever you want."

Antony nodded. "It's a celebration, right? Let's do it up."

"Yes." Kingsley leaned back, smiling at his son. "Rundown too. Plantain chips. Festivals. And pudding for dessert."

"Where do you suppose we'll put it all?" Evelyn laughed.

"In this growing boy. And we'll pack what's left if we need to." Kingsley grasped her hand under the table. His eyes, the twinkle in them, even after all these years, made her stomach flip-flop, made her able to fool herself—just for a moment—that life had turned out the way she'd envisioned. Kingsley looked to Antony. "Place the order?"

"On it."

Once Antony was out of earshot, Kingsley turned to Evelyn. "How much longer do you think we can hold off driving lessons?"

"Not long."

"Where did de time go?"

A grin spread across Evelyn's face, for the double nostalgia, the lilt and hardened *the* that had slipped in, such a rarity these days.

"Wish we'd had more." He sighed before bringing back the grin. "But if one is all we get, what a one!"

Evelyn forced a smile, the now-familiar guilt what flipped her stomach this time. It was a choice they should have made together. But also, it was her body. She who would have had to go back to lugging a stroller through these crowded streets, take time off work, endure the looks she received in this city—which held more vitriol for some reason when it was a baby she held in her arms rather than a child who walked beside her. And so she'd gone to the doctor. Such tiny pills— that let her determine her own life. That let her deceive this man who, in every other way, she loved more than herself. "What a one, indeed."

Antony leaned against the counter, grinning at the young girl who worked the cash, who clearly was enamoured of their son despite being at least five years his senior. It was hard not to be enamoured. Antony. Vivacious. Smart. Passionate: as a child, about G.I. Joe, Transformers, and oceans, equally; as a young teen, about track and basketball and the harms of pollution, making them set up recycling stations throughout their house, urging them to reduce and reuse; and in the past year, about Jamaican culture, about politics, opportunity, civil rights, anything and everything about what it meant to be a Black man in the world, about making the world better for Black people.

Antony plopped a tray with three waters on the table, splashing the liquid. He sat, legs spread, slouched, one arm dangling over the back of his chair. Kingsley, with his proper posture, proper presentation, held back the criticism that would typically pour from his lips. Evelyn squeezed his knee in appreciation.

"Pretty lady there," said Kingsley, winking at Antony. "Know her name?"

"Sure. Lily."

"Seems to have an eye for you."

"To joke." Antony grabbed a straw, ripped the paper, then played with it, folding it in his hands, looking at it rather than Evelyn or his father.

"What do you mean?" Kingsley leaned forward.

"I mean . . ." He scrunched up the paper, then tossed it on the table. "She knows I'm a zebra."

"A zebra?" Alarm flared through Evelyn.

"Girls like her," said Antony, seemingly missing the question, "aren't likely to get with someone like me. Which is the weirdest thing, because *in* Jamaica, it's not such a big deal, right? There's lots of mixing?"

Kingsley looked to Evelyn, his jaw tightening, his eyes softening, then back to Antony. "It wasn't uncommon, no."

"Yeah. Exactly." Antony laughed, the sound brittle and short. "Isn't that the motto? *Out of many, one people?*"

Kingsley nodded.

"Here it's like . . . I don't know. They can't be sure whether I'm white with black stripes or Black with white."

"You're neither," said Kingsley. "You're a man, not an animal. You don't have stripes."

"A man?" Antony straightened, eyes wide. "That's the first time you've said that."

"Well, you are," said Kingsley. "Or you will be soon."

Evelyn's chest tightened. A zebra. She'd not heard that one before. Oreo. Checkerboard. Whitewashed. She wanted to smack the smirk off whatever kid had called her son that. She wanted to take her family to a place where none of this mattered, where they could teach him to drive—the only words of caution to make sure he was conscientious and careful, rather than to make sure he was aware of how his skin, his hair, his clothes could draw undue attention.

"A man drives," said Antony, snapping Evelyn's attention back to the conversation.

"A man drives." Kingsley nodded. He tapped his fingers on the table, staring at their son. "I'll take you out this weekend."

Antony whooped, pulling his fist down to his side in victory.

Evelyn inhaled, wishing the impossible, that they were back in Jamaica—not the country that existed now, but the Jamaica that they had intended to live in—raising their children, many instead of one.

She sipped her drink, her gaze on her son, his tan skin, a perfect fifty-fifty mix between her and Kingsley. And her anger simmered to a thread of hope. If that girl over there saw him as different, not "one of them," maybe the people she worried about would, too. Maybe life here wouldn't be so bad for him or as hard as it'd been for Kingsley.

A zebra. A checkerboard. A coconut.

Maybe it would help.

Violet

When did you first notice the symptoms?"

The symptoms?

Me gaze travel from the hazy poster on the wall, grotesque in its intricacies of the female anatomy, past another, displaying the inner workings of the lungs, the stomach, intestines, over some cluttered mess of items—pens, me think, and swabs most likely, a baby's scale, more. This not be like the clean, sterile clinics of home. At last I stare at the doctor. There, sitting so confident, like he got ne'er a care in the world. Like he never been hungry a day in he life. Never walk down the street afraid of too many things to count.

The symptoms.

They started long, long ago. Back when me own grandmammy be picking in the field, in the too hot sun. Not having choice. Not knowing there be anything better. Then me think, no, farther back than that. Maybe to me grandmammy's grandmammy, far off, someplace in Africa. When someone fooled, cheated, stole her. However it all came to be.

But I know that not what the doctor asking. So I smile, real-nice-like.

Like it no big deal, 'cause that what I taught to do, even though it one of the biggest deals I can think of.

I say, "Me think it been 'bout two years now. Maybe three?" Which is a lie. It been closer to five. And him look at me, silent. Lips pressed, so I can hardly tell where those thin lines end and his face begin. And that look make like me so small, like me could jump out the keyhole in the door.

I know he nice man. I know he feel bad for me, for whatever reason there be I wait so long. Probably he think I too stupid, too poor to know better. I none those things. I just busy, scared. Tired. Once I had four children, three daughters. Now I have two. And they, these two, they not even mine. Not really.

All me own babies under the ground. Still, there be these two, and I try to take care of them. I owe them that, with all that be stolen. So I delay, put off, pretending, like I taught to do, like we all always taught to do, because being here, sitting in front of this clean-cut, bright-eyed, young-enough-to-be-my-grandbaby man mean I got to admit it . . . maybe someday soon, it going to be them have to take care of me.

No wonder it take me so long.

Kareela

As the group from the rally leaves the restaurant, there are hugs and fist bumps, *catch ya' later*s, hands firmly placed on shoulders with a gentle squeeze, and me, standing amidst it all, not sure what to do with myself. Jasmine materializes beside me, and then Carson is in front of me, inviting me to come to a meeting next week. "To learn a bit more about what we do." He smiles. "Jasmine said you're an amazing asset to the community, that her adviser says you're one of the best young social workers the department has, and also"—he grins—"that before last week, you didn't even know there was a BLM chapter here."

I shake my head, the compliment nothing compared to the embarrassment that seeps through me—that I didn't know. That I'm so out of touch. I try to push the feeling away, tell myself I belong, or that I could, but it's replaced with fear, that the more time they spend with me, get to know me, they'll see I'm not who they think I am, who Antony was. That I don't even want to be.

"No pressure." He drapes an arm around Jasmine's shoulder. Squeezes. "We're a laid-back bunch . . . until we're not." His eyes hold a hint of laughter and my stomach flutters, an entirely different sensation from the one I felt earlier.

I nod without commitment. "Maybe."

He's called away and Jasmine squeezes my side, then bounces off in the other direction, linking her arms through the arms of two women I've met but can't recall the names of. "Up Home girls," says Jasmine, before she flits off.

People disperse in twos and threes and fives. I walk down Quinpool Road, the sea of Black and Brown faces trickling away as an ocean of dread seems to fill its place: Thomas at home—who I told not to come, whose child I'm carrying—waiting for me.

My phone buzzed in the restaurant. One call. Four texts. I didn't answer any of them. Didn't even look. Now, as I stand outside our building, the dread builds, starting in my toes and slowly rising upward, like sludge from an overflowing sewer. The guilt rises, too. For not telling him as soon as I suspected, even though it would have meant a long-drawn-out discussion, and probably missing the rally. Though really, there's no point in telling him at all, not until I've made my decision, and it's my decision to make. I think. Or so I've been told. Because it is my body. And I agree with this. Mostly.

Still, the guilt grows, because I'm pretty sure what his opinion will be. Already he talks of marriage, like it's a foregone conclusion. I cut the conversations short, nod or smile. Yet he talks. *When we're married . . . our children . . . our house.*

I pull my phone out, tap the notification window, see his last few messages:

Call me.

In the beginning, all I cared about was that he loved me. Wanted me.

Or text.

Now I'm not so sure.

This isn't for a friend, is it?

My brow furrows, the sludge surging up as I press my hand to my forehead, try to force the realization away. He knows. The open tabs on my web browser. The fact that Thomas's computer keeps crashing, and when it does, if he doesn't have time to wait for a reboot, I've told him he can use mine.

Don't bother doing any of those things. Just come home!

A stream of air makes its way out of me. I swallow, then take the steps to our apartment, walk through the door, hear the smack of feet on aging hardwood before I see Thomas's grin, eyes bright, like a little boy on Christmas morning.

"You're pregnant."

My mouth contours—lips wide and slightly upturned, teeth exposed, yet not a smile.

"Well, are you?"

I shrug. "Probably? Yeah. I mean, I think so?"

The space between us closes and I'm in his arms, spun in a circle, set to the floor, then squeezed again. This is what I hoped for. A man who loved me. Who would be thrilled when he learned this news—the start of our family.

But not yet. Not like this.

He steps away from me, his hands grasping mine as he leads me to the living room, pulls us both down to the couch. "What do you mean, you think so?"

"Well, I mean, I haven't tested or anything."

His eyes narrow slightly, his brow getting that little crinkle. "Why not?" Now his lips scrunch, too. "When I saw the articles, I started thinking about it, realized you hadn't, well, you know . . . that you must be, well, pretty late!"

I nod.

"So?"

"Around two weeks. Maybe. I'm not sure."

He squeezes me again. Grins. "What? Were you worried I wouldn't be thrilled?"

An invisible hand reaches out and clamps my throat. I sputter. "I don't know. I mean—" I'm worried he isn't the man I want to do this with. Even more, that I'm not the woman he'd want to do it with, if he really knew me. Which he doesn't. He can't. I don't know me.

"This wasn't the plan, obviously." He leans against the couch. "And when I figured it out, I'm not going to lie, my first emotion was terror. But screw plans, right?" He laughs and throws his fist in the air. "I'm going to be a dad!"

I swallow, not sure how to label the mess of emotions roiling around inside of me. "Well, I mean . . ."

"What?" His head whips to zero his focus in on me.

"I mean, like, these things aren't always, I don't know, sure things."

He shifts closer. "Do you have any of those symptoms the articles were talking about?"

"Well, yeah, but, I mean—" I want to squirm away, take the time to figure this out, weeks, months if need be, without Thomas's smiling face, Thomas's expectation. "It's just, something like twenty-five percent of women end up losing their babies. So I figured, why not wait and see?"

The crinkle in his brow deepens. "That can't be right."

"No, it is."

He shakes his head. "So twenty-five percent of women, that's counting women in their thirties, forties, even. Women with health problems and conditions." He reaches for my hand, and the touch, though meant to comfort, seems to expand, wrap around me, a boa bent on constricting. "You're twenty-four. And healthy. You don't need to worry about that. Let's get a test. Find out for sure. Then you can book a doctor's appointment, make sure everything's fine."

I plant my lips together, let the tiniest stream of air emerge. "No."

"Babe, it's going to be fine. We're going to be fine. It'll be an adjustment. It'll take work, but . . ." He hesitates. "You seem . . ." His expression shifts. "You're scared of more than losing it. You're scared of having it."

"Of course I am!"

He nods. "It is scary. This was not part of the plan. Not yet." He shrugs. "Like I said, I was scared, too. But then I thought . . . it's me and you. We're young. But we love each other. We can do this. We can make this work. We'll—"

I pull my hand out of his grasp, stand. "I didn't even want you to know yet. I need time to think. To decide if I want to keep it, so there's no point in—"

"What?"

"I mean." My heart pounds. I can't look at him: the love in his eyes for this false woman he sees in front of him. I turn to the window. "Like you said, we didn't plan this, and we're young. And the world is shit, so who wants to bring a child into that anyway, right?" I laugh, kind of, and slump into the desk chair across the room.

"The world is—?" His voice cuts off. And in the silence, I dread his next question. "So you're thinking of what, exactly?"

Pressure builds in my throat. Thomas is kind, and sweet, and ridiculously good. And everything we've said is true, about the world, our ages, how this was not part of the plan. But it's more than that. I'm not sure I want his baby—what having it would mean, being connected to him, his world, forever. Because unlike I'm implying, I do want a baby—a child who belongs to me, who I belong to. One day. When I'm ready. When I've stopped being such a mess and know how to make the world, my life, a lot less shitty. For my child, at least.

"I was so excited I didn't even think." He sighs, and I swivel in the chair to face him. "The rally, was it . . . ?" He offers a smile, the compassion of a saint on his face. "I mean, are you okay, or . . ."

I bite my lip, thankful for this shift of focus, then shrug through my words. "The rally was okay. I mean, intense and hard and kind of awful, right? That there's even a need for it."

He nods.

"But it was also kind of wonderful." I pause as that sense of connection comes back to me. "All of us there, together, feeling part of something."

More nodding.

I turn my gaze back to the window, the blue jay I've come to know a focal point, living his life, unaware of the way I watch him, yearn for such simplicity. His rich blue plumes bring back the eyes of one of the officers. "A couple of the cops. I don't know . . ." The pressure in my throat intensifies as I see those irises again, the hate behind them, the fear that flared in my belly, making me want to run, making me wonder if that's what Antony had seen, just before . . .

Moisture builds behind my eyes, knocking me off balance. I lean on the arm of the chair and pull my gaze from the window, directing it at the rich brown of the aged and gnarled hardwood beneath my feet. "They made me think of Antony, you know? If . . ."

Thomas crosses the room. "Ree, I can't imagine." I keep my gaze on the floor, refusing to see his so similarly tinted eyes. The shittiness of the world is no longer a false distraction as I imagine all the things I generally try not to: filling in the blanks of my brother's last moments. Because when it comes down to it, I know almost nothing about that day. I simply know it happened—that one afternoon Antony was alive, and the next, he wasn't, and it had something to do with a rally, with standing before a crowd for what he believed in.

And now people sit in bars and say my brother's name. A name that scrolls on a website I found, constantly, forever and ever until time ends, or the internet is obliterated or whoever pays for the hosting forgets to update their credit card information.

It is shitty to bring a child into a world capable of that, of trying to erase all these names, which aren't just names, but people—who had mothers and fathers, friends, little sisters.

If I brought Thomas's child into this shitty world, it would be a lot less likely to be a target of that kind of hate, could be as light skinned as he is, but how would I explain all those names?

Antony's.

At my silence, Thomas lifts me from the chair and wraps his arms around me. I sink into him. Into how safe it feels to be in his arms. But this safety—it's short-lived, maybe not even real.

My teeth clench. My head aches, thinking of my brother and all the pain that came after. In my family. In other families. So many others.

Today is too much. Too everything. I raise my gaze, so I'm looking into Thomas's eyes, which aren't so similar to the officer's after all, because of the hope that lives there, the concern, the yearning for an answer to a question I don't even want to think about, since it means thinking about so much. About Thomas. And whether I should stay in his life, whether I want him in mine.

"Listen, Ree, we don't have to figure this out today. Or even talk about it. We have time."

Weeks. I have until twenty weeks. And then, if I haven't made a choice, it'll be made for me.

"Okay?"

A tsunami of exhaustion crashes over me. I raise on tiptoe, kiss him, taking a quick moment to pretend this is all there is—us, with no complications—then pull back. "I have a headache. I'm going to lie down." I step away before waiting for an answer, head to our bedroom, and close the door. As I settle onto the bed, an undulation in my abdomen greets me. I try to will the sensation away, what it means, but the thoughts crowd in. Who would this child be? What would he or she look like? What label would be placed upon this unsuspecting soul?

Possibly the same one placed on Thomas—who, most of the time, doesn't even have to think about it. And where would that put me? Separate, from my own child. On the outside, as I've been my whole life.

I roll onto my side and wonder if most women would call their mother at a moment like this—ask for her thoughts, her advice, her assurances. Even with my mom, it's hard to remember a time when I felt I belonged, felt accepted and loved. A time when those tendrils of frustration, of anger, didn't mix with everything else—with the wanting.

I smooth my hand across my abdomen, letting it settle inches above the place of expansion, wondering, too, what my father's response would have been: pain rises, because I'll never know, because if I decide to keep this child, two of the people I love most will never meet it.

The world *is* shitty—I look to the hand cupping my abdomen—but it's not this little bean's fault.

Footsteps sound outside the door, then, less than a minute later, I hear the sound of Thomas walking away. I pull my knees up to my chest, squeeze. In the ways it matters most, I'm still a kid. I don't know who I am, what I want, where I belong . . . it doesn't seem right that some cluster of cells should make that decision for me. I close my eyes, knowing that when I wake, Thomas will have placed a glass of water and an acetaminophen by my side. Knowing that he, at least, loves me, wants me . . . Or at least the me he believes me to be. I rub my belly again, whisper, "Not yet" to the growing and separating snippets of our mixed DNA. *I'm not ready.*

Evelyn

After dinner at Dulcie's, her belly full of too many festivals and more meat than any person should eat in one sitting, Evelyn lay in bed, thinking of the boys she'd taught in Jamaica: politically minded, like Antony. Loose-limbed and cocky. Marching to Vale Royal, protesting a government that cared only for itself. Boys who came home beaten, bruised, or not at all.

She and Kingsley had left for a reason. A good reason.

Yet there were those other boys and young men—here in Canada, and the US. Ones she'd never met, their faces—on TV screens, in the paper—like the face of her own child.

Evelyn rolled toward Kingsley and wrapped her arm around him, her the big spoon, him the small, which he loved, and she loved, too, though it didn't work quite so well as the opposite arrangement. He shifted into her, pulling her arm tighter around his torso.

"Do you think it's a good idea?" Evelyn whispered, that familiar fear bubbling up again. "Antony on the road, with the way things have been?"

Kingsley sighed, turned so their faces were inches apart, so they breathed each other's breath. "He's got to learn sometime. I'll hammer

31

in how important it is to be cautious, obey the rules of the road to the letter, that when he gets stopped, he needs to be mannerly, calm, and it'll be a hassle, but beyond that, he'll be fine."

Obsequious. That's what Kingsley would tell Antony to be, what he always was himself. Evelyn was thankful for it, but she feared her son would see it differently. Balk at the injustice. Try to teach the officer about the error of his ways, the inherent racism in pulling him over because he was Black—which Antony had taken to calling himself more and more. They hardly used the words in their home: Black, white. She and Kingsley had never had a distinct conversation about it. They simply focused on people's humanity, taught their son to do the same . . . though Evelyn often wondered, silently, if they were doing him a disservice.

Antony seemed to think so. Her son, so bold, so smart, refusing to accept—or care—about the way things worked, that many would hate him for his boldness, want him to know his place.

Kingsley cupped her cheek, kissed her softly. "If he doesn't learn from me, he'll learn from one of his friends who might be cocky, a show-off, teach Antony to be the same way."

"You're right." Evelyn continued to breathe her man's breath as their eyes locked. A familiar yearning stirred in her. "You know"—a smile spread across her features—"we've yet to christen this room, this bed."

Kingsley grinned. "Woman, you don't have to ask me twice!"

Several weeks later, Evelyn took her X-Acto knife and slid open one of the few boxes she hadn't gotten to over a month ago. You'd think she would have been upset by it—having to pick up every few years, leave her community, her friends. Except there were no friends to leave. Acquaintances here and there. But not friends.

Black women seemed resentful of her taking one of their successful Black men. White women seemed suspect, looking at her like she was an outcast. As if Evelyn had betrayed something . . . her race? A sense of propriety? The way things should be? Or as if she'd sullied herself—and them—bringing the entire white race down. Asian women simply seemed confused—and tended to stick to their own anyway, Koreans with Koreans, Japanese with Japanese. A lot of Black women were like that, too. Caribbeans mixed, but not with Africans or those from the US. Everyone had someone. Except her.

The looks and sly comments had faded in recent years, but she couldn't be certain: Was it because they'd stopped, or because she'd stopped looking so intently? Stopped trying to find a place to belong?

Evelyn pulled out one of the few pieces of art they'd brought from their home in Kingston. A wave of nausea stilled her hand. As the wave crashed upon her, she stared at the tile, wondering if this feeling was from something she'd eaten at last night's school fundraiser; wondering, too, what had happened to their other art, abandoned on the walls of their Kingston home.

Evelyn held up the framed tiles: two faceless men, hands beating djembes, hair flying with the intensity of their playing, in between faceless women dancing, their skirts high and full, their head wraps contrasting with the rich colour that danced through the background of the scene.

A wedding gift from Violet. Tears had sprung to Evelyn's eyes upon opening the gift, which she knew must have cost too much, which seemed to say, *You're my daughter now, my kin.*

Evelyn had mounted the artwork proudly in their Kingston home, wrapped it carefully for the flight, then mounted it again in their first Toronto apartment—a salve against the loneliness that had enveloped her when they'd first stepped off the plane in Canada and a reminder of where they'd come from, where they'd return as soon as Kingsley had his doctorate. Back when she still hoped they'd return, when she held hope about her prospects here, too, thinking the women on buses, in grocery stores and parks, couldn't represent the women everywhere. That, with time, the isolation surrounding her would be replaced with friendship.

Hope had blossomed when the ladies at her new secretarial job invited her to their book club. On her night to host, she'd baked and dusted and polished. She'd instructed Kingsley to keep Antony, then three years old, in the bedroom, to not disturb their lively discussion.

The women oohed and aahed at the tile image. *The vibrancy of it! How ethnic!* Asking where she'd gotten it. *You lived there!* they exclaimed. *You taught! How adventurous. How brave. How exciting!*

And then, halfway through their discussion on Morrie's wisdom, Antony's feet had pounded up the hall, curls bouncing, eyes bright. As the women's smiles tightened and faded, Evelyn realized she'd spoken of Kingsley, studying to get his doctorate. Of Antony, whip-smart. Yet her desk was small, always full of papers her boss wanted her to sort and file, so she'd never put up a photo.

The meeting continued, less animated than before. The following meetings were scheduled for the one night of the week Evelyn said she couldn't do.

Borders meant so little. In the moment Antony had run into the room and the women's faces changed, she'd thought of a trip she and Kingsley had taken to Florida, where they'd walked hand in hand, her little baby bump on display, in a state where over a decade earlier, their love would have been illegal, where the looks of hate made it clear people weren't ready for this change, for the offspring of their love.

Today, Evelyn smoothed away a piece of fluff caught in a groove of the wood on the top of the frame, the hurt still fresh after all these years. A mosaic, the city boasted, but not within an individual family. That was where acceptance stopped.

Evelyn reached for the hammer and a nail, turned as she surveyed the living room, then tossed both hammer and nail on the couch, another wave of nausea cresting, and ran to the toilet, flipping the lid just in time. Her insides emptied as she knelt, grabbed a tissue, then wiped the spittle from her lips. She sat back, and rather than feeling worse, as would have been likely with some sort of food poisoning, she felt better. Too much better.

Evelyn leaned against the tub, remembering the two days of pills she'd missed in the harried, frantic disorder of the move. Apparently, two days, after over a decade of never forgetting, was all it took.

Evelyn

T he living room, to the master bedroom, to the living room again. Evelyn paced. Only two pills. She put a hand to her head. Paced. She was thirty-seven years old. Too old to be a new mother. Antony only had two more years of high school left. People would laugh. People would balk. Evelyn sank to the floor, her back against the wall. She felt her abdomen, knowing and not knowing. Wanting to believe it was all those foods from last night. Not food poisoning, but an array of spices and herbs her body simply wasn't used to.

She and Kingsley had made it. They were here, now, where they'd wanted to be so many years before. Where, now that they were no longer renting and Kingsley's job was relatively secure, Evelyn felt she might pull out the dream she'd held secretly for years—a degree of her own. Social work. A chance to dive deeper into the work that had taken her to Jamaica in the first place: her urge to help make the world a better place aligning with her desire to get as far away from her father as seemed humanly possible.

And now this. A baby. Which would mean Evelyn would have to leave work—not for her own education, but to change diapers and wipe a runny nose, to be kept awake, night after night, by a crying infant and her doubled fears—afraid for the safety of not just one child, but two. Two children for whom life would be harder than she'd ever anticipated when she'd married a Jamaican man in a country where their unusual pairing hadn't been an issue, hadn't even been that unusual.

Here, she was all too aware of the fragility of her child's safety. Simply existing, here, held risk.

Zebra.

Risk not only from one side, but both.

Risk. It was why she'd started taking the pills. She'd gone to her doctor just days after she'd heard the first hint of the war on drugs, the war that people made clear was going to be a war on men like Kingsley, like her son. She'd lived her entire childhood fearful for her own safety, watching her mother cower in the corner, cover her bruises with too much makeup. Three years after her mother's death, when her fears for herself had been realized, Evelyn—bruised and battered—had collected her bags, walked out of the house, made it her mission to get as far from that fear as possible. And she had . . . only to end up back in a place where her child would grow up in fear, too.

She was sick of it.

A part of her itched to pack her bags again. Leave. Start a new life. But she couldn't leave what was already a part of her. A baby: After all these years of lying to her husband, hiding the pills, making him believe that rushed, terrifying hour of labouring Antony, which ended in so much blood, had broken something inside of her. After turning away from his questions that maybe she or he, or both of them, should see a doctor. After telling him if it was meant to happen, it would.

Evelyn's breath came quick. The lie could continue—if she wanted. It was legal now. Safe. She wouldn't even have to risk her life, go to some back alley on some dirty table, where she was likely to bleed out.

Evelyn stared, the patterned paper on the wall pulsing and twirling before her eyes. In the hall, she turned, sank, back pressed against the wood panelling. The front door opened and Kingsley's footsteps sounded through the living room, the kitchen, back toward the hall.

"Evelyn?" Worry tightened his throat; dread hers.

She wanted to pretend it wasn't true. Maybe, even, make it so. She wanted to live a life that wasn't only about her family, but her, too. A career, not a job. She wanted less fear, not more. But as she looked at her husband after so many years of lying, she couldn't lie anymore.

"Evelyn?"

She stared, her breath frozen.

"Eve—"

"I think I'm pregnant."

Kingsley whooped. He ran to Evelyn, pulled her to standing, then wrapped his arms around her and lifted her. She yelped as her foot banged into the wall. "Oh, I'm sorry, sorry. Darling, are you all right?"

Evelyn nodded, thankful for the pain. The way it presented a reason to wince, rather than burst with joy.

"This is incredible. Pregnant." His eyes lit with the type of energy she remembered. He took her hand, drew her to the living room, thrust the hammer aside, and pulled her down beside him. "I thought it was impossible. I thought—" He paused, his brow crinkling in concern. "You said *think*. You're not sure?"

"Pretty sure." Evelyn's chest constricted. Why had she spewed it out like that? Why hadn't she made certain first?

"Well, we can find out, can't we? You don't even need a doctor's appointment anymore. The pharmacy. I think—" Kingsley turned from Evelyn, tapped his hand on his knee. This was why she'd blurted the words. So Kingsley would know the same moment she did. So there'd be no possibility of keeping it from him, continuing the lie with an act he would never forgive. "Yes"—he nodded more to himself than her—"without a prescription or anything. People just go to the pharmacy, pick up some test, and know in minutes."

Evelyn exhaled. "That's right."

"A baby." The skin around Kingsley's eyes crinkled. Moisture made them glisten.

Guilt pulsed and throbbed.

"After all these years."

For the lie.

Kingsley wrapped Evelyn in his arms. He pulled back, then kissed her long and hard. He hugged her again. "Let's go." He stood and put out his hand.

She looked at it, fear like a noose around her neck. "Now?"

"Of course now."

Evelyn met his gaze. She was so old. The world was so awful. And she wasn't sure she would have had even one biracial baby, let alone two, if she had known she'd be raising them here.

Kingsley took her hand, pulled her up, and laughed.

Kareela

I lie still as the door opens, ensure my breathing is deep and even. Soft footsteps, and then the pad of feet to the closet, the slight creak and rustle as Thomas reaches for his paramedic uniform and bag. It must be after seven. I've slept for four hours, another indication that a pregnancy test is unnecessary. I've never been a napper.

More pads, another pause, longer this time. I concentrate on my breathing as I sense Thomas above me, then feel the barely there touch of his lips on my forehead. The door closes and I roll onto my back, guilt swirling through me—for not opening my eyes, kissing him back, thanking him for his concern.

He'll be at his practicum until late into the night, long after I've gone back to bed, and then I'll be up, out of the house and on my way to work before he wakes. A three-day-a-week routine he laments, but that, lately, I don't mind . . . too much.

Today's ships-passing-in-the-night routine will grant me at least twenty hours before I'll have to live through the continued conversation I know is coming. I lie in bed until I hear the click and various clanks of the locks sliding into place, wait another five minutes for good measure, then crawl out of bed, stomach rumbling. I drink the water waiting beside me but leave the acetaminophen untouched, slide my feet into the massive bear claw slippers that Thomas always chuckles at, wrapping his arms around my torso, kissing my neck, teasing me that the Caribbean blood must be strong in me if I need slippers throughout the year.

I head to the kitchen, which is clean, Thomas's dinner dishes washed and stacked to dry. A smile crosses my face. It's my night, but of course he did them, my sweet man. Another rumble, and I know just what I need. I reach into the cupboard, then open the fridge, setting down tools and ingredients—coconut milk, flour, salt, *unsalted* butter, brown sugar, bowls, a pan, sifter, and last of all, yeast—lining them up the way Gran showed me, her voice in my head, *Yuh gat to do it right, now, yuh hear? None of dis running fah dis, running fah dat.*

I pull out a baking sheet, rub the bar of butter over a sheet of parchment paper and then a bowl, greasing them, *just suh.* I heat the coconut milk, testing the temperature with my finger—an action that raises Thomas's eyebrow and gets him booted out of the kitchen anytime I make what Gran calls "home food." But it's an excuse, really. Cooking together is our thing, yet when it comes to Gran's recipes, making them, letting her movements become my own, I appreciate solitude.

I proof the yeast, mixing in the sugar, salt, a slab of butter, *just suh,* and am transported to the first time she invited me into the kitchen, almost a year after Antony's death. How every time she visited, the pain of it seemed a little less, and every time she left, it was like losing my home, the only remaining true sense of family I had.

Next comes the flour, my arm jutting forward and back as I pour the powder over the sifter, *smooth like, yuh see.* Another belly rumble. I mix the wet and dry, set the ball of dough into the greased bowl with a cover over it, then set an hour on my timer. Coco bread wasn't a practical choice, but I need that sense of Gran's presence, Gran's food. My relationship with my mother may be a wreck, but me and Gran, we're perfect.

I open the fridge, grab a container of cut carrots and Thomas's home-made hummus, then head to the couch, open my laptop, and navigate to a password-protected folder full of case files. It's work I should do at the office, but that we all do at home—because there are never enough hours, never enough of us for all the hurt out there. Hurt we're told not to take home, but do anyway.

When the jingle of the alarm sounds, I'm in the middle of Destiny's file. A nine-year-old girl with a life that exemplifies my earlier thoughts. The world is shitty.

I've only met her once, yet her face is clear in my mind, even without the attached photo in her file, like all the faces are. Her smile—lit with so much joy, so much energy, despite the dump of a life she was dealt—seems to scream that despite all the shittiness, we should keep on. Because if this girl can smile the way she does, maybe there is hope.

Still, I wonder about the trade-off, continuing the propagation of the human race when it's this massive mess, knowing future generations will face such pain and hardship simply for the rare moments of good.

I punch the dough, Gran's invisible hands on the back of my elbow, my waist, guiding me to use the strength of my body—*nah too ruff*—but with smooth, sure power. Kissing her teeth when I do something wrong, then kissing my temple, hugging me to her side, letting me know it's okay, I'll learn.

I go through the rest of the steps with the warmth of her lingering over me. My hands become her hands, the motions a meditation.

While the dough rests, I open the freezer, knowing Gran would tut, telling me store bought and frozen is no patty. But it's after eight thirty now, and the carrots and hummus won't cut it much longer. Everything in the oven, I return to Destiny's file, making notes, ensuring I have a plan in place for tomorrow's visit. It's never fun to remove a child from her home and I'm hopeful this won't be the case. Her mother loves her, I can see that—envy it. The answer, then, is to help Tanisha see that her child needs her more than she needs the slime of a man she's dating.

I brought it up last time, indirectly, as I was taught to do during initial visits, emphasizing Destiny's safety and well-being, the importance of a secure environment, people she could look up to rather than be afraid of.

Tanisha leaned back, her brow raised, her mouth twisted. "What? You think I'm you?" She spread her hands to flow down the length of her. "You think some nice white boy gonna see me, see *this* place, these kids, and whisk me away?" She shook her head. "Nah, nah, nah—"

I stepped back, swallowed, ready to reply in line with my training, when she cut me off.

"I saw you. I *seen* you. You're friends with Jasmine. At the club just a few weeks ago, trying to act like you one of us, like you down, though you can't even move yo' hips. Then you're picked up by some bougie white boy, going hand in hand down the street, as we all gotta wait round forever trying to flag some cabbie who's not too afraid to pick up a group of Black girls."

"I don't see how—"

"That's why I'm telling you. You here, dancing around your words, telling me without saying it that I should get rid of my man if I wanna keep my kid. Well, that man brings food. He brings money. And he ain't never touched one of my babies, no matter what you trying to say."

I looked to my file, more to break away from her gaze than to find the notation I didn't need to read. "There was her bruised arm," I said, "characteristic of twisting. And a few months later, her broken—"

"She tripped," said Tanisha. "I told Social Services that. She a klutz."

I nodded, my chest tightening, my arms too. Because her words about me are true, words I've heard said in different ways, through looks and gestures and unmistakable intonation my whole life. I'm not one of them. But I'm not who she thinks I am, either . . . not quite. And all of it was irrelevant, because I was there to do a job, not to get shaken by my own insecurities.

"So do what you gotta do," she said. "Take your little notes, do your little assessment, but you're not taking my kid, and you're not telling me what to do." She paused, looking down at me, even though we're almost the same height. "Not you."

I inhaled, hating the way her gaze, her tone, ripped me of my training, sent me back years, to another part of the country, sitting cross-legged on the floor of my best friend's house, a place I thought I was welcome, belonged. A place full of laughter, rubbed shoulders, whispered admittances of crushes we were nervous but also excited to share, because the risk was so low. The boys in the pages of the magazines we spread out on the floor couldn't reject us, tell us our hair was too nappy, our noses too big or lips too plump—not to mention our skin, which I would never point out, my hand being so much lighter than the one that turned the pages.

And then the moment—along with that month's issue—was ripped from us. "People should stay with their own." My friend's mother, towering above us. "Makes me so angry. Not a single Black boy in this magazine." Looking at me sideways, as if the sight of me put a sour taste in her mouth. "White boys are what our girls are taught to want, what their girls are, too. And yet, white women trying to take all our men. Our *good* men. Ones with solid jobs and education. They make them think they're better than us. Well, I'll tell you this." She stared at her daughter, then slammed the magazine down on the table. "Stay with your own. Be interested in your own." At the last moment, her gaze met mine, stayed there, before she walked away.

Stay with your own . . . the words echoed in my mind, echo now, have echoed countless times in between. *Stay with your own.* But where does that leave me?

The oven's timer rips me out of my thoughts, and I jump, finally noticing the sweet, spicy-warm scent that always feels like a hug. Tonight I wish I could sink into it, bathe in it. I pull the warm buns out of the oven, set the pan on a cooling rack, then reach for the patty, hoping the leftover buns will be a peace offering. Of all the home food I make, coco bread is Thomas's favourite.

I slump onto the couch, about to take a bite, when my phone dings. It's Jasmine.

Impromptu BLM meeting tomorrow night to discuss the success of the march, plan next month's events, etc. etc. I know you're resistant for some reason, but just come, okay?

Before I can even think to reply, another ding.

Not taking no for an answer, so see you after work tomorrow. We'll take the bus together. No need to reply, because your reply is Sure, Jasmine! Wouldn't miss it! 😊 *xoxo*

I drop the phone to the couch, something between a laugh and a sigh in my throat. At least it'll let me procrastinate the conversation with Thomas even further. He won't be happy. But when I tell him why I'm not coming home, he'll act okay with it, supportive even, though when he sees my text, he'll get that momentary look he gets whenever I mention I'm doing something with Jasmine. Fear, maybe, that she'll draw me away from him, to a world he can't enter.

Not willing to wait another second, I bite into the coco bread and patty sandwich, the flavours settling my shoulders, relaxing my forehead, making me feel, as Gran always does, that there's at least one place, with one person, where I'll always belong.

Evelyn

Evelyn passed a hand over her rounded belly, then lowered herself onto the not-nearly-soft-enough subway seat. She'd accepted it. This baby was coming.

Yet fear still gripped her. For this child. For all the things that could go wrong. For Antony, when she'd be too tired to keep an eye on him while tending to the constant demands of a life whose existence relied solely on her, too tired to do what little she could to assure that, each night, he came back to her.

Evelyn raised her gaze to a woman pushing a stroller, shoulders drooped, eyes harried and vacant, but nodding thankfully at the passenger who rose from his seat to let her fall. That terrified her, too: the exhaustion that was to come. Last time, Violet had been there to help in the early months, neighbours and friends, as well.

Last time, she'd planned for it, wanted it, prepped their little brown house just outside of downtown Kingston as if she were a mother hen building her nest. Seeing that home in her mind's eye—the chickens in the yard, the clothes on the line that dried nearly instantly any time of year—a wistful smile twitched her lips.

It hadn't all been idyllic, but the good memories were the ones that surfaced. Casseroles showing up on the stoop in the last month of her pregnancy, and Violet, who came from her mountain village—speaking so fast and fluid Evelyn could barely understand her, despite her growing knowledge of patois—who'd been there, whether standing at the stove, wringing clothes before hanging them to dry, or washing all those cloth nappies.

In the hospital, too, she'd put a cool cloth to Evelyn's brow, helped her through it.

Despite the sway of the subway, Evelyn was in that sterile room again, the fear so potent she felt frenzied, desperate, and kept forgetting to breathe as her body was torn in two.

Her labour had started calmly. Cramps that were more than mild, but bearable. In between them, she had time to go over her list of items to bring: extra clothes, sanitary napkins, laxatives—which made her wary—enough cloth diapers for a minimum of two days, cotton balls, and a mason bottle that she'd fill with boiled water to rinse off her nipple before each breastfeeding.

And then the contractions got stronger. Closer together. Not alarmingly so, but enough that it was clear she'd need to get moving long before Kingsley would be back from his exam. She considered calling the school, getting someone to find him—the exam hadn't started yet—but labour took hours, days sometimes. He'd miss the test he'd been studying for for months, maybe have to do the whole class over. Most likely for nothing. Violet had come from the mountains a week early, in case the baby did, too, but she was off somewhere, visiting relatives, so Evelyn slung her hospital bag over her shoulder, slipped into her comfiest sandals, and made her way down the street to a neighbour who had three young ones of her own, but who she hoped would drive her to the hospital.

"It irie." Cherry had smiled when they'd arrived at the hospital and the staff wouldn't let her wheel Evelyn through the inner set of doors. "Trust, yuh hear? Everyt'ing going to be all right."

Evelyn tried to smile, to trust as her friend walked away, leaving her on her own. A deep groan erupted as a porter wheeled her through doors and then more doors, the sound coming from a place within her she hadn't known existed.

The sharp scent of bleach stung her nostrils as she was forced into a bed, pierced with a needle, connected to a drip. Nausea crushed upon her, weariness hazed her vision. The nurses told her it would be a long wait yet—six, maybe seven hours. That her husband's exam would be done. That he'd be here, right by her side. That she should rest.

And then they were gone, too, and she wanted to tell them to stay but could barely speak. She rolled over, tried to sleep. Like firecrackers erupting through her pelvis and lower back, the contractions came harder and faster, the baby's head pushing so that she felt certain she'd explode.

She screamed and a nurse's head was between her legs, a yelp sounding from the end of the bed. Within moments, two more arrived, one of them turning Evelyn over, saying she'd rolled onto the drip and the medicine to induce contractions was flowing far faster than it should have, saying there was the baby's head, and the doctor had left for dinner.

Evelyn was screaming, the pain more than seemed possible. The nurses were yelling, trying not to, the sound of their voices like wind through a straw, telling her not to push, that, "De doctor come soon."

Then another voice shouting at the nurses. "Yuh be crazy, don't yuh know a baby when yuh see it?" A hand gripping Evelyn's, caressing her forehead, telling her, "Me here for yuh, girl. Me here, now. And it time to push." Telling her she could do it. Violet's eyes focused on hers. Violet's voice calm. "Yuh can and yuh will."

And afterward, Antony in Evelyn's arms, Violet beside them—
caring for the baby, caring for Evelyn, too, in the hours after she'd
lost so much blood, she could hardly lift her head. In the weeks after,
when they'd left the hospital and the days and nights blurred into one,
Violet was there. Cooking food, cleaning house, walking or rocking
the baby so Evelyn could steal precious moments to sleep or shower
or relieve herself. Being the mother Evelyn had yearned for all these
years. The mother she hadn't realized how much she needed.

The subway slowed and Evelyn grabbed the railing at the announcement of her stop, hoisted herself to standing, glanced back at that
wearied mother, then pressed through the doors.

She wished Violet were here now. When this baby came, Antony
would be at school. Kingsley would be at work. Evelyn had no close
friends, no family, and was a decade and a half older than she had been
the first time. She felt her age in her muscles, her joints, her inability
to bounce back from a restless night. How much worse it would all be
with a baby in her arms. For over ten hours a day, every day, she would
have to do it all on her own.

Evelyn

L aughter sounded through the air, mixed with the trill of the robins' and cardinals' songs, the pigeons' coos, the scolding squirrels dissatisfied at the birds trying to steal their stores. The sound of traffic filled the air, too, but in the distance, far enough away that Evelyn could pretend they were removed from it all, in a small town, perhaps, similar to the one Evelyn had grown up in, but kinder, more welcoming to outsiders.

Not that they would ever leave. Again, Kingsley was being considered for tenure. This time, he felt certain they couldn't deny him. And, with only two years left of university, there was no chance Antony would come with them, and no chance Evelyn would leave her son to navigate this city alone, to sink deeper and deeper into the passions Evelyn feared would swallow him.

And then there was Dani. Evelyn turned to her friend, whose gaze was focused on their children. Hands on either side of her mouth, she shouted to Asher to wait his turn, and who did he think he was, anyway?

They'd met in their seventh month of pregnancy, Evelyn so afraid of the days and weeks with only her and this child in the house from sun-up to sundown, that she'd gone to a prenatal class hoping to find someone, anyone, with whom she could share the burdens, help multiply the joys. Fear slowed her steps as she'd approached the building, but she walked forward, hoping the years had changed people or that most of the slights had been in her head. This time, she resolved, she wouldn't let them be.

The small room, in the basement of a church that smelled faintly of mould and heavily of stale coffee, held a dozen women. Mostly white, but two Black, one Asian. All of them almost certainly in their twenties, maybe one or two having just entered their thirties. Except Dani. She tapped Evelyn's shoulder, grinning.

"Is this your first?" she asked, her tone making it clear she hoped it was.

"Second." Evelyn shifted from one foot to the other, the pain in her ankles making her transfer her weight as if she were on a teeter-totter. "But my son is seventeen, so it feels as if I'm going through it for the first time."

"Ah." Dani's eyes held mischief. "Seventeen. So I was right. You're one of them, too."

"One of?"

"A *geriatric* mother." Dani said the word in an overly loud whisper, then laughed. "I don't even mind the term. For years, I thought this day would never come, and here it is. I'm tickled pink!"

Evelyn laughed. She'd heard the term, too, feared and hated it. But the way Dani said it, it seemed an accomplishment.

Dani had linked her arm in Evelyn's, then squeezed her wrist. "You and me, we're going to stick together."

And they had, at that class and the next and the next, Evelyn never mentioning Kingsley's background, or Antony's. Telling herself she wasn't hiding it, that it simply hadn't come up, and fearing the moment it would. More than once, Dani talked about the future—the playgroups they'd attend, the daycares they should apply to, how they should show up to that first day of school side by side, looking down their noses at all the young mothers who thought they were the bee's knees.

Then, when Evelyn was counting down the days, anxious, uncomfortable, wanting the pregnancy to end, to finally meet this kicking, flipping bundle of life she'd come to love, but also fearing that moment, Dani rushed over at the start of the class, eyes wide with a plan.

"I've had the most wonderful idea!"

A dinner party—just the four of them, so their husbands could meet, become the good friends Evelyn and Dani already were. The good friends she was determined their babies would always be.

Evelyn met her friend's gaze as a shiver pulsed through her. She'd nodded along at Dani's suggestions, hoped they'd come true, without quite believing it, despite Dani's enthusiasm to see the friendship grow.

"Your son can come, too," said Dani, "but he'd probably be bored out of his mind, so I'm guessing just the four of us. This Sunday. I know it's soon, but next Sunday Charles has some law conference he'll be travelling for. Besides"—she grasped Evelyn's arm—"if we wait any longer, it could be the five of us. Or six! Which would be fine, but for this first time, I think four is right."

"Oh." Evelyn stepped back, dread hovering above her. This was it, another potential friendship ruined.

"Oh, what?" The excitement in Dani's eyes dimmed. "You'll come, won't you? I'm positively bored. It's been so hard to make friends since we arrived in this city, and even harder with this time bomb growing inside me." She laughed. "As thrilled as I am, it's like everyone is afraid to get to know me, because they think I'll disappear off the face of the earth as soon as I have a baby." Resolve coated her features. "But that won't be me. Oh, no! I've seen enough mothers in my time—friends and cousins, all three of my sisters—to know you can be a mother *and* have a life, if you want to."

"You can." And Evelyn had, in what felt like another life, when she'd dropped her baby boy off at daycare on the way to work. When, in the heat of the afternoon, feeling as if she had it all, she'd sit in the courtyard with the other teachers, marking papers and tests, sipping tea, laughing at the lizards scurrying this way and that, perching on typewriters, stopping to stare, then puffing out their gullets.

"I don't know." Evelyn eased herself into a seat. "Kingsley's so busy. Working for tenure, you remember?"

"The man has to eat."

"I just . . ."

"Evelyn! Spit it out."

Evelyn massaged her hands, the dread a physical pressure now, so certain of the way Dani's expression would shift, how she'd lean back in her seat. "I didn't just meet him in Jamaica. He's from there, and—"

"And he's a Black man?" Dani shook her head. "Oh, Evelyn, you think I'd care?"

"Well, some—"

"Some schmum." Dani laughed. "I couldn't care less. I saw you two last week. Outside the grocery on Eglinton East. And Charles won't care, either. We're basically an interracial couple ourselves."

"But I've seen Charles." Waving from the car as he dropped Dani off at a café. "He's—"

"A Protestant. And I'm a Jew."

"That's not—"

"You ask my father about that." Dani laughed again. "Or Charles's old man. As far as they're concerned, as far as most Jews or Protestants would be, we're interracial, all right."

Evelyn laughed, too, then shook her head, relief and a flicker of hope growing. She agreed to go, then had continued going, and even hosted on alternate months.

The men were friendly, but Evelyn and Dani, all these years later, were family.

"Asher!" Dani stood, gaze toward the slide, hands on her hips. "Wait your turn!" She turned to Evelyn, flashing an exaggerated grin. "Oy vey! This child!" Dani sat, shaking her head. "And how are you doing? With your worrisome child."

Evelyn sighed and stared at Kareela, her angel, this girl whom she'd feared, whom she'd prevented for so long, but who was just as marvelous a gift as her son.

"When this interest developed, I thought it was going to be another one of his short-lived passions. But every day there's more talk of how hardly anything has changed since this continent first started talking about the race problem, how when it comes down to it, those in power still see Black people as ignorant, lazy, criminal. Barely more than savages. I don't know how many times I've heard those terms. It's as if . . ." Evelyn shook her head, gaze still on Kareela, laughing, running, blissfully unaware of the world that awaited her.

"Well, he's not wrong," said Dani.

"But he's not entirely right, either." Evelyn understood him. She hated the world as it was, too. But she'd seen what fighting against it could bring. How fragile life was. She turned to Dani. "And all this anger, this passion . . . his grades are suffering, because injustice is all he can think of, all he focuses on. He wants to be the one to change the world."

"Someone has to."

"Not him."

"No . . ." Dani knit her brow. She patted Evelyn's knee. "At least it's a good passion. A positive one. Something to be admired."

Evelyn sighed. "A degree is what he should focus on. Becoming a lawyer or a judge, someone to make policy, help shape it."

"You sound like Kingsley."

"Well, Kingsley has a point. All Antony wants to do is write pamphlets, shout in the streets."

"He's young." Dani waved a hand, as if dismissing a fly. "This intensity will fade. He could still become that policymaker yet. He probably will."

If he doesn't let his grades fall so low he loses his scholarship, thought Evelyn, *or drop out altogether. If he doesn't follow his beliefs so far he ends up in jail—or worse.*

"Listen. It's risky," said Dani. "It's scary. I see that. And I won't claim to understand what life is like for your son . . . or your husband. But I know something of what it's like to be viewed as inferior, to not get the opportunities you deserve, to be seen as less." Dani stopped. "Asher, if I have to tell you one more time!" She turned back to Evelyn. "I've seen that frustration, that anger in my father, my grandfather. How, if a man does nothing about it, it can eat away at him. Make him believe he's less, if only because he didn't fight. Antony, at least, won't face that."

Evelyn had seen it, too, in Kingsley. Though he wouldn't say it— never mentioning race each time he got turned down for tenure— he must think it, fear it. Must feel the pressure he'd never spoken in so many words but that she'd seen in millions of actions, or lack of action, the way he made himself smaller than he was.

She didn't want that for Antony.

"Asher Daniel Thompson, you cut that out right now." Dani threw her arms in the air, stalked across the playground, grabbed the hand that had just shoved another child to the ground, and practically dragged her son back to Evelyn. Kareela ran behind them, her puff of a ponytail bouncing. "My goodness." Dani shook her head, her voice firm, but laughter in her eyes. "How parents are supposed to discipline without spanking, I've yet to figure out." She looked to Asher. "No ice cream tonight."

"Noooo! Mama, no!"

"Yes." Dani winked at Evelyn. "That ought to teach him."

Evelyn chuckled, then took Kareela's hand as Dani waved and walked away.

"Mama."

Evelyn crouched to Kareela's level.

"Do I get ice cream?"

Evelyn stared at her girl, seeing the same wide eyes Antony had had at this age, the precious nose, all he had turned into and all she might. She wished, for the millionth time, that it was easier to protect one's children—from scrapes and bumps, from name-callers, from hurt feelings and disappointments. From the way the seriousness of all those pains grew as they grew. She kissed her daughter's cheek, nodded, then placed her forehead on Kareela's.

"Heads!" Kareela laughed.

Evelyn grinned, then pressed her nose to Kareela's.

"Noses!"

Evelyn touched her cheek to her daughter's.

"Cheeks!" Kareela's sweet, clear voice rose into the air before they both broke into giggles.

Evelyn wrapped her arms around her daughter as Kareela's wrapped around Evelyn's neck. She tried to focus on her girl, but in her mind's eye, she saw Antony standing in front of the TV screen a few nights ago, yelling. Turning to Kingsley. "They call us apes!"

During the year Kareela had grown in Evelyn's belly, a young man had been shot nine times while sitting in his vehicle. It shook Antony, taking an interest and exploding it into an obsession.

"What if they do it to me?" he'd asked after hearing the news. "What if they do it to that baby?" He'd pointed at Evelyn's belly as she stared back, unable to answer, to reveal it was her fear, too.

When, several months later—after Kareela was in her arms, after Antony's face turned wan and tired from following the trial, spending the days and nights he should have been focused on his studies searching instead for instances of punishment after police brutality, for hope—the ruling came that the cop was cleared, Antony sank to the couch.

"We have to make it stop, Ma," he cried, leaning into her, her full-grown boy, letting Evelyn brush away the dreads that now reached his shoulders, then wrap her arms around him. "We have to make it stop."

Kareela

The bus ride to the Black Lives Matter meeting takes us over the Macdonald Bridge, into Dartmouth, and through to Preston. It's a long ride, one I've never been on before, and Jasmine gasps when I admit this.

"Why would I?" I shift in my seat. "I finished my schooling in Halifax. Now I work there."

"Oh. K." Jasmine shakes her head. "You're about to get an introduction."

I raise a brow as the bus stops in what looks like the middle of nowhere. Jasmine gives the little shake of her head that means *Don't worry, I got you.*

We step down from the bus and onto a gravel shoulder, with no houses discernible in either direction. "How is this even—"

"We're here."

I turn to see Jasmine, phone to her ear, hip out, a grin on her face.

"Get us first . . . yeah, yeah. *Pleeeease.*" She rolls her eyes then chuckles, a laugh seemingly for me rather than the person on the other end of the line.

She hangs up, the grin increasing. "You were so scared."

"What? No, I—"

"Yeah. You were so scared. Like, what is this homegirl up to, some kind of *Get Out* shit?"

"Get out—what?"

Jasmine rolls her eyes again. "Sometimes, Kareela, I swear, it's like you grew up under a rock."

Before I can respond, a car speeds over the hill to our left, slows, then stops. The back door swings open. Jasmine bends over to look through the front window. "Hmm." She gives cut-eye to the young woman in the passenger seat, then steps into the back, motioning for me to follow. "Kareela," she says, as she's buckling in, "this is my cousin, Dwayne."

Dwayne clears his throat. "And Sasha, his girlfriend."

Sasha turns, a sweet smile on her face. Her weave, shiny and smooth, swishes in front of her face like a fan. "Jasmine doesn't like me."

Dwayne reaches over to squeeze Sasha's leg. "Jasmine likes everyone. She's just jealous you always beat her out in—"

Jasmine knocks the seat. "See me spilling your business, D? 'Cause I could. Just watch. And don't be trying to tell anyone how I am or am not. You don't know me."

"I only changed your diapers."

"Once!" Jasmine leans back, eyes rolling, arms over her chest. "He messed it up, too, Ma said. Gave me a rash."

"I was six!"

"Excuses."

Sasha and Dwayne laugh. I try not to but can't help a grin. Minutes later, Dwayne pulls into a driveway with four cars already in it and another seven or eight lining the street in front of a large, time-worn house that may not even be from the last century.

"We usually meet in the North End," says Dwayne, "but renovations."

I nod as I step out of the vehicle, the thick scent of pine and burning wood hitting my nostrils.

"So next time," says Jasmine, looking back with a wink as she makes her way up the driveway, "it won't be so far to come. But tonight"—she does a little hop—"is gonna be way more fun." Through the ground-floor windows, people appear and disappear. Voices and laughter carry on the evening breeze. My steps hesitate as Tanisha's accusations come back to me—*You trying to act like you one of us*—and the implication behind those words.

Tonight, I want to fit.

The rally was great. I move up the driveway, nearing the door. The restaurant, too. I felt welcomed. Not like I belonged, exactly, but welcomed. Though, there they knew about Antony. Of course, probably most will here, too. Some may even know more about what happened to him, and why, than me.

We step into a wide, open foyer, with faces of smiling children on the wall and furniture that's likely older than me. Voices and laughter travel around us. The crowd is mostly young—forty and under, though a handful of older people are spaced throughout the rooms. A woman I recognize from the rally and restaurant, with the most fantastic dreads I've ever seen—coiled on her head in a way that suggests chaos and careful control—stands against one wall of the living room, with a couch and collection of armchairs, kitchen chairs, and folding chairs angled toward her. She rings a vintage-looking kitchen bell, and within moments, the voices and moving bodies cease.

Her posture is that of royalty, though her words, her tone, are casual, friendly, inviting. I try to focus on what she's saying, but she's going over the minutes—items I know little about that can't compete with the desire to scope out the faces in the room, wonder what it is, exactly, that's brought each one here. I notice, too, the shades. A few are lighter than me. One woman could pass, though I can see she has Black in her. I shift my gaze, aware of how many times people have looked at me the way I'm looking at her now, and how much I hated it.

The voice of the woman at the front is replaced with a deeper one, and I turn my head to see Carson. It's not until he speaks that I realize there was quiet chatter before. Now, the room is truly silent, every head turned. He talks about a mission. A calling. About what brings us here tonight, unites us, what should: the dismantling of all forms of anti-Black racism, the liberation of Blackness, the importance of Black healing, the freedom to love and self-determine and live—in safety.

It's this last point that sticks with me as that promise to my mother rings in my ears. The desire to keep me safe is what prompted it, despite so much that now indicates she couldn't care less.

But before I can sink into the complex feelings of being here, Carson moves onto a more specific mission. One I've heard plenty about, but I'm not sure I fully understand. I lean forward, arms on my crossed knees as he talks about the billions of dollars that go to police services across the country, the routine surveillance of Black and Indigenous people, the daily harm and injustices: the unwarranted cardings and arrests, the beatings, the murders.

An agonizing buzz thrums through my body. I stiffen at Jasmine's hand on my leg, try to ignore the all-too-familiar tsunami of grief that threatens. Carson's gaze meets mine, barely, before it travels on.

This is why I didn't want to be here. This is why I said no every other time Jasmine asked. But despite the despair that accompanied me at the rally, there was also the joy, the connection, the yearning that maybe, just maybe, change would come.

"All across the country," continues Carson, "for people of colour, the simple act of stepping out of our own front doors is one that involves danger and fear of being harassed by police. Heck"—he raises his arm—"we don't even need to step out the door. They target us in our homes. Our beds."

A murmur of agreement sounds through the crowd. I'm staring so hard at Carson—afraid of letting my gaze travel anywhere else, of seeing the eyes that are probably looking my way—that my vision blurs. I blink, try to focus again on Carson's words as he talks about the fact that Black communities deserve better, Indigenous and LGBTQ2S+ communities deserve better, *all* communities deserve better.

As he talks about the ways to create this "better," the silence behind Carson's voice fades. Grunts and mm-hmms of acknowledgement fill the space. And I can see why. It sounds good. Really good. Like why-in-the-world-is-this-stuff-not-happening-already good. *How* is it not happening?

Some of it must be . . . or is. I know. I'm a part of it every day at work. But not in the way Carson is talking about. Not in a way free from the systemic injustices that make my job feel as if I'm Sisyphus, pushing a boulder up a growing hill every single day. His words are inspiring, important, but also . . . not enough. Which is why we're here, I suppose. Why Antony marched.

We can't change what most needs to be changed: the way they see us. That, more than anything, is on them. But we can stand against the injustice. Show the world who we are and what we want.

As the sounds of acknowledgement continue and heads nod, I look around the room again, less afraid of the eyes that may be trained on me—the sad eyes, the bright eyes, the angry eyes—feeling a part of these people, because of the way I've been targeted, too, because of how much I want the world to be better.

My phone buzzes against my backside, pulling me out of this myth of oneness. Like a coward, I'd waited to text Thomas until I was halfway to

Preston. Now, according to the buzz in my pants, he's seen the message, knows I blew off our dinner plans to come here. It's not the first time I've chosen Jasmine and my growing group of friends over Thomas, without even an invite for him to join, and guilt courses through me. But guilt is better than sitting across from him would be, seeing in his eyes the plea to make a decision: the decision he wants me to make. I send a quick message, apologize again—promising we'll talk once I get home—then silence the phone and bring my focus back to Carson.

Evelyn

A s her foot landed on the front steps, Evelyn stiffened. The shouts were muffled, enough that the neighbours wouldn't hear, but already Evelyn could make out the tension in their voices, imagine the standoff: her two men, so similar and so different. Each unable to see through the other's eyes.

She gave Kareela's hand a squeeze, put her key in the lock, and stepped inside, knowing in mere moments she'd have to decide whether to step between them.

"Education doesn't solve everything!"

"It solves a lot." Kingsley's voice, on the edge of anger, trying to hold in a full yell, trying to seem reasonable, calm, and even-tempered.

"Oh, really? Like what?"

"Respect, Antony. It gets you respect, a place in the world, and from there—"

"From there you get passed over, year after year, and you smile, their little lapdog, their Uncle T—"

"Antony!" At Evelyn's voice, the two men turned, Kingsley's jaw and fists clenched tight, his back ramrod straight; Antony slouched, shifting foot to foot, a mix of sheepishness and determination on his face. He kissed his teeth to the side and cast his gaze away from both of them.

"Let him talk," said Kingsley. "He thinks I'm an Uncle Tom? That's what you were going to say? Why? Because I'm not yelling in the street? Because I'm putting food on our table, a roof over our heads? Your head, while you live here, rent free. Because I'm not yelling 'Racism!' every time the world doesn't go exactly as I'd like?"

Antony stepped forward. "That's not—"

"Kareela." Evelyn peeled the girl's arms from around her leg, then crouched so she was eye-level. "I think Holly doll needs a nap. Why don't you go to your room and check?"

Kareela looked between the men, her eyes taking it in . . . her ears, too.

"Go, sweetie." Kingsley smiled at his daughter, gestured toward the hall, and she scampered off. He turned to Antony. "I'm not saying what you're doing is wrong. I'm not saying you shouldn't do it." He sighed, the sound thin yet forceful, like wind squeezing through attic eaves. "I'm just saying find other ways. Safer, more practical ways. Yes, change sometimes comes from yelling, from marching in the street. But it also comes from getting the notice of people in power. More change. Safer change. So finish school and finish well, then go further. Become one of those people."

"What?" Sarcasm dripped from Antony's voice. "Like you did?"

"No." Kingsley stopped, lips tight, everything still clenched. "I'm a medical sciences instructor, not a policymaker or politician. But if that's where your passion lies, become someone who enacts change through the proper channels."

Antony stared, slumped again, his whole body a sigh. "I never said I was dropping out."

"But you're planning to miss an exam to prep for a rally? I've seen your grades lately. You're better than that. Do better."

Antony looked from Kingsley to Evelyn, back to Kingsley. Evelyn wanted to reach out—for all the pain she saw in him. To tell him they'd support him, no matter what.

"Do both, if you must," continued Kingsley. "But not one at the cost of the other."

She wanted to side with Kingsley, too, to help keep Antony far away from all the activists drawing dangerous attention to themselves.

"I have to go." Antony crossed between them, the front door closing with a thud.

Kingsley looked to Evelyn, his hands raised in surrender. Evelyn stared at the door, then turned to her husband. "His exam is tonight?"

Kingsley nodded.

"Do you think they'll let him retake it?"

Another sigh. "I may be able to pull some strings, but I shouldn't have to." Kingsley sank to his armchair. "This boy just doesn't understand. If he knew, really knew, what it was like, what it can be like. If he could see . . ."

"Maybe you should tell him what it was like." Evelyn perched on the edge of the chair, taking her husband's hand in hers. "Why we left."

Kingsley looked across the room, his gaze focused on something Evelyn couldn't see. He'd witnessed so much more than she had, experienced the horror, the pain, in ways she hadn't. And maybe if he shared—

Kingsley stood, their hands pulling apart. "We left so he wouldn't have to know."

HOURS LATER, THE house quiet and dark—Antony, who knew where, Kareela asleep in her bed, and Kingsley in his office—Evelyn crossed to the living room, her shoulders heavy with the weight of memories, with all their son didn't know, with the loneliness of not being able to tell him, to talk about it with Kingsley, even.

If they'd stayed in Jamaica, Antony's skin colour would have been an asset, helped him rise through the ranks and become one of the powerful people Kingsley was talking about . . . if he'd survived that long. And that's why they'd left. So he'd survive. Be safe.

She sat in the rocking chair. The same one they'd bought in their first months in the city—similar to the one that had sat in their home in Kingston, where she'd nursed and rocked her baby boy.

She'd rocked throughout her pregnancy, too, the chair placed strategically to catch the evening's breezes, as she tried her hand at knitting. Once Antony had arrived, the nurses laughed at her haphazard attempts, told her she couldn't put a baby "in dese t'ings." Cotton shifts—lightweight, breathable—was what he needed. Antony had been in one of those shifts, months later, while she rocked him to sleep after returning home from a visit with friends. Remembering the bin of laundry ready to be put away, she placed Antony in the bassinet by her bed, then stood, folding clothes, moving from the bed to the dresser to the closet, thinking of the visit, how her friends—fellow teachers, most from the island and some from away, like her—had cooed over Antony, all smiles. Then, as Evelyn probed about their lives, those smiles had faded.

Evelyn, in the haze of life with a newborn, had known little of the state of things. How politics, the upcoming election, had transformed the parish into a war zone. There was no more staying late after class. The whistles from men were now the least of the women's worries. Just last week, one of them had been attacked, her purse stolen, her necklace ripped from her throat, watch from her wrist, earrings from her lobes. The woman pulled her hair from the side of her face, revealing thin scabs.

"I was lucky that's all they did," she said. "A few scrapes and bruises, the money and jewellery lost, but a student found my bag in a ditch. I got all my papers back."

"The police did nothing," said another of Evelyn's friends.

"The police aren't even police anymore. They're militia."

The women nodded.

"The officers shrugged," continued the one who'd been attacked. "Didn't even ask for descriptions. Told me to stop walking by myself. That beyond that, they had more important things to deal with."

"And they do," said another. "War in the streets. Barricades. Road-blocks of garbage, and people gunned down." She shuddered. "It's desperate out there—jobs lost, men with families to feed and no concern for anything but that."

A chill had run up Evelyn's spine. It did again as she folded Kingsley's undershirts, stacked them neatly, the faint barking of the dogs growing louder. Their dogs, who hadn't been there to greet Evelyn when she returned home. She froze at the sound of shuffling—yet Antony was fast asleep. The barking was thunderous now, nails scratching at the loose latch of the back screen door.

A groan mixed with a curse sounded beneath the bed, followed by more shuffling as two hands, then a head, a shirtless torso, khaki pants, and bare feet thrust themselves out from under it and fled the room, not looking back but running toward the front door just as the dogs burst through the back door.

Evelyn chased after the dogs, watched the animals leap against the front door: howling, scraping. She stood watching, terror raising the hair on her arms, wanting and not wanting to open the door, let the animals rip to shreds the man who'd lain underneath her bed, her baby boy just an arm's length away. But she was frozen.

Evelyn

After the break-in all those years ago in Jamaica, Kingsley and Evelyn had sat at their kitchen table, dinner uneaten, staring at each other as they imagined all that could have happened. All that may happen in the days and weeks to come.

"You called the police?" Kingsley had nudged his untouched plate away from himself.

Still trembling, Evelyn nodded.

"And they didn't come?"

She shook her head—trying not to relive that blast of fear at the shuffling under the bed, the terror that followed as the man scrambled out from under it.

Kingsley's voice lowered to a growl. "Those dogs."

"It's not their fault." Evelyn reached her hand out, resting it on Kingsley's. When she'd gotten the animals to settle, she'd seen traces of fur, meat, and blood in their mouths. Drawn away, most likely, by an accomplice with roadkill who figured he'd left enough time for his comrade to get in, raid the place, and get out, unaware that Evelyn had arrived home in the midst of it, leaving the intruder trapped.

Kingsley's fist clenched, the veins in his arms rising into long, angry cords. Evelyn uncurled his fingers and rubbed hers along his palm. "It could have been worse. We're lucky."

"Exactly." Moisture glistened in Kingsley's eyes. "It could have been so much worse. He could have done anything—to you, to him." He gestured to the bedroom, where Antony lay in his bassinet. "It's getting bad out there. Scary. You don't know."

"I know."

Kingsley's voice deepened, the urgency of it making the hair on the back of Evelyn's neck rise. "You don't." He told her what her friends had. The bodies he'd seen. More. How every day, the tensions were building. How in the past few months, it'd risen to a fever pitch. "I've applied to City University," he said. "In Toronto. For my PhD. I've gotten in. With a partial scholarship."

The air around them buzzed and pulsed, muffling words she wished she hadn't heard. "Toronto?"

"I didn't tell you. I know I should have, but I thought it was such a long shot. I thought . . ." Kingsley hesitated. "I know you said when you married me that this was your home now, that you had no intention of going back."

"I don't."

"But we have to. We have to get out. There's no life for us here, no future."

"You don't know that." Evelyn pulled her hand from his, the air still thick, weighted with the bitterness of betrayal—that he'd made the choice to apply without her, that, as far as she could tell, they'd be leaving whether she liked it or not.

"I'll get my degree in a few years. And if things get better, we can return. If not, with your citizenship, we should be able to stay."

"You don't know what it's like." Evelyn stood. She turned from him, paced this house *she'd* chosen, in the country *she'd* decided to make her life in, raise a family in, leaving everything from the past behind. "The cold. You couldn't handle it."

"We'll get parkas."

"I don't just mean temperature-wise." She turned back to him. "I did my training in Toronto. People don't talk to each other. There's no community. It's dirty."

"We'll figure it out."

"How? We'll have no money. No support." Evelyn sat back down, placing both her hands on his. "The gals were telling me the government has gone crazy. We'd have to leave the house. We'd only be allowed to take a hundred dollars each out of the country. We'd have to start over with nothing!"

"But we'd have a start," he said. "We'd have our lives. And there are ways to get more money out."

"Illegal ways."

"Then we'll break the law."

Toronto. Canada. A place she'd fled, vowing never to return, the entire country tainted with the memories of her childhood—her father's fists, her mother's cries, her own perpetual fear. Growing up, she thought she'd never have children, never have her own family, for fear that any man could one day morph into her father, and that even if he didn't, her father, always, could find her, hurt her—and them.

But then she'd stepped off the plane in Kingston, and all that panic seemed to melt away. She'd felt safe. She'd felt far enough removed that the looming shadow of terror her father cast couldn't reach her. She'd met Kingsley and known, within days, that he could never be the man her father was. That with him, she would be safe. That any children they had would be safe, too.

She turned back, hands on hips, anger and understanding swirling within her as she stared at the man she'd put her trust in, who was asking this of her: to keep them safe. "I don't know . . ."

"You're right. You don't know." Kingsley's voice broke, his eyes closed. "Omar."

"Wha—"

"Cherry's son. He went into town for some produce. The people were protesting. The bullets started—"

"No!" A sharp burst of anguish shot through Evelyn's core. "He's twelve."

Kingsley yanked his forearm across his eyes, smearing the wetness there. "If we want to keep our lives"—he gestured down the hall again—"keep his, we have to leave."

Evelyn had nodded, then put her hand in his once more, entwining their fingers. And in the days and weeks to come, as their community shrank, she saw, more and more, the truth in his words. Many fled. Others didn't have the chance: her director at the Red Cross, one of her fellow teachers, two more neighbours, caught in the crossfire.

EVELYN JUMPED AT the sound of her name, then turned to see Kingsley, suddenly two decades older, standing in the shadows. She leaned forward in the rocking chair, her gaze on him as he crossed the room, then sat. "I think of those days a lot," he said. "The weeks and months before we left."

"This isn't there," she whispered, the memory of that night at the kitchen table, her hand on his as he'd revealed his decision to bring them here, so fresh in her mind.

"It could be."

"Here," she said, "police don't stand on corners with machine guns.

Here, people don't run through the streets wielding machetes. Here, it's safe." She paused. "Safer."

"But not safe enough." Kingsley shook his head. "Where does it come from? This political obsession. This . . . I don't know." He slumped. "I just want to shake it out of him." Kingsley held up his arms and shook them.

Evelyn met the eyes of this man she'd loved almost since the first moment they'd met, with whom, despite the struggles, the secrets, the ways in which they hardly knew each other at all, she'd made a life, a family.

She wanted to comfort him, but also, she wanted to see him heal the fractured relationship he had with the son they had upended their lives to protect. "Maybe we shouldn't fight him on this." She spoke slowly, her tone soft, hoping it would help him listen, consider. "Maybe we should try to meet him halfway."

"It's foolishness!" Kingsley cut his eyes at her. "The boy missing an exam for a rally. Not even a rally, to prep for it. As if what little difference they could make would compare to throwing away his life, his future."

"Do you want to lose him over it?" Evelyn leaned forward. "Have him stop coming home? Or, maybe worse, do you want to win, and see the passion fade from his eyes?"

Kingsley's head shook.

Evelyn interlaced her fingers with his, the same way she had that night a lifetime ago. "I don't think we could stop him, even if we tried. We're definitely not going to yell it out of him, so maybe . . ." She hesitated, torn between wanting to support both of her men, not knowing how, but desperate to figure it out. "Maybe we try to understand him, listen instead of argue, and help him understand us, what we've been through, what we know that he doesn't. We came here to protect him from that, but maybe protecting him now means letting him know."

"I don't want to dredge any of that up. He's not stupid. He's so interested in the past. He must know what happened in Jamaica, the fighting, the killing. Know and not care. Know and think he's immune." Kingsley clenched his fists. "It's too dangerous, what he's doing. And where will it lead?"

Evelyn inhaled, choosing her words carefully; their best bet of reaching Antony was to remain a team. United. "Your father wanted certain things for you, and mostly, you listened. But maybe that's because those were the things you wanted for yourself. Antony's different than you, than us, and maybe that's okay, if the path he takes isn't—"

"We've worked so hard to make a life for him here, to provide a future."

"One missed exam won't destroy that."

"It's a pattern."

Evelyn nodded, seeing it, too, fearing it, but fearing more the loss of her son, the resentment that could build from these arguments, that could one day push him so far away they'd be lucky to receive a card at Christmas. "Well, maybe it's a pattern we can alter. Suggest he finish out this semester with focus, there's only a few weeks left, then next semester take fewer classes, giving him time to focus on his future and his passion. Like you said, both, if he must."

Kingsley shook his head, brow furrowed, but didn't argue.

"So we try," said Evelyn, despite his actual agreement. "Pose the suggestion. Say if he graduates, he can continue to live here, rent free."

"And if he doesn't?"

"We cross that bridge when we come to it."

Kareela

When the official portion of the Black Lives Matter meeting ends, it seems it's time to eat. The array of food would normally tantalize me, but tonight, it prompts the urge to heave. The nausea is inconsistent—not morning sickness, but whenever-it-rears-its-head sickness. I turn away from the buffet-style table and right into Carson.

"Kareela." His smile is warm, strong, confident—just like the way he holds himself. "So glad to see you tonight. Based on the other day, I didn't think we would."

I let out a little chuckle and tilt my head toward the opposite side of the room. "Jasmine didn't exactly give me a choice."

"Yeah." The warmth in his expression spreads. "She's always been one to get what she wants. Ever since she was a baby."

I offer a closed-lip smile, trying to not let the nausea win, not zig and zag through the crowd, in search of the nearest bathroom. Realizing this smile is only making it worse, I open my mouth and breathe gently.

"What did you think?"

"Hmm?" I see an open window less than fifteen feet away and wonder what reason I could find to take this conversation toward some fresh air.

"Of the meeting. Of us?" The dimple in his left cheek prompts a flutter to mix with the sickness. Is this what it is to carry new life? Hormones so messed up you don't know whether you want to yak or fall into the arms of the near stranger in front of you?

"It was good." I rub an arm, willing away the flutter and the sick roil of my gut. "Interesting."

His smile stays firm, lips closed. I know what this is. I was trained to do it when trying to get a client to open up. *Don't rely on questions,* my mentor had said. *Silence is sometimes the best way to get genuine answers.* It works. Is working.

"It seems like a lot," I say to break the silence, stepping back as a stream of laughing children run between us. "I mean, great and all, but maybe not very . . ." I let out a puff of air, my weight shifting from foot to foot. "I don't know, realistic? I mean, in theory, yes, I could see how it would work, be so much better. And I can see how some of it's totally doable, but other parts—" I look away, the children in a circle now, playing some hand-clap game, giggling, happy, safe. "Just—" I look back. "It's a lot, when our society is already set up the way it is."

Carson's face remains unchanged, his gaze focused on mine. Attentive.

"Like disarming the police," I continue. "Most of the time, it would be fabulous. It would, well, prevent . . . like, so much. But how would that work when they're called to a scene and the . . . uh, assailants have guns? How would they protect themselves? And knowing that scenario would happen, who would want to become an officer in the first place?"

Carson nods, his grin broadening. "Those are excellent questions.

Important ones. And when we have a bit more time, I'll get you the answers."

I shrug. "That'd be good."

"It'd be great. And especially with your experience in social work, we'd really love you to volunteer. We're always looking for—"

"I don't—"

"Listen." Carson raises a hand. "You've got a lot of questions, and I've got answers. There isn't time or space for a proper conversation tonight. But I'd love to talk to you more about it. A group of us are meeting later this week to hand out petitions to defund the police, do some canvassing. Why don't you join us?"

"I don't think—"

His hand falls on my shoulder. "Don't answer right now. Think about it."

I look away from him. Attending a rally was bad enough, but even attending this meeting feels like stepping over the line. A betrayal. It is. Volunteering, being a part of this movement out in the open, would send my mother reeling—or would have, back when she pressured me to make that promise.

"I get if you're afraid," he says, his hand still on my shoulder. "And I'm not trying to say I know you or what you went through, what your family did. Because I don't. But I know enough to know that sometimes the thing you're afraid of, that you step away from, is exactly the thing you should step toward."

As a familiar and painful sensation creeps in, I swipe my hand under my eyes and glance around to see if anyone has noticed. Frustration at this decades-old hurt, coupled with the more recent loss of my father, makes me ache for escape. "It's late," I say. "And we've got a long ride back. Work tomorrow."

"Dwayne's going to drive you and Jasmine into town. But you're right, it's late."

I release a sound of agreement, slip out of his grasp, and cross the room to Jasmine, who stands amidst a group of people, her hands gesticulating the way they do, her voice carrying above the others'. I turn at the last moment, find a bathroom, breathe deep, realizing the nausea has left but that I'd prefer it to the feelings Carson erupted in me, the fresh, confusing whirlpool of grief and guilt. I stare into the mirror, seeing what my mother sees every time she looks at me—why she must find it so hard to look. Antony—or at least aspects of him. His nose. His eyes. The distinctive rise of his cheeks.

I splash my face and turn to the door, determined to find Jasmine immediately, to get the hell out of here.

WHEN I SAY my farewells to Jasmine, Dwayne, and Sasha and step into my building, it feels like an odd repeat of yesterday's approach to the door. Today, however, rather than rushing at me with excitement, Thomas is cautious. He asks how the meeting went, though I'm sure it's the baby that's forefront in his mind.

"Interesting." Discomfort trickles through me, at wanting and not wanting to talk about this new part of my life that's so separate from him.

"What was the reason," he says, his tone tentative, "for going? Did the rally prompt something, or . . . well, you seemed upset about it."

I hesitate, knowing he's thinking about that night, my colleagues' gaze on him, his gaze on me. How, ever since, things have shifted between us, the closeness waning. I can't very well tell Thomas I largely went to delay seeing him, so I use Carson's words instead.

"Maybe that's why I should go," I say. "Because it's upsetting. Because in all these years, hardly anything has changed. Because it should."

He nods.

But it's more than that, I realize. Working with the community I'm working with, and seeing not just my colleagues' passion but the passion of the people they fight for, has been inspiring, has opened my eyes to so much I hadn't taken the effort to see. But it's also the way my colleagues view me as part of it. As one of them. I want more of that. "Plus, I was invited," I say. "And it felt good to be." It felt good, too, to know that I was doing the thing my father wanted us to do, taking it a step further, even if it was too late for him. "I just never had that 'in' before, you know? That clear path. And now I do."

"That makes sense."

I sigh, knowing it's paining both of us to delay the inevitable. "About last night . . ."

"You had a right," he says, "to keep it to yourself. I didn't mean to pry. To snoop, or, well—"

"You didn't. Your computer froze, right?"

"Yeah." He reaches to the floor, pulls up a brown paper bag. "I know you said there's no point yet. But I really want to know."

I reach into the bag, certain what I'll find, then stare at the box. "I think I'm supposed to wait until first thing in the morning."

He shakes his head. "Not when you're this far along."

I raise an eyebrow.

"I asked at the pharmacy. You can take it right now."

"I don't see the point in knowing"—I drop the box back in the bag—"when I haven't even decided what I'll do about that knowledge."

His lips press together and his nostrils flare with a long intake of breath. "Okay. I get that. But maybe actually knowing will help you figure it out."

I shake my head, push the bag away.

"So when you say what you'll do about that knowledge, do you mean . . . well, what do you mean? Adoption or . . ."

I shrug. "Or."

"Uh-huh." Thomas nods. "That makes sense. The easier solution, I guess." He's silent for a bit. "I don't know." He chews his lip. "Just, like I said, the first thought was terror. Like how the hell will we handle this? And I thought . . . I guess I just thought you would want the baby. Or in case you did, I needed to be on board, you know? Make sure I didn't ruin the moment. Be happy. And that seemed crazy. I've just started this new career path. My hours are insane. They'll continue to be. But lots of people in worse situations than ours have kids. And they make it work. So I tried to think about the good things. A little person, made up of us. Cuddles and trips and seeing this new human grow."

He stops, rakes a hand through his hair. "It's no secret that neither of us had the picture-perfect family. Your parents checking out, all that shitty I don't even know what to call it between you and your mom. My dad starting over—whole new family, whole new life. And that put the terror in me more—we don't have the best role models."

"Your mom's amazing."

"Yeah." He chuckles. "She is. But she wasn't always so great, not the first couple of years after Dad left. And I know how hard your dad's passing was for you—the way he went."

I nod. The ache rising—sharp and complicated. Nearly two years, and this pain, when it comes, feels as fresh as the day we found him.

"Anyway, we've both had it rough in different ways, but then I thought, even with the crappy hands we've been dealt, look what we've accomplished. You're killing it at your job, I'm on the road to. We've got this decent place, a bit of money in the bank. We're making it work. So we can make having a baby work, too. If we want. If we try. We can give this kid a way better life than either of us had. And maybe that, in itself, is a way to make the world a bit less shitty."

Affection swells within me at how earnest he looks. How vulnerable. And he has a point. But a decision like this can't be made on simply having a point.

"So will you test?" He holds up the bag. "And then at least we know if this is a conversation to keep having, or if all this talk is nothing more than hypothesizing."

I take the bag, a lump in my throat.

Minutes later, I step out of the bathroom, hold up the stick, and Thomas's arms are around me. Not congratulatory, exactly. But weighty. "This is happening," he says, and I'm not sure what exactly he means. The baby? The need to keep talking? To decide?

I stare at the stick, amazed at how knowing something in your gut and seeing the undeniable proof of that same thing can prompt such distinct sensations.

"We better book a doctor's appointment," he says.

"Not yet."

He presses his lips. "I'm guessing you don't want to tell our parents."

I shake my head, my gaze back on the stick.

"Do you even have a GP? Here, I mean? I bet we could get you in at mine if—"

"Thomas." I put my hand on his, draw my gaze from the stick. "Not yet."

A mix of emotions I can't quite read swirls behind his eyes. "I know you're scared, Ree. About the world. Maybe about being a parent so young. But I'm telling you, we can figure this out. We can make it work."

"Thomas," I say again, trying to say it in a way that will make him finally hear. "For me, figuring it out might mean stopping it."

His eyes twitch, just the slightest bit.

"I have time." I swallow. "Weeks to decide. So . . ."

"You looked it up?"

"No." I shrug. "I mean, it's legal until twenty weeks. So based on how far I must be . . ." My voice trails off.

He nods, lowers his head, and then raises it again. "Maybe I'm being silly," he says, "maybe I let the goal to get on board get away from me. It's just, like I said, when I started thinking about the good, the potentially fun and wonderful parts about having a child with you, I don't know." He shrugs, the corner of his lips rising. "I guess I fell a little bit in love with the idea. With this baby, that's ours."

Something thick and uncomfortable rises within me—that he could be right. That this could be a chance to do things better. But I push it away. "My career is just starting." I step back, increasing the distance between us. "It's intense. Yours hasn't even begun." I pause. "And I think I'm going to start volunteering. That will take up extra time."

"Volunteering?"

The words were out before I had a chance to think about them. But it makes sense . . . or it might, if what Carson said was true, that we need to step toward the things that scare us. So much of the reason I'm unsure about this baby is that I'm unsure about myself, and so much of that is connected to Antony, and my Blackness, or lack thereof. Maybe connecting with people like him, with the side of myself that feels like a stranger, is exactly what I need to figure things out. I take a breath, wear a smile that holds more confidence than I feel. "Yeah. At BLM."

He scrunches his forehead, his expression inscrutable.

"We have time to think about what we want to do," I say, and can tell from Thomas's injured expression he knows I mean "I," not "we." "So let's just, I don't know, table this. For a few weeks at least. I need time to think and I don't want to talk about it constantly."

He says nothing, only stares, wanting, I'm sure, to say that talking is how we'll figure it out. That this, after all, is a part of "the plan," just a little out of order.

His plan, though. Not mine.

I step into the bathroom, toss the test and packaging into the garbage, then turn back toward him. "I appreciate your enthusiasm. Really." I pause, the thump of my heart too palpable. "But just because you can make something work doesn't mean you have to, or that you should."

Evelyn

velyn stood at the counter chopping vegetables, adding them to the pot one by one. The onions and garlic, thyme and tarragon had already simmered, filling the room with the scents of her childhood. Hodge-Podge, the one dinner she remembered clearly, her mother's go-to because you could make it once, have enough to last for days, add to it if necessary.

It wasn't necessary today, but something had made her think of it, of her mother's hands, ornamented only by a thin gold band, chopping, rubbing the thyme between her palms, sniffing, handing Evelyn a spoon and asking whether she thought it was "just right."

Evelyn looked to Kareela on the floor with her legs tucked beneath her, one hand propping her up as the other held a puzzle piece. Her daughter's brows knitted, just the way Kingsley's would, as she stared at what Evelyn could clearly see was the eye of an octopus. Kareela looked from the pieces already joined on the floor to the piece in her hand, back and forth, back and forth, until her face lit up and those little, able fingers found the correct spot. She lifted her gaze to Evelyn and smiled before returning her focus to the puzzle.

Evelyn's hips swayed to a soft beat on the ancient dial radio she kept above the stove, the same one she'd brought in her suitcase from Kingston. The sound of the front door opening and then closing travelled to her ear, followed by Antony's voice. "Hodge-Podge?"

"You got it!" Evelyn beamed as her son walked into sight, dreads now hanging below his broad shoulders and, despite the difference in their style, looking more and more like Kingsley every day. He was a graduate, at last, only one year late, though he was putting off his law school acceptance to champion the fight against racial injustice—which seemed more muted lately. Meetings. Posters. Presentations at local schools. But no big rally since the one a couple years ago. He came around behind Evelyn, kissed her cheek, then swiped a carrot, crunching loudly at the corner of his mouth.

"What's up, Doc?" he asked of Kareela, who looked up and giggled, adoration in her eyes. He knelt on the floor beside his sister, analyzing the puzzle, handing her a piece, asking her what she was thinking about the prospect of Grade One, whether she thought her teacher would be super cool or just all right.

"Oh, Ma!" He stood, reached past her to the radio, twisted the dial until the hip-shaking beat filled the room. He spun, swayed back and forth, his teeth showing, then grabbed Evelyn's hand. She batted him away, laughing. "Ma." He tilted his head, gave the wily smile he'd been giving since he was Kareela's age, which Evelyn found impossible to resist.

Evelyn let him pull her to the centre of the kitchen and spin her. She laughed again as the moves her friends had taught her over two decades ago, on hot nights, barefoot in the sand or at rec centre parties, came back to her. She twirled and dropped it low—or lower, at least.

Kareela popped to her feet, clapped, and jumped, as Antony grabbed her hand, too, then dropped Evelyn's to focus on his sister.

"Like this, KeeKee!" He put his hands on his hips, did a little two-step, swayed. Kareela copied him, giggling all the way. Antony turned back to Evelyn, then grasped her hand and gave her another little spin.

"Dad always said you could dance"—he laughed—"for a white girl. But Ma, wow!"

Evelyn shimmied.

"Now, my ladies, try this." Antony put his hands to his hips, squatted. "To the right, front, left, back. To the right, front, left, back."

Evelyn shrugged and put her hands on her hips, then Kareela did, too.

"Smoother, now. Get that chest going. They call this the wine!" The music played on as Evelyn and Kareela mirrored Antony, Kareela's giggles catching, so they were all laughing now. "We wining, we wining!" called Antony.

Evelyn tried to drop it low and collapsed to the floor.

"Ma! You all right?" Antony turned down the music and crouched to her, a hand extended.

"Yes!" Evelyn laughed and pulled him down beside her. "Just not as flexible as I used to be."

"So." Antony's expression turned serious, though there was a glint in his eye. "You could get low." He paused, the smile clearly struggling to break through. "At one point in time."

"I could get low," said Evelyn, as Kareela plopped in her lap.

"What was it like?" Antony leaned back on his hands. "Living in Jamaica. Meeting Dad. I was born there, and I have no idea."

"It was wonderful." A smile tugged at Evelyn's lips. "Not all of it, of course. But a lot. So much when it related to our own lives. Our inner world."

"Tell me."

"Tell you what?" Kingsley stepped into the room, his satchel still slung over his shoulder, his brow lifting high. "And tell me what's going on here."

"He's asking about Jamaica." Evelyn reached her hand to him, gesturing for him to join them.

"Ah." To her delight, Kingsley looped off his satchel and sat cross-legged on the floor across from them. "Well, the best part was meeting your mother." He winked.

"But how was it different?" asked Antony. "How was it the same? Was it a huge culture shock for you, Ma?"

"It was." As a memory crept over Evelyn, she laughed. "The time I was served chicken feet."

"They have that at Dulcie's."

"Yes. But I'd never had it. I didn't even know it was something people ate."

Kingsley leaned back. "That was at Ma's, wasn't it?"

"It was." Kingsley had taken her to the mountains, the farthest she'd ever been from Kingston, to a village where not just some but every eye turned to watch as she walked by, mouths hung open. "Your uncle was there." Evelyn grinned at Kingsley. "He went and got the chicken, right from the yard." Kingsley nodded and chuckled. "Chopped its head off, right there in the dirt."

"What!" Kareela squealed. Her hands flying to her cheeks in shock.

"I know, I know." With a laugh, Evelyn placed a hand to her throat. "I was scarred!"

"Oh, come on, they weren't slaying chickens in Juniper Cove?"

"They were." Evelyn looked to her husband. "But not right in front of me." She turned to Antony. "So your grandmother, she plucked it right there, on a table in the backyard, under an awning. Talking away."

"You couldn't understand half of it."

"I couldn't!"

"You can't understand Granny?" said Kareela.

"Not then. She was speaking full-on patois."

"Probably to throw you off guard," said Kingsley. "See how much sticking power you had. She could have toned it down enough for you to understand."

"Well, she didn't." It all came back to Evelyn: Her nerves at meeting this woman who'd given birth to the man she loved. The sweet scent of tropical flowers, ripe guava, and soursop. The sharp tang of blood in the dirt. "And it's hard to make conversation when you catch maybe two words out of twenty." The land came back, too, so lush. So vivid. Greenery like she'd never imagined. A sky that went on for miles.

"So dinner is served," Kingsley continued, "and the guest of honour—"

"Gets the chicken feet." Evelyn put a hand to her mouth, just as she'd done then, the horror alive at the memory. "I had to try not to heave when I saw them floating in my bowl. I didn't know about this 'guest of honour' thing. But I looked up at your father, and his eyes told me to grin and bear it."

"So you ate it?" asked Antony.

"I did." Evelyn shivered at the memory. "And I never have since."

"Do you like chicken feet, Daddy?"

"I do." Kingsley leaned forward and grabbed at Kareela's toes. "Such a delicacy. And little girl feet are even better."

"No!" Kareela pulled her toes away with a laugh.

Antony leaned to the side. "What else?"

"I don't know," said Evelyn. "It's just so different there. Life moves at a different pace."

"With the seasons," said Kingsley.

"Yes." Evelyn laughed, attempting her best Jamaican accent. "When mango season come, yuh put up pot."

"What?"

She looked to Antony. "A saying. In mango season, you cook far less. You eat the fruit until your belly aches."

"They'd rot, otherwise," said Kingsley.

"Nature provides. And you let it."

"Did you feel like an outcast? Or like you didn't belong?"

Evelyn looked to her son, her heart aching as she heard his own experience in his words. "I did. At times. With the Jamaican born. There was such a sense of community, of history. And people were kind, welcoming—so much so—but I was always aware I was a bit on the outside. Not quite one of them."

He nodded.

"The children loved you," said Kingsley.

"I was entertainment. Not a day could go by without a child touching my hair, wanting to feel it slide through their fingers."

"And the women were so scared you'd burn. Cover up, Miss Godfrey. Cover up."

"They became family, though." Evelyn met Kingsley's gaze. "More than I'd ever experienced before. I didn't want to leave." A sharp yearning reared up in Evelyn, for that feeling: Family. Belonging. Acceptance. The sense of being home.

"Why'd you go?"

"Hmm?" Evelyn looked up at Antony.

"To Jamaica. Of all places."

"Oh." To get away. She'd been holding off until graduation, biding her time, trying to stay far from her father's wrath—working as many hours as she could at a local pub or holed up in the library whenever she didn't have shifts, searching for an escape. "I saw an ad, that the Red Cross was looking for teachers, that the training was only six months for a yearlong teaching position, with the possibility of renewal."

It lined up well; the training would start two weeks after she got her diploma. Only, in those last days, as she spent time at home figuring out what she could and couldn't live without, it meant more time around her father. She'd arrived black and blue for her training in Toronto—the makeup barely masking her bruises—and firm in the conviction that the past was simply that, and her real life was about to begin.

"So you just wanted an adventure?"

"I did." Evelyn smiled, willing away the bad, focusing on the good. "And to help people. To do what I could to make the world just a bit better."

"And why'd you stay?" asked Antony.

Kingsley laughed. "Do you really have to ask that question?"

"Your father," said Evelyn. "Of course. But it was more than that. I never felt like I fit in, in my town. Not in the way I wanted to. But in Jamaica"—she looked to the ceiling—"there were people from everywhere. The Red Cross was practically a United Nations, and then the locals. As I said, they were so friendly, and loving. It was like returning to the home I'd always wanted but never known, like, finally, I belonged."

Antony stared at her—a question in his features.

Kingsley reached for her hand, knowing all the details of her past she didn't speak: that Jamaica also held the security of knowing her father couldn't reach her, that he had no idea where she even was, and that for the first time since childhood, she'd felt safe.

"I wish we could go back." Evelyn looked to Kingsley. "Maybe we could. For a visit, at least. It'd be safe enough now."

"We should." Kingsley nodded. "Soon."

"Please don't let that just be words," Antony pleaded. "And when you do, you better take me!"

"Of course."

"And when we do"—Kingsley's gaze met Evelyn's, love so deep in his eyes it made her heart swell—"we'll dance." He pulled her up, then turned to Antony. "It wasn't like you kids today. At clubs. We went to friends' houses. Rec centres." He grinned, motioning for Antony to turn up the music. "It was community. It was celebratory." He winked as the music rose, then stepped away from Evelyn, the way he used to. "It was how I made your mother fall in love."

Evelyn laughed, waving a hand at him.

Kingsley spread his feet, adopting the slouch Evelyn remembered so clearly. With a smile tickling at the corners of his lips, he held out his hands, snapped, lifted his shoulders, then shuffled and swayed, two-stepping island style, almost as smooth as all those years earlier, and focused his gaze on her, just as he had back then. Antony whooped. Kareela stood, bouncing. "Daddy! Daddy!"

Kingsley extended his arm to Evelyn—"Me lady"—and pulled her close. He drew her in and sent her out, spun around her.

Antony clapped, his grin wide. He pulled his phone out of his pocket, flipped it open, then froze, his expression falling.

Evelyn dropped Kingsley's hand and straightened. "What? What is it?"

Evelyn

TORONTO

2004

After returning his phone to his pocket, Antony strode across the kitchen, waving Kingsley and Evelyn to follow, then went to the living room and picked up the remote. The screen lit, and he changed the station, stepped back. BLACK BOYS BEATEN read the ticker. "One is in critical condition," said the reporter, "in the ICU. The others sustained serious injuries."

Antony sank to the couch, fists on his knees, and leaned forward as the reporter described the altercation—three boys, mistaken for suspects, unarmed, walking home from school and all now in hospital. When the segment finished, Antony turned off the screen. The remote fell to the floor. He turned to Evelyn and Kingsley. "That's why I'm out there!" Tears streamed down his face. "That's why this matters." He shook his head, his dreads swinging, paced to the window and back. "They treat us like dirt. Did you hear how the reporter talked about it? Never laying blame on the cops, making it sound like those boys got what was coming."

Kingsley cleared his throat. "I don't think—"

"What?" Antony spun to his father. "You don't think what?"

93

"I don't think that's necessarily true. She said the boys were unarmed. She said witnesses stated they weren't being aggressive."

"She also said they were 'known to police.'" Antony raised his fingers for air quotes. "Known to police! What Black man isn't, what Black person!"

"Well, I'm certainly—"

"Pa! How many times have they pulled you over?"

"I don't know. But it doesn't happen so much anymore."

"You're known."

"What?"

"That's what it is. That's all it has to be. Driving while Black your only crime, and you're in their databases. Fu—" He glanced to Kareela. "Frigging walking while Black. That's what street checks are all about: getting our names, our dates of birth, our addresses. Making us *known* so when something like this happens, they can make it seem like we're trouble. Like any little slip-up, any little *anything* represents a pattern."

"Well, those boys should have been compliant." Kingsley stepped toward their son. "If they had, it all would have gotten figured out and none of this would have—"

"No!" Antony shouted. "They were right." Kareela ran to Evelyn, climbed up on her lap. "No. If they had, then the cops would have their fingerprints, too. I know you don't get it, how bad it is out there." The muscles and veins in Antony's neck bulged. His arms shook, the tears still streaming. "They were boys. Just boys. Walking in their neighbourhood. They were boys, Mom." He caught Evelyn's gaze and her heart wrenched. He turned to Kingsley. "They were me."

"They weren't you."

"You just watch." Antony turned from his parents again, hands to his head. "They're going to get away with it. Those officers are going to be lauded as heroes. For what? Beating up three kids because they 'looked like suspects,' because they didn't bow down and cower like frightened animals when the cops told them to listen."

"There's probably more to it," said Kingsley. "Not that it's right, I'm not saying—"

"There doesn't have to be more to it!" A sound of pure pain erupted from Antony's throat. "Don't you get that? Don't you see? Their crime was walking while Black. Being in a part of town the cops didn't think they should be. That's all it takes. They stop us. Identity checks, searches, seizures, hauling us in. And that's the *easy* stuff. They beat us. They kill us, simply for existing. Our very *being* makes us suspect, no matter how good we are, how smart, no matter how we try to fit in. You know it, Pa. You live it. Don't tell me you don't. You live it every day."

Kingsley shook his head. "No one's ever—"

"Okay, so you've never been beaten. But you've been stopped. And professors ten years younger than you have tenure, while you're still scrambling."

"I've focused on teaching. Not done as much research as I should—"

"That's what they tell you. But you know, Pa. You—"

"Well, it's true"—Kingsley cleared his throat, shifted his feet—"for now, maybe, we have to work twice as hard to—"

"Stop! Just stop. Please. Open your eyes. Black men can't go anywhere, do anything in the white man's spaces without being suspect. We're scrutinized constantly. Walking home from school, I've been accosted, threatened. And Malik—he was beaten so bad it hurt to breathe."

"What?" Evelyn slipped Kareela off her lap, stood.

"And why?" Antony continued, his gaze still on his father. "Because they didn't believe a Black boy could be telling the truth that he lived a block away, that he could have a right to be anywhere but the gutter."

Kingsley stepped forward. "What are you talking about? When did this happen?"

Antony cast a hand to the side. "Years ago. When I was fifteen, maybe sixteen."

"Did they hurt you?" Evelyn moved closer, remembering a night Antony had come home sullen and tense, the muffled sobs she'd heard through his bedroom door.

"They shoved me, warned me to stay out of the park at night if I didn't want trouble, then Malik got between us, and—" Antony's jaw clenched. His lip trembled. "And I just stood there."

"Antony, it wasn't your—"

"You were just walking?" Kingsley interrupted. "Home? Across the park? That was all?"

Antony nodded.

"Was Malik okay?" Evelyn asked. "Did his parents know?"

"After a while, physically, at least," said Antony. "He told his parents he got mugged and didn't want to report it."

"Is that . . ." Evelyn hesitated. "You and Malik, you were so close, and then . . ."

Antony nodded. "He didn't like being around me after that. He became what they thought we were."

"Why didn't you tell us?" Kingsley reached for Antony as he shrugged him off.

"Like you would have believed me?" Antony laughed. "Even now, you can't believe it. Can't believe me."

"No, I do. I—"

"You would have thought we were doing something we shouldn't have or had lip. You would have questioned, thinking we must have done something to provoke it. Just like you questioned now."

"Son." Kingsley's voice tensed. He couldn't deny it. Of course he would have asked. Not as justification for the officer's actions, but to understand. At the time, Evelyn would have wanted to understand, too, but after the past years of listening to Antony, watching the news with him by her side, she understood without any explanation needed. "You should have reported it. We'd have gone in with you." Kingsley rubbed a hand across his hair. "Not just for you, but for Malik."

Antony's shoulders fell. He shook his head and exhaled. "Nothing would have come of it. Two cops we didn't know the names of, against us, two inconsequential Black boys? I decided, instead, that I'd change it."

Evelyn and Kingsley stared at each other. Evelyn wished she could turn back time, be there for her fifteen-year-old boy who must have been terrified, who didn't think telling them would make a difference.

Antony raised his hands, then let them fall. "I was walking. Chatting with my friend. Laughing. That was all. And that's what I want." His jaw quivered. "To walk. Not just for me, for Malik, for those boys." He gestured to the screen. "For all of us, to be able to go for a walk, stroll through a park without fear. Without being looked at as criminal." His voice shook. His eyes closed. "That's not too much to ask. It isn't. But it's not going to happen unless people fight for it. So I started learning all I could, meeting people who—" His phone buzzed. He whipped it out, read, then raised his gaze, fire in his eyes. "We're moving the protest up."

"What protest?" Evelyn went to the rocking chair, motioned for Kareela to join her, then pushed her foot to rock, hoping the action would help her resist the urge to dart across the room, hold her son and cradle him in her arms the way she was cradling Kareela, to try to make all this hurt go away.

"We've been trying to get the word out, gather thousands. And this will help. It won't just be a protest but a rally call, a sit-in, to make it clear this can't keep happening. We'll camp outside city hall and make the people who run this city hear that we won't stand for the way people of colour are treated—the disproportionate incarceration rates, the abuse, the systemic and institutionalized racism. We'll stay for days if we have to, weeks, until they acknowledge that there needs to be change, until they determine to enact our plan."

"What plan, Antony?" Kingsley stepped toward him. "What plan, exactly?"

Stop! Evelyn wanted to yell. *Don't question him. Support him. Hold him!*

"We're working on it," said Antony. "We'll have a list of demands, of—"

"I'm sorry for what happened to you." Kingsley put his hand on Antony's shoulder. "I'm sorry for what happened to these boys. But you can't be working on it—"

"Pa."

"You have to know. If you want change, you have to know and understand how change happens. This is why you need to go to law school. This deferral you took . . ." Kingsley lifted his hand and sighed. "Antony, write them, call, I'm sure it's not too late to get in for the fall semester."

"Pa."

"Kingsley!" Evelyn said at the same time. They'd discussed this. Agreed they'd support Antony's passion, so long as he got his degree. And he had. Then he applied and got into law-school. A year wasn't so long to wait.

Kingsley turned from her pleading eyes, back to Antony. "I'm not saying you're wrong. You're not. Change needs to happen. But go about it the right way. Don't yell in the street, don't—"

"Pa!"

"Son."

They stared. Evelyn's mouth opened and closed—wanting to support Antony, as they'd said they would, but not wanting to go against Kingsley, especially when she, too, wanted Antony to have as little to do with these street politics as possible.

"Come with me, Pa."

"What?"

"Tonight. We're holding an emergency meeting. And come to the protest. See what it's about. See what and who we're fighting for."

Kingsley raised his arm the way he always did before a lecture and Evelyn wished, just for one moment, that he were a puppet on a string and she the puppeteer, so she could close his lips, extend that arm to embrace their hurting son. The fingers of one of Kingsley's hands hit his opposite palm. "This is not the way to do it. You need to—"

Antony flung his own hand in the air. "I'm out of here. My people . . . *our* people, need me."

Kareela

I step out of the office after a long day of too many clients with too many problems that are never easily fixed, and am hit by a heat that makes me want to skip the BLM headquarters and find my way to the beach. But the renovations on the new meeting space are almost complete, and I promised to help set up for next week's meeting and scan and upload the latest batch of signed petitions.

It's the third time I've shown up to help in as many weeks, this time and the last without Jasmine by my side. And as I think of Carson's smiling face, his passion, the passion that must have pulsed from Antony as well, the beach seems less appealing. It's not just Carson's passion though . . . it's everyone: mothers who stop by after work, despite having four or more kids in tow, because they want to do whatever they can to ensure those kids make it to adulthood with no time behind bars; grandfathers who remember what the world was like before, who acknowledge how far things have come while hardly changing at all; and young people like me, who just want something better, to be less afraid, to be seen for who we are, to feel we can breathe and move and exist without each step feeling so weighted there are days it's hard to keep stepping.

I manoeuvre around a group of kids spread out on the floor, playing some card game I don't recognize—joking and yelling and safe. Carson waves me over and directs me to the scanner. A satisfying pile awaits, at least fifteen to twenty pages containing approximately fifteen signatures and complete addresses each. The members have been busy.

Over an hour later, after I've finished scanning and categorizing more files Carson laid out for me, the place seems oddly quiet. I lock the filing cabinet, then, keys in hand, walk through the empty meeting space as disappointment creeps over me. I've been forgotten. Here, where I was finally starting to feel I belonged. I rub a hand over my upper arm, the keys dangling from my fingers.

"Kareela?"

I whip around, my bottom lip clenched between my teeth, my eyes wide at the shock Carson's given me.

"Sorry." He chuckles. "I didn't mean to startle you. Was on a call. You all done?"

I nod.

"Thanks so much. So helpful." He reaches out his hand and I drop the keys into them, my shock turning to something else as our fingers graze. My eyes trail over his face, the breadth of his shoulders. How many years separate us? Six, maybe? Nine? And here we are, alone. I take in the dimple in his cheek, the couch on the other side of the room.

I need to get out of here.

"Hey."

"Yes?" my voice yelps.

"Have you eaten?"

I shake my head.

How different would life be with a man like Carson? So much easier in some ways. Harder, likely, in others.

"If you don't have plans, why don't you come to my place? There are a few things I'd like to talk to you about, and I'm starved."

My mind races. Jasmine assured me Carson was a good guy. The best. So, in the rare chance he has something other than conversation in mind, all I'll have to do is say no. Which I will.

"Sure." A smile spreads across my face. "Sounds great."

The drive, which takes us across the harbour, is less than ten minutes. My hands work in my lap, fingers squeezing, interlacing, then breaking apart as Carson chats about his meeting with someone from the mayor's office.

He pulls into the driveway of a house that's small and well-kept. The paint is fresh. The driveway free of cracks. The yard maintained, with an array of flowering bushes and a small garden in bloom front and centre. "Lilacs," I say, as we pass by the tree across from the front door, the scent both wonderful and full of pain. "We had one at our old house. In Toronto."

He nods, his dimple prompting that all-too-recurrent flutter. "I've always liked them."

My mouth goes dry, and I curse myself for not thinking to refill my water bottle. He opens the door and I almost blurt the word no!, ready to start rambling about how I'm not hungry or I forgot I have some work I need to do, or that I'm pregnant with a baby I can't decide whether I want, with a man I feel the same way about.

But Carson calls out before I have the chance, and two kids come racing.

"Daddy!" One of them leaps into Carson's embrace while the other wraps her thin arms around his side. Carson hugs the boy, squeezing him into his chest, kissing his temple, then sets him down to give the girl a proper hug.

As I follow Carson down the hall, I hope the laugh that bursts out of me doesn't sound as embarrassed as I feel. "Rania," he calls, "I brought company."

The woman from the BLM meeting in Preston, with the dreads and regal yet inviting air about her, walks into view. "My queen," says Carson. He kisses her firmly, gives her side an affectionate squeeze, then turns to me. "This is the girl I was telling you about. Jasmine's friend. Kareela."

"Welcome!" Rania crosses the space between us and wraps me in a hug so warm, so inviting and motherly, that a spritz of moisture builds behind my eyes. I smile brightly, damning these hormones.

Dinner is grilled chicken and spiced potato salad, with corn on the cob so sweet it doesn't even need butter—though we slather it on, anyway. The kids are talkative and precocious—aged twelve, seven, and five. When we're about halfway through the meal, after the children have told Carson all about their day, Rania looks to me. "Carson said you have questions about how disarming works. Defunding."

I look between them. Nod. "Well, yeah, I mean . . . I just, like in theory, it sounds so great, but in practice I wonder how it would work."

"And it makes sense to wonder, to ask questions rather than shrug it off as a pipe dream." She tells me that disarming police doesn't mean disarming *all* police or disarming them entirely—most would still have pepper spray, night sticks, possibly tasers—it means keeping firearms reserved to specialized units who are only called to the scene when necessary, who are rigorously trained on when and how to use the weapons and when not to, who have regular mental and emotional assessments to ensure they're still fit to carry those weapons.

As she continues to explain, calmly listing numbers and examples, explaining the ins and outs of what sounded like an unrealistic dream, it all makes sense, so much sense I'm equally in awe and enraged that this type of system doesn't already exist.

I shake my head, stare at the table.

"Kareela?"

If it did exist, if it had existed eighteen years ago, my brother would still be alive—my father, too. I swallow, the anger exploding in a frenzy of emotion I struggle to keep down.

"Are you—"

"It makes sense!" I yell, and snap my gaze up, disgust and frustration blazing. "It makes so much sense." I pause, look between them again, see the faces of the children, wide-eyed at my outburst. And like wet fingers to a wick, the fire that blazed is extinguished, leaving wispy fumes of rage tampered by embarrassment. "Do you think it's possible?"

Rania shrugs, her hand extending until it rests on my still-clenched fist. "I don't know. Probably not in my lifetime." She glances to the children. "Maybe theirs. Hopefully. But change is possible. Better is possible. It's already started in some places."

I nod again, pull my hand away, not looking at any of them but lost in that hazy sight my mind so often goes to. Antony in his last moments: Sometimes he's alone. Sometimes he's in a crowd. Sometimes he's standing tall. Others, I watch him fall.

There are things I know: A collection of sheets found among my father's effects. The things he knew—words written in a script so different from what I remember. Hen scratches. Scribbled over and over again. As if by writing them repeatedly, maybe they'd make sense.

Seven bullets. Three cops.

Four of those bullets found their target.

I don't know whether Antony's body convulsed with those impacts like a puppet on a string or stayed still with the shock of it, then slumped to the ground.

Three of the bullets found no exit.

I don't know whether he died instantly or bled out.

When he reached the hospital, he was pronounced dead on arrival.

Dead. Before he even reached the age I am now.

The cops' names. First, middle, and last. Their badge numbers. That none of them received disciplinary action.

I don't know whether, in the privacy of their own homes, they feel guilt. Or pride. Or that it was just a day on the job, nothing to think about beyond that.

"Kareela?"

My jaw quivers, and I realize Rania or Carson must have shooed the children away, because they're getting up from the table, feet shuffling quietly to the living room.

"That's why we do this," says Carson. "Antony is why we do this. You are. Your mother, your father, all the people who've lived what you've lived through, who've died, who will keep dying if nothing changes."

I squeeze my moist eyes shut. Damn hormones. Damn hormones. Damn hormones.

Rania's hand is on my shoulder. "It's happening every day," she says. "And it's horrible. Not just the deaths, but all of it." She squeezes. "It's okay to be angry. You *should* be angry. It's okay to cry. The whole world should."

But I don't cry. I was taught not to, for the sake of my father, my mother, the classmates it would have made uncomfortable. I wipe a rogue tear away and sit straighter.

"We're angry, too," says Carson. "And we're so glad you're with us. Antony, this anger and pain, it's why we hope you'll become even more deeply involved."

I look up. "What do you mean?"

"You've been through a lot," he says, "more than anyone should have to go through. Which means your words, your voice, hold more power than most."

A weight seems to settle in my stomach.

Rania, with her hand still on my shoulder, looks to Carson. "I don't know if this is the time."

He leans back in his chair with a slight nod.

"Time for what?"

"We've got another rally coming up. Televised this time, and I thought you might want to speak . . . but Rania's right. And there is something else I wanted to talk to you about."

A sense of dread settles over me as Rania's hand falls from my shoulder.

"I made some inquiries a couple of weeks ago," says Carson. "Jasmine mentioned you didn't know many details about what had happened with your brother. Which didn't surprise me. They hide as much as they can—from the families, the media—especially back then, but I know of a journalist in the Toronto chapter who's been documenting, researching, trying to put together a fuller picture of exactly how much we've suffered, who we've lost, and how, over the years, the details of those losses have been kept out of the papers, how the files in the public reports are hugely redacted."

My hands clench in my lap, the possibility of new knowledge tantalizing and terrifying. Growing up, I'd heard tidbits from schoolmates, neighbours, but I was too afraid to learn more, to ask questions. Then, after my father's death, I read everything I could find in archived newspapers about Antony. Most of it obvious trash. Lies. The person they wrote about could not have been the brother I knew.

"He's sent me a bit of info already," says Carson. "Not much. But he's working on getting more."

Something cold and tight pulses within me. "About Antony?"

He nods.

"About what really happened?"

Another nod.

"But how? I thought—"

"There were some people there who were afraid to speak up or were pressured into silence, but they aren't so afraid anymore. There are official records that were unavailable to the public at the time."

That strange pulsing spreads through me. Fear, but more than that. Yearning. Uncertainty.

"A lot has changed," says Rania. "Regarding information. And now that things are coming to light about how real and insidious the systemic racism was . . . *is* . . . people who were afraid, and so kept silent, are willing to speak."

"About Antony?"

"About so much. We now know in Montreal, police used photos of Black men as target practice," says Carson. "I know one of those cops. A good guy who gets sick just thinking about it, remembering how he pulled his trigger beside everyone else, too afraid to speak out. But the more people who speak, who tell their stories—stories from both sides—the sooner change will come."

I stare.

"So, I'm getting that info on your brother. What I need to know is, do you want it?"

My mouth opens and closes. Opens again. Rania's eyes are kind and supportive. Carson, this man who Antony could have been . . . would have been, maybe, who I thought brought me to his home with questionable intentions, yet had this intent instead—to offer me information, ask me to use it, which is questionable in another way.

I shake my head, want to rise from the table and run. But I stay seated. Laughter lifts from the children in the next room. The eldest has her head in a book. The two younger ones pull and smack and twist a toy I'm pretty sure might be older than I am—Hit It! Or Bump It! or something like that.

The slights over the years crash upon me. The "Brown People Posse" at school in Toronto, how I wanted to be a part of it so badly, but they wouldn't let me, at first saying Jamaica wasn't really a part of the West Indies, but then, when I countered that, saying I had to be Black, *really* Black, to be a part of the posse, not just half. How in Juniper Cove I faced the opposite problem. That even to those who welcomed me, I was the *Black* friend. How any time I had an issue with anyone about anything, everyone always assumed it was because of that Blackness.

And now here these people sit, wanting me to represent them, regardless of my mix—all that white blood coursing through me. Regardless of the fact that if I did that, if I spoke of my mother's gunned-down child, she would know of my betrayal . . . which I'm starting to care less about. She's betrayed me in so many ways.

But, more important, what they're asking me to do is what Antony would have done. And he died because of it.

Their eyes are on me as I blow out a small stream of air.

Not only do they want me to represent, they want to give me the details to do it more accurately. Details I've wanted my whole life. Details that, if his incoherent mumblings were true, my father craved almost as much as he craved the drink.

To know. To actually know and, maybe, to understand.

"Kareela?"

A thrumming sounds between my ears, the roar sickening.

To know. To finally know. And once I do, to be expected to do something with that knowledge.

"Don't even think about what Carson was saying," says Rania. "Don't worry about that. Not yet. Just . . ." She looks at me with such compassion I want to fold myself in her arms once more, let the forbidden tears come. "This isn't about that. What matters is whether you want to know."

She waits.

Carson's voice is soft, hesitant. "Kareela?"

I turn my gaze—the roar like a windstorm—wanting and not wanting to know. Fear sweeping through me. "I'm not sure."

Evelyn

As the door closed behind Antony, Evelyn slipped Kareela off her lap, then crossed to Kingsley, who stood frozen. He tensed at her touch but didn't shrug her off, and, after a moment, leaned into her. "Hodge-Podge is on the stove," she whispered, wanting to say so much more. "Just another few minutes and we can eat."

Kingsley nodded, raised his hand to hers, and squeezed before walking down the hall to vanish behind his study door. Evelyn's heart seemed to pulse in her throat. She looked to the front door, fighting the desire to pass through it, run after Antony, and throw her arms around her aching boy. She smiled at Kareela. "You have just enough time to finish that puzzle before dinner. What do you think?"

Kareela stared at her, eyes wide. Evelyn kept her smile firm, wishing she knew how much her daughter had understood. She crouched down. "Honey, your brother . . ."

Kareela crossed the room and sat before her puzzle. She picked up a piece of a fin. Evelyn looked to the door again, seeing Antony's anger, his hurt. What must it have been like, at fifteen, to be harassed by the police? Beaten and bruised. And then too afraid—or ashamed? defeated?—to tell his parents. Regret passed through her, for not being a mother he could come to, a mother he could trust with his pain.

Evelyn turned to the counter and braced her hands against the laminate. She turned down the bubbling brew, picked up her knife, and was taken in time to another kitchen, where she stood, prepping the same meal. Ella stood near her, looking so much like Kingsley, leaning in, laughing, saying she wasn't sure about this Maritime dish. It looked weak.

Later that night, Evelyn, Ella, and Violet sat on the back porch in the low evening sun, laughing at the chickens chasing each other through the yard. In the distance, the neighbour's children chased each other in much the same way, their voices carrying on the breeze. Antony, who should have been sleeping, was enjoying the show, and getting passed back and forth between the laps of his aunt and grandmother, the two of them not able to get enough of him.

The peaceful moment went out with a sizzle when Ella told Violet she wasn't returning to the mountains, but staying in Kingston—to find a job, to help the struggling people. That she'd stay in Kingsley and Evelyn's house. Prevent squatters from claiming it.

"Girl, yuh not." Violet tsked. "Here where grown men fightin in de street like boys in de schoolyard!"

"Ma."

"Yuh brain a sieve? Yuh not hear what me just say? 'Bout dis warrin, fightin, killin?" Violet stood. "Yuh brother's got sense enough to leave, and yet yuh tellin me he settin it up for yuh to stay? No!"

But Ella had made her decision, despite what Violet thought, what Kingsley and Evelyn thought, too.

Three days later, after Violet returned to her village alone, Ella had held them tight, her teeth gleaming within the breadth of her smile. "Yuh have a wonderful adventure," she told them. "And come back soon. But not too soon, nuh?"

All these years later, as the Hodge-Podge on the stove sizzled and popped, Evelyn could still hear the sweet timbre of Ella's voice. That was the last time they'd seen her alive, and Evelyn always wondered if the threat of getting an apartment in the city centre had been a bluff. If, without a ready, free place to live, she would have returned to the mountains with Violet. Been there still.

Evelyn turned off the burner and slid the pot to the back of the stove. "Dinner!" she called, wishing she hadn't made Hodge-Podge, which might remind Kingsley of that night, of the guilt they both held over not urging Ella to return to her village. Evelyn could still see the two of them in her mind, brother and sister, heads angled toward each other as they sat on the porch laughing, while Evelyn watched their outlines growing fainter with the setting sun.

THAT NIGHT IN BED, Evelyn waited for the click of the door, the thump thump of her son kicking off his shoes, the shuffling down the hall as he tried to be quiet. The next morning, never having heard it, she peeked into Antony's room. The sheets were tousled, as always: no way to tell whether he'd come late, left early, or not been there at all. The next night, she waited again. The next morning, she checked, with still no obvious answer but a suspicion that the sheets remained unmoved.

A flare of frustration rose in her: That he wouldn't at least check in. That he was fine with leaving things so sour. Still, there was no real reason to worry. He was a grown man. And he was angry, too. So, though tempted to call his mobile and plead for him to get in touch, she prepared Kareela for daycare, herself for work. It was better, maybe, to give him his space.

After the third night of not seeing him, Evelyn called Dani, suggesting they meet at a playground after work.

"You're not worried, are you? That something happened?"

Evelyn shook her head. "He was home today. He took some clean laundry I left in his room."

"Tracking his movements, are you?"

Evelyn shrugged, reliving the frustration that flared when she realized she'd missed him. That he must have intentionally come at a time none of them would be home.

Dani laughed. "He's twenty-three." She waved her hand. "He's revved up. About the protest, the fight with his father. Give him time."

Evelyn stared at the children on the swings, each pumping their legs as hard and fast as they could. Last year, this was a challenge, yet now they soared. She looked back to Dani. "He won't answer his phone. Hasn't returned my messages."

Dani raised her eyebrows and narrowed her gaze. "How many have you left?"

"Two."

"Restraint. That's good." She patted Evelyn's leg.

"I've wondered about texting." Evelyn looked to her hands. "I'd have to buy a mobile phone first."

"Evelyn!" Dani laughed. "If you're going to join the rest of the world, join us, but not so you can send your son one text message."

Evelyn swallowed, wishing she could explain her fears. The things they'd seen in Kingston. The people they'd lost, and how, to not go against Kingsley, she'd never explained it to Antony—why they were so resistant to his politics.

Dani reached for Evelyn's hand and squeezed it. "The protest was on the news. It's going to be big. Why don't you go? See if you can get Kingsley there, too."

"To a protest?" Evelyn looked again to the children, tried to imagine it: Her, in an angry throng. Her, going against her husband, against her own fears. But this wasn't Kingston. And Kingsley had gone against her in arguing with Antony the other night.

"Yes," said Dani. "Like Antony said. See what it's all about. See his role in it. And then, at least, you'll be able to tell him you did."

"Me at a protest." With Antony. Standing up for Antony. Being that mother he could trust, who he knew would be there for him, no matter what. A smile spread across her lips. "Maybe."

"Asher!" Dani stood and rushed to her gap-toothed son. "You jump from that swing again and I swear, you'll wish you hadn't!"

Evelyn watched as Dani lectured, as Asher crossed his arms and stamped his foot. At some point, she had to let Antony go, let him make his own mistakes, learn his own lessons, didn't she? And if she were going to, at least she could be close by, in case he fell.

Evelyn

The next afternoon, Evelyn dressed in jeans and a T-shirt. She wore her hair in a high ponytail, something she hadn't done in years, then threaded the ponytail through the opening in a cap, wanting to look youthful, to mix in with the crowd.

Not wanting Kingsley to know what she was up to, she walked Kareela to Dani's. Just last night, he'd railed in frustration upon seeing the upcoming protest on the news, seeing Antony's face on the screen in a crowd of half a dozen. Evelyn had hushed him, gestured toward Kareela, reading a book in the corner of the living room, where she had draped sheets over a table and chair.

Kingsley lowered his voice. "Evelyn, it's dangerous."

She nodded, shoulders tight, jaw clenched, and refrained from telling him, again, that this wasn't Jamaica in the late seventies. Wasn't Jamaica now. It was dangerous, yes, but not as dangerous as he thought. And if trouble did break out, Evelyn would be there to find Antony, get him away from it as fast as possible.

Now Evelyn's steps quickened as she rose from the underground and made her way to Nathan Phillips Square. A sea of people stood in front of city hall. At least a thousand. Evelyn made her way through the mass, her chest tight, nervousness and the faintest hint of excitement pulsing through her as she scanned for Antony. She'd expected a cacophony of noise—shouts of anger, hate—but the crowd was oddly silent. A hush, rather than a roar, buzzed through the space as posters and placards waved in the air, calling for peace, equality. There were images, too, those three boys, mostly, but others as well. Faces she'd never seen but recognized for what they could have been, for what they weren't now, either their lives or their innocence gone.

Though it became more difficult to press through the mass of bodies the closer she got to those two iconic curved towers, Evelyn kept on, desperate to see the face that she knew best. In front of the building, rows of officers stood with the protesters less than six feet from them, separated by makeshift barricades. Evelyn caught sight of a young woman who'd been to their house once or twice, with some of Antony's other friends, piling in spaghetti like one of the boys. She racked her brain, tried to remember her name, but the crowd seemed to swell and shift, and the woman was lost. Evelyn turned with the shift, saw what she was looking for, and then heard. Her boy. His voice smooth and eloquent, speaking over the crowd.

Evelyn's jaw quivered with pride at the sight of Antony before all these people—his posture, his presence, his words, which she'd been hearing for years, had heard less than a week ago. Here, in this place with so many listening, they didn't sound like impossible dreams.

After he'd barely begun, Antony stepped down—not the main event, it seemed, but there to introduce the man who'd been speaking the other night on the news—a Bahamian professor. By the look of him, nearly as old as Kingsley. His voice rang with an island lilt.

Evelyn tore her eyes from the man, looking for Antony, now lost in the throng that had pressed in front of her. She continued to search as others rose to the makeshift podium—mothers and friends of the boys who'd been beaten. Of others who'd suffered attacks by the police. After one boy stepped up, face still swollen, arm in a sling, instructions were given for those who wanted to help keep the protest alive. They'd sleep in shifts, so that a presence would be there until the mayor and chief of police agreed to hear their demands, to acknowledge that change needed to come, that cops couldn't beat people in the street, kill them with no repercussions. Until they agreed that the city needed not only investigations but public trials.

When the crowd thinned, Evelyn pressed forward, searching, then stopped.

It didn't make sense to approach Antony here, where she wouldn't know what to say, or even more important, whether he'd calmed down enough to listen. Besides, hours had passed since she'd dropped Kareela off and Dani would be expecting Evelyn back by now. Evelyn turned, following the flow of people to the subway, jostled in the crush that sank below ground.

Hours later, once Kareela was home and in bed and Kingsley was busy in his study, Evelyn picked up the phone. "I was there," she spoke into the voicemail service. "I heard what you said, really heard it this time. And Antony, I'm so proud of you. Of your passion. Your commitment to stand for what you believe in. They're good beliefs. A good cause. It scares me. I can't deny that. But I won't fight you on it anymore."

She hesitated, thinking of Kingsley, how he'd view her words as a betrayal—and what that could do to their marriage. Thinking, too, of the inspiration her son had sent ricocheting through the crowd, how it lit a spark, making her think maybe now was the time to pursue a degree for herself, a life for herself. In the fall, Kareela would be in school full days, so Evelyn could work part time or take night courses.

Maybe one day she could work alongside her son. Work for change. "We can explain it to your father together." She smiled. "We can help him see." She stopped again, seeing her boy up there, so confident, so sure. "I'm proud of you, Antony. And I love you." She hung up the phone, hoping she'd said the right thing, hoping Antony would call, or even better, come home.

YET AGAIN, EVELYN lay in bed, the phone beside her, her ears tuned, knowing it wasn't likely Antony would be home anytime soon. But she hoped for a call at least, acknowledgement that he'd heard her message, would come home when his shift at the sit-in was over. She looked to the clock: 11:43. He wouldn't call this late. She should close her eyes, try to sleep. There was no reason to walk through tomorrow like a zombie.

As she drifted into sleep, Antony's face loomed in her mind: the way he spoke with such authority and conviction in front of that crowd of people. A smile turned her tired lips. Then, at three loud bangs, she jolted awake.

"Evelyn?" Kingsley's voice in the darkness, the sound of shuffles beside her, the bedside lamp flicking on.

Evelyn thrust off the sheets and stepped into her slippers. "It must be Antony." She waved a hand for him to stay in bed. "I'll get it."

Kingsley stood, pulling his robe around him. "Antony has a key."

Evelyn froze, the possibilities shooting through her with an icy blast. The two of them padded down the hall to the door, Evelyn telling herself it could be anything, anyone.

Three more wall-shaking knocks.

Kingsley peering through the small diamond-shaped glass, then stepping back. The door opening.

The words. Words. Words.

Sounds that seemed to come from a throat other than her own. Pain like she never imagined pulsing through every pore. Heavy hands on her shoulders. Then her own arms around Kareela, sinking to the floor with her child. Her one remaining child.

Violet

When I get the call, the first thing me think of is Femi. Why she and not Ella? Who to say, except that she be the first. The first time one of me babies, who supposed to outlive me, did not.

And now me grandbaby. All shot up.

Femi. Me girl. All burned up.

That was before the store, so I been out working, cleaning some fancy lady house, morning to night. Ella be cooking, watching the young'uns. Something distract her, and she come back to the stove, flames licking the walls. So she throw the pan out the window, forgetting that where Femi like to play, tending to her little garden, making villages for the mice and the fairies.

Ella say she hear the scream, and just like that, she know, before she even see she sister running down the yard, across the field, arms flailing. She scream for the girl to stop. But Femi don't stop. She run. And Kingsley, playing nearby, he run after her. And even though Femi younger than he, she legs so long, she so fast, he say, she fast like she crazy. The pain, he say, musta make her lose she mind. Why else she not run toward the house, the well?

So it take him too long to get to her.

He tell me this, tears in he eyes, looking so guilty, like it he fault for not being faster, stronger, though he only six. A baby heself. "Me catched her, Mammy," he say. "Me knock her down. Me pull off me shirt. Me beat the fire." And then he stop. He can't tell me no more, he tears too heavy. He tears take he voice away.

It don't matter. Me know the rest. Me little baby. Me precious baby. Blacker than black in spots. Skin crusted ash.

She held on. That the worst of it. That the fire didn't take she quick.

She held on three days. No crying. Just whimper. Like an injured animal you know you need to put down. But I couldn't put down me girl.

And now this. Antony.

At least he, me first grandbaby, be gone quick.

There be comfort in going quick.

Ella went quick.

Ella and Antony. The rest of us, we go slow.

Kareela

Two weeks pass, during which I make excuses to avoid entering the BLM headquarters, too wary of what Carson has offered me, what he's asked me to do with it. But, at last, missing the camaraderie, I go. Within minutes, Carson draws me into his office. A file folder sits on his desk—which I find odd in this digital age. The information, I'm sure, was sent through email, or some cloud-based service; split apart, then pieced back together again.

He motions for me to sit, then does the same. His hand taps the folder.

I stare at it. "That's the info?"

"I thought it might be easier," he said, "if you could look at it in private. Take it wherever you want. A park. Your home. I can be with you, or someone else, just . . . however you want."

"If I want."

He nods. "Well, it's yours, whenever, if ever, you want it." He lays both hands on the folder. "There's a jump drive, too, interviews of people who knew Antony. Who were there. But my contact, he transcribed everything on it."

"You listened to it? Read it?"

Another nod.

"And you think I should."

He sighs, long and heavy and filled with things I can't quite decipher. "I think you should do whatever you feel is best for you."

My heart pounds.

"My father would have wanted to know."

Carson is silent, and so am I—my father's want pressing upon me, the way he would have grabbed for this folder, read its pages hungrily. I breathe out, my gaze on the folder, tempted to say more, to tell Carson that if my father had had these pages, had the answers I hope lie within, maybe that would have been enough. Maybe we could have read these words together—worked through the pain of them— and then continued working. But Carson may not even know my father is dead. I mentioned it to Jasmine once, but not how or when or why. Not that the best part of him died over eighteen years ago, a part I saw only glimpses of, like seeing the shadow of the person you yearn for, rather than their actual being.

The folder seems to throb. It's thick, though the jump drive may be giving it false girth. I imagine photos—from the morgue, the crime scene. I imagine an explanation.

Would it have been enough? Or simply too little, too late.

"The meeting tonight. I don't think I'll make it."

"Okay."

I raise my gaze to meet Carson's, the throb making its way through me, mixing with the ache of knowing that none of the knowledge my father held was enough. That I wasn't enough. "Got to catch up on work. And my boyfriend, he said he's making a special dinner for us. He got a great mid-course review on his practicum. So he's excited. Trying a new recipe or something. He likes to cook."

A pause sits between us, and then, "You should bring him by sometime."

My brows knit. Does he not know? Not care? Thomas wouldn't be the only white person to enter these doors, but my guess is he'd be the only white person without Black family. My hand gravitates to my abdomen before I think to stop myself. Carson's gaze darts to the movement, then raises back to my eyes. I've told no one. I didn't even tell Thomas, technically, but Carson has seen me rush to the bathroom more than once, maybe even heard the retching I imagine the fully open faucet couldn't mask.

I stand and reach for the folder. "Thanks. For this."

"Of course." He rises, places his hand on mine before I can lift the pages. "You might need someone," he says, "to be with you. Or after . . . I mean, I know you have your boyfriend. Or your parents. But if you need anyone else, call Jasmine . . . or Rania. She had me put her number in there. On a Post-it note." He keeps his hand on mine. It's the closest we've been, our faces no more than a foot apart, and the look in his eyes makes me wonder how I ever thought he could have been interested in me sexually. He sees me as someone to guide and protect, to groom, possibly. And right now, he's frightened for me.

"And Kareela, what's in here, whether or not you look at it, it's about you, not about speaking at the rally." He stands upright, releasing my hand, and a moment passes before I lift the folder, hold it to my chest, then offer a smile in thanks before leaving the office.

BACK AT THE APARTMENT, the folder sits in my bag, out of sight and yet filling the room. It blocks out most of Thomas's words as he talks excitedly about his supervisor's praise, that he has a natural knack for the work, an intuition she hasn't seen in years.

I smile and try not to avert my gaze to the bag across the room, try to be the attentive girlfriend I led him to believe I was. He cooks as he talks and pulls me into the effort. I peel garlic and cut off the ends before squishing them through the press, watching the masticated pulp plop into a clear glass bowl he's set out. But my mind is on the folder.

I move on to the peppers, slicing them in long, even strips, until all I can hear is the sound of the knife on the board, the sizzle of onions in the pan. I turn to see Thomas staring at me, a mix of concern and frustration in his expression.

"Did you hear me?"

"No. Sorry." The knife is still in my hand, held out between us. I twist to place it on the cutting board. "What did you say?"

"Where were you?"

"Just thinking."

"About what?" His voice is tense. "You're not here half the time anymore—even when you are actually here. You don't want to talk about the baby. Fine. But does that mean we can't talk about anything? That you can't give me five minutes of your attention?"

A shudder reverberates through the room. Another crack in the bedrock of what we built between us.

"Work's busy." I turn back to the cutting board, but he crosses the kitchen, places his hand on my hand in such a similar way to Carson's that it takes me back to the office, the folder—though in all the ways that matter, I've been standing in that room all night.

"Is it the volunteering?" His voice softens. "I know it's important. But other things are important. We are." He pauses. "I said that my supervisor wants to offer me a position after graduation. Right here in Halifax."

"That's great. I'm so proud of you." A rush of guilt enters me for missing this news, and I reach on my tiptoes to kiss him. When I pull away, he doesn't. His arms grip me tighter. His hands smooth their way down my back and his lips find mine again, latch on—urgent, almost desperate, as my own desperation rises up to meet his so violently that it shocks and thrills me. It's been weeks, my nausea and uncertainty always giving me reasons to shift away. But now this distraction is all I want. He releases one arm to switch off the stove, then spins me, pressing my back against the fridge door. We fumble to peel off each other's clothes, not fully succeeding but getting far enough, and only make it to the living room before it's too late to continue the journey. Our bodies lock, and as we move, I'm reminded of the things that drew me to him. His smile, his kindness, his generosity—in so many ways, but especially in this, ensuring pleasure like no man I've ever met.

When we're done, breathless and sweaty, I kiss his brow, his nose, his lips, and lay there, half on the couch, my legs dangling off it, my arms clinging to him, to what we once had, what part of me wishes I could have forever. He kisses me back, sighs, and nuzzles his head against my neck.

"You know," he whispers, his voice lazy and content. "This job offer is perfect timing. It would give me a few months to get settled in the job before the baby comes . . ." He hesitates. "If the baby comes. It takes one less worry off the table—that I'll find a full-time job, whether or not I would have to move to find it. We wouldn't have to worry about bills, even if you decided to take a full mat leave."

The hormones that allowed this momentary coupling, this forgetting, fade, and everything I'd been feeling, fearing—about the baby, Thomas, Antony—rushes back. I shift, and his arms grip me tighter. The urge to peel myself away rushes through me, but I don't, fearing that if I do, I'll never be in this position again and, despite everything, it feels good to be here in his arms. It feels . . . not safe, exactly, but comfortable. Tinged with a nostalgia I want to let myself sink into.

So I lie here, not replying to his comment, his point, which is a good one, but not good enough. Wishing I could tell him about the folder, that in this moment it is weighing on me far more than this wisp of a child. But I can't bring myself to say the words—and that, out of everything there is to be afraid of, is maybe what scares me most of all.

LATER THAT NIGHT, after we've eaten and Thomas is sleeping for his early morning shift, I sit cross-legged on the couch, the folder in front of me. For eighteen years, I've wanted to know. For eighteen years, I've wished someone would tell me the truth about what happened that night. Why.

And here it is.

My palms sweaty, my mouth dry, I open the folder. There are photos, but not the ones I feared. Antony smiling. Antony's mug shot, something I didn't even know he'd had taken, just a few weeks before the shooting, when he'd been brought in for unlawful assembly and causing a disturbance on municipal property.

I turn a page to see each of the officers, looking serious. Stoic, for their official work photos. I stare at their faces, my breath shallow and thick, then draw my gaze to the written text.

The words blur with the sound of intermittent traffic outside the window, the gentle whir of the fridge in the kitchen behind me, the whoosh whoosh of blood thumping through my ears.

The day it happened is the clearest memory from my childhood. Not after—that's a blur—but before. At least I think it was the day . . .

memories shift and merge. Antony—tall, thin, with shoulders that seemed to broaden with each day, taking the shape of my father's—was a ball of energy. He came into the kitchen, where Mom was making something on the stove. Broken up sea creature puzzle pieces lay out before me on the floor. Music was on the radio, and then it changed, got louder, and Antony stepped away, grinning. He pulled Mom from the stove. She batted him away at first, but then they danced. I was dancing. And laughing. Shaking my hips the way he did, she did, all of us smiling.

He lifted me up and we twirled.

The words in the file blur hopelessly. I blink, rub the back of my hand across my face, and pile the pages together. Phone in hand, I punch in the numbers and a plea pours out. "I can't do this. Not on my own. Can we meet?"

Evelyn

Evelyn stared at the door for hours, waiting for Kingsley to return, to tell her it'd been a mistake, that some other parents' son lay on a cold slab. Or even better, for Antony to saunter in, still buzzing from the crowd, the energy of all those people who wanted change.

It couldn't be true that her boy was dead. His heart stopped, his eyes vacant. It couldn't be true that he was gone and she lived on. How could she live on?

She continued to stare, Kareela in her arms, the girl's chest rising and falling in a perfect, unending pattern. Evelyn should put her in bed, pull up the sheets, but Kareela was the only explanation for why Evelyn's body hadn't disintegrated into a million pieces the moment Antony ceased to be; this child, this firm, breathing body, the one thing keeping Evelyn tethered to the earth.

As streams of sunlight crept around the ruched edges of the curtains, the door opened. Evelyn stood, hoping.

But there was no hope. No words. Only their eyes, speaking everything they'd never be able to say.

Kingsley turned from Evelyn with a shake of his head, down the hall and into their room, leaving Evelyn still standing, trembling, with Kareela asleep in her arms.

Several hours later, Kareela asleep on the couch, Evelyn walked to their room and stood before Kingsley's open eyes as he lay on the bed, waiting for him to move, cry, yell. At lunchtime, she came again to that vacant stare, whispered his name.

Her chest didn't seem to rise and fall the way it should, her limbs felt numb, broken. She returned to their daughter, who needed food.

"Mama," said Kareela, setting herself on a kitchen chair, "what is shot?"

Evelyn's body stiffened.

"Mama?"

"Hush."

With a clatter, Evelyn placed a bowl of cereal on the table and stepped to the window, her hand on her throat. When evening came, she placed that same hand on Kingsley's shoulder, jostled it. He lay as if paralyzed, eyes still open, red and raw.

Evelyn's mother had lain under the covers for days at a time, that first time, when Evelyn wasn't much older than Kareela. Before that, Helen's middle had grown large, so big Evelyn couldn't fit on her lap. A pile of twin hats, sweaters, and booties grew along with her mother's belly, with her smiles and winks. A secret. A big surprise. And then the mound was gone, along with the whispers, the smiles, the knitting, the needles. When Evelyn shook her mama, her body jostled then settled, jostled then settled. When Evelyn caressed the bruises on her mother's pale cheeks and arms, it was like caressing a soft doll, rather than a living thing.

The next morning, Evelyn got up, because Kingsley didn't. After making Kareela peanut butter on toast and sending her to school, she called her office to say she wouldn't be in. When their phone rang, she answered it, and spoke to the receptionist of Kingsley's department. "A family issue," she said, her shaking voice seeming to amplify in the cavernous void that hovered around her. "I'm not sure when he'll return."

That afternoon, Evelyn set a ham and cheese sandwich and a glass of water beside Kingsley. Less than forty-eight hours earlier, she had stood watching their son, letting pride flow through her, when she should have been wrenching him down from that podium, dragging him home.

"Mama, when will Antony be back?"

Evelyn spun. Kareela leaned against the door, feet bare, hair a mess, lips pulled together and cocked to the side. "The policeman said he didn't make it. What didn't he make?"

Pain squeezed like a vise—her heart closing in on itself. "Kareela, shh."

She guided her daughter out of the doorway and across the hall. She tucked her into bed, then lay beside her all night, Kareela's torso pushing and retreating against Evelyn's, along to the rhythm of their breath. The way Antony's once did.

Had he heard her voicemail, words to bolster his courage? If he hadn't, would he have dropped to the ground with the rest of them? Would he be here now?

In the morning, she took Kingsley's sandwich away, leaving the water. The phone rang and kept ringing, but she didn't answer. She turned the TV on, tuned to the Family Channel and its promise of a constant stream of animated figures and sassy tweens.

Kareela curled into Evelyn's lap, and Evelyn, for the first time, realized she hadn't thought much about those two lost babies. What it meant to her mother—never meeting them. The reason why. Evelyn had thought, instead, of the shift. Her mother going from living to existing. Her mother not really her mother anymore. Hiding in the room. Doing the bare minimum. Her father out longer and later, and when at home, angrier and rougher.

She'd thought of herself. How she hated it. Hated her mother, sometimes, for caring more about the loss of those babies than about her. Evelyn lifted her arm and wrapped it around her own baby. Squeezed.

"Mama." Kareela looked up, eyes and cheeks wet, a plea to her voice, as if she'd been saying Evelyn's name over and over. "When is Antony coming home? I want to see Antony."

"Sweetie." Evelyn wanted to scream, to crawl into bed, too, and turn out the light. She wiped Kareela's cheeks, wishing she could draw away all the tears from her daughter's eyes, all the pain. "Antony's not coming back. He is dead now. So he will never come back."

"But Mama."

"No questions." Evelyn rocked in the chair she'd always rocked her babies in, her eyes burning. "Please, sweetie, no questions. Not right now. And no more tears."

Less than a week later, Evelyn imagined rain falling on warm earth, a ceiling of umbrellas above them, something to hold on to, to shelter them. But their hands were empty. The day shone as brightly as it did on the day of Evelyn and Kingsley's wedding, on the day of their son's birth. A good omen, she'd thought then. But today Evelyn wanted rain so hard she could almost see it. She wanted, too, for the crowd to disperse. His schoolmates were fine, people who'd filtered through their doors over the years, sat at their table. But all these other people. People who knew an Antony she'd only gotten that one glimpse of. People who shook her hand, Kingsley's, who promised they'd continue the fight, do it for Antony. All in the name of Antony. She wanted them gone. She wanted them to stop.

No! she screamed with no sound emerging. *Go home. Stay alive.*

She nodded, murmured thanks, accepted hugs.

An altercation. Except it wasn't, said one young woman. "They're lying." She shook her head, jaw clenched and quivering. "They're lying, like they always do. Antony didn't cower. He didn't lie on the ground like the rest of us. He stood, that was all. He stood, hands raised. He spoke. He took one step forward."

Evelyn focused on her legs, keeping them rigid enough to stand, wanting and not wanting to hear the words as waves of some foreign feeling flushed through her, some seed of an emotion, a thought, growing. An altercation, the officer at the door had said. Self-defense, when Kingsley had gone to the station after the morgue, demanding answers.

Their son, the aggressor. Their son, nothing more than a political criminal, according to all those talking heads on the news.

The woman—a girl, really—moved on and Dani's arms wrapped around Evelyn, as they had so often these past days, in between organizing the casseroles that arrived, calling the funeral home, arranging a service, sitting with Evelyn as she rifled through photos, then deciding for her which one to have enlarged.

A pastor who knew none of them spoke about Antony as if he knew him. Spoke of his bright future. Of his passion. The papers had said the opposite. Said he and his compatriots ignited unrest, put lives in danger. That the officers, as always, were simply doing their jobs. Protecting themselves. Protecting society. The young man's death was a tragedy, of course, but . . .

But.

As the earth fell, Evelyn gripped Dani's hand, wanting to grip Kingsley's, but his were full of Kareela, the girl clinging to him, head nuzzled in his shoulder. The doll Violet had slipped into Kareela's hand when she arrived from the airport dangled from the girl's fingers. Upon seeing it, Kareela had pulled it to her chest instantly, clung to it as if the doll's dark skin and dreaded hair weren't that of a toy, but of her brother reincarnated.

Evelyn stepped toward the hole in the ground, stopped, knowing she couldn't fling herself into the grave. That they'd pull her out. That even if she kicked and screamed, it would do no good.

Still, she wanted to, to protect her son from those lumps of earth. If they had to fall on him, she wanted them to fall on her first.

The crowd thinned. Flowers fell, mixing with the loose earth as Evelyn stood, her hand still gripped in Dani's. Kingsley, less than a foot away, felt thousands. Violet wrapped her arm around her boy, leaving Evelyn separate, disconnected from the only family she had left.

Eventually, after it was only the five of them and the gravediggers, after Kingsley had set Kareela down, grabbed a shovel, and joined the men hurling pile after pile of earth on their son, each thump of dirt on the casket prompting an internal scream within Evelyn, after Kingsley moved so vigorously that the diggers stepped aside, it was done. Kingsley handed the shovel to the nearest digger. They all turned. Evelyn looked back, expecting it to be a dream. Expecting Antony. Knowing, as she stepped away, a part of her would stay here always.

Evelyn

Evelyn's gaze focused on the black lace of her dress, the shine of her shoes, shoes that should have been left by the front door. A spasm of pressure tore through her chest as she thought of the dirt she may have tracked onto the rug—dirt she wouldn't want to get rid of, because it would feel like getting rid of the last small connection to her son.

Kareela's laughter sounded through the room, impossible, cruel, confusing. Violet—tickling, singing, laughing, too—made Evelyn want to scream.

Evelyn's jaw hung loose as she tried to make sense of their smiles. Maybe she'd gotten it wrong, and it had all been a dream. A nightmare. Maybe Antony was fine and Violet was here for some other reason: time had fast-forwarded and Antony was getting his law degree, or it had rewound and Violet had come for his undergraduate graduation, like they'd hoped she would.

But the image of Violet arriving early this morning was stark and clear in Evelyn's mind. Violet stepping through their front door silently, taking her granddaughter's hands in hers, as if she knew more of her than photos in the mail, a voice travelling across land and sea, and one brief visit, years ago. Hugging her close, then whispering, voice as raw and rough as sandpaper, "Me love. Me sweet, little love."

It couldn't be a dream. The air hung heavy with the scent of casseroles, several on the counter because the fridge and freezer were full. And all three of them, from neck to knee, were covered in black. Why, in the middle of summer, would a girl be all in black, if not for death? Her brother's death.

Evelyn, hands shaking, knees weak, moved to the hall but couldn't remember why. She stopped, returned to the armchair, watched as Violet sat, wide-eyed, telling her baby a story about her other baby—Antony as a toddler, chasing after lizards. The way his chest puffed out and his smile blossomed as he brought his first capture. Such a pretty one. How, when the lizard's bright orange dewlap popped out, Antony hollered, dropped the poor thing, then cried as it scurried away.

"Antony cried?" Disbelief dripped from Kareela's voice as she held the dreaded doll to her chest. The child had hardly let it out of her hands since Violet had given it to her. Evelyn wished she would. She wished she'd throw it in the trash.

"He just a pickney then. Yea high." Violet raised her arm.

"Smaller than me."

"Much smaller than yuh."

Kareela's lips pursed. "Yes. Two is smaller. I'm six."

"You sure is."

Evelyn shifted her gaze, remembering. They'd been in Jamaica for Ella's funeral, risking the still simmering urban warfare, risking the possibility that they'd never make it back to Toronto, to Kingsley finishing his degree. Grief hung on all of them like a shroud. Fear, too. But for Antony, Evelyn had worn a smile. She'd wrapped him in her arms, rocked him. Told him she understood. It was painful when you lost something you cared about. But he would catch another lizard one day, and when he did, he would know about the dewlap, and not be afraid.

Antony's laughter danced that day as he set out again, hunted for almost two hours, came back as the sun started its slow dip to the horizon, running with a wobble due to his clasped hands.

Always so determined. Always so . . .

Violet was talking about something else now. Kingsley. How he was a boy "too big for he britches." Intrigued with the word, Kareela repeated it—"Britches. Britches"—getting Violet to explain what it meant. Violet, who had lost two of her own children. Smiling. As if the death of Evelyn's baby hadn't stolen every reason to smile again.

"Why was he too big for he britches?" Kareela knelt on the couch, as if this was any other day, as if her brother, Evelyn's son, was not in the ground.

"He t'ink he know all t'ings about all t'ings. He t'ink he smarter than me. Smarter than he big sister, he father, de man down de street, and de women up de road."

"What!" Kareela leaning forward, incredulous.

"He come to me. He say, 'Mama, I gonna start a mango store. I gonna pick all de mango and sell it to de people pon de street.' Me laugh. Me say, 'Boy, mango fall from de tree. No soul gonna pay yuh to pick it.' He say, 'No, mango fall from de tree, it get bruised. I gonna climb up. I gonna pick it. And everyone gonna buy it. Everyone gonna say, *Kingsley, yuh a smart boy. Yuh a businessman.* I gonna get me rich, buy me a bicycle.'" Violet shook her head. "Me say, 'Kingsley, yuh do what yuh want. But me tell yuh, yuh not gonna get one sale.'"

"And did he?" Kareela bounced on her knees.

"Patience, now, yuh hear? I'm getting to it." Violet smiled. "Yuh daddy, he climb all de trees around. He get buckets of mangoes. He set up he stand and write up he sign. He sit there morning and night. Morning and night. Well"—Violet leaned back—"I be wrong. Eventually a neighbour up de way, he come by, he say, 'Master Kingsley, me ah gonna buy one mango. And me ah gonna pay yuh for de price of ten to stop dis foolishness and go inside to bed.'"

Kareela's laughter grated, shredding Evelyn's heart.

Violet smiled, her voice soft, her hands rubbing each other as she looked toward something Evelyn couldn't see. "Yuh daddy. He took de pay for dat one mango and say no to de rest. He come inside waving he money, saying, 'See. See. Me sell it.' He sit out dere three more days, never selling another." Violet lowered her head. "He not determined in de same way after dat. He mix sense into he determination. A clear plan, a proven path to success." She raised her gaze. "But your brother, he like he daddy was then. So determined."

Even with gun-wielding officers standing in front of him. Always just so—

Evelyn stood again, the heat behind her eyes a fire. Her gaze met Violet's, who stared at her, compassion in her look, a hand on her heart. Evelyn turned, not knowing where to go, what to do, wanting to fall into Violet's arms but knowing if she did, she'd fall apart— maybe for good. So, she turned, left. She couldn't stay in this room hearing these stories a moment longer.

Kareela

In the BLM headquarters, Rania sits on one side of me, Jasmine on the other. I imagine Antony leaning over my shoulder, urging me on, but can't feel his presence.

"Have you read any of it?" asks Rania.

"Only a glance." I look at her. "Have you?"

She nods.

I stare at the folder, now sitting on the coffee table in front of us. The room smells of meat and spice, with the faintest hint of something sweet. I want to be alone, but not alone. I want to take in every detail, but also to throw this folder and everything it contains into a fire and never look back.

"You could start with one page," says Rania. "And if that's all you want to look at tonight, that's all you look at."

"Maybe an account of what happened?" I say. "As in, technically . . . who shot, why, etc.?"

Rania nods and reaches for the folder. She rifles through the pages, then pulls a couple out. Rather than handing them to me, she sets the closed folder back on the table, the pages on top of it. "Jasmine and

I could head to the back," she says, "start compiling some of the new petition forms from tonight. If you like."

"Okay." My gaze stays on the pages. When they're halfway to the office, I pick them up, thinking again of what I know and don't know, and what I want to know. As he lay on the ground, did he realize he was dying? Or was he gone instantaneously? All that he was. Gone.

The music comes back to me. The laughter and life that used to fill our home—my parents' eyes. The joy I'm not sure I actually remember or simply made up. A hope. A dream.

With tense focus, I lift the first page, read that the shooting happened not at the rally, as I'd believed, but later. After clearing away dropped signs and other debris, Antony and a few of his "compatriots," as the report calls them, were on a nearby side street where a protester's van was parked. They were storing the signs for future use and loading the garbage to cart away. The witnesses said the police came after them, harassed them about the protest, about the law, said that if they tried something like this again, made even one slip, they'd be sorry. There are four accounts of what happened in the report from Carson's contact. All slightly different, but all affirming Antony was not armed and held nothing in his hands.

The police report from the three cops is less clear on this point.

"'He had a gun,'" one officer had said. Then, when pressed, "'Well, we thought he had a gun.'" A little later in the report, the same officer clarified, "'He could have had a gun.'"

Another said Antony was clearly dangerous. Aggressive. His mission was to incite unrest. Violence. And the meaning behind the man's words are clear without Carson's contact having written them out. Of course he could have had a gun. Of course he was dangerous. He was a Black man in a place they thought he shouldn't be, doing things they thought he shouldn't.

It was his own fault is what they've said, without actually saying it.

I pick up the folder and flip through more pages: faster, eager. Desperate. The reports from the police. From the investigator placed on the case. The disciplinary committee, which doled out no discipline. The Special Investigations Unit, who decided that the officers had a reasonable assumption of fear for their lives, so laid no charges. My eyes burn. The sound of the scanner and the faint murmur from Rania and Jasmine mix with the rushing throb in my ears.

I think again of those words behind the words. In some ways, the officers were right. Antony was where he shouldn't have been. Doing what he shouldn't have been doing. He forgot who he was—in their eyes. He'd done the thing none of us should do, if we want to preserve our lives—see ourselves through our own gaze, not theirs.

One witness, Deja, speaks with such conviction, such passion, about how she should have been braver. Stronger. Saying they all should have stood up with Antony instead of dropping to the concrete under threat of those guns, that the police wouldn't have shot them all. That, in the days following, they shouldn't have cowered in fear, bending to the officers' pressure and threats to hide the truth. Antony was brilliant, she says. And brave. Headstrong, maybe. But that's not a crime. He was murdered, she continues. Plain and simple. He was murdered. And none of us did a thing about it.

I reach the medical examiner's report. Four bullets, as I already know. But the locations are new to me. His chest, his shoulder, his hip, his head. Two aimed to kill, two maybe not. And three more, missing their target entirely. I scan the pages, itching to see if there are any more statements from the cops, something to explain more clearly, have it make sense. But it's only the witnesses' words. Antony, they said, stood tall in front of the officers. Told them everything the group had done was peaceful, and within their rights. When the officers told them to scram, empty out the square, not try it again, he stood firm, asking why? On what grounds?

Unlawful assembly, said one, and disrupting the peace. Another referenced Antony's status as an immigrant, adding on an incorrect and defamatory word. Which was typical, said one witness: "We're all the same to them." All four witnesses report what came next differently. One says Antony took a step toward the police. Another said he started to lower his hands. Another, that it all happened too fast. The fourth, that Antony said something back to the most aggressive cop—the one doing most of the talking, who had an Irish, or maybe Scottish, accent—something about him being an immigrant, too. And that's when the shots fired.

None of these things seem enough.

Yet the shots fired, one officer, a fraction before the others, pulling the trigger. Why?

Fear for his life? Fear that the split second it would take to see if my brother was reaching for a gun, or something else, or nothing at all, would be the second that cost him his life?

Or was it hate? Plain and simple.

The report doesn't say which bullet came from which officer.

His chest, his shoulder, his hip, his head.

One in the van. Two in the wall of the building behind him.

It doesn't say which bullet entered first. I close my eyes, hoping for the head—for instant death, no pain. But then, maybe, Antony would have wanted that second or two for a final thought. To think of Mom or Dad or me. To remember his first kiss. To have time to hope.

I scan the pages again, thinking maybe I missed it and it'll be there—who shot first. I need to know who shot first. To find him, ask him why. I clench my teeth, resist the urge to scream as the not knowing haunts me, has haunted me for nearly two decades. Who shot first? Why? Because one had to pull the trigger before the others. One had to decide. And if he hadn't, maybe the others wouldn't have, either. One finger, triggering all the others.

His chest, his shoulder, his hip, his head.

I focus on those stray bullets—in the van, the wall, imagine at least one of those shooters missed on purpose, hoping the others would, too. Imagine he lies awake in bed, even now, wishing he'd been braver, stronger. Wishing he'd tackled the other officers, stepped in front to diffuse the situation. Wishing, if that's what it would have taken, he'd turned his gun on his colleagues.

A cry erupts from somewhere deep within me, a guttural yawp as I throw the folder to the table, double over on myself, my head in my lap.

Did his body jerk and spasm? Did he fall to the ground instantly? Was there pain?

Or was he just gone? All that he was, in an instant, gone.

"Kareela."

I raise my head, blink, and see Rania on the couch beside me, sense Jasmine.

"Are you—?"

"It's not enough." The words spew out of me. "This, all of it. It's nothing."

A long breath. Rania's hand on my knee. "I can see that."

"What was Carson thinking?"

"What did you know before?" Rania asks in a whisper.

"I don't know." I clench my fists, my chest tight, my frustration too large for this small, ineffective body. "Nothing." The heat behind my eyes is unbearable, my body a steam engine. "I knew he was shot. I knew—" And there's nowhere to release this anger, this grief, this helplessness. "They made him sound like a villain. Like he was dangerous and aggressive. Like the police were doing a community service."

"Yeah." A long sigh. "That's typically how it goes. You'll notice none of the news reports that imply that are in here."

"Were you sent them?"

"We were. Carson figured you'd know all about that, and if you didn't, there was no need to see it."

The steam trickles out, a slow warbled breath between my trembling lips. A few casseroles came. But not enough. At six, I had to figure out how to make peanut butter and jelly sandwiches. Sometimes, for snacks, I chomped on whole carrots, too scared to use the knife that slipped and rolled when I tried to cut that unwieldy vegetable. And my father, who had been so robust, withered, his clothes hanging loosely, all of him so much smaller than before.

Silence is what I remember after Antony, only broken by the sound of the television, which never seemed to shut off.

"It wasn't like it is here," I say, looking to Jasmine, who clasps my hand in hers, squeezes. "There was no community. There was no one."

Rania makes a soft noise that indicates she's listening. That she's here now.

"People turned away from us. Their smiles, if they smiled, weren't the same. It was like . . . like . . ."

"You were infected?"

My shoulders slump as my eyes drift closed. "Yeah. And my parents . . . it was like they didn't see it. Or didn't care."

"The conversation was different back then," says Rania. "Your parents likely wouldn't have had this information. If they went into the station, they were probably brushed aside. In every word, every action, the goal would have been to make them think Antony was the villain, a criminal, a lowlife who got what he deserved."

"But—" Jasmine blurts, then shakes her head. "Sorry . . . I mean . . . nothing."

"What?" I ask.

"It's just, this wasn't the thirties. This was after the civil rights movement. No offence, Kareela, but it seems like what you're saying, Rania, is that her parents just, like, had no agency? No ability to even have it?"

"No. What I'm saying is you don't know their pasts, their situations, their fears. We're taught, or at least the powers that be try to teach us, that *they* are infallible. That the police are knights in shining armour, there to protect us, to make everything all right. And so if they do something . . . like what they did, what they do, we're told it's part of their mission to serve and protect, which implies the people they're protecting us from are the ones in the wrong."

"Antony wasn't," I say. "He wasn't . . . I mean . . . violent or anything. I know that."

"I'm sure he wasn't."

"And my parents knew that—" I turn to Rania, a current of furious resistance tingling my limbs. "They're not stupid people. I don't buy that they would have just accepted this was Antony's fault. I don't understand why they didn't push, fight! The cops all stayed on the job. No punishment, no nothing."

"Again, your parents didn't have the information we have, the networks, the easy ability to see and know this kind of thing was going on so often, everywhere."

"But it's not like this was before the internet," says Jasmine.

"No, but it was before the rise of social media," says Rania. "Anyway, that's not the point. The point is your parents were already brave, stepping outside of the norm, whether or not they saw it that way. A Black man and a white woman married in what, the late seventies based on Antony's age? And here they are in a country that declares vehemently there is no race problem. Which means the problems are with individuals. Individuals like Antony.

"Listen, I don't know the situation. I don't know your parents. All I'm saying is you don't know what they were facing. You don't know how hard it would have been to stand up to societal views, all those negative stories being spread about their son. Maybe even violence toward them, or the threat of it, for raising this 'terror,' as one article referred to the protesters, a Black group spreading terror, creating a nightmare in the city's streets." Rania pauses, then continues, the tension in her voice rising. "Despite the fact that there was no vandalism, no violence. It's a system of cover-ups, lies, false reporting to justify and make acceptable the killing of Black and Brown people. So no, you don't know what it would have been like for your parents to fight that, especially with a young daughter at home to protect. Especially with a grief that's more intense than you can imagine."

She stops and rests a shaking hand on my shoulder. "Sorry. It works me up. Anyway, I know you've had your share of grief, but so have your parents, and probably they were trying to survive as best they could while most everyone around them would have been saying—or thinking, at least on some level—that this was Antony's fault. Their fault."

I turn my head from her, look to the table, trying to imagine what it would have been like, if what she's saying could be true, while also trying to work through the realization that I'd never considered any of this before, never taken the time.

"So don't judge them for not fighting when you don't even know whether they did. You were, what, six? Maybe they did fight. Maybe they fought and lost. Either way, trying to blame them won't help anything. Especially not you."

My shoulders tense, the steam inside rising again. A current of shame hits me—shame for thinking so much about myself and so little about them. For the way my father had stood, wanting to fight, and how I had been the one to tell him no.

Had he tried before? Failed? According to these papers, Antony's "compatriots" were harassed when they tried to make their story heard to the police, the media. They were threatened, some even temporarily put behind bars. And if my parents had done any of that, suffered any of it, I wouldn't know. I'd never asked.

I should have asked.

"Why did you give me all this?" I gesture to the papers before us. "Why did Carson? He said it wasn't about me speaking, but . . ."

Rania smiles, pity in her eyes. "Because you have a right to know."

I look away, the steaming fury and confusion and shame causing my head to ache.

A right to know.

I thought knowing would give me the answers I'd been looking for, a way to make sense of Antony's death. But it was senseless, could never have been justified. So instead of having answers, there are only more questions, more mess.

Evelyn

Antony's body had been in the ground eight days when Evelyn was back on a streetcar. It swayed and jerked as a vision of her surfing boy materialized before her—gap-toothed, proud, laughing. She blinked, and he was gone. Weary with the weight of his absence, she pulled out her compact, checked her hair, her makeup, knowing it was entirely possible she'd forgotten to tend to either before stepping out the door, then dropped it in her bag. Antony appeared again, a young man too cool to surf, sitting across from her, legs spread, body slouched, taking up almost three seats with his sprawl, and grinning.

She turned to the window, though it didn't matter where she looked. Her son was everywhere and nowhere.

Two weeks, and her bereavement was supposed to be over. Life was supposed to go on as normal. For her. For Kingsley. Both due back to work this morning.

Evelyn pulled the trolley cord for her stop. She stood, catching another glimpse of her boy before he vanished into the ether. She stepped down from the streetcar and was taken back to the funeral, to the throng of people rushing to offer condolences.

"A terrible business," said one of Kingsley's colleagues, who'd started five years after him, yet gotten tenure five years ago. "Such a terrible business." As if that's all it was. The death of their son. Business. The officers doing their job. A hard, unpleasant job, certainly, but a necessary one.

"It's awful," said a neighbour. "Just awful. Now you've got to carry on, and we all need to teach our children how to react in these situations. Hands up, following the officers' directions."

As if the fault lay with Antony. With Evelyn, for not instructing him better in the ways of the world.

Then that young woman's voice. "They're lying." One hand clasping Evelyn's hand, the other on her wrist, as if entreating her. "He stood, that was all. Hands raised. He spoke."

Swept forward with the rush of people on their morning commute, Evelyn heard the words again. *They're lying.* She froze. *He stood, that was all. He spoke.* She turned against the crowd, walking first, then running. Breathless, she burst into Dani's office. "I need to see Charles."

"Evelyn." Dani stood, a nervous smile cast to her office mates, ushering Evelyn out of the room. "What are you doing here?"

"I need to see Charles," said Evelyn, again. "I need to fight this."

"Fight . . ." Dani shook her head and pulled Evelyn into the hall. "I don't under—"

"The officers are going to get away with it, like they always do. For murder, Dani. This was murder."

"No, it—"

"Do you think, do you honestly think Antony deserved this? That he was a threat or—"

"Of course not. It was a misunderstanding. And awful." She led Evelyn toward the fire exit, then closed the door behind them. "A tragedy. But you've talked to the police. They thought he was armed. That he was reaching for—"

"No."

"Evelyn. You're upset. I understand."

"You don't!" Evelyn pulled away. "He wasn't reaching for anything. A girl at the funeral. She told me. He had his hands raised. He didn't cower. He didn't lie on the ground like the others, but he had his arms raised. All he did was speak, take one step forward."

Dani's brow narrowed, her lips following suit. "You're sure?"

"I'm sure that's what she said. And Antony, he's not stupid. He knows what they're like. He wouldn't have reached for anything. And what would he have been reaching for? He was unarmed. The police confirmed that."

"Well . . ."

"Dani, I need to speak to a lawyer. When can I see Charles?"

"Tonight." Dani nodded. "After work. Come over to the house."

"Thank you." Evelyn embraced her friend. Taking the officers to court wouldn't bring Antony back. But it'd be something. It'd continue his work. She'd find that Bahamian professor—who wasn't there when it happened, but would know more than her about what to do. She'd find the people who were there. She'd do whatever she could to make sure those officers lost their jobs, their lives as they knew it. She'd find justice for her son.

Outside Dani's office, Evelyn got on a bus heading toward the 52 Division police station. In the precinct, the noise and hustle shook her. She'd expected order. A calm rigidity. The opposite of what she'd seen on late night crime shows. But the shows were more accurate than she'd imagined. Movement. Uniformed men. Some women. People in cuffs.

She stepped slowly, making her way to reception. "Excuse me." She spoke louder, stepping closer. "Excuse me. Miss!"

A young woman, blond, blue-eyed, looking like she could be Evelyn's daughter, raised her head. "Sorry, sorry." She half laughed, half sighed. "Such a hectic morning. What can I do for you?"

"I'd like information," she said. "On my son's . . . case."

"Is he up for trial?"

"No."

"You're probably looking for an incident report, then. Is he here with—"

"No. He's . . ." Evelyn had only said the word once. To Kareela. She'd since found other ways when she needed to relay information, but now—

"Dead. He was shot by police. He's dead."

"Oh!" The woman's eyes widened, the words seemingly not what she'd expected—from a woman like Evelyn. "Oh. Well . . . do you have an appointment?"

"No."

"Hmm, well"—the woman looked down, shuffled papers—"you'll have to put in a request. That's not here. You'll need to go to police headquarters, on College Street."

"But . . ." Evelyn's resolve wavered. She should be at work. She shouldn't have come here, not knowing what she was even looking for. But how many more young men would be killed if she waited? How many boys? She leaned on the desk, and the woman leaned back. "It was two weeks ago. Surely the information is still here. Or accessible, at least. Can I talk to one of the officers? They must be still . . . uh, assessing the case? Compiling witnesses? Building a—"

The woman shook her head, distaste passing over her features. Of course she knew about Antony. The entire city did. Thought, probably, that Evelyn was what the papers were not saying, exactly, but implying. The mother of a thug. A threat to society. That young Black man, that "political Black man"—as if those words beside each other auto-matically meant criminal—a Black activist, who got what he deserved. "There'll be an incident report," she said, her blue eyes looking at Evelyn with no sympathy. "Witness statements as well. The officers' accounts, but . . . you'll need to go to police headquarters, as I said."

Evelyn opened her mouth, her limbs tightening. She closed it. Opened again. "Thank you. For your help." She turned from the woman, anger coursing through her, urging her to turn back, yell, *You're wrong about him!* She pushed through the doors. *He wasn't a thug.* She turned toward her office, the mental tirade continuing. *He was a person.* She'd be an hour and a half late, maybe two. *He was my son.*

She increased her pace, realizing the risk she'd been taking—going to see Dani, to the station. She couldn't afford to lose this job, so she'd visit the professor during her free time. He worked at City University. She could call reception, figure out his office number. After work she'd go to Charles and Dani's, figure out the best steps, whether she should make the request for information herself or have Charles do it. She'd find answers, find justice. For Antony.

"I CAN'T, EVELYN. I'm sorry."

Evelyn sat across from Dani and Charles in their living room, the sounds of the children's laughter wafting up the hall. Her head shook. "What do you mean you can't? This is what you do. Try criminal cases."

"Yes, but—"

"But what? I'll find the woman. She said Antony wasn't aggres-sive, like they said. There'd be others who could corroborate. He was unarmed."

"Yes, I know."

"So what's the problem?"

Charles sighed. "I'm about to be made partner."

A bead of sweat trickled down Evelyn's spine. The three glasses of lemonade Dani had set on the coffee table between them sat untouched, condensation slipping down the edges.

"So I can't . . . I just." Charles looked to Dani, who gave him a tight smile. "I've been working toward this for over a decade, Evelyn. I can't take on a case that . . ."

"That what?"

"That will take on the Toronto police. It'd be a career killer."

Evelyn swallowed, the damp heat closing her throat. She reached for the lemonade. Gulped. With her throat opened, Antony's words poured out. "They'll get away with it, like they always do, unless we fight."

"You don't know what happened."

"I know my son didn't deserve to die!"

"You're right, of course you're right." Charles leaned forward, but it was dismissal, not conviction, Evelyn heard in his voice. "You may find someone who's willing to fight. Request the incident report, the witness accounts, the autopsy. Go to the witnesses themselves. You may find someone."

Antony's words, up on that podium, streamed through Evelyn's mind. *They look at me and see drugs. They see violence. Danger. But I'm not violent. I've never hurt anyone.*

"Do all of that, Evelyn, if you must. But I have to tell you . . . there's a reason I'm not helping. A reason it'll be hard to find someone who will. The police are a force. And that force is supported by the judicial system, the government. They look out for their own. Nine times out of ten, heck, nineteen times out of twenty, maybe more, the police win."

But they think I'm dangerous. They think my existence, my feet walking along the street, through my own neighbourhood, warrants suspicion. They think they can do whatever they want.

Evelyn's bottom lip trembled. Her eyes burned. She thought back to that first dinner invite. The fact that Dani said they "couldn't care less" that Evelyn's husband was Black, that her child was.

"So, what you should do is take that girl of yours home," said Charles. "Hold Kingsley in your arms. Try to move forward. Try to move on."

"What if we sued?" said Evelyn. "Not a criminal case, but—"

"The prospects aren't better. No matter what route you take, it won't be easy. It'll be awful, and almost certainly doomed to fail."

Evelyn shifted her gaze. "Dani?"

Dani licked her lips, bit them, then shook her head. "I think he's right, Evie. This is horrible. Tragic. It never should have happened. But bringing this upon yourself, trying to fight it—" She turned to Charles. "It could go on years, you said? Years, and in the end, Antony will still be gone." She turned back to Evelyn. "And most likely, nothing will have come of it. Nothing but more misery, more stress."

"Charles, please!"

"She's right, Evelyn." Charles wiped the sweat from his brow. "These are battles that are fought but not won. The cost, the time. We all know it's horrible; we all know it shouldn't have happened, but it's a fight we won't win. It'll make this tragedy stretch out. Putting you, your family through that? I won't do it."

"You don't think it'll stretch out, anyway? That we won't be feeling it every minute of every day?"

"Not like that," said Charles. "Evelyn, believe me, you have no idea what it would be like. No idea what *they* would be like."

A hollow made its way into Evelyn's middle. Her breath caught. "Kareela." Evelyn raised her voice. "Kareela!"

Footsteps down the hall, her girl, face expectant. Evelyn stood. "We're leaving."

"But *Mommy*."

"Now!"

"Evelyn!" Dani stood, then stepped toward Evelyn.

"Thank you for taking the time to see me." Evelyn nodded at Dani, and then Charles. They "couldn't care less," but she felt certain that if her son had been white, they, the judicial system, the government, the media, would have cared a lot more. She stepped toward the door, fighting tears, her chest weighted with the expectation that this would be the last time she'd ever step through it. "Good night."

Evelyn

The front door looked the same as it always had, but Evelyn's body stiffened at the sight of it. Although on the outside, nothing had changed, on the inside, her home was transformed. Foreign, without Antony.

Inside, Kingsley sat in front of the TV, a plate in front of him. Violet had left two days earlier, leaving the fridge as full as it could be, and the scent of food Evelyn and Kingsley hardly took the time to make anymore still filled the house, making every blanket and throw potent with the smell of home. Evelyn put a bowl of rice and peas and stewed beef in the microwave for Kareela and debated putting a bowl in for herself. She should. She'd had to pull the belt buckle of her skirt an extra notch this morning.

She waited for the ding—staring at her daughter. The first time Violet had cooked, Kareela scrunched her nose. "What's that?" Today, she was two-stepping in front of the microwave and accepted the bowl with eager hands. "Take that to your room," said Evelyn, the mask of a smile firmly in place.

"My room?" Kareela's eyes widened. "Am I in trouble?"

"No, sweetheart. I just need to talk to Daddy."

"I want to talk to Daddy."

"Go to your room, Kareela, please."

Kareela's expression fell, displeasure coating her features, but she went, always the dutiful child.

Evelyn closed her eyes—failure tugging at her, but also yearning. Antony wouldn't have gone. Antony would have protested, said he would not eat alone and there wasn't a single thing they could do about it. Antony never gave up.

She went to the living room and sat across from Kingsley. "I want to fight this."

He turned to her. "Fight what?"

"The police. Getting away with it."

Kingsley looked at her like she was crazy. "What?"

"It shouldn't have happened. And now they should pay."

Kingsley set his plate on the coffee table. "You want money? For our son?"

"No. I want justice. I want them to lose their licences. I want to see them on trial. I want them in prison."

"That's not how it works."

"It could be."

"No."

"Antony would have—"

"Antony's gone." He gestured to her, her blond hair, her blue eyes, without saying what he was saying. "You think you won't be next, but you could be. Or, more likely, me."

Evelyn's chest hitched. "I—"

"Drop it, Evelyn. It's over. He's gone."

Kingsley turned his face to the screen. Evelyn turned hers, too, but not her thoughts.

She entered the kitchen, hands on her hips. She spun, looking for a task. But the kitchen was clean. Her stomach growled, though the thought of food made her sick—eating, when her son never would again. She slammed the side of her hand against a cupboard, then froze with shock, waiting for Kingsley or Kareela to call out, ask what happened. After one breath, two, she held her throbbing hand to her chest, so she wouldn't do it again, or pick up the dishes from the counter and hurl them, throw the chairs across the room, the table to the floor.

She stood, imagining the chaos, the relief there would be in falling apart. But she didn't have the luxury. She called to Kareela, her smile firm, and asked her what she wanted for dinner.

"I just ate." Kareela tilted her head, that little nose scrunched again.

"Right. Of course." Evelyn forced a laugh. She turned to the sink and braced her shaking arms upon the counter. Justice. It didn't matter what Charles said, or Kingsley. Justice was what she'd focus on, the one thing in this nightmare she'd make sure she'd get.

THE NEXT MORNING, Evelyn called into work. Said she needed extended leave. Her boss sighed. He was a good man. He didn't like it, she could tell, but he said, "Two more weeks."

Evelyn thanked him, said she hoped she wouldn't need more, but she might.

"I can't give you pay for this extra time," he said. "And if it goes longer than that—"

"Thank you," said Evelyn, not waiting to hear what would come after.

Notebook at the ready, with a list of all she set out to do, Evelyn finished getting Kareela ready for daycare. She dropped her off, the directions to police headquarters in hand.

The sounds of the city beat against Evelyn's thoughts, the cacophony amplifying the hot tension that thrummed in her chest. The man at reception was pleasant. Not much older than Antony. He nodded while Evelyn spoke, his eyes sympathetic. "A terrible thing," he said.

Evelyn's throat caught, surprise and thankfulness flooding her at the admission. "Yes." She straightened. "Yes. It is terrible."

He nodded again. "We'll get you all we can."

"Thank . . ." Evelyn almost smiled. "Thank you. I appreciate it."

She stepped out of the building, a burst of accomplishment adding purpose to her steps. It was something. A yes instead of a no. A confirmation that the truth was coming. She walked the short distance to City University, deciding visiting Dr. Knowles in person was the way to go.

Usually within moments of stepping onto campus, a peace overtook Evelyn—she loved these old buildings: the cornices, the vines, the stones that had stood long before her and would stand long after. But today, the history offered no comfort.

She navigated the tree-lined pathways, thankful as she travelled farther and farther away from Kingsley's building.

The door to Dr. Knowles's office was half open. The man behind the paper-strewn desk rested his head on his hand, a pencil between his teeth, the lines on his forehead meeting in deep grooves.

"Hello."

Dr. Knowles looked up. The pencil fell from his lips. As he stood, the lines stretched out and raised to meet what should have been his hairline. "Hello! . . ." He swallowed, clasped his hands in front of him, and came around the desk, shortening the space between them. "Hi."

Even in those few words, Evelyn could hear the gentle lilt. "I'm Ev—"

"Yes. I know." Dr. Knowles extended his hand, then released hers so quickly it was as if her touch had burned him. He rubbed a hand over hair that was no longer there. "I'm sorry I . . . uh . . . for your loss, Mrs. Jackson. I'm sorry."

Evelyn gave a slight nod as he gestured to the chair in front of his desk.

"Please. Sit."

She did, thinking how in another life she could have been here for office hours, pursuing a dream, instead of meeting this man because of a nightmare. He shuffled back around to his own seat, not looking at all like the strong, powerful, confident man she'd seen speaking in front of hundreds. His lips trembled and his eyes moistened. "I . . ." He put his head down, made a deep, almost coughing sound in his throat, then raised his head again. "I'm sorry, too, that I didn't say it . . . at the funeral. I wanted to. I tried to. I couldn't."

He lifted his gaze to the ceiling. "I keep thinking . . . maybe if I'd been there. I sent the kids. And maybe if I hadn't. Maybe if I'd gone myself."

Evelyn reached her hand out, then let it fall. "I don't blame you." Though maybe she should. Maybe she did. They were kids. And he was a grown man. An educated man. Someone who should have known better.

"I came here today"—Evelyn straightened, and pulled her hand back—"to see what you know about what happened. What the next steps should be. And to get the names and contact information for the people who were there."

"Oh." He looked down again, piled several stacks of papers to the side, placed his hands in the cleared space. "Oh. Well."

Evelyn waited. "Have you talked to the people who were there? Do you know who they are?"

He nodded, his gaze narrowing. "Mrs. Jackson, we're all incredibly sorry for your loss. All of us. And we all wish things had turned out differently. We loved Antony. He was a wonderful young man. Bright. Kind. Passionate. It is a great loss."

"It is a crime."

"Yes."

Evelyn licked her lips. She bit the bottom one as she shoved down the anger that built at his words. "And you fight these kinds of crimes. This kind of injustice. That's why my son is dead. Because he was fighting. With you."

"I know, Mrs. Jackson. I know." Dr. Knowles gulped air, his smile quivery.

"So . . ." She kept her gaze level. "What are we going to do about it?"

"Uh . . ." He rubbed a hand along the back of his neck, looking sheepish. "We're having a memorial to remember him, honour him, but I'm stepping away from the protests, for a time at least. This has been hard on all of us: the students, me. I think it's best if you step away from this, too. It won't bring Antony—"

Evelyn stood. "Stepping away? What do you mean?"

"Please, Mrs. Jackson." He half stood, leaning toward her over the desk, a hand out, palm down. "Please. Sit. People will hear you."

"What people?" Evelyn stayed standing.

"Look." He kept his voice low. "I'm on probation. With the university. Because of what happened. I have three kids at home, a wife who needs the health insurance this job provides." His voice lowered another notch. "And they, well, I guess there's no other way to say it. They threatened me."

"The university?"

"No. Well, yes, in a way, with the probation. But I meant the police, they . . . they said they could make things bad for me. For my family. I have a brother who . . ." He pressed his lips tight, let a stream of air blow from his nostrils. "I'm not giving up the fight. I'm just shifting the way I fight. Re-strategizing. Biding my time. And you . . . you should do the same."

"I'm not fighting the system," said Evelyn. "I'm fighting for my son. Justice for my son."

"And to get that," said the professor, "you'd have to fight the system."

"Isn't that my choice?"

"It is." He placed his hands back on the desk, fear behind his entreating eyes. "But I wish you wouldn't." His voice shook. "They . . . Mrs. Jackson, you have a young daughter at home. So the best thing to do, for all of you, is to move on as best you can, to remember Antony and—"

Evelyn stepped back, her body tense. "You have a rally, a protest, for those boys, those strangers. But for my son, who was one of you, nothing. You decide not to fight. To stay silent."

"We're having a memorial."

"Which will accomplish nothing. Change nothing."

"It will help people remember. It will inspire—"

Evelyn hefted her purse to her shoulder. "Do you have the names and contacts for the people who were there?"

Dr. Knowles leaned away from her. "I do."

"Will you give them to me?"

He sighed. "I will. But my guess is not many, if any, of them will talk to you. Not once they realize what you're after."

A roiling heat swirled in Evelyn's belly. These people had stood and fought—with their words and their presence. Had spouted beliefs. Yet now that it mattered, according to this man, they wouldn't stand.

"Give them to me, please." Evelyn crossed her arms, waiting.

Dr. Knowles nodded. He tore a piece of lined paper from a notebook and started writing.

Kareela

After leaving the BLM headquarters, the file on Antony a weight in my bag, I tiptoe into the apartment. My eyes moist and stinging, I thank the darkness as I crawl into bed. Thomas rolls over, drapes an arm around me, and pulls me close. I shape my body into his, wanting and not wanting to tell him of the folder and everything in it. Wanting and not wanting to stay in his arms forever. This man, this wonderful, kind, beautiful man who has no idea of the fear I feel, the anger, the pain. Who never could. Not in the specific way Rania and Jasmine do, that Antony did.

My body wants to shake, to let the sobs take over. I take deep, slow breaths and force my mind to focus on tomorrow, the best order to address each task. I breathe, and plan—what I should and shouldn't say to each client—plan and breathe, until sleep creeps upon me.

When I wake, alone in the bed, I determine to put the words in the file behind me, pretend they don't matter.

Yet all through the day, as I speak with client after client, meet with my adviser, who emphasizes how pleased she is with me, I see those words, my mind never stopping, continually yearning to piece them together, to have even the smallest aspect of them make sense. I see, too, my parents in a way I'd never considered—that I'm afraid to, because of the uncomfortable itch it brings that although all these years I've thought they failed me, maybe, in a way, I've failed them, too.

As I pull my body up the stairs to our apartment in the early evening, the words in that folder, the questions and revelations they prompted, are still there, swirling, merging, threatening to exit my mind and form a chain around me, restricting my movement, my ability to live.

Inside, the scent of onions and garlic and beef takes me to Gran. *Yuh brotha,* she says, *he loved his food, and aye dat boy could eat. Just like yuh daddy. It hard to fill dem up.*

There are things I remembered, but memories are uncertain, like the fragments of a dream in the moments after waking. So I asked Gran to tell me about him. She only knew him well as a baby. She remembered his cheeks. Chubby and round, with one dimple. His laugh. High pitched and squeaky. The way he toddled on that one visit back island. Five years passed before she saw him again. Then another. Her memories of him end before mine begin.

"Babe?"

In the kitchen, Thomas smiles, his pleasure at seeing me radiating, and it reminds me of the first time I saw that smile, over a year and a half ago. How when he looked at me, talked to me, it was as if he was focused on me and only me. Not some Black girl. Not as a way to carve one more fetishized notch on his bedpost. But me. He pulls me in with one arm, kisses me long, bringing back yesterday's intimacies.

"How was your day?"

I hoist myself up on the counter, legs dangling like a child's, remembering how I did this same thing on our first official date—surprised at my immediate comfort in his apartment. "All right. My supervisor's pretty pleased with my work."

"We're both killing it!" He grins, then turns to the stove, jostling the food around, prompting fresh pops and sizzles, and the memory continues. How he grinned as he looked at me, propped up there on his counter, told me just because he'd offered to cook for me, that didn't mean I got to sit there looking pretty and do no work.

He lowers the heat, turns back, smiling, and motions for me to join in, like he did that night. He'd given me the job of kneading the dough for the pasta, hoping, I imagined, that I wouldn't quite know how to do it and he'd have to sidle up behind me, place his warm hands over mine, and whisper directions, his breath on the back of my neck. It'd been the best foreplay I'd ever had—emphasized by the fact that he extended it not just through the preparation of that meal but for weeks, drawing it out before that first explosive night between the covers. With each subsequent date, he let me fall deeper into his laughs, his smiles, the way he made me feel more wanted, more seen, than any guy I'd ever dated—never mentioning the bigness of my hair or shade of my skin, or asking what my background was or whether I usually dated white guys or Black. I felt so secure; it prompted me to do whatever I could to keep that feeling. Keep his interest alive.

"I called my doctor's office today," he says, jolting me back to the present. "They agreed to take you on. They have an appointment next Tuesday, at four, which I can make. If you can get off work about a half hour early?"

My body stiffens as all those tender memories from the early months of our relationship drain away. He speaks as if we've discussed this— beyond me saying I'm not ready—as if yesterday changed everything. "I don't want to see a doctor."

He sighs. "I know, okay. And maybe I shouldn't have called without talking to you, but you don't want to talk about it, and Ree, this is the responsible thing to do."

I stare at him, trying to figure out the last time I felt secure—though I know it's me that's changed, me that's looking at myself differently, not him.

"I don't mean having the baby," he continues. "I know you haven't made your decision yet. I get that. But that means your decision may be yes, and if it is, well, then you want to make sure that you're healthy. The baby's healthy."

I shift from thinking about our relationship to what's growing inside of me. He's right, but I wish he wasn't . . . because this baby, right now, may be the safest it will ever be, and I don't want to know if it isn't.

"Like you said before, maybe we're going through all this, and it's nothing, not even a baby, just a conglomeration of cells. Wouldn't it make more sense to know?"

No, I say, but only in my mind, as I tense at the thought of this being not a conglomeration of cells, but a potential person I have to decide whether to keep or not.

"Even if you—" The tone of his voice tightens my chest. "I mean, it's your choice, obviously, and I don't want this to happen, but . . . well . . ."

"Spit it out!" I snap, surprised at the forcefulness of my tone.

He flinches. Clears his throat.

"Sorry." I place a hand to my forehead, battling to expel the fear, the uncertainty that revealed itself in anger, out of my voice. "What is it?"

"I've been thinking." He leans against the counter. "And honestly, it feels like all I'm thinking about lately. And I know this seems crazy. And I know it would be asking a lot. So much, but . . ."

He trails off, and my voice is softer this time, but still tight. "But what?"

"I've been thinking about my dad," he continues. "And what it felt like when he abandoned us. Me. I know this is totally different. I get that. But I don't want to abandon this child. I don't want to be a person, like him, who decides life would be easier without their kid, so just . . . I know it's not the same—"

"Of course it's not the same. What are you even saying?"

"I . . ." He rubs his hand through his hair, uselessly, as the blond strands settle over his eye again. "Well . . . if you don't want the baby, and if you're willing to . . . well . . . I was thinking that I still want it. To keep it. Even without you."

I hear his words, but they don't quite make sense.

"I mean, I want you *and* this baby. I want to be a family. But if you decide, as it is your choice, that you don't want this baby, and again, I know it'd be asking a lot, but would you let me have it? Raise it. On my own. Totally on my own, if you wanted. Or you could have some role. A small role. A big role. Whatever you want."

I step back, almost feeling the earth shake as another invisible fissure widens between us.

"I'm in, is what I'm saying. All in. Whether it means having this baby with you or without you." He takes a step toward me. "As I said, I know it would be asking a lot."

"A hell of a lot."

He flinches. "Yes." He rubs a hand along his opposite forearm. "And I don't want that, as a first choice. I want us. But I also want this child. And I recognize it's your choice. It's your body." He hesitates. "But it's my child, too. And as I said, already I've started to fall in love. So I want to know if it's there, real, and growing as it should. If being a father, a good father, is even a possibility."

I turn from him, step out of the kitchen, the beat of my heart firm against my chest, and place a hand on my abdomen, imagining the life that is and isn't there, is and isn't real. If I go to the doctor, hear a heartbeat, I fear this thing inside me will stop being a potential person, but become an actual one. And I'm not ready for the reality. I can think about ending the life of a concept, but to end the life of a being with a beating heart, made up of my blood, my father's, the blood that flowed through Antony . . .

To end the life of a child I've always wanted, but don't want yet.

I turn back, wondering if what he's asking, though it seems so unreasonable, isn't. Except he's gone. Silence filling the space: no more sizzle. No more pop.

He sits on the kitchen floor, back against the counter, elbows on his knees, hands folded as if in prayer or supplication, gaze straight ahead.

"I'm sorry," I say.

His head nods slightly, turns toward me. "Why don't you want it? And me, do you—?"

"I want you," I say, because what else am I supposed to? None of this is his fault.

His lips lift the tiniest bit, on one side only. "Are you sure? You've been so—"

"This isn't about you." I speak before he can finish, knowing, at least in part, my words are a lie. "We're young, the—"

"The world is shitty." He pushes himself to stand. "We don't have our careers solidified."

I press my lips, look to the window, my thoughts again on Antony— how senseless it all was. On my father, who, when it comes down to it, died from those same bullets. How Thomas's words are truer than he could ever realize.

"But we have each other." He steps closer, the pain in his voice a rushing wave upon me. "And we can figure out the rest."

I swallow through a lump so large it hurts. Despite this shit world, he has a point, at least about the ultrasound. It makes more sense to know. And, perhaps, I owe him that much. "I'll see the doctor."

He nods. "Thank you." We stand there, one breath, two. So close, but horribly distanced. He gestures to the stove. "You hungry?"

"Yeah." I'm not. But food is how we connect, so I give him this.

Evelyn

TORONTO

2004

Three women. Four men. Evelyn had waited to unfold the sheet Dr. Knowles handed her until she was out of his office. She sat in the hot midmorning sun and struggled for a full breath, the sheen of pollution already darkening the horizon. People would die today. Asthmatics in high-rise apartment buildings with no AC who had to open their windows, let all that poison in. Likely some homeless people, too. A number of elderly. There wouldn't be justice for their deaths, no specific people or entity their loved ones could blame.

With Antony, it was different. With Antony, individuals were involved. The ones who'd specifically done it, and the ones who'd led them to believe they could, to believe they'd get away with it.

Paper clenched in her palm, Evelyn stood. The back of her dress stuck to her thighs. She tugged and the fabric peeled free.

It would be easier to go home, to call from the comfort of her living room. But in case any of these people were on campus now, could meet her now, she didn't want to miss the opportunity. She returned to the Faculty of Social Work, remembering a rare pay phone she'd seen in the lobby.

Antony would grin if he saw her. *Told ya.* Laugh. *Wouldn't a mobile phone be handy right about now?*

Pain hit like a tidal wave—to never see that grin, hear that laugh, again.

Evelyn rifled through her purse, searching for the baggie of coins she kept for this reason, then pushed one in.

"Allô?"

"Hi. Hello." Evelyn's voice jumped. "Is this Sylvie?"

"It is." The girl had an accent. Québécois, by the sounds of it. "How may I help you?"

"It's . . . well . . ." Evelyn should have planned her words, determining how best to avoid the reaction she got from Dr. Knowles. "I'm Evelyn Jackson. Antony's—"

"Antony's mère. Oh, mon Dieu. Why . . . I mean . . . hello?"

Evelyn took a moment to breathe. To think. She shouldn't blurt it out, her request. If the girl was scared, that would—

"Madame. Are you there?"

"Yes, I am. Yes." Evelyn clutched the phone to her ear. She evened out her voice, trying to even out the beat of her heart as well. "I was hoping we could talk." Silence. "About Antony."

"Oh . . ." Sylvie muttered something unintelligible. "Oh. I am sorry." Her voice quavered. "I did not know Antony very well."

"I see, but . . ." Evelyn closed her eyes, fighting disappointment. It wasn't the reason for the call. But she had hoped this woman had known her son. Could share snippets of his life Evelyn hadn't been privy to. "You were there, though, weren't you? When he died."

"I was, oui. I mean, yes. Yes, I was."

"So maybe—"

"No, I . . ."

"Please, Sylvie, it would mean—"

"Non. I am sorry, Madame Jackson." A low quick sound—like a sob but strangled. "I am sorry about your son. But non."

"I—" Evelyn held the phone away from her ear at the sound of the click. She slammed the receiver into its holder, then breathed, picked it up again. She dialed the next woman's number. No answer. And the next, voicemail. She straightened, recognizing the soft cadence. It was the woman who'd told her the police officers' stories were false. Deja. Evelyn left a message, telling her the number she could call to get in touch. And if that didn't work, to try Antony's mobile. She didn't have it on her now, but she'd turn it back on when she got home, have it with her going forward.

She tried the next numbers. Two answered. Two didn't. Both men were as short as Sylvie, as shifted and frightened as Dr. Knowles. One talking about his family, how the police threatened him, them. The other saying he was here on a student visa. He didn't want any trouble. *Then what were you doing there?* Evelyn yelled internally. *Why were you protesting, fighting the system, in the first place?* "I'm sorry," he said, sounding it. "But if I say what happened, rather than what I was *told* happened, they promised me there'd be trouble. There's already been trouble enough."

Evelyn slammed the phone into its holder when the man hung up. She slammed again, then slumped against the wall. Were none of these people the ones who'd shaken her hand, who said they'd continue the fight, do it for Antony?

Why was it her son, and not these men, these women, who was six feet underground? But she knew the answer, if what Deja said was true. He was the only one who'd stood when the wise choice would have been to drop to the ground, who spoke, when all the others stayed silent.

Evelyn pushed herself from the wall, her fist aching and red. Had she punched the brick? It didn't matter. She needed to get home, get near the phone, get Antony's mobile charging. One of the witnesses she'd left a message for may still be willing to talk, to fight, for Antony.

EVELYN WALKED INTO a quiet house, her stomach cramping. She'd forced herself to eat a banana this morning, the only item since yesterday's lunch. Her eyes closed. Her jaw, her shoulders, and her hands trembled as moisture sprung behind her lids. She walked to the kitchen—she didn't want to eat—and braced herself on the back of a chair. She didn't want to live. Not in a world without Antony.

But the world still held Kareela. She blew out a stream of cold air, gave herself a little shake, and crossed to the fridge. While she waited for the leftover rice and peas to warm, she remembered the phone. Moments later, she stood at the door of Antony's room. She'd only entered once since the night they'd heard the news, the bag the police had returned to them in her hand. She'd felt as if she were desecrating something and sat gingerly on the bed. The bag was light; his clothes hadn't been returned. Too damaged, the officer said. Too bloody, Evelyn heard. She'd taken out his wallet, then his watch, which she and Kingsley had given him for finally getting his degree. She closed her eyes, saw his smile as he crossed that stage, Kingsley's as he sat, his back ramrod straight, chest puffed.

And then she reached for his phone.

Today, Evelyn flipped open the phone, which sat on his dresser beside the wallet and watch, and pressed the power button. Nothing. She surveyed the room, then remembered having seen the phone resting on the bedside table the many times she'd peeked in to call Antony for dinner or ask how his day had gone. She stepped over, bent down to look for a charger behind the table, and caught the scent of her son. Evelyn shook from her core. She eased to the bed, her head on the pillow, her arms around it, breathing in the smell of Antony. His cologne—spicy, with a hint of musk. The oil he applied to his dreads—sweet, a bit fruity. The distinctive scent he'd had since the day he was born. She breathed, inhaling as deeply as she could, wanting to take this smell into her. Knowing it wouldn't last long.

The microwave beeped, and then another sound. The phone. Not Antony's. She pushed herself to standing and raced to the kitchen.

"Hello."

"Hi, uh . . . I'm . . . uh . . . is Mrs. Jackson there?"

Deja.

"Hello, yes. This is she." Evelyn sank to a chair, gripping the phone like a lifeline. "Deja, right? Thank you for returning my call."

"Yes. Uh . . . yep. It's me. What . . . uh . . . what can I do for you?"

"I'd love to meet. Anytime that's most convenient for you. I'd love to talk about Antony."

Silence.

"You knew him, didn't you? My son."

"I did, yeah. We . . . uh, we were pretty close. Not . . . I mean, well . . . I cared about him. You know?"

"Yes. Yes, I do." A pause. "So can we talk? Maybe a coffee shop or somewhere on campus. Anywhere you want, really. Anywhere that's convenient for you."

"I'm just on my break at work. I finish in about three hours. It's not too far from you, actually. You're at home, yeah?"

"I am. Yes."

"How about the Tims on Danforth and Birchmount? You know it? I could meet you there at three thirty."

Evelyn gripped the phone tighter, hope welling in her. "Yes. Tim Hortons at three thirty. I'll be there."

The microwave sounded again as Evelyn said goodbye. She crossed over to it and, stomach clenching in pain, hands shaking with anticipation, dumped the food in the trash.

Evelyn

More than half the seats in the small restaurant were filled, the air heavy with laughter and the sweet, warm scent of baked goods. Evelyn sat in a booth by the window. She'd arrived almost ten minutes early and stood in front of the cash, not knowing whether to buy something for the girl, fearful of making the wrong choice. So instead she sat, nothing in front of her, her hands folded on the table, then on her lap, then back on the table again.

When Deja stepped through the door, a half-open backpack slung over one shoulder and a jean jacket tied around her slim waist, Evelyn stood and waved, nerves tingling.

"Sorry, so sorry." Deja rushed over. "I thought I'd be here early, but my boss, he's like, the worst." She bit the side of her lip, smiled, shy and awkward. Beautiful, too. Evelyn hadn't noticed at the funeral. But behind her bedraggled clothes, which Evelyn imagined were a conscious choice, wild hair that spread around her face in gravity-defying curls, and an alarming amount of black eyeliner, this girl was gorgeous. The instant the thought arrived, another one joined it— what *had* Deja meant when she said she and Antony were close? Like a movie before her eyes, Evelyn saw a different life. This girl showing up at their door, sitting at their table, laughing with Antony, the two of them curling up on the couch, arm in arm. Years down the road, a wedding. Grandchildren. Evelyn blinked, gave her head a little shake, and replaced the smile she'd let slip off her face.

"No need to apologize. I'm just so glad you came!" Evelyn gestured to the front. "What can I get you? Anything you want. My treat."

"No. Oh, no!" The girl waved a hand in front of her face, her tan skin flushing slightly. "That's okay."

Evelyn leaned forward, smile firm. "I insist. Thirsty? Hungry? Both? Whatever you like."

"Okay. Well . . ." Deja shifted her bag strap higher on her shoulder. "Maybe a black coffee and an everything bagel with cream cheese and tomato. If that's not too much. The tomato is extra."

Evelyn's heart seized, her smile transitioning to something genuine. "That's not too much at all. Just a minute." She stood in line, then glanced back at the table. Deja had plopped onto the bench, her backpack spread across the table, her head in her hands. The girl looked exhausted. Overwhelmed. Evelyn snapped her head to the cash, not wanting to risk being caught staring. She placed her order, getting the same as Deja, and adding a box of Timbits to share, as well as two bottles of water.

Minutes later, she set the food down as Deja raised her head, straightened her spine. "Thanks so much, Mrs. Jackson." Deja unwrapped the bagel and was about to take a bite when she set it back down again. "Oh, God. I didn't even . . . I'm sorry, you know? So sorry for your loss."

"You said it," said Evelyn. "At the funeral."

"Oh, yeah, well." Deja looked down. "I think it . . . like, bears repeating."

"You knew him well?"

Deja kept her head down.

"Deja?"

A sound like a rodent's squeal escaped from her lips. "God. Sorry." She raised her face, tears sliding down her cheeks. She rubbed those cheeks with her fists, so childlike. Evelyn wanted to cross to the other side of the booth, take the girl in her arms. But she sat still, fearful that if she followed her instincts, she'd embarrass the girl, or worse, cause her to clam up.

"We weren't, like . . . you know . . . he wasn't my boyfriend. But I think, maybe soon, he would have been. I hoped, anyway."

"Oh, sweetheart."

"God!" Deja exclaimed. "Don't pity me, okay? I'm just some silly girl, falling in love with a boy I'm not even sure felt the same way . . . but, well . . ."

"I'm sure he would have been lucky to have you."

Deja let out a sad little laugh.

"He was shy," said Evelyn. "When it came to girls, anyway. It took a lot for him to work up the courage to ask a girl out."

Deja's face scrunched, as if not believing Evelyn.

"It's true." And it was. Though not because of a simple lack of confidence. If the girl were Black, Antony would fear she'd think him not Black enough; if she were white, that she was merely interested in the thrill of "stepping out," as Antony had referred to it more than once. Deja's skin wasn't much darker than Antony's, but Evelyn doubted she was mixed-race. Antony would have mentioned it, as he often did when learning of someone like him. There were so few.

"I know he seemed confident," said Evelyn. "But not when it came to that."

"You think?"

"I know."

Deja lowered her head, biting the side of her lip again. "Not that it matters now." She looked up, her eyes still moist. "I'm sorry. This isn't meant to be about me. What, exactly, did you want to know? Just like, about Antony?"

"Yes," said Evelyn. "But, more specifically, about that night. The night he . . ." She wanted to say *was murdered*, but if Deja was anything like the others, she'd been warned off, too. "The night he died."

"Oh. Uh . . ." Deja shifted in her seat. "That."

"You said, at the funeral, that what the police said wasn't true. That Antony hadn't been acting aggressive. That he hadn't reached for anything in his pocket. Hadn't lunged forward."

She nodded.

"I want to fight this," said Evelyn. "I want to let people know the truth."

Deja's face scrunched again—in what looked like fear. "I shouldn't have told you that."

"Of course you should—"

"I couldn't see. I mean, I was lying on the ground."

"But you said . . ."

She leaned forward, her voice a whisper. "I tried, too. I went in. Told the police what the news was saying wasn't true. That that's not what happened. They put me in a room with a couple of the officers who . . ." She trembled. "And another one, too, who wasn't even there that night. They told me I didn't know what I was talking about. That I was on the ground. That I couldn't see."

"But you did see."

Deja looked to the ceiling, her lips tight and twisted. She returned her gaze to Evelyn. "The officers said I was wrong, confused. That from where I was lying, there was no way I could have seen what happened. They said they'd testify to that if I tried to make any trouble."

Evelyn leaned forward, her hand inches from the girl's, anger and frustration brewing—at the officers. For this girl. "Did they threaten you, Deja?"

"I don't know. Kind of. Yeah . . . they're cops, okay. Their word is law. And obviously, we're trying to fight that. Or we were. But if I say one thing and they say another, who's going to listen to me?"

"The media?" said Evelyn. "A judge?"

Deja shook her head. "I act like I'm all big. Out there protesting, marching, planning. But I'm just a kid. I still live with my parents. My mom needs me. To finish school, to help more with the expenses. I've got three little brothers, and my dad walked out a couple of years ago. I can't go making waves. Not those kinds of waves, anyway." Deja stopped. Swallowed. "They knew my brothers' names. Each of my brother's names."

Evelyn nodded, wanting to press, wanting to shake this girl, tell her she *should* make waves. For Antony. That she should bring a tsunami down on the whole police and judicial system, if that's what it took. But she was just a girl. A child, really.

Burying her disappointment, Evelyn unwrapped her bagel and smiled at Deja. "Then why don't you tell me good things. How did you and Antony meet? What was it about him that caught your interest?"

Deja's smile shone through fresh tears. She took a sip of her coffee, then began.

SEVERAL DAYS LATER, Evelyn answered her door. Dani stood, Asher beside her, an uncertain smile on her face. "Playground?"

Kareela ran toward the door, squeezing around Evelyn's hip. "Yes, Mama! Can we, please?" She looked up at Evelyn, eyes aglow.

Evelyn put a hand to Kareela's chin, caressed it, then looked to

Dani, unrestrained irritation in her voice. "I guess we're going to the playground."

The women walked in silence as the children chattered, several steps ahead of them.

"You haven't returned my calls," said Dani, once they'd crossed over the street and stepped onto the park grounds.

Evelyn inhaled.

"I'm sorry about Charles." Dani reached for Evelyn's hand, grasped it.

"It wasn't just Charles." Evelyn sat down on a bench, taking the excuse to pull her hand away.

Dani gave an embarrassed smile. "How are you?"

"How do you think?"

Dani sat silent beside Evelyn as the children shouted and laughed. "Are you still . . . trying? Charles called Kingsley the other day—"

"He what?" Evelyn snapped her gaze to Dani. "Why?"

"To see how you all were. Since I wasn't getting through. Kingsley didn't sound good."

"He's not."

"He said all you do is look at old archives on Antony's computer. Cases. That he suspects you're at the library in the day, looking up papers. That you come home with ink on your fingers."

Evelyn slipped her hands under her purse, surprised Kingsley had noticed.

"I know it's hard. I mean, I don't know. How could I? But I imagine. And I get why you would want justice. An answer other than this being a horrible misunderstanding. An honest mistake."

"An honest mistake is giving someone the wrong change. Not shooting them four times."

"I know. That's not what I meant. It was more than a mistake."

Evelyn returned her gaze to the children, but she could imagine Dani's expression. The pinched lips, the tight brow.

"I talked to Charles more about it. Tried to convince him that maybe it was worth, well, a try. He said if it were, he'd try. But that this isn't something one man could take on, one family. That it would take multiple complaints with the money and the manpower of a whole firm. And even then, it could take years, decades, to make a lasting change. To get true justice for Antony. And during that time, it'd be horrible. For you. Your family. For anyone who went along with you."

"He makes it sound like I'd be up against the mob."

"No." Dani let out a strangled chuckle. "From how he talks, the mob isn't nearly as powerful."

"Listen, Dani—"

"No. You listen." Dani shifted toward Evelyn. "I know this is the absolute worst thing that could have happened. And I can't even imagine your pain. But this, throwing yourself into this lost cause instead of processing the tragedy, letting yourself grieve? It's not going to help you. It's not going to help Antony. And it's not going to help that little girl over there."

Dani stopped, huffed, as if debating whether to continue. "Sometimes bad things happen, and sometimes there's no clear reason why, nothing we could have done to prevent it and nothing we can do afterward to make it right. So all we can do is move forward, as best we can, try to believe there is still good in the world. Because there is." She gestured to Kareela again. "She's got to be your reason now. Not trying to launch a case against an entire system."

Evelyn opened her mouth to speak, but Dani held up her hand.

"I get it. I get why you're doing it. And if I were in your shoes, maybe I would try, too. But not being in your shoes, being able to see it from the outside—Evelyn, this mission you're on, as much as I wish it weren't, is a battle you're destined to lose. And even if, by some miracle, you won, you'd lose so much else in the process. You just need to keep living. You can't use this impossible fight as a distraction to hide from the pain. So, please. Stop."

Evelyn kept her gaze on the children, laughing as they chased each other, the happiest, freest, she'd seen her daughter in weeks. Her daughter, who was not the reason she should stop, but, as much as Antony, the reason to keep on. Evelyn spoke slowly, to give Kareela more time. She wouldn't be seeing her friend again soon. Maybe ever. She turned her head toward Dani, the loss already pulling at her throat. "You're wrong about so much." Her voice wavered. She pushed her shoulders back and held her words steady. "This wasn't a hurricane or a malfunctioning car leading to an accident. There are reasons why it happened, and it could have been prevented." She stopped, saying an internal goodbye to the years of laughter and commiseration . . . of friendship. "I can't bring Antony back, but maybe I can set a precedent, prevent this from happening again. Maybe I can bring Antony justice and make him proud." She turned her face and stood. "Kareela, time to go."

"But we just got here!"

"Evelyn." Dani reached for her hand. She pulled it away.

"Kareela. Now."

Kareela

On the weekend, Jasmine drags me to a house party in Preston. Though if I'm truthful, dragged is not the right word. I'm happy to go, to be distracted, to lose myself in a dark room with pounding music to drown out my thoughts. To hide. There's no hiding at home, where Thomas's eyes are never silent—asking, pleading, wondering—while every other part of him pretends he's patiently awaiting the doctor's appointment, to see if this thing in me really is a thing at all.

It isn't a dark room we enter. It's many. And lit. As we step through the front door and into the heat, I'm not merely Jasmine's tagalong. I'm greeted and hugged and waved at as we weave through halls and corridors, then linger outdoors, where two men sit around a bonfire—one with tight white curls, the other with salt and pepper dreads—pounding away on djembes with the vigour of men less than half their age.

Children of five dance as heatedly and skilfully as the women of sixty. I watch, mesmerized, the rhythm so good, so sweet I feel swept away before Jasmine grabs my arm and pulls me back inside. People know my name. Several call me sister. And with all that's gone down the past weeks, with these hormones that still creep up on me at the most annoying times, tears burst to my eyes. This feels like family. Like home. The one I'd dreamed of, yearned for.

I belong.

In a large, open-concept living room, with all the furniture pushed to the walls, the bass pounds. Jasmine, my hand still in hers, spins me. Laughs. Our bodies intertwine, then part, then meet again, a dance that goes back generations.

And for a brief moment, I wonder—had Antony found this, too? Is this what drew him in? This incredible sense of oneness and ancestry I've never felt elsewhere? Is this why he stood—so impassioned to protect it—when everyone else dropped to the ground?

The DJ mixes the beats seamlessly, hip hop, reggae, old-school funk, then eases in, so smooth, to a song I've never heard but that prompts a roar of excitement from the crowd. The bodies on the makeshift dance floor rearrange themselves and I'm shuffled among them as people lean forward, back, one foot out, and then the other.

"You don't know it?" Jasmine shouts in my ear as I stand, tempted for only a moment to hurry off the floor, watch from the sidelines.

"No," I yell.

"Follow me." She stands close, shouts directions in my ear. I stumble, almost trip, my moves disjointed, a beat behind, until they're not. That other dance party drifts into my memory—Antony, Mom, Dad, and me. Grooving. Joyous—that moment melding with this as we slide forward, twist back, spin, jump, hands in the air for a collective *whoop* before we go through the motions again. It's an orgy of joy, of belonging, of letting go of my insecurities and fear. It's as if for the first time since that afternoon in my family's kitchen, there's no worry, no uncertainty. I simply am.

The beat shifts again and it's over all too soon, but I'm glowing. I'm on fire, and am tugged off the floor as the bodies rearrange themselves for a slow reggae beat.

"Look at you!" Jasmine leans against a wall in the den, the music muffled enough that she doesn't quite have to shout. "Moving and grooving!" She winks, pulls me further, until we land in the dining room, the table spread with chips and dip, chicken wings, an assortment of cakes and squares, a plethora of liquor bottles, and a keg on the floor beside it.

"Better than a club, huh?" She laughs again, picks up a bite-sized square, and pops it in her mouth. She closes her eyes, her face an expression of ecstasy. "Oh, these are Mama C's. Yes. I was so hoping these were Mama C's."

"Mama—?"

"Sasha's granny." Her eyes open. "I'm not a fan of how she makes grandbabies, but her Coconut Toto is pretty much heaven on yo' tongue. Try it." She grabs a piece, and before I've had a chance to take it from her, it's inches from my mouth and I open wide just in time. "Heaven?" She grins and I can't quite smile, my mouth full of wonder, so I nod. Heaven. "What are you drinking?" she asks. "There's quite the array tonight."

I chew and cover my mouth with my hand. "Rum and—" I stop. A quick chill shooting through me. "Just Coke, actually."

"Rum and Coke? Let's see." Jasmine searches through the bottles.

"No." I finish chewing, then swallow, put a hand on her arm. "And don't worry." I spy a Coke bottle and grab it. "I'll get it myself."

"Mm-hmm." She steps back, sizing me up, a hand on her hip. "Well, we know you're not driving."

I ignore her, grab a cup, and pour.

Her hand lands on my shoulder, prompting a twitch. "Obviously, your business is your business. But if this is business we should be celebrating, I'd love to celebrate. And if it's not, if you're uncertain, or scared, or upset, or whatever, and you want someone to talk to, if you don't already have someone, well, I can be that person."

I rub a hand along my hip, wipe off the condensation from the Coke bottle, bide my time. At last I turn to her. "You're gleaning this from the fact that I don't feel like drinking?"

She laughs. "Gleaning! Girl, the words you use. And no, I'm *gleaning* it from the fact that the stomach bug you had a couple weeks ago lasted way too long. And your breasts: those knockers are *huuuge*."

Although I haven't had a bout of nausea in almost a week, my stomach twists.

"So you are, huh?" Her expression sobers. "You know what you're going to do?"

I shake my head.

"And this with all that info about your brother? Damn." She crosses the space between us, wraps her arms around me, and with that brief mention of Antony, of the file, of the impending reality of this baby, all the joy from tonight seeps out of me. "You wanna talk about it?"

I shrug. "It's a party. Not exactly—"

"Don't worry about that." She grasps my upper arm, her eyebrows scrunched to almost meet in the middle. "But first, libations." She winks. "How do you like that one, wordsmith?"

I let out a little laugh.

"Okay. Coke for you." She takes a cup, the bottles, then pours. "Rum and Coke for me."

A few minutes later, we're in the basement rec room—on one of two long couches. Here, the music is low enough for conversation, but loud enough that if we speak softly, the few guys playing pool on the other side of the room won't hear us.

"How long have you known?" Jasmine asks.

I bite my lip, rub one hand over the other. "Officially, a little over a month. Unofficially, a bit longer."

"So you're . . . ?"

"About ten weeks. Maybe eleven."

"Girl, shoot! And you're not sure if you're going to keep it?"

"Well . . ."

"You don't have a lot of time."

"I do. Until twenty weeks at least."

"Na-uh." Jasmine twists her lips. "Not here. Fifteen weeks six days in Nova Scotia, and you've probably already missed the pill option, if you're right about your dates."

"What?" The news hits like a slap. I turn my gaze to the carpet: bright orange shag. "How do you know this? Why don't I?"

"Clients. Friends. I'm guessing you never had a reason to know." She pauses. "You're not drinking."

I look to Jasmine. "Well, in case, you know?"

"Yeah." Jasmine's cheeks puff before she blows out a long stream of air. "That makes sense. Though I think if you really didn't want it, you would have made up your mind by now, and you would drink without worrying about it . . ."

"Not necessarily."

"No, not—"

"Thomas wants it."

Jasmine raises a brow. "It's not really his choice, though."

"He wants it even if I don't. He says he'll take care of it, that if I don't want to, I don't have to have anything to do with the child. Or I can have some role, whatever I want."

"Damn. Really?" Jasmine leans back. "Maybe I need to be giving this white boy a bit more credit . . . but also, that's a truckload of pressure."

A flare of defensiveness rises within me. "He's a good guy. A great guy. I'm lucky to be with him."

Jasmine's smile softens. She places a hand on my knee. "I'm sorry. I'm sure he's great. It's just . . . you don't talk about him much. If ever anyone brings him up or asks if he's coming to stuff, you always, well, it seems like he's really busy. Like he doesn't have much time for you, or like you don't want him around."

I shake my head, a short laugh erupting. "It's not that. It's—I hardly fit. Do you think he would?"

She stares at me, something like pity in her expression, but no confusion. "You fit, Ree." She shakes her head. "Did you not see yourself out on that floor?"

"No." I draw out my voice. "I did not *see* myself."

She pushes my shoulder. Laughs. "Anyway. You could bring that boy if you wanted to."

"You remember the staff party?"

"What?"

"The way people looked at us. Their faces shifting when they saw him on my arm, learned he was my boyfriend."

"So wha—?"

"Yours did too." I cut her off, take a sip of Coke, focus on the sweet tickle over my tongue.

"Well." She shrugs. "It was a bit of a shock."

"Disappointment, more like it. That's what the look was. Distaste."

"No. No." Jasmine looks away. "Well, not really. Not for me. And honestly, it wasn't that surprising, you all proper and shit. It's just— and I'm not saying I think this, but maybe others do—it's just a choice, right? And it's a choice that will determine so many others."

I nod, thinking of how, at the time of choosing—before having an entry point into this tight-knit community—it didn't feel like a choice in the way she's implying.

"Like there are white people here tonight, but more likely you'll be pulled into his world, not him into yours."

I look back to the shag as tiny razor blades seem to pulse behind my eyes, in my throat, pressure building in my chest as she says all the things I've been saying to myself for weeks now. Months. Before I even knew about this baby.

"Which isn't a bad thing," she continues, "necessarily. I'm not saying that. It's just . . . a choice."

The music thrums, deep, slow. Male laughter erupts across the room.

"Obviously, if you stay with Thomas, have this child with Thomas, your world will shift. But maybe that's what you want?"

The razors slice as I resist the pain, resist the rising moisture.

Jasmine squeezes my knee. "It doesn't *have* to be one or the other," she says, but the way she says it, I can tell she's not sure. Just as I'm not. "I guess the important thing is, do you love him?"

"I don't know!" I yell, not realizing I have until the male voices stop. I whip my head to look, and theirs whip, too, back to each other.

"All right. Green in the corner pocket," says one, louder than needed, as he leans over the pool table.

Jasmine squeezes my knee again.

"I love this," I whisper. "Finally feeling as if I'm starting to belong somewhere. At last."

Jasmine nods, her eyes softer than usual, like she truly cares for me, loves me. Like Gran's. "You do belong." She jostles my knee with the hint of a grin. "And I get how it'll be scary. Like I bet you had to explain to him why you *must* use a silk pillowcase."

I throw my head back and laugh, the tears falling over in a way that feels good. "I didn't even know I should be using a silk case until you started talking about your new one."

"Girl, please." She raises an eyebrow. "No. You serious?"

I nod, laughing harder now, because the emotion needs to get out somehow. "My mom's white. My dad . . . well, he didn't know. My grandma braids and wraps. But our curls are so different, and Gran tried to get me to braid and wrap, too, but I couldn't sleep like that."

"Has your life been transformed?"

"It's a whole new world."

She shakes her head, her smile broad. "I wonder what else you've yet to learn?"

I wonder, too, something within me swelling at how Jasmine has opened my world to so much, taught me things I didn't even know I didn't know. I haven't told her, but since leaving Toronto, she is my first Black friend. In Juniper Cove, it wasn't even an option, my friends making it clear I was their *Black* friend—because there were no others to be had. In university, none of the Black people I met—mostly Africans and Caribbeans who kept to their own—became more than acquaintances. So my few friends were white—people I loved, but who stressed the way their parents would freak if they were to bring a Black boyfriend or girlfriend home, emphasizing that it wasn't because they were racist or hated Black people, just that the races were inherently different. And how hard would that mixing be for any future children?

Children like me.

"Earth to Kareela."

I lift my head to attention. Jasmine smiles and rubs her hand along my arm with a squeeze. "What do you want to do? Dance? Leave? Look up baby names and see if something in you suddenly snaps one way or the other?"

I take a sip as I try to force away the memories and the tense shame of saying nothing to those friends, of knowing I should have, but also that I couldn't.

"Dance." I set the cup on the table, hoping the music will help, needing it to. "Definitely dance."

She downs her drink, slams it on the coffee table, then stands, grabbing my other hand to pull me up. "All right, my love. We dance!"

Evelyn

Over the following weeks, Evelyn kept up the pursuit of justice. She'd had to go back to work, her boss threatening to let her go if she didn't, but in the evenings, she sat at Antony's computer, searching cases of police brutality throughout the Western world. It might not make sense—it was possible only the cases here, in her own city, would matter—but it also couldn't hurt. And there were so many. Someone should be compiling them.

She'd been back to the library a few times—quick stops after work, taking advantage of the extra hour Kareela's daycare allowed, which Evelyn had rarely used before now. When she got home, she sat Kareela in front of the TV, so she could continue her research. Several times, she'd come out of Antony's room, for a drink or to use the washroom, and found the girl eating—cinnamon toast, cereal, whole carrots, once an egg in a basket, the way Antony used to love.

"Who made that for you?" Evelyn asked, looking to the kitchen, wondering if Kingsley had arrived home without her noticing.

"I did, Mama."

"You—?"

"I took the stool to the stove."

Evelyn's insides clenched, a chill trailing over her. "You used the stove?"

"It's okay, Mama." Kareela looked up with a smile, that dreaded doll perched on the couch beside her. "I'm a big girl now. I can do it."

Evelyn sat beside her daughter. She looked at her, her puffs of hair two matted balls at the sides of her face. "You ask me next time." She put a hand to one of Kareela's neglected pigtails. "How would you like braids this weekend? We can take you to that place An—" She couldn't say his name. "Your brother went to tidy his dreads."

Kareela nodded, her face aglow. "Just me and you?"

"Just me and you."

Evelyn walked to the kitchen. The stove was off. The frying pan sat in the sink. She returned to Antony's room, her hand rubbing against her aching neck, and dialed again, the one witness she still couldn't get ahold of. Hoping he, unlike all the others, would be willing to speak the true story. It rang and rang, then went to voicemail, as it always did.

The sound of the front door opening travelled down the hall, the shuffle and bumps of Kingsley setting down his briefcase, kicking off his shoes, the groan as he settled onto the couch, his arm probably around their girl, where it would stay for five minutes, maybe ten. Next he'd stand, scrounge for something in the fridge, retreat to his office until one or the other of them put Kareela to bed. They traded nights—a one-day-on, one-day-off schedule—as they had done for years. They didn't talk, passing each other in the hall, the kitchen, like ghosts of their past selves—inhabiting the same space, but hardly aware of the other's existence.

And yet Kingsley had talked to Charles. Expressed concerns to

Charles. But not to her. Not then. Not now, weeks later. Evelyn watched his thinning frame pass by the door, mourning him—them—almost as much as she mourned Antony.

He needed to do this with her. He needed a cause, a reason to keep on. Keep them keeping on, together.

She would talk to him tonight. See if she could get him on board. See if, maybe, he knew someone braver than Charles, someone to help her make sense of all this research, establish a clear and focused plan of attack. What to do, how to go about doing it.

She'd visited five law offices. Each one reacted similarly to Charles, looking at her like her pain, her tragedy, may be catching, a look she was getting used to—at the grocery store, the daycare, anywhere she was recognized.

EVELYN WAITED WHILE Kingsley put Kareela to bed. Not that it took long anymore. She'd started getting her pyjamas on herself, without prompting, then brushing her teeth, knocking on one of their doors and telling whoever's night it was that it was time to tuck her in.

Evelyn used to read a chapter or two of whatever story Kareela had on the go—the girl had abandoned simple picture books months before—but a few weeks ago, Evelyn had drifted off mentally, lost in considering all the lives she was learning about, people killed or harmed at the hands of officers.

Mama.

Not just Black people. But Indigenous, Latin, white, too.

Mama.

So many people. So little justice.

Ma—

Evelyn had jerked back to the present when Kareela tugged on her wrist, not knowing how many times the girl had called or where she was on the page.

Never mind. Kareela grabbed the book from Evelyn's hand and threw it to the floor, a burst of anger flaring across her features.

The next time Kareela came knocking on Antony's door announcing it was bedtime, she said she'd already read. All she wanted was a good-night kiss and for Evelyn to turn out the light . . . and Evelyn didn't have the energy to argue.

Tonight, Evelyn stepped into the hall when she heard her husband passing. "Kingsley?"

"Hmm?"

"Can we talk?" How long had he had those bags under his eyes, those deep grooves on his forehead, such slumped shoulders? "In the living room would be fine."

They sat on opposite ends of the couch. "I'm sure you've noticed I've been researching."

"I asked you not to."

"I know."

They stared.

"Antony was right, you know. The injustice out there. The power the police wield, how they're backed by the judicial system. It's mind-blowing. It's horrible." Evelyn shifted. "We need to do something about it."

Kingsley's expression was so similar to the one he'd shown to Antony. *We need to show them,* their son had said. *Show them every day that we're not who they think we are. That we're people. Just like them. Just as worthy to live, to have rights, to be safe.*

Not by yelling in the streets. Kingsley had said. *Show them with your position. By being worthy. Being someone to respect.*

I am! Antony yelled. *Why can't you see? I don't need to* become some-

one worthy, someone who deserves respect. I am. Everyone is. We're born that way.

"I would like you to help me." Evelyn took a deep breath, resolving to stay firm, despite the frustration in his eyes. "For us to do this together."

"Anything I could have done, I should have done before, with him."

"It's not too late."

"Evelyn."

"It's too late to save Antony." Evelyn could hear the desperation in her voice, but the situation *was* desperate. "It's not too late for change. Someone has to fight. Someone has to try."

Kingsley's expression shifted to one of outrage. "You've seen what trying gets."

"We won't do it in the streets. We'll fight in the courts. By the book, like you said. Show them we have a case."

"That's not what I said."

That's what gets you down! Antony shaking his head, disappointment shrouding him like a cloak. *You think you have to prove to them you're worthy. That you deserve respect. That's why your colleagues zoom past you. If you fought the board's decisions, if you called out their racism, they couldn't just ignore you. You ache for their approval. The white man's approval. You'll never get it. Not unless you take it.*

Kingsley had stepped back as if struck. Antony stepped forward. *You're amazing, Pa. I've heard the students talk. You're one of the best professors your department has, and you do more for the department than half of those lazy, tenured schlumps. But why would they raise you up, increase your pay, your status, give you a permanent position when they know if they don't, you'll just sit there and smile? Sit there and let them treat you like a second-class nobody. Like less than that.*

Come with me, Antony had continued, saying what he'd said so many times before. *Come and see.*

Kingsley turned his head to the TV. "I had my chance." The reporter's face was grave, but not too grave. Bad news was good news, after all, was ratings. "If I was going to help him, stand by him, I should have done it then."

"Do it now."

"No!" Kingsley yelled, and Evelyn pulled back. "There's nothing I can do. Nothing you can do. He's gone!"

A tremor made its way through Evelyn. A chill settled over her arms.

"He's gone, Evelyn. Accept it."

"But Kareela's not. Do it for her, so she—"

"No." Kingsley slumped against the couch, sobs racking his body, shaking him as Evelyn sat frozen. "They shot him up." A primitive wail. "Like he was danger. Some threat." The sound, the words, pulled at something in her—pulled her to let go, too, to crumble. But instead, she eased herself over, settled one arm around him. He lunged forward, pulling her body against his own, sobbing into her shoulder as she hugged him close, her back rigid, her throat tight.

Eventually he stopped, sitting still as the minutes passed. When at last he pulled away, he grabbed a tissue from the table next to the couch, wiped under his eyes, his nose, then clenched the Kleenex in his hand, staring, again, at the TV. "This is the world we live in, Evelyn. And it's not going to change. We keep our heads down. Be silent. That's what we have to do to survive." He turned to her, the pain in his eyes unbearable. "Antony was wrong. Has it gotten better? Did people like King, X, make it better? Sure. A bit. But ultimately, it's not going to change."

"Kingsley—"

He gripped her shoulders. "Please, Evelyn. Stop. For me. I can't take it. I can't see you doing this, poring over papers, dredging it up, day after day. I can't cope." His hands dropped. "I've tried to do my best for this family. I've worked hard. I haven't made waves, because I've seen what making waves does to men like me. How budgets suddenly get cut, and they're so sorry, but they just can't keep us on anymore. And suddenly a man's career is gone. He's working at a gas station or driving a taxi."

Kingsley's head drooped. He shook it. "Dr. Knowles called me to apologize. He said you'd been by. He tried to defend himself about why he wasn't standing up for Antony the way he stood up for strangers. But I knew. I knew what he was facing." Kingsley stopped, gaze to the floor. "I've tried so hard. I've done what I was supposed to do, what I was expected to do. I tried to teach my son the same thing. But still—" His voice caught. "He was gunned down. For trying to make the world better. For doing something, when his father refused to. Refused to stand beside him."

"So stand for Kareela. So the world she—"

Kingsley kept talking, as if he hadn't even heard Evelyn. "I should have never let him storm out of this house. I should have held him in my arms, and if I couldn't have stopped him, I should have been there beside him, thrown myself in front of those bullets."

"Kingsley."

"It's too late, Evelyn. It's over. This is our life now. Don't make it worse."

Evelyn's chest swelled. Her throat burned for all she wanted to say—that maybe he was right. Maybe he should have been there. But also, maybe she shouldn't have, shouldn't have made that call.

They couldn't change the past. Only the future.

Or, at least, they could try, because there was still Kareela. Still the hope of changing things for her. For Antony, too, so he didn't die for nothing.

Yet Kingsley would never listen. She saw that now. He turned off the TV and walked toward the hall. After enough time had passed that whatever door he'd entered would be closed, Evelyn stood and went back to Antony's room. Rather than returning to the glowing screen, she climbed into his bed, clothes still on, as she'd done more times than she knew. For days, now. Maybe weeks. Caressing the sheets the way she'd caressed his head, his back, so many times before. His smell wasn't gone, but it almost was. It would be soon.

Evelyn

The next evening, the conversation with Kingsley still thrumming through her bones, Evelyn pushed through the front door. She let Kareela's backpack fall to the floor, the weight hardly seeming to lift from her shoulders. Without even asking, Kareela headed to the couch and pressed the button on the TV's remote.

The screen came to life. What had they done in these hours just months ago? The playground. A walk. Meeting Dani and Asher. Making an elaborate dinner, while Kareela drew or worked on a puzzle, just feet away from Evelyn. A swim, perhaps, at the neighbourhood pool when it was a scorcher, like today.

"Kareela."

The girl turned her head.

"Want to go for a swim?"

Confusion spread across Kareela's face, as if she hadn't heard correctly, or the words didn't make sense. "A swim?"

"Yes."

"At the pool?"

"Yes, sweetie."

"Me and you?"

Evelyn let out a sound that was half laugh, half frustration. Not at Kareela. But at herself. Remorse reared its head—had it really been so long since she'd done anything with her daughter that this simple proposition seemed perplexing? Forcing a smile on her face, Evelyn crouched to Kareela's eye level. "Yes. Me and you. At the pool. It's so hot out!"

"Okay!" Kareela jumped from the couch and headed down the hall. She ran back, laughed, turned off the TV, then sped down the hall again. Evelyn watched as her daughter grabbed a bag from her closet, her swimsuit, goggles from one of the dresser drawers.

"This is going to be so much fun!" Kareela giggled and Evelyn tried not to cry. Kareela looked up at her. "Mama. Get your stuff." She stopped, her hands falling at her side. "You didn't change your mind, did you?"

"No." Evelyn shook her head, her smile firm. "No. I didn't."

"MAMA! LOOK AT me. Look at me." Kareela, holding on to a flutter-board, kicked vigorously, water splashing up around her.

"Good job, baby!" Evelyn clapped. And laughed. And attempted to push away the memories that fought their way in: Antony at this age, Antony last summer on the other side of the flutterboard, cheering Kareela as she made her way across the width of the pool toward him.

"Mama. Watch this." Kareela held her nose, sinking under the water, her body twisting and turning, her legs flailing in what Evelyn knew was meant to be a somersault.

"Excellent."

Kareela shook the water from her head, the puffs now two thick wilted pigtails.

"Race?" Kareela's grin was broad, sun glinting off her goggles.

"Race." Evelyn gripped the edge of the pool, one foot braced on the side as Kareela did the same, the flutterboard in front of her.

"One. Two. Three. Go!" They kicked and Evelyn paddled with her arms, keeping even with Kareela until just before the end, when she fell behind enough to let Kareela's hand slap the other side of the pool first.

Kareela whooped. She spun. They went again and again, then lounged on the pool deck, licking frantically at the overpriced pink Popsicles dripping onto their fingers.

Towels slung around their shoulders, they walked home, hand in hand. Kareela squeezed, and Evelyn squeezed back, realizing, for a moment at least, she'd felt happy—for the first time since the night he was taken away. The pain reared up again. But something small and fragile existed beside it. Hope. Maybe.

"That was great." Kareela nodded as she spoke, a bounce to her step. She stopped, then squeezed Evelyn's side. "I love you, Mama."

Hope, like a whisper. A possibility. "I love you too, sweetheart."

Kareela bumped into Evelyn. "Sides." She looked up and grinned.

Evelyn crouched. She pressed her forehead to Kareela's. "Heads."

Kareela laughed.

At home, Evelyn stepped out the back door and hung their towels on the line. As she stepped back inside to ask Kareela if she wanted a bath or shower, a knock sounded. Evelyn pulled open the door, her face falling at the sight of a man. He wasn't in uniform, but something about the spread of his shoulders, the lift of his chin, the firmness of his feet placed on her doorstep, more than hip-width apart, made her suspect.

"Evening, Mrs. Jackson."

"Good evening."

"Wondering if I could step inside."

"I . . . well . . ." Evelyn looked behind her. Kareela was nowhere in sight.

The man whipped out a badge. "It will just take a moment. I have something for you."

"I . . . okay." Evelyn stepped back as the man stepped forward.

He lifted an eight-by-eleven envelope, tapped it against his hand, but didn't pass it to her. "I heard you've been . . . investigating"—he said the word as if it brought a rancid taste to his mouth—"the incident with your son."

Evelyn's heart beat against her ribs.

"I understand, Mrs. Jackson. Truly, I do. You loved your son. It's hard to accept the truth. That he was a danger. Involved in things he shouldn't have been. That he threatened the lives of good and honest officers. That they had a right to protect themselves."

"He was unarmed."

The man stepped closer. "Your son was a big, powerful man. The body, Mrs. Jackson, is a dangerous weapon."

His breath hot against her cheek, she stepped away.

"Mama?"

Evelyn whipped her head around. "Go to your room, sweetie."

"Lovely girl you have there."

Evelyn didn't speak.

"Lovely home. Lovely life. Mrs. Jackson, you don't want to bring trouble upon yourself."

"I have a right to—"

"Or against your husband."

Evelyn cast her shoulders back. "Are you threatening me?"

"No!" The man smiled. Laughed. "Not at all, Mrs. Jackson. The opposite. I'm letting you know you should be careful. That the world is a dangerous place. And the best thing to do is to focus on your family.

The family you have left. Live for them. Protect them. Don't get your nose into things you know nothing about. Don't try to stir up trouble."

"I'm not—"

"Going to the library. Pulling newspapers. Talking to lawyers. Trying to, what? Reopen an incident report? Turn it into a case? Something more?"

"There were witnesses."

"And none of their written statements go against what the officers attest happened."

"He was unarmed."

"And aggressive. Using threatening language. Lunging at the police. Reaching for what very well could have been a weapon."

"But he was—"

The officer took another step as Evelyn withdrew, the tension in her chest making her dizzy. Her back bumped the wall as the officer's arm shot out, his hand landing just inches from her head. With the other hand, he raised the envelope, held it there until she grasped it. "I would hate to see anything happen to you, your husband, or that sweet little girl. That's all I'm saying. People love the men in blue. And if they feel someone is trying to attack us, punish us for simply doing our job, they may get—" He hesitated, smiling, leaning his head side to side. "Upset. Aggressive. Vengeful, even. Not officers, of course. Civilians. People who believe as strongly as we do that our role is to serve and protect. Believe it so strongly, not even a child would be safe from their passion."

He stepped back, smile still strong. "I hope you've appreciated this front-door service. Usually a request like this comes in the mail, but I wanted to place it directly in your hands, Mrs. Jackson, seeing all you've been through. You have a right to know the truth." The officer started to turn, then stopped. "I should offer my condolences. For your loss."

Once he was gone, Evelyn rushed forward and turned the lock. She kept her hand on the door, her pulse racing. After several breaths, she stepped back, back, back, then stopped. She tore open the envelope and yanked out the sheets. Six pages. So much of it redacted. What was left, apparently, was the truth. Their truth. Which indicated Antony was the aggressor. That the officers believed he was reaching for a gun. That the officers were acting in self-defence. Doing their job.

Evelyn let the papers fall to the floor as she stood, shaking. This had been her last hope. Her last chance at evidence she could take to a lawyer, to convince them she had a case. She'd expected inconsistencies in the officers' stories as they'd tried to justify their actions. She'd expected internal investigations about why an unarmed man, just standing there, had been shot four times.

She picked up the pages and stuffed them back in the envelope. Fearful of how much Kareela had heard, she ran to her room. Empty. "Kareela!"

Evelyn rushed down the hall, checking the bathroom, their bedroom. "Karee—"

A whimper sounded.

Evelyn turned and made her way to Antony's door, which sat ajar. She pushed it open. Kareela lay curled on the bed, knees up to her chin, doll tucked into the curve of her arm. Panic leapt within Evelyn. She wanted to pull Kareela off the bed, tell her to leave Antony's stuff alone. But she also wanted to wrap her arms around her daughter, hold her close, protect her always, from men like that officer, from the ones who'd shot Antony, from the whole wide world.

She stood at the door, afraid that if she held her baby she'd unravel, and if she did, she wouldn't ever stitch herself back together. "Sweetie." Her hand clasped the doorframe. She braced herself against it. "What are you doing?"

"Is Daddy gone now, too?"

"What?"

"Last time a strange man came . . ."

"No!" Evelyn dashed to Kareela. She sat next to her and placed her trembling hand on Kareela's back. "No. Daddy's fine."

"I didn't like that man."

"Me neither." Evelyn lowered herself, so she was cradling her daughter in her arms, the scent of chlorine strong against her nostrils, overpowering the scent of Antony. Evelyn tensed, wondering if this would be it—the chlorine lingering until any trace of Antony was gone. A sob worked its way up her throat, but she pushed it back, the officer's words echoing in her mind. The threats, which, according to him, were friendly advice. Bile rose in place of the sob. "Bath or shower?" she whispered.

"Bath."

"Okay." Evelyn gave Kareela a squeeze—her one remaining child, who with her research, her pursuit of justice, Evelyn had put in danger—then eased off the bed.

"Will you stay with me, Mama? Read to me while I play?"

"Of course." Evelyn put out her hand. Kareela stared at it a moment, then grasped it and stood.

LATER THAT NIGHT, Evelyn returned to Antony's room, remembering the officer's face, inches from her own. His threats. She lifted Antony's pillow, the stinging scent of the pool hitting her nostrils. A tremor made its way along her arm. She set the pillow down, then turned to the envelope the officer had given her, cast to the desk at the sight of Kareela earlier that day, and placed it in the bottom drawer of Antony's desk. She gathered the piles of research she'd been compiling—

the printouts and clippings, notes in a repurposed duotang—and added them to the drawer. She closed the open web pages and Word documents on Antony's computer, then powered off the device. The machine whirred and seemed to gurgle before shutting down with a whoosh.

All of them were right. Kingsley, Dani and Charles, Dr. Knowles. It was too late to protect Antony. She needed to protect Kareela. And this mission of hers—clearly—was only inviting more harm.

With a painful lump in her throat, Evelyn stood and crossed to the threshold, her hand on the doorknob as she surveyed the room where Antony had lived, the room where she'd tried to make his death have meaning, the room she was abandoning, in the hope that this— despite what she'd thought, what she'd worked for—was the surest way to keep her daughter safe.

Kareela

On a blessedly breezy Sunday morning, I step out of the apartment while Thomas is still sleeping. The air is cooler than I've felt in weeks, and as I walk up Summer Street, then turn into Camp Hill Cemetery, the sudden tree cover makes me shiver. Rather than cut through the centre path to the other side, as most people do, I weave my way between the rows and rows of headstones, gravitating to the old and crumbling ones, with words so faded some are impossible to read.

I come here often. Knowing it's silly. But it's the closest I can get to Antony—walking among these people who, in some distant realm, may be walking along with him. After my talk with Jasmine, fresh fears dominate, and my throat tightens with thoughts I wish I could bury as deep as these lost souls. I stop before an unreadable headstone, then kneel and place my hand on the cold, moss-spotted granite, the way I used to place my hand on his. As the cold seeps into my skin, so does the memory of that polished tablet, how it seemed so impossible that this was all that was left of him. I think of the coming rally, trying to determine what Antony would tell me to do. Before the shooting, the answer would have been clear. But after . . . would he tell me it was worth the risk, that he'd be proud for me to follow in his footsteps no matter the cost? Or would he want me to be safe, above all, do everything I could to preserve my life? The way he didn't.

I dismiss the thought, knowing another decision, right now, is so much more pressing. "I'm pregnant." I whisper. "And I don't—"

I jerk at the sudden blare of my phone in this hushed place.

"Hello, Kareela?" My mother's voice is loud, with an energy she reserves for salespeople, the kids at school, her boss. "How are you?"

I swallow as the tight, pulsing tension that so often appears at the sound of her voice spreads over me.

"Fine, Mom. Good. How are you?"

"Oh, you know."

And I do know. She hasn't been fine in eighteen years.

"And Gran?"

"Well." The word is firm, decisive, full of something that makes me want to slam the phone on one of those headstones, watch it shatter. "You know"—the attempt at light and loud and falsely cheery has faded, as if that little burst of energy was all she could muster—"I need to talk to you about that. So I thought I'd drive to town, we can have lunch, and I'll tell you all about it?" She's trying again, and her school voice is back. "When's the last time we did that?"

I lick my lips, place a hand on my bent knee, and raise myself to standing. "A while." Except the true answer is, as far as I can remember, we've never gone for lunch just the two of us. "Gran, is she—" My voice catches. "Is she okay?"

She hesitates. "We'll talk about all that at lunch."

"Are you bringing her? It'd be great to see—"

"How about that café you've shot some grams of? Dolly's or Dahlila's or—"

"Dilly Dally?"

"Yes, that's it!" She lets out a tinny, self-conscious laugh.

I hesitate, surprised and slightly thrilled that she's paid that much attention to my life. "You see my Instagram posts? You've never—"

"Well, who wants their mom liking their posts? I'll see you there. Twelve o'clock."

She hangs up before I can answer, and a sense of disorientation and fear flows through me.

MOM SITS IN a back corner of the café, as she does in any public place, wanting the spot where she can see the most people, where no one can sneak up behind her. She holds a teacup. Not a mug, but an actual teacup, which she always asks for—something about her mother, about life needing some sense of refinery. It shakes, slightly.

I stand in the entry to the shop, between the two glass doors, watching her through the glass wall separating them. If I stay here, watching this woman who birthed me sip tea as if nothing is wrong, maybe it won't be. Maybe I can back out, slip through the door, and pretend she didn't avoid my question about Gran. One devastation at a time, please, I'd say to life, and it would listen. Maybe.

I open and step through the second door, take a breath, and try to put on a natural, easy-looking smile. "Hi."

"Kareela." Mom speaks my name as if I've shocked her, as if those eyes that were cast in my direction, dark hollows around them that the makeup can't fully hide, didn't see me approach.

I hesitate, waiting for her to rise, put her arms around me, though I know she won't. After an awkward beat, I sit. I come to Dilly Dally often, a world with scents meant to tantalize, to encourage its patrons to sit, stay awhile, order more than they intended. A fear flares. If the news is bad, if Gran is sick, or worse, dead, will I ever be able to come here again?

A steaming mug sits on the table between us.

"I saw you post about the London Fog Latte," says Mom, in a tone and with an expression that seems almost normal. Motherly. "That it's your favourite."

I nod. Beside the tea is a morning glory muffin, complete with a knife, plate, and generous pat of butter. I'd posted about how much I loved that, too. Moisture settles behind my eyes at the hope that maybe she does love me. Does care, at least a little. Yet in addition to talking about Gran, this is supposed to be lunch, a visit, and no food sits in front of her.

She leans forward. "How's that boyfriend of yours? Tom?"

"Thomas."

"He seems like a keeper." She hesitates. "Though, really, you're too young to think of keeping."

"You were already married when you were my age," I say, without saying the rest . . . *You already had Antony.*

Though she's right. I am too young. Too young for marriage, too young for a child. I resist placing a hand on my belly. Hope my flouncy shirt will hide my swollen breasts.

She nods, sucks and probably bites the inside of her lip. I lift the tea, wrap my hands around the ceramic. This is the benefit of a mug. Warmth. Something to hold firmly. I take a sip, preparing myself for whatever has prompted this show of interest in my life—a tactic to either soften or distract from why we're really here. "Is Gran okay?"

Mom looks away, gaze focused across the room. She wants to delay it. To not speak the words.

She'd been brave once. The day I was surrounded. At least ten boys, smoking in the high school courtyard. Yelling. Cursing. Laughing.

Saying the word I imagined had been spoken about me many times, but never to my face.

"Mom." I make my voice soft, nonthreatening. "Tell me about Gran, please."

She presses her lips, preparing.

That day she stood tall. That day she fought. For me.

"Mom."

"She's blind."

"What?"

"Or nearly." Something resembling exasperation seeps from my mother's voice. "Apparently, she's been going blind for years and decided to do nothing about it. To go on, day by day, as if nothing was happening."

I lean back, the force of realization slamming into me. Layers of dust coating the shelves and trinkets during recent visits. Crumbs on the kitchen counter. Dust bunnies on the floor and a slight ring around the tub. I'd thought Gran was tired, old, grieving Dad too much to care about dust and dirt—not that she couldn't see.

I take another sip of tea, swallowing back the sadness. The fear. Gran—sweet Gran, who rises from work in her garden to watch the sunset, who examines fruit or her beloved vegetables as if she were an art dealer assessing a rare find. I sip again, distracting myself with the taste of vanilla, lavender, steamed milk.

"Okay." My voice is clear, strong, the way I want it to be. "So she's going blind. She's not blind yet. Is there anything the doctors can do to stop it?" I slice my muffin in two, spread the butter, focusing on the ease of it sliding across each side, watching it melt, willing the fear to not consume me.

"No."

I nod, take in the information. Nothing can be done. Gran, who spoke of the curl of her newborn baby's hair, the sun glinting over the trees, the way, when cooking, the nose was important, the fingers, but the eyes, only second to the tongue, were pivotal—noting the sheen of the dough when it was ready for shaping, the brown glaze that meant a dish should be freed from the oven.

Mom holds her tea in one hand, fingers delicately grasping the handle. "I'm putting her into a home," she says. "I've decided."

Evelyn

The rays from the streetlights streamed through the gaps in the curtain that Kingsley, yet again, hadn't properly closed when he'd slumped into bed just minutes before Evelyn. He'd been in his office, she in the living room, some sitcom she couldn't even recall the name of flickering in the dim light.

Evelyn rolled over, trying to get comfortable, but was distracted by the incessant whir of cars on the not-too-distant highway. Nights like this, it seemed impossible that anyone in this city could sleep. Or fall back to sleep, rather. Most nights, Evelyn was out to the world within minutes of her head hitting the pillow, but then two, three, sometimes four hours later, she'd wake with a start, usually in a cold sweat, the vision of Antony—bullets riddled through him, blood spreading on the pavement, or what he must have looked like after on a frigid slab, before they'd hidden him beneath the locked lid of the casket—in her mind.

If it wasn't these nightmares that woke her, it'd be Kingsley, lost in his own dreams, calling out Antony's name, Femi's, Ella's. All the people he'd lost violently.

Oddly, sleep had been easier when she'd lain in Antony's bed. But since the night the officer had arrived, months ago now, she hadn't opened the door to his room. So, every night, she lay beside Kingsley, each of them tossing and turning, leaving and returning, failing at this, one of the simplest and most important tasks to ensure continued existence.

Evelyn tiptoed out of the room and crossed the hall to Kareela's door. She peeked through the crack, staring until she was certain of the barely noticeable but rhythmic rise and fall of her daughter's chest.

She'd done that with Antony, too. Even when he was a grown man, when he'd come in late, thinking everyone was asleep, and flop into bed, smelling of alcohol or marijuana, though she'd never seen him obviously drunk.

She'd ease open his door, look . . . because what if this time he'd gone too far? What if he'd vomit and choke on it? A few times, she'd entered his room, smelled his breath, and when she caught a whiff of alcohol on it, rolled him to his side, despite his complaints of "Ah, Mom," "I'm fine," or "Let me be."

Evelyn closed Kareela's door and put a hand to her raised, all-too-prominent collarbone. Her hunger only reared at night now. She'd have yogurt, or a piece of toast with butter, and that would settle it. She was cooking for her family again but mostly pushed the food around her plate as she questioned Kareela about her day, desperate to establish some sense of normalcy, of family. That was, at least, when they sat together. Most of the time, Kingsley sat behind the closed door of his study or, occasionally, in front of the TV. Kareela would join him, press into his side, as Evelyn sat in the kitchen alone, for a minute, two, before scraping her barely touched food into the compost.

"Mama?"

Evelyn jumped. Kareela stood between the living room and kitchen, her pyjama top reaching only three-quarters of the way down her arms, the pants barely skimming her calves, the doll Violet had given her now ratty as it hung from her hand.

"What are you doing?"

"Oh." Evelyn looked at the bare plate in front of her. She tried to think of what she would have said before. "I had the munchies."

Kareela sped over, her bare feet barely making a sound on the tiles. "Can I munch, too?"

"Uh-huh." Evelyn stood. "What do you want?"

Kareela plopped the doll on the table. "Cereal?"

Evelyn turned to the cupboard, brought down a bowl and a box, then opened the fridge.

"Mama."

"Yes, sweetie."

"We're not putting up the tree this year, are we?"

"Tree?" Evelyn turned.

"For Christmas. It's in three days."

"Three days?" Evelyn turned back to the counter. She shook the cereal into the bowl, poured the milk, set the spoon in with a clink. Three days. She'd seen the decorations on her way to work, heard the music in the grocery store, but had thought they had weeks. "We'll put it up tomorrow. When Daddy comes home from work. I'll ask him to get off early."

"Mama."

"Yes?"

"There's no school tomorrow. And Daddy's been home all week."

"No, he . . ." Had he been? She hadn't heard him come home the past few days. Only heard him come out of his study. She turned to the calendar. One more day of work for her. Since she'd last entered

Antony's room, her days had blurred together, with no clear focus or direction. But still, how had she missed this?

She looked back to Kareela, whose eyes were so wide, so concerned and uncertain. Evelyn forced a smile and imitated a tone of excitement. "When I get home from work, then. All three of us. We'll put on music and decorate the tree."

"With hot chocolate?"

"Of course."

"Mama?"

"Yes."

"What about the stockings?"

Evelyn froze.

"Will we put out Antony's stocking?"

Her heart beat fast and frantic. Back in their Kingston home, she'd embroidered his name on the oversized sock as he slept in a bassinet beside her. Today, she fought to keep the excited smile on her face. "I don't know." Her voice cracked. "We'll have to think about it."

Kareela tapped her spoon against the bowl, a crease in her brow. "I think we shouldn't. It may upset Daddy. And anyway, I don't think Santa would bring presents for a dead person, do you?"

"No." Evelyn sat down across from Kareela, a weight crushing upon her. Presents. Three days to Christmas and no presents. A stocking that couldn't be hung. "I don't think he would."

Evelyn

The next morning, Kareela still sleeping, Evelyn knocked on the door of Kingsley's study. He swivelled in his chair as she entered. "I forgot it was Christmas."

Kingsley nodded, his expression as unconcerned as if she'd forgotten to pick up milk. Evelyn's chest expanded and tightened. She fought the urge to scream. To cry. This shouldn't be all on her. It couldn't be all on her.

But . . . she had always been the one to get the kids' presents.

"I'll go out tonight," she said. "After we put up the tree."

Kingsley nodded again, then turned back to his desk. *What are you doing?* she silently yelled at his stooped shoulders. *School's out. Why are you staring at that screen?* She almost said it aloud, but turned away, remembering how he'd collapsed into her arms. His sobs shaking them both.

Later that evening, after they'd played the music, after they'd hauled the tree up from the basement, inserted its branches, pulled out the garland and lights and decorations, Evelyn stepped off the bus in front of Eglinton Square mall. Her stomach clenched, despite the relief of stepping away from her family, from the loud, cheery music that hadn't done enough to mask the long stretches of silence. Instead, it had emphasized the memories attached to each decoration and highlighted the falseness in Kareela's smile, the way, so quickly, she'd learned to be delicate with them, as if she didn't need any delicacy herself. Evelyn had thought Kareela was fine. Was managing, almost too well, in a world without Antony. But had Evelyn simply been blind? Had the horrible, all-consuming pain of loss numbed her to all else? She was doing the bare minimum to keep her daughter alive. To keep her job. To ensure Kingsley was fed—the only thing she could do to aid him in keeping his too.

It wasn't enough.

She turned, placed her hand on the door, stood for one breath, two, the pain hitting like a hurricane. "Excuse me." A woman rushed past, opening the door beside Evelyn, and Evelyn stepped back. She turned around, trying to resist the brutal force tearing through her, trying to remember what she was doing here, why. Kareela. She was here for Kareela, who couldn't wake up to an empty tree. Who, after accidentally dropping one decoration tonight and breaking Rudolph's antler, had ripped five more from the tree, shattered glass and ceramic spreading across the floor before Kingsley threw his arms around her, stopping her fit with a bear hug, catching her angry fists and then her tears with the breadth of his chest.

In the massive complex, surrounded by stores, and people, too, Evelyn froze, not knowing where to go, what to get.

Pyjamas.

The girl definitely needed those. The three-quarter length pair she'd been wearing the other night wouldn't do, especially as the nights were getting colder.

She headed to a kids' clothing store, passed her fingers over the racks of animal and princess and multicoloured designs, then held up a pale pink set with unicorns boasting purple manes. But the size. She didn't know her daughter's size.

Kareela was six. She'd be seven in . . . Evelyn froze. She was seven. Kareela was seven, as of last month. Evelyn spun, looking for an escape as a wave of torment pressed against her. She tossed the pyjamas on the top of the rack, ran to the change rooms, and slammed a door behind her. She crouched to the floor, her hands pressed against the wall as sob after sob erupted. Kareela had lost her brother, and then Evelyn had not only forgotten Christmas, but the girl's birthday, too.

"Ma'am." A knock on the door.

She'd forgotten her daughter's birthday.

"Ma'am? Are you all right?"

"I'm fine!" Evelyn croaked as she turned and pressed her back against the wall, trying to control her sobs, her hitching breaths.

"Ma'am."

"Just a minute. I'll be out in just a minute."

"Can I call someone, or—"

"No!"

Evelyn closed her eyes. She concentrated on breathing. In. Out. In. Antony was gone, and Kareela . . . could Kareela have forgotten, too? Her own birthday? The year before, she'd talked about her birthday-extravaganza plans a full month in advance. And yet this year, she said nothing. To save her parents? To not put a burden on them?

"Ma'am?"

"Size seven!" Evelyn yelled, the grief like a boa, wrapping itself around her. The shame. "Girls'. Five sets of pyjamas. Several T-shirts. Short- and long-sleeved. Three or four pairs of pants. A zip-up hoodie. She likes pink and purple. Turquoise, too."

"Ma'am?"

"And sneakers. Size two. Something with glitter if you have it."

Silence.

"Take it up to the cash. I'll be there in a few minutes to pay."

"Ma'am, are you—"

"Go!"

Violet

Ella be such a brave girl. She think she the mammy half the time. She think, just 'cause she cook and clean while I at work, it make she the boss of everyone. Of me. This way of seeing the world, it benefit her. It mean she don't let no one give her grief. She work hard. She be sure she get what she deserve.

Me first baby. The one to make me a mammy.

Her birth derailed me life. Turning me from a good girl to a sullied one. The community's darling to the community's shame. Making it so her daddy feel justified in having another woman be he wife, raise he legal family.

But not once did I regret it, regret her. That smiling, chubby, full-o'-life girl. Screaming as she enter the world, transforming me from a child into a woman with she first breath. Then, so soon, running around the house, acting like it hers. Acting like she some big woman before she even know how to wipe she bottom. So sure of sheself, she own way of being, not even the threat of the Duppy coming to steal she voice enough to make her quiet down or listen when she told what to do.

Oh, she make me laugh just as much as she make me proud. She start work too soon, like we all did. But she act like she been in the hustle a decade before. No low wages for she. No bosses saying, *Ella, do this*, and *Ella, do that*, when it not her job. No, she decide she going to be the boss one day.

She would have, too. She on her way. Fancy job in Kingston. Working with politicians, though me told her, that no job for no one. Not in those times. With all that strife.

But, Ella, she the boss. Boss of she own life and anyone else's she can be. So when those hooligans came in, trying to be the boss, touting Manley's name, Manley's words, she didn't walk away. She didn't surrender. She told them to get out. She stood when she should have cowered.

Me first baby. The one to make me a mammy.

Quick death.

That what I told meself. At least it be a quick death. No suffering, said the others, who be cowering on the floor, listening to everything those men waving their machetes say. Watching it all.

No suffering, the doctor confirmed.

For her, at least.

Kareela

The chatter of Dilly Dally's customers forms a sort of halo around our silence. My mother looks cagey, embarrassed, almost, as I register what's happening. Gran is blind, or nearly. My mother is putting her in a home.

"She's putting up a fuss." Mom exhales, as if the weight of this news has worn her out. "She insists she'll go back to Jamaica before being dumped in a place like that." Mom turns her teacup on the saucer, though she still hasn't taken a drink. "She says she'll go to her own home, where she knows every inch of the house and property, where she'll be fine without sight. A ninety-year-old woman who's half blind and could be fully within the year. Who has next to no money. She still has a house, she says." Mom closes her eyes and gives her head a little shake, as if she's fed up with an unruly child—and tired, oh so tired. "A house that's been boarded up for almost a decade. In who knows what state. And with the store sold, how would she support herself? That would be the cruel thing. The wrong thing. No." Mom looks to the window and I can't tell whether she's talking to me or herself. "A nursing home is the only option. A nursing home is the right thing to do."

Despite the warm tea that works its way down my throat, a cold settles over me. It can't happen. Gran—who grew up in the mountains of Jamaica, raised her children there, who never saw a white person until she was a grown woman and a mother of two, never saw snow or highways or people looking at her like she was nothing, worse than nothing, because of the colour of her skin, the lilt of her voice—trapped in a place where hers would likely be the only face of colour, where the people she'd be trapped with would be some of the same ones who taught their children, their children's children, to hate faces like hers.

"Mom—"

"What I was wondering"—Mom sets down the tea she hasn't yet sipped—"is if you thought it would be better to put her in a home here, so you could visit her more easily."

So I won't have to are the unspoken words. Anger flares within me. The woman who cared for my mother's child when she couldn't has become obsolete, a burden, so it's time to get rid of her. I put down the mug, lean forward, think of my mother that day I was surrounded. We never discussed the incident again—I've never talked about it with anyone—but, like it was yesterday, I remember how she rushed out of the car, wrapped her arms around me, then released me to walk down the long path to the courtyard. How her back was tall. Her head held high.

"Why can't you take care of her?"

How the minutes passed as I sat there, not knowing what to do, shaking with the fear that had shaken me again just weeks ago when I saw those officers' eyes, when Carson asked me to speak. I froze that day in the courtyard, dumbstruck at the boys' words. *That* word, and how instantly I understood the menacing power it held in a way I never had before. How I understood, viscerally, why she'd had me make that promise, how easily a life you felt secure in could become anything but.

Mom brings the cup to her lips. "I'm going to move. Maybe work part-time somewhere until my pension kicks in."

She was brave that day, as she stood for someone other than herself. The mother I'd once known, barely remembered, returned.

"Or maybe not. Maybe I'll sell the house and just travel."

Then she had the car accident, and all that hope faded away. She became a person who acted, again, like I was a burden. Like Gran was. "Since when do you—"

"I travelled to Jamaica." She smiles—wistful. "As a young girl. You know that. But then I met your father. Married so young. This will be the first time in my adult life—you could hardly have called me an adult back then—that I can go off on my own."

She became a person whose hands shook, who sat, as she's sitting now, in a place with an easy path to the exit.

"I don't see the point of prolonging things. So if you want your grandmother closer to you, say the word, and we can find her a place here. But say the word quickly, because I've called around, and the good places in Halifax have waiting lists. But close to home, I could get her in next week if—"

"Next week!" My voice raises and Mom's eyes narrow. Her gaze darts to and fro, as if she's afraid someone will come chastise us. *We don't make scenes in public*, I can almost hear her saying. *We don't make scenes anywhere.* I sigh and wonder why I'm surprised by this news. For years now, there's been this unexplainable tension between them that, any time I asked, Gran always brushed off. Saying it was nothing, that my mom was just tired. Busy. That the job at the school took too much out of her.

What's surprising is that Mom let Gran stay this long after Dad's death. Probably it was the pandemic, and that Gran still cooked and cleaned, that it was easier to do nothing than make a choice.

"The ones here are more expensive, too." Mom's voice lowers several notches. "But I'm willing to pay, because a home close to you will be better for her. For you. She says she'll do fine on her own. That she can make her own way. But she can't. To leave her in that condition would be elder abuse." She shakes her head. "But I'm not spending my final days stuck taking care of a woman who . . . who . . ." She looks to her hands.

Who what, Mom? I want to say. *Who's taken care of you all these years? Of your family?*

"Let me know by end of day tomorrow"—she raises her gaze— "whether you want to find her a place here. And if so, we've got to get her name down on wait-lists, we've—"

I look away, the anger burning, and think of the women Gran has told me about: Aunts. Cousins. Friends. Jamaican mountain women, most of whom have passed now, but who lived into their hundreds. Which means Gran could live that long, too. Could be stuck in a home for a decade. More.

The answer creeps into the corners of my mind, but I don't let it formulate. My life is too much already. Everything too much. I close my eyes, my heart breaking for Gran, stuck in this country, with this woman who clearly has no love for her, with a granddaughter who hasn't called in weeks, visited in months. With all her children under the ground. Two grandchildren as well. And this is what she gets.

"Don't put her in a home in the Valley."

"So you want me to look for one here?"

I nod, not able to commit with words. I want Mom to take care of her. I want this to not be happening.

"Don't look at me like that." Mom's shoulders slump, her hands clasped and pulled into her lap. "As if I'm abandoning her. As if she were some great saviour who came to pull us all out of our torment. Yes, she came here to help us, but also, it was to help her. She was out there in the country, the mountains, for goodness' sake. No running water. No electricity. Alone. Travelling over two hours a day to get to and from that store. So I asked her to come. Told her it was to help. But it was to help her, too. Out there alone, she could have been found dead in her home, weeks after the fact."

I don't think Mom's words are true. Aunt Chevelle was still living, though how much care she could have given, I don't know. But then there were friends. Family. Gran wasn't alone. Gran didn't need to come. Mom needed her. Dad needed her. I did. And because of that, now she has no one but us.

To the outside world, Mom always gave the appearance of functioning. She got dressed, did her hair, showed up to work on time. But there were weeks sometimes, when Gran wasn't living with us, that I had to make my own meals, pack my own lunches, wash my own clothes, tuck myself in at night. And now, this is what she wants for her. "Why do you hate her?" I ask.

"Don't be ridiculous." Mom laughs, but in the sound, I hear the lie. Maybe not hate, but something close. She bolts upright, jostling her chair. "I need the facilities. I'll be right back."

As I watch her walk away, I want to yell out, tell her to get back here and answer the question. In the beginning, there'd been love between them. Closeness. Sometimes at night, I'd lie in bed, lulled by the sound of their whispered voices. With Gran there, Mom helped with the cleaning, the cooking, had more of an interest in me. With Gran there, after we'd moved, leaving the constant physical reminders of Antony behind, Mom had smiled more. Laughed. Been attentive.

Then the accident.

And like an integral piece of a puzzle clicking into place, revealing what's to become of the mess of pieces strewn around you, I see more clearly now. Mom was doing better and then the accident. That's when the flip switched—from a mother who was coming back to me, to one that left again, never to return.

She'd spent almost two weeks in bed, hardly speaking, hardly moving, which seemed extreme for a broken arm and some scrapes and bruises. There'd been whispers—Dad voicing concern, Gran dismissing his fears, telling him a brush with your own mortality could do this. And then, when Mom finally rose from her bed, she wasn't the same, as if the person she'd been trying to become had shrivelled up. There was no more genuine effort to show interest in my life. No more dog-eared magazine pages about how to overcome grief or move on after tragedy. She was cold with Gran and barely acknowledged Dad. She became jumpy—sometimes on edge, sometimes as if she were walking around in a fog, barely processing anything. The vacant look in her eyes intensified, and she never held my gaze in the way she used to, to the point where, to pass on pertinent information, sometimes I had to snap her out of what almost seemed a fugue state, hoping she wouldn't tune out again before I'd finished speaking.

This disconnection happened slowly. Over years. Yet now, I realize, the start of it was all at once.

I'd been angry—that she was checking out again. That I wasn't enough of a reason to try to get better. That, in public, she gave the appearance of being okay, but at home, it was different. Sometimes on weekends or holidays, she'd disappear to her room, spend the whole day in bed. Confirming Gran's words, she said she was just tired, that work took so much out of her. Dad tried to make up for it, I think, taking me to lunch or to the local video store to pick a movie. But it hurt that she had energy for work, but not, apparently, for us. At the time, my pain blinded me. It was all I'd thought of, but . . .

I sit waiting, working up the courage to ask her, *What really happened that night? Why did—*

But before I make up my mind, she returns, words already on her lips, as if there hasn't been this long pause to the conversation. "And if you think I hate her, maybe you should do the looking, set it all up, make sure I'm not just dumping her off somewhere."

My face falls, as if I've been gut punched. Is this what she wanted all along? To cast this off on me, wipe her hands of it so I become the one to make the calls, visit the facilities, convince Gran one of these places should be her home.

"I don't think you'll dump her," I say.

"Then we'll start looking here. We can—"

Keep her with you, I shout internally, but stay silent as she speaks on, my mind back and forth between Gran and Mom, my body hinting at things I'm not ready to hear, not sure I'm able to give.

Mom sets down her tea, lifts her purse from where she'd hung it over the chair, stands, then stares at me, as if I'm the one acting weird. "What are you doing? Let's go."

I blink, realizing I must have tuned out her words. She puts on a smile—her public-facing one, and I wonder, was it a relief for her, those early months of the pandemic? When what was supposed to be a weekend visit turned into us all being trapped in the house together for over two months—no work for her, no training for me—when she didn't have to pretend for the world and didn't bother for us?

"The facility I was talking about is a few blocks away. So let's pop in."

Did she regret when the restrictions eased and suddenly we were out in the world again—masked, but out there? Regret even more when those masks came off?

"It's beautiful, Kareela." That smile, again, so unconvincing to me now. "The photos online are great. It has activities. It's not like that awful place we saw on the news during the first lockdown."

I bite the inside of my lip, the same way she did earlier. "I haven't finished my muffin."

She clenches her purse to her middle as one breath passes, two. And I see that something about being here in this public, tightly spaced place is hard for her. Something that goes beyond her discomfort with me. But this tenseness—fear?—she hasn't always had it. So it can't be just about Antony. And it didn't start right after I was surrounded. So it must have been—

"Can you take it to go?"

I look at the muffin, to save myself from looking at her, to give myself time to figure out how I should ask.

"Kareela!" She's frustrated. On edge.

"You said we were meeting for lunch." I swallow, wanting and not wanting to know. "And you didn't even eat."

"I can't . . . I need . . . Look—" She huffs, pink blotches blooming over her clenched knuckles. "I need to get back, to transcribe meeting notes for work."

Work she's planning to abandon as soon as she gets rid of Gran.

"We can pop in later," I say, not wanting to, ever. Wondering what Dad would think of Mom's plan, whether he'd have had the strength to stand against her, stand up for Gran. "Let me eat. Stay. Chat. You haven't asked me about my job. My life. It's been five months since we've seen each other." *Spend time with me* says a rising feeling, too primal for actual words. And then, maybe then, I'll work up the courage to pose the question.

She sits carefully, with a quick 360 glance. "The phone line goes both ways, Kareela. The roads, too."

Guilt, my training tells me, is behind this tone, these words, these actions. Grief. Frustration at a life she never intended. Which means there may be some small fraction of love left. But not enough. And it hurts. It transforms that feeling of yearning to one of rage. *You're the mom!* I think, but don't say. *You're supposed to be my mom.*

I shouldn't be the one to have to ask questions. I glance down at the table, take a bite, think of her grandbaby, swimming and flipping inside me, and wonder if she'd care, if she'd help me work through the pros and cons, or if Thomas being the father would be all the pro she needed.

She never exactly told me not to marry a Black man . . . but in the offhand comments and looks, the straightening of my hair, the modification of my speech, the guidance around my clothes, what I listened to, watched, she might as well have.

"If you have to go, go," I say, hating my tone—that of a petulant child—furious that I don't have the answers I crave. Furious that she's the only parent I have left, and I her only child—yet still, there's this distance between us. "I don't want to visit a home today."

She stands again.

"Just don't book Gran anywhere without talking to me."

She nods.

"Thank you for the tea and muffin." My voice rises, hopeful she'll change her mind, sit, take me in her arms.

The corners of her lips lift. She pats a hand to my shoulder, lets it rest there for the briefest of moments, as if it's painful to touch me, but she knows she should. She looks at me the way she has for years now, with a distracted, tense energy, as if the sight of me makes her uneasy. As if, whenever she looks at my face, some other, terrible thought lingers on her mind.

What is it?! something in me yells, again. It had to be that night. The accident. *What happened?*

She walks away without looking back, the way a stranger would—yet taking so much of me with her. And the other question that's plagued me for as long as I can remember rises. *Why wasn't I enough?*

I put my hand to my abdomen, thinking of how my mother lives like she owes me nothing, like I'm a burden, a responsibility she's barely responsible for—thinking that maybe we're not so different after all.

Evelyn

On December 27, Evelyn stood outside of an old church with a brick facade and steps leading to two massive wooden doors. She glanced at the flyer in her hand, though she knew this was the right building, right day, right time. She knew, too, that as much as it scared her to step inside, risk people not understanding, risk it not helping—which would mean there was no help left—she had to try. For Kareela.

Evelyn pushed open one of the heavy doors and stepped into a cold foyer.

The steps to the basement led to a large open room, the floor some type of linoleum made to look like tile, the walls wood panelled, the air warm with the scent of cinnamon and coffee. A man approached, his belly hanging so far over his pants Evelyn couldn't see the buckle. His smile spread, wide and genuine, but with a pain behind his eyes she recognized. "Good evening." He took her hand with both of his, didn't shake, but squeezed before releasing. "It's so great to see you."

"Oh, uh, thank you."

He pointed to a circle of chairs, several already occupied. "Take a seat if you like"—he gestured toward the back—"or help yourself to some tea, coffee, or treats." He leaned in. "I made the cinnamon rolls just this evening. My specialty."

Evelyn smiled, clutching her hands so they wouldn't shake, and made her way to the back. She reached for a mint tea, not wanting caffeine to delay those first few—and only—hours of sleep she managed to steal each night, and took a cinnamon roll to keep her hands and mouth busy, each little bite something to focus on, an excuse not to contribute.

"This is a hard time," said Arthur, the cinnamon roll man, once nine of the twelve chairs were occupied. He chuckled. "All times are a hard time. But Christmas." He shook his head as others murmured their agreement. "Everywhere around us, reminders of the good days. Of life when it felt like life, instead of struggling to live." He let out a sigh that transitioned to a chuckle. "I'm sure that's why you're here, out on a night like this."

To Evelyn's left sat a woman whose son was riding his skateboard and didn't look before entering the street. Next, a man whose daughter was attacked while walking home from her job late one night. Across from him, a mother whose son was the night manager at a convenience store and had been shot during a mugging. Arthur's child died in a car accident, when a truck went through a red light and rammed into the side of the family's car. The others didn't say. Evelyn didn't say.

"It's a complicated grief," said the convenience store mom. "The suddenness of it. The complexity. I'm not simply grieving my son. I'm dealing with the hate for the person who took him. And for what? A few hundred dollars? My son's life. That's what it was worth to this person." She lowered her head. "And so I try to ask myself why. I try to find sympathy. The shooter was never found. Maybe he . . . or she . . . had their own pain. Maybe they needed that few hundred dollars to feed their children. Or for a loved one's medical expenses. But why shoot? Why not take the money and run?"

"Fear that your son would have called the police?" a man offered. "That they'd have that much less time to get away?"

The woman pivoted her head, glaring.

"I don't think it was an actual question," said Arthur softly. "I think Lenora was just expressing."

"Oh." The man shrugged.

"I've been reading about disenfranchised grief," said the woman whose son died on a skateboard. "About how there are all these expectations around grief. And I mean, obviously society, the people around me, understand why I'm grieving my son. But not how long. They all want me to move on. That's why my husband left. He was so angry that I wouldn't move for his new job. That I kept our son's room 'a shrine.' But how could I change anything? How could I leave? It's been seven years, and people think I should be over it. Go back to work, they said after a few months, see your friends. Like his death should be some private little sadness I put on a shelf somewhere."

"Two weeks my work gave me," said another man. "Like, oh, that should be enough time to get over the loss of your child, right? My boss even said, when I asked for more time, that it would be good to have something to focus on, to distract me from my grief—work during the day and my remaining two children at home. Focus on what you have, he said. That'll get you through this. As if I *wanted* a distraction, as if it were even possible. And my other children, I love them. But . . ." The man sighed. "I hate them, too—for being the ones to survive—almost as much as I hate myself."

Evelyn tore a piece of roll, then another.

"I've been coming for twelve years," said one woman. "Twelve years of this meeting one week, AA the next. And it doesn't get better. Just different. You learn how to live alongside the pain. That's all I can do."

Evelyn stood, one hand holding the cinnamon roll and the other the tea, as the eyes in the room shifted toward her. She crouched and set the items on the ground. "Sorry, I . . ." She shook her head, pulled her purse strap up over her shoulder. "I have to go."

"Come again!" Arthur called out after her. "Any time. We'd be happy to—"

Evelyn lifted an arm in farewell. She dashed up the steps, then yanked the wood door as a flurry of snowflakes danced and swirled, her hair caught up in the tumult. She wrenched her toque out of her coat pocket, pulled it onto her head, then swept the rogue strands firmly under her hat.

Twelve years. Hating their children. Living alongside the pain that never got better, only different. She was living alongside the pain already. If that's all the group would give her, she could figure this out on her own. She would. For Kareela—who was struggling, who was furious at the neglect, but tried so hard to hide it. Evelyn tramped through the accumulating snow. She didn't hate her daughter. She didn't wish she had died instead. She wanted both her children. But since Kareela was now all she had, Kareela was who she'd live for, who she'd remember birthdays for.

A car tore around the corner, careening in the slush, fishtailing to correct its path as Evelyn jumped back from the thick wet spray. She stood a moment, breathing, realizing a part of her, for a moment, wished she'd been in the vehicle's path and all her pain would have ended. But she was still here.

She'd say goodbye to Antony, if that's what it took to carry on. Evelyn looked both ways, then stepped into the street. With a hand to her brow to block the icy wind and flakes from blurring her vision, she continued on. She'd find a way to live, to get better, to keep her daughter safe.

Kareela

After my mother leaves the café, I pick at my muffin, its moist deliciousness lost on me. Putting my complicated feelings and questions about her aside, I focus on Gran. Blind. I swallow through a dry throat, take a sip of lukewarm tea. Gran, in a nursing home, strangers around her.

At least in Halifax, there'd be the chance of Black and Brown faces—with stories similar to her own. People who immigrated for family. Maybe even other Jamaicans, descendants of the Maroons. They could talk about that. That they were kin, though hundreds of years apart.

I step the plate away. Maybe Mom's right, and it's not like that exposé. Gran could like it. Companionship. Community. She certainly didn't get that in Juniper Cove: not since Dad died, since I left.

That's the core focus when she talks about home. How everyone, regardless of blood, is considered family—taking care of your neighbours, your neighbours taking care of you.

I step through the two sets of café doors, wanting to call Gran, see her, drive to the Valley right now. But if I called, she'd hurry me off the line, no time for *talking 'bout dese t'ings*. If I showed up, aware of her blindness, like the tender awareness of a fresh wound, I'd fall apart.

So I return home, where Thomas and I have been flitting and weaving around each other for days, acting as if everything is fine, while he places a prenatal vitamin beside my breakfast plate or bowl each morning, while I dutifully swallow, knowing since I haven't decided, I should be living as if either decision were possible.

"Where've you been?" he asks when I step through the door. "Out with Jasmine?"

I listen for something behind his words—fear, frustration, jealousy —something to tell me he's not as good as he seems. But hear only curiosity.

"No." I turn from him, open the fridge, stare as if gazing into an abyss. "With my mom, actually."

"Your . . . ?" He sidles over, his back against the counter, his gaze on mine. "Did I know she was coming for a visit?"

I close the fridge door, the action in place of a sigh. "I didn't know."

"Is everything—"

"Gran's blind. Or almost. She will be soon. Mom wants to dump her in a home."

"Oh. Wow. Wow." He nods, clearly processing this information. "It just . . . came on?"

"Apparently she's been hiding it for years." I stop, remembering her skin on mine, papery thin yet full of such substance, her hugs, the scent of her food—tantalizing, sharp, spicy—which smelled like love, which was. "And I didn't see it. I didn't even know."

His hands land on my shoulders, guiding me to the table, setting me into a seat. "You have your own life, Ree. A busy life. And if she was hiding it . . ."

"I know." I swallow and a ball of stress squeezes down—painful and hard. "Mom was talking like she's going to put her in some nursing home near Juniper Cove," I say, "because it's cheaper, easier, faster. And Mom's moving. Which means Gran would be alone. Like, really alone out there. But I don't even think that's what it's about. I think she just said that so she could put her in a home near me and it would seem like a favour, like this good option. So—"

"Wait, what?" Thomas stops me. "Your mom's moving? Where?"

"She didn't say. Just away. To start over. New job. New life, and—"

"In her sixties? And she has no idea—"

"Thomas." I let my hands flop, not wanting to make space to think any more about Mom, about what this move would mean—if her leaving also means she intends, once and for all, to leave me. "This is about Gran. About what's going to happen to Gran. Not my mother."

"Did you tell her about . . ." He leans in, trying to keep the hope from his voice.

"No." I rub a hand along my arm, imagining, again, how that conversation would have gone.

"Well, maybe you should. Maybe, if we decide to keep the baby, she'd move here. Wouldn't that be nice? And maybe your gran could move into a home here, or even, with you close by to help, maybe your mom would reconsider and—"

"It wouldn't be nice." My shoulders stiffen as I try to keep the annoyance out of my voice. To remember that he hasn't lived my life and so is speaking from the perspective of someone whose mother is wonderful—who cares. "And she won't reconsider."

He nods. "The blindness is awful. But the move to a nursing home here, you'd see her way more, most likely. So that's a good thing, right?"

The answer hovers in my mind, not in words, but a feeling.

"Kareela?"

I breathe in, out, not meeting his eye.

"Kareela?"

"I'm not sure."

"Not sure about . . . ?"

I shake my head, stand, not able to articulate the solution, even for myself. "Gran says she wants to move back to Jamaica, where she knows the land, her house, her property. Where there are people who could help her. Not family. I don't think there's any left. They all emigrated to the States or the UK, or disappeared never to be heard from again, or died. But neighbours. Friends who are like family."

His voice is slow, cautious. "Is that a possibility?"

I keep my gaze averted. "Gran doesn't know who is and isn't still there. There was no phone line when she left. No internet . . . satellite maybe." I turn back to him. "It's everywhere, isn't it? And cellphones? But Gran doesn't have their contacts. She hasn't spoken to most of them in a decade."

"So?"

"I'm hungry." I place a hand on my belly with a smile, as if I mean something more by my words, as if my raging hunger is something to be excited about, as if I'm not merely trying to end this conversation, to give myself time to process the past hours. "How about we go out to eat. Maybe take a harbour walk after?"

He stands, clearly not duped, but taking the hint: this isn't something I want to discuss. Not now, anyway. And he doesn't want to upset me, not with the ultrasound in three days.

Evelyn

S hivering from a cold that had worked its way into her bones, Evelyn put her key in the lock. Large chunks of snow fell from her coat and hat, and as she hung them, she paused to let the hook hold a fraction of her weight.

The living room was empty; the kitchen, too. Kareela was likely in bed, Kingsley in his study. She stared at the closed door, trying to imagine what work could keep him so cloistered over Christmas vacation. She had a mind to burst through the door, tell him to get it together. Start living. Disenfranchised grief? Well, it didn't have to be an excuse. They could choose to be acceptable. Grieve how society expected. Go on with their lives, even if life had stopped feeling worth living.

She stepped toward the door, stopped. She couldn't tell him what to do, how to handle this grief that could not be handled, just as no one could tell her. They were separate now, the bullets that tore through Antony tearing through the union she'd once thought unbreakable.

She turned, her hand on the door of the shrine she'd unwittingly allowed Antony's room to become. Five months since her son had entered this room. More than three since she had.

Evelyn slipped inside. She started with the wall. Posters of Martin Luther King Jr., Mahalia Jackson, Billie Holiday and, finally, Dudley Laws and Charles Roach, local activists Evelyn had only learned about in her weeks of research. She wondered, staring at the images of these two men, if they were who she should have gone to. If they were the ones who could have stood beside her, started a rally cry. If they were even still living.

But it was too late for that now. She took down the posters, folded them, piled them on Antony's bed, then started for the closet. She pulled out sweaters and shirts, jeans and sweats. She emptied his drawers, making trips to the kitchen and then the basement for bags and boxes. Returning to his desk, she opened the drawer she'd stored her research in, then piled the papers in a box marked for recycling. Another drawer held folders, binders, and duotangs full of old schoolwork. She kept the essays, depositing them into a box she'd labelled "Antony" in big black marker. She discarded the tests and math equations and note-papers, then opened another drawer full of pens and markers, rulers, tape, and whiteout. It made sense to keep them, let Kareela use them one day, use this desk, too. But would she be able to look at her daughter, sitting at the same desk Antony had? Could she crouch over her to help with homework, knowing her son had held the same pen?

She closed the drawer. She'd decide later. She went to the bed, picked up the pillow, pressed it to her face. Not even the faded scent of chlorine from Kareela's curls lingered. She let the pillow fall, then pulled off the quilt, the sheets. She should wash them before putting them in a bag for Goodwill, but that was asking too much—all that water and soap flushing away fragments of Antony, his DNA, that still lingered. She held the fabric against her, then spread her fingers to the edges, snapped, folded, and stuffed the sheets in a donation box. Someone else could be the one to send those last remnants of her son down the drain.

She returned to a bag of clothes, rooted through, finding Antony's YMCA sweater, which he'd gotten the summer he was a camp counsellor. He wore it so much over the years, the fabric was threadbare. She added it to the Antony box, then continued working, until the room, too, was threadbare, nothing but a stripped bed, desk, dresser, and a pile of bags and boxes.

Waves of something she couldn't quite label—heavy and uncomfortable—pushed along the muscles of her chest. She opened the door and dragged two of the bags up the hall.

"Evelyn?" Kingsley stood in the living room, the TV flickering behind him. "Where were you? When did you get home?"

"A while ago." Evelyn yanked the heavy bags, then thrust them up against the wall by the front door.

"What are you doing?"

"Cleaning out his room."

"What?" Kingsley stepped forward, his eyes wide and frantic.

Evelyn looked up at him, her hands on her hips, her heart thumping from the effort of dragging the too-full bags. "Cleaning out—"

Kingsley rushed past her. He stepped through the half-open door. Evelyn followed, watching his shoulders rise, then fall. He spun. "Are you insane!"

"We're not—"

"How could you . . . without even talking to me?"

"I—"

"You just packed him away." He stepped back, as if from some terrifying threat. "Why?"

"Because why wouldn't we?" Evelyn's arms fell to her side. "Are we going to leave it like this, untouched, unused, collecting dust for a year? Two? Ten?" She paused. "So if not, why not now?"

"Why ever?"

"Kingsley."

"I use it." He turned from her, his hand on the wall where the Billie Holiday poster had been, the paint slightly brighter than the rest. "I come here."

"What?"

"I look at his yearbooks. I sit on his bed. I touch his clothes."

A shiver of uncertainty spread through Evelyn.

"Not every day. But I do. I have." He turned to her, achingly fragile, his expression sending stabs of guilt, like pinpricks to her heart. "So what if it's a shrine? What's wrong with that? He deserves a shrine. He deserves a place we can remember."

Moisture sprung to Evelyn's eyes. She reached out, wanting to breach this chasm between them. "I . . ." Her hand fell as he stared at her with something, not hate exactly, but something too close to it for comfort, in his eyes. "I'll put it back. All of it."

He turned from her. "There's no point." And she heard what she'd been hearing for months, the refrain that had been playing in her mind, in her sleep, from the moment she put away her research and closed Antony's door. *No point. No reason for any of it. Their son had died for nothing.* Kingsley surveyed the room. "You were just going to get rid of it. All of it."

"I kept a couple of boxes." She pointed to the two marked Antony. "Keepsakes."

He nodded, his shoulders drooped. "Let me look through, before getting rid of the rest. I may have my own things to keep."

"I should have asked. I should have thought."

"Just . . ." Kingsley paused, his face looking as if it were about to crumble. "Why?"

How to explain? She'd have to start with forgetting Kareela's birthday. Then on to the church basement, all those sad people who, as far as she could see, had succumbed to their grief, not even looking for a way out. How that couldn't be her. She had a child to take care of, a house to pay the mortgage on, a family to keep.

It would take more words than they'd exchanged in months, and, inevitably, those words would fall short.

"Violet," she said, the idea forming like a light rising out of the fog. "I thought we could invite Violet. And if we were to invite her to stay, we should have a place for her. A place that could be her own."

Kingsley stared blankly, as if she spoke in some unknown language.

"An extended stay. It could be good . . . for all of us. You always said you never really got a chance to know her—being taken from her home when you were just a boy. Plus, Kareela is her only grandchild now, and she's only met her twice. She went back so quickly last time."

"She had to get back to the store. And Chevelle. You know Chevelle can't manage on her own too long. It's too much burden on the neigh—"

"Maybe it's time Violet sold the store," said Evelyn, the idea spreading like salvation. "Or found a long-term manager." So Violet could be here to help take care of Kareela, of Kingsley, of her. "And Chevelle has a fella now, doesn't she? I'm sure he could look out for her. It wouldn't have to be so rushed this time." Violet, to help lighten the load.

Kingsley scratched his head, exhaustion drawing down his features. "I don't think she'd want to. Jamaica's her home."

"But we could ask. Tell her we have a room for her. Tell her we want her."

He sighed, his eyes travelling over the bags and boxes. "We can ask. Just"—he stepped forward, his hand gesturing—"don't take anything out. Not yet. I'm too tired tonight. But I'll look soon."

Evelyn nodded, then stepped aside as Kingsley walked into the hall. She leaned against the doorframe.

Violet. To remember birthdays and Christmas. Violet, who'd lost two children of her own but still managed to smile. Violet, who during Evelyn's time in Jamaica, had become the mother Evelyn hadn't even known how much she needed.

Kareela

We step into the crowded restaurant, where photos of the city's finest line the walls. The underground venue, about halfway between campus and the harbour, is one of Thomas's favourites. A place for "bros," Jasmine would say. I do a quick scan, see that mine is the only non-white face in the crowd—though there may be others, behind a divider or the uncertainty of hair or a hat. It's been a decade since leaving Toronto, and this division still shocks me. I'd heard Halifax was diverse, been excited, and it is, and it isn't. In one part of the city, mine could be the only Black face in a whole evening. Then in another, the palest one in the crowd.

We continue past tables. A sprinkling of undergrads dot the place, but it's mostly people our age and older, grad students and a smattering of those who've put their schooling days behind them and are working their way up in their chosen professions or flitting from one to another, desperate—but never letting on that's the case—to find their calling.

"T-Dog!"

A guy Thomas has known since elementary raises an arm, shouting above the crowd, waving us over.

I nod to the group: the men with their polo shirts, tight tees, or button downs, their chiselled arms and soft middles; the women with long straight hair, unblemished skin, and smiles, half of them making themselves less to make their men seem more.

As we sit, I'm asked how I am. I smile and nod, return the expected pleasantries, and try to recall if I've ever felt truly comfortable with this group. They laud Thomas for his paramedics course, call him a hero. One of the best. A girl sighs wistfully at the mention of Thomas's career change. "I just want to find what brings me joy," she says. "My parents don't get it. They said if I don't choose a 'career path' soon"— she does the air quotes—"they're going to make me pay rent."

"Waah-waah," replies one of the guys, laughing, and I can't help but think how young they seem. Half of them still live with their parents. I moved out at seventeen, came here, took extra courses during the school year and all through summer, graduating a year and a half early because I didn't want to rely on my mother and father. Because when you're grown, shouldn't you act it?

The bro who called us over wraps his arm around his girlfriend and pulls her close. "We weren't planning to announce tonight, but since almost everyone is here . . ." His girlfriend, no, fiancée, shoots out her hand in a way that seems practised, the glittering diamonds so bright, so obvious, it seems impossible no one has noticed them before.

"We haven't made it social media public yet," she says as the women closest to her yank for her hand and examine the ring, oohing and aahing. "So this is in the strictest confidence."

There are congratulations, mine included, as Thomas wraps his arm around me, pleased, I can tell, thinking somehow this will help, show me we're not too young, that the world isn't so shitty. But the thought of a ring like that on my finger, Thomas boasting that I'm his, makes me desperate for air.

With his friends all around us, the uncertainties that started scraping at my mind months ago seem more pronounced than ever. I slip out of the booth and stride past the tables, feeling as if I'm slipping and sliding between two realities, never fully belonging in either. I thrust my back against the bathroom wall, thoughts of that ring, this baby, what Carson asked of me at his dinner table, whether Thomas and I make enough sense to even try to make it work, and of Gran, slamming against me.

For some reason, it's Gran that looms largest, not only her eyes going, but eventually her mind, her heart. All the questions I never asked seem to surge, along with what she revealed anyway, intricacies of her own life—the joys and trials—handing them to me like ripe tropic fruit: full and juicy and delightfully foreign from the life I was living.

I return to the day she told me of my grandfather. "Oh he nuh me husban," she said, "nuh in de way yuh t'ink." She leaned back, the dishcloth she'd been wiping across the counter twisting between her fingers, a dreamy girl's glow on her face. "Me wanted it all." She smiled. "De weddin, godmotha and godfathas, de procession all through de village. De cakes. De booth and de songs. De sprinkled rum—all de evil spirits sent away to have dem own revelry." She sighed. "But me eldest, she showed too soon for all dat. And me had me own house, yuh see? Me parents already in de ground. So yuh grandfatha, he just move right in. Then out and in, out and in, until out for good, to get a proper wife, proper family."

I spin to the sink, then stare at my face in the mirror, trying to see what Gran always saw—her girl, her granbaby, *perfek, just as she is*—and realize I never asked how she felt about it: the father of her children coming and going, never marrying her, then marrying someone else. Taking her son, stealing him, as Gran's tone implied.

Despite everything she's been through, she was there for me, and the answer that's been thrumming through me all day, that I couldn't let myself fully articulate, even in my thoughts, settles on me, so clear, so obvious, it seems ridiculous that I ever tried to deny it. It's my turn to be there for her: I'm taking Gran in. I close my eyes, the moment of expansion in my womb taking this instant to pulse and settle, pulse and settle.

Back at the table, I ignore Thomas's questioning look. I smile, laugh, eat. The woman with the ring turns to me. "You have to join us at the club next weekend." She flashes the ring, her fingers flickering. "To celebrate. Just us girls." Something about the word *have*, although I know that's not how she means it, makes me hold back a cringe. Because last time I went—"just us girls"—was fun, until I realized I was a statement, a showpiece, like a high-end purse or earrings, to flash in the crowd. They emphasized my name to each new person they showed me off to—pressing me forward, hands on my shoulders, almost petting—*Ka-ree-la*. As if without this emphasized enunciation, no one would possibly understand.

"Maybe." I smile. "Work's been so busy. And I've been dealing with some family stuff."

She nods, clearly disappointed, but polite enough not to pry.

If Mom were here—back when she still took the time to notice these things—she'd nudge me: *Fit in. Be liked.* Tell me these were the friends to have, friends who were safe, not even considering the particular dangers they bring. The way all the little offences, unintended or not, made existence so weighted.

The party breaks up, with talk of work and courses tomorrow. Although dinner has taken at least an hour longer than expected, I insist on the harbour, because, at last, I'm ready to talk. Thomas and I head toward the water, hand in hand, the city buzzing around us. And it takes me back to the first time we walked here, fingers linked, high on the giddiness of falling in love, of feeling, at last, we'd found our someone.

Two girls, their hair a mess of blond ringlets, tackle the harbour walk's painted obstacle course with such intensity you'd think a gold medal was waiting at the finish line. Across the splashed rocks, people sway in orange-roped hammocks. The food court, shut down for the night, is eerie with its silence, and it's only as we near the submarine playground, the few lingering laughs of children travelling on the breeze, that I turn to Thomas. But before I can speak—

"Were you okay back there?"

"Huh?" After finally resolving to spit my decision out, I'm thrown.

"In the restaurant. You were in the bathroom for a while. Was it nausea again, or . . ." He hesitates. "You seemed pretty rigid about the engagement."

I look away from him, try to sync my breathing to the lapping waves.

"It wasn't nausea."

He waits. "Karee—"

"I'm taking Gran in." I throw the words out like an attack, though this isn't what I intended. His hand tightens around mine, and I shift my head, see his jaw has tightened, too.

"What do you—"

"I can't have her in a home," I say, my voice softer now. Kinder. "She's my family. She's—" Her face in my mind's eye, that smile, that touch, as she holds my head in her hands, kisses my forehead, gives me the love my parents stopped being able to give. "I won't have her stuck with strangers. So I'm taking her in."

Thomas draws me to the wooden stage, the children's laughter still sounding in our ears. "This was a shock"—he sits, hands in his pockets, and I settle beside him—"learning about your Gran like that. You might just need time to process."

I breathe in the faint hint of salt, breathe out my resolve.

"Table this for a few days," he says. "Maybe let her move into a home. A great one, and she may love it. It may be the best thing for—"

"She left her life, her friends, her country to take care of me. To raise me, when my parents were too grief-stricken and broken to do it."

"Our apartment's too—"

My hands shake, but my voice is firm. "I'm taking her in."

He's silent as he looks at me. My statement is unfair. Is not the way to make decisions in a relationship. Because if this is a relationship, this shouldn't be my decision to make. Not on my own.

"You're not sure if you want a baby"—tension throbs in his voice— "if that's too much responsibility, if we're ready for it, and yet." He pauses. "Have you even thought about what taking her in could entail? What kind of responsibility that is?"

"It's an entirely different situation." And it is, and isn't. But Gran exists. Gran is here, now. "I need to do this." I keep my gaze locked on his, knowing this choice I'm making may inadvertently lead to a host of others. "I'm going to do this."

His nostrils flare. "You told me we'd table the baby conversation." His hands reach for mine. "I'm telling you we'll table this. No decisions tonight."

He isn't asking me a question, so there's no need to answer—and those fissures, I can almost hear the cracks and groans. At a loud hoot of excitement and fear, we turn our faces toward the harbour's most iconic sculpture—a 3.6-metre steel-and-concrete wave. A child, breaking the rules, scrambles to the top. If she took a few steps too far, she'd take a potentially deadly fall to the ground. But the girl turns and slides down the way she came, squealing before running back up. I wince. "It's not that dangerous," Thomas says, hardly veiled annoyance in his voice.

But it could be.

Evelyn

TORONTO

2005

E ven after all these years, the terminal still felt like a city. Enclosed. Futuristic. Too large to be an airport. Too sterile to be anything but a place of passing. Evelyn placed one hand on Kingsley's shoulder, the other on Kareela's. Her daughter's eyes were wide, her head swivelling back and forth, her hands pressed up against the glass, watching the jets taxi in and out.

"Is that Granny's plane? How about that one?"

The hustle of the airport, the crush of bodies, put Evelyn on edge. What must it be like for Violet, this airport so different from the place where she walked across the tarmac, took movable steps, rather than a jetway, into the plane? The memory of Evelyn's opposite journey years ago eased into her mind, the hot balmy air such a contrast to the frigid wind she'd left in Ontario. Eighteen, and never so far from home. She'd been scared, but eager. Full of hope for this new life. And then there was Kingsley, a volunteer driver for the Red Cross, holding a sign, his smile buoyant. A flurry in her stomach seemed to say, *him.*

His swagger, suaveness, was something she'd only seen on the silver screen, and as a result, his slight accent was less of a surprise than it should have been. He reached out his hand, and it lingered around hers. The intimacy of their touch converting that flurry to an electrical current.

"When will Granny be here?" Kareela stepped away from the glass, a pout on her lips.

Evelyn gave a sharp inhale, shocked out of her reverie.

"Soon." Kingsley placed his hand on Kareela's head with a tenderness Evelyn herself hadn't felt in months. He pointed at a screen to the left of them. "Her plane has landed. It'll be any minute." He stood tall, his shoulders back, his chin lifted, the way it used to. "Let's go over there and wait."

"I hardly know my mother," he'd told Evelyn after their first time together, as they lay in the sheets, covered in residual sweat, the faint breeze through the window a soft caress. "I left her when I was eight."

"Left?"

"Was taken." Kingsley rolled onto his back, one hand resting on her bare stomach. After lovemaking, she later learned, was the only time he'd speak about his past. "My father came one day." His voice was soft in the dark room. "I hadn't seen him in several years. He took me. Just me. Hardly looked at my sisters beyond a pat on the head. Said I was going to the city to be a man. To better myself, the family."

Kingsley had lain silent while Evelyn waited for more. In future moments of intimacy, she'd learned about the death of Femi. Of Chevelle, how she was never quite right, and no one knew why, but he loved her anyway, loved her more, maybe, because of it. Of how difficult it had been, being torn away from her like that—from Ella, his mother, everything and everyone he knew. A country boy in the city, in uniform, in a proper all-boys school, with rules and ways of speech that seemed foreign. Without the only family he'd known—his mother, sisters, cousins, aunts. A boy in a world of women, suddenly in a world of men.

In the terminal, Kareela stepped forward as dark-skinned passengers came their way, the colours they wore as bright as their smiles.

"We need you," Evelyn had said when she called Violet. "Kingsley and Kareela need you."

"In a month," Violet said. The tourist season was coming to a close. Her cousin could manage the shop. She'd come. For one month, two maybe, if they needed her that long. "How yuh doing?" she'd asked at Evelyn's silence, the lilt of her voice pulling back to over twenty-four years in the past when, seeing Evelyn sleep-deprived and at a loss, Violet had asked the same question, became the mother Evelyn had lost too soon.

"I—" Evelyn faltered. "I need you, too. For as long as you can stay."

"Me ah gonna come," said Violet. "Soon as me can. For as long as me can." She'd paused, the silence stretching in the miles between them, Evelyn gripping the phone, wishing she could step right through it, emerge on the other side. "It hard in a way nothin can prepare yuh for. But de sun still rises."

Today, Kareela rushed forward. "Granny!" she cried. Kingsley grasped Evelyn's hand—the movement so unfamiliar now it sent a surge of hope through her. She looked at him, offered a smile. He waited while the old woman and young girl embraced, then dropped Evelyn's hand to step into his mother's arms. After several breaths, Violet stepped away from her son and turned to Evelyn. Evelyn sank into her arms, a small portion of the weight she'd been carrying seeming to slip aside.

"Me here for yuh, girl," Violet whispered. "Me here, now."

Kareela

The clinic is in a part of the city I've rarely ventured through, in a strip mall not far from where Thomas grew up. The waiting room is clean, but dated; most likely, it was pristine when Thomas was a boy. It's sparse compared to what it likely would have been, with the majority of appointments still by phone, the distanced chairs, never more than two beside each other. We sit, not talking, the tension from a couple of nights ago at the harbour still sizzling between us. He's angry and has a right to be, but doesn't want to say it.

I almost wish he would.

"I delivered this one," says the doctor after waving us into her office. She grins at Thomas, then gestures to my abdomen. "Maybe I'll deliver this one, too."

She asks me several questions, which I answer as I hoist myself on the table, knees together, ankles crossed. She asks me to lie down, pull up my shirt. "We got a new ultrasound machine." Her smile is the wide-mouthed, bright-eyed grin of a child at Christmas. "We only had dopplers before. This is nothing like the quality at the hospital, but you'll get to see your baby."

My breath catches, my throat tightens, my muscles clench.

"Really?" Thomas rises from his seat on the other side of the office, the tension on his face transitioning to that same kid-at-Christmas grin. "Today?"

"That's right." The doctor lifts a tube, flips off the top, tells me I should expect it to be cold.

I sit up, yank down my shirt. "Hearing's okay," I say. "That's all we expected." The doctor's expression falls. Thomas's brow scrunches, his lips tighten. "I mean, ultrasounds can be dangerous, right? Too many of them? So might as well save it for when we can get a good look, you know?"

Her smile returns, softer this time. "It's fine," she says, "really." She lays a hand on my arm. "Where you're not positive of your dates, and we haven't even done a blood draw, this is an important time to do an ultrasound. If I don't do it, I'll have to send you to the IWK Health Centre for an ultrasound in the next week or two, anyway. But if we get a good image today, you won't need to go for another six to eight weeks. Lie down, sweetie."

I do, wondering how she'll possibly hear the baby's heartbeat over mine. The machine is small, the screen maybe eighteen inches. I flinch at the cold gel, the pressure on my abdomen. The doctor manoeuvres the wand for a few seconds before holding it still over what is, unmistakably, a baby.

"That's it?" Thomas steps closer.

"That's it." The doctor shakes her head, smiling. "This is one of the best angles we've gotten yet." She glances at me. "We've only had the machine two weeks."

"The head and the nose"—Thomas points—"those are the feet?"

"You've got it." She pulls her cursor across the screen, a yellow line spreading as she measures, as the feet kick and a hand waves. She must be taking a picture because the screen freezes, and she continues measuring.

"Look, Kareela, the nose? Do you see that cute little nose?"

Movement again. The doctor points to a flicker on the screen. "And there's the heart." She presses a button and noise fills the room, fast and loud, like the sound of a dog panting after a long run.

"Is that—?" Thomas's voice rises in alarm. "Is that all right? It's so fast!"

The doctor laughs. "It's fine. It's perfect." She records the pace, lowers the volume. "You're measuring just under thirteen weeks," she says. "A little off what you thought, but that's normal, especially where you said your cycle had a bit of a range."

I stare at the image, which twists, so it doesn't look like a baby at all, then moves again, suddenly recognizable. Suddenly mine. I try to push the faint sound of that beating heart out of my mind, pretend this isn't happening. Pretend I still have time to decide whether it's real or not.

"How much time do I have?" I blurt.

"It's listing your due date as January third." The doctor grins. "A New Year's baby . . . or Christmas, if you're early."

"No." I knock aside her hand with the wand, grab the towel she tucked into my underwear, wipe, and rise to sitting. "No . . . how much time do I have to decide if I want to keep it?"

"Ah." The doctor cleans the wand, nods, as Thomas steps back, tension filling his body, his expression shifting, as if I've just killed our child.

"My friend said fifteen weeks, fifteen weeks and, uh, six days?"

"That's right." The doctor sets the wand in its holder. "If you want it done in Nova Scotia."

"And could I come here, to you, instead of—"

"No." She goes to her desk, grabs two pamphlets, then hands them to me. "But you can ask any questions you'd like today. You are already past the point of a medical abortion, which means you'd need a procedural abortion in hospital. A D&C. Do you know what that is?"

I nod.

"It'll be more difficult now . . . all around." I can almost see the judgment in her face, hear it in her voice, but she's fighting it—and for that I'm thankful. I refuse to look at Thomas. I've already seen what he thinks of this. "Even if you haven't made your decision, with the timeline, you'll want to move forward. Visit the Sexual Health Centre, where you can talk things through with a counsellor, maybe even book an appointment, to ensure you don't miss the deadline."

"But booking an appointment before she's made her decision—" Thomas's voice is tight. "That doesn't make sense. It—"

"It makes sense if she doesn't want to end up going to Quebec or Ontario," says the doctor. "Which would mean travel and accommodation costs, and a lot more stress."

"I'll take the baby," he says, almost yelling. "Shouldn't I have *some* choice here?"

The doctor inhales, her lips in a firm line. "Thomas. I realize this is difficult, but I'm going to ask you to step outside, please."

"But—"

"This is Kareela's appointment, not yours."

He looks at me. "Kareela?"

I shrug, as if to say, *She's the doctor, she's the boss*, which is cruel and weak, but I'm afraid if I speak, my voice will break. He shakes his head, exits, closing the door gently behind him.

"Has he been pressuring you?" the doctor asks. "Is that why it's taken so—"

"No," I squeak, then swallow, a bitter dryness in my mouth. "I mean, not really. He wants it. He said he'd take it, that I wouldn't have to have anything to do with it, but . . ."

"But you'd still have to go through another six months of pregnancy and then know, for the rest of your life, that you have a child out there."

Emotion wells within me. "Exactly."

"It's ideal," she says, grabbing her chair, rolling it over, sitting so she's looking up at me, "if partners can make this decision together. But, ultimately, the choice is yours." She puts her hand on my knee. "You want to be sure. Counselling, talking about your options is great, but I'm guessing you know your options. So you also need to know the choice is yours, and yours alone."

I nod, wishing it wasn't. Wishing someone could make this decision for me. Wishing it could just be that—a decision. That it didn't need to feel political. That it didn't need to determine whether I would or would not have a future with Thomas. Wishing that I was making this choice ten years from now, when I hopefully would have figured out my own shit—what I want, what I don't, who I am and who I want to be.

The doctor hands me another pamphlet, and I take it blindly, thinking of caring for Gran and a baby simultaneously. I try to force the thoughts away long enough to look at the pamphlet, take in the words, then thrust the paper back. "No. It's not like that," I say. "He's not abusive."

"Sometimes it's hard to tell," she says. "Sometimes it's subtle. Emotional. It wouldn't do any harm to give it a read."

"No." I hold the paper out. If anyone is emotionally abusive, it's me, for how much I've withheld from him, the way I've lied. The pamphlet flops between us until she takes it from my hand.

She stands. "The decision is yours," she repeats. "But you have to decide soon, Kareela. Very soon."

Evelyn

Evelyn sat at the kitchen table, papers spread in front of her, a laptop to the side. Violet was here again, which meant life was easier—homemade meals instead of frozen or take-out, perfectly clean countertops, a tender, patient, undistracted ear for Kareela. She'd been coming and going for years. Since Chevelle's death, she'd stay for months at a time, then go back to the island before tourist season to help her now full-time manager handle the shop. Her presence assuaged the guilt that picked at Evelyn constantly when Violet wasn't here. When Evelyn, despite her best efforts, knew she was failing her daughter.

But this problem, Violet couldn't help with.

Evelyn put a hand to her head, feeling as if another one was on her chest, pressing in. The last of Kingsley's severance had run out two months ago and her own salary wasn't enough—not for the mortgage, food, hydro.

"We know you've been through a lot," the dean had said in reference to the pile of increasingly negative student assessments Kingsley had received over the years. "We hoped in time, you'd get back the joy you once had, the talent."

The severance had lasted a year. And in all that time, Evelyn had heard nothing of a job search, receiving only mumbled utterances of some book Kingsley was working on whenever she dared to ask.

She clicked open the file with their investments. She could withdraw them, but they'd run out soon, and the bills would keep coming. She turned to the letter that had arrived last month. When she was rifling through flyers and bills and had seen the return address, her hands shook, a cold sickness spreading through her.

It had been difficult to find her, her uncle wrote. But he remembered the wedding announcement clipping Evelyn had sent to his daughter years ago, and through that, he had her new last name. But it hadn't been enough. He'd had to hire an investigator. In the search, he'd also learned of her "son's demise" and expressed his condolences.

Her father was dead. Without a will, the house was hers. Her uncle, who now lived in Alberta, would keep it until he heard from her. He didn't want to sell it without her permission, but, living so far away, wasn't able to manage the upkeep. *Six months,* he wrote. *And if I don't hear from you, I'll sell and put the money in savings, in case you need it one day.*

They needed it now. But how much would it be, the cash for a house in rural Nova Scotia? An old house, possibly falling apart. What they needed, instead, was the money their current house would get, and a place to live where, if necessary, her income would be enough.

Evelyn placed both hands on the edge of the table and stood. She held the letter in her hand, though she wouldn't read from it. A prop. Something tangible, to remind her, and her family, that this offer was real.

She entered the living room. "We need to talk."

All three heads turned. Evelyn reached for the remote, lowered the volume, then, thinking better of it, pressed the power button. She clutched the letter. "We can't afford this house anymore. This city."

The eyes stared.

"We're getting behind on our bills."

"We have investments," said Kingsley, his voice drawn, the way it so often was now. "I'm working on something. I'm—"

"Investments meant for Kareela's education. For our retirement." Evelyn stuttered, her stomach tightening. "We . . . we need to sell the house."

Kareela's mouth dropped as Kingsley looked at the bottle in his hand. Two more sat on the table.

"This neighbourhood has boomed. We'll get a good amount for it. Maybe over half a million." She held up the letter. "My father died."

"Oh, Evie." Violet leaned forward.

"Your father?" Kareela raised her brow, her expression perplexed.

"He left me the family house. It's large. Old, but with the money from selling this one, I'm sure we could take care of any fixes. The cost of living will be much less. We could get by on one income." She hesitated, seeing the shame in Kingsley's expression. "If needed. And without the full pension we expected from the university, we'll need the extra money for our retirement and"—she shifted her gaze to Kareela—"your schooling."

"I thought your parents died years ago," said Kareela.

"My mother did. When I was around your age. My father wasn't someone I wanted in our lives."

Kareela crossed her arms. "What if I want—"

"That's not what this is about," Evelyn snapped. She softened her tone. "You wouldn't have wanted to know him."

"Where?" Kareela's voice shook with fear, but also anger. "Where is this house?"

"In an area called the Valley. In Nova Scotia. It's beautiful country.

Ocean views less than a ten-minute drive from the house. And in the surrounding area—farmland, apple orchards, vineyards."

"If it's so beautiful, why have I never heard of it?"

Evelyn's throat tightened. This was hard enough: the thought of going back there, to a place she'd been so desperate to escape. She didn't need—

"Why have we never been there?"

Evelyn sighed. "I told you—"

"This is my home." Kareela stood, her voice sharp and loud. "Where my friends are. My school."

"I'm sorry, but—"

"I'll get a job. I'll help." Kareela turned to Kingsley, desperate. "And you'll find a job soon, won't you? Dad?"

Kingsley took a sip of his beer, eyes averted. Guilt pierced through Evelyn, for exposing his failure to provide in this way, but the conversation couldn't have been held in private. Kingsley would have turned to her with his sad eyes, his assertions that things would get better, that he'd find work soon, that this book he was working on would pay off. And she wouldn't have been able to say no. Just as she hadn't said no to the ever-increasing number of bottles hauled out each recycling day. To the way, most nights, his head lolled above his desk in the study, or fell against the couch, a half-finished drink staining the coffee table.

They would have stayed, burning through their finances, their future, and ended up old and riddled with debt. Destitute.

The move was for Kareela, too. As she got older, craved more independence, it was hard enough to let her out alone in this city of threat. But then there'd been another shooting just last month, which brought up Antony's name, and her classmates began to probe and pry. She'd cried for hours. And it would keep happening, again and again . . .

"We need to leave," said Evelyn. "We can no longer afford this house. We can't afford anywhere decent in this city. So it'd be an apartment, likely too small for the four of us, in a neighbourhood we'll be scared to walk in at night." Evelyn swallowed. "I don't want that for us. I won't have it."

"So the decision's been made? Just like that?" Kareela's chin jutted.

Evelyn clutched the letter harder, willing her resolve not to crumble. As Kareela's shoulders squared, Evelyn caught a glimpse of Antony. Kareela had stopped asking for details about his death years ago. Stopped bringing him up at all—knowing how much it hurt Kingsley and Evelyn. She had protected them. Now it was time for Evelyn to protect her.

"It's the best thing to—"

"I'm not moving!" Kareela ran toward the front door, the slam as it closed shaking Evelyn to her core. Kingsley put his head in his hands.

"It's the only way," Evelyn whispered, that familiar crush of failure rushing over her, mixing with the absence that, despite how she tried, she just couldn't overcome. "To keep this family together. Safe and together."

Kingsley raised his head long enough to meet her eyes, then lowered it again. He nodded. "My book probably won't sell, anyway. I've had four rejections."

Evelyn wanted to reach out, wrap her arms around him. "Maybe in Nova Scotia, you can teach again. Someone with your qualifications, you'll find a job in no time."

Kingsley stood. Evelyn flinched in shock as his hand landed on her shoulder. He squeezed it, then let his fingers fall.

THE SOLD SIGN sat in the yard less than a month later. Evelyn had given her notice, and boxes sat throughout the house—some to ship, some to give away. Violet had left to pack up her own home, sell the store. To meet them in Nova Scotia. To stay. Evelyn pulled an item out of a bin, the fabric soft and pale, the faint scent of baby powder floating in the air. She turned to Kareela. "You came home from the hospital in this."

She smiled, remembering the sweet new baby in her arms, whom she hadn't wanted initially, but loved just as much as her first.

Antony had held Kareela that day, a shy look on his face, his arms tense, as if he feared he might drop her, his eyes full of more wonder than she'd ever seen.

In the past weeks, Kareela's rage had dissipated into a quiet bitterness. She stepped forward and took the item from Evelyn's hand, examining it.

"Anto—"

Kareela's head snapped up, her eyes shocked and expectant. Sometimes, Evelyn could think of him now, without pain being the only emotion. Sometimes, there was joy in the memory. But to speak his name aloud . . . "Nothing."

"I hate packing." Kareela dropped the sleeper. "I don't want to move."

Evelyn nodded, her gaze on the other items in the bin. Dresses and onesies. Tiny shoes and tiny socks. A lovey. "We should take this whole bin. You may want it one day, for your own child."

"Do you hear me?" Kareela shoved a box of old toys to the floor, the thump causing Evelyn's shoulders to tense. "I don't want to move."

Evelyn raised her gaze. "I know. But the house is sold."

"And you made a ton, right? So let's find another place in the city."

"We made a lot. But not enough."

"This neighbourhood's becoming swank, like you said. I'm sure we can find somewhere else . . . without it being the ghetto."

Evelyn shook her head. She wanted to take her daughter in her arms. But she knew the motion would be awkward, unsettling for them both. It'd been so long.

The more Kareela grew, the more she looked like Antony, moved like Antony. Making touch painful. Making the fear grow—the fear that one day, Kareela would be taken away as well. A car accident. A disease. Another hate-filled attack. And so Evelyn kept her love distant, at arm's length. *You'll be safe there*, she wanted to say, in a place where Evelyn never remembered seeing a Black person in her whole eighteen years of life. Or safer, at least, with no police beatings, gang shootings, multicar highway pileups. *I'll be able to hold you*, she thought. *Love without so much fear.*

"Think of no smog," said Evelyn, instead. "The ability to see the horizon for miles."

Kareela flopped onto the couch.

"It's gorgeous," said Evelyn, aching to rub her hand along Kareela's head. "Cool summer breezes that don't carry toxins into your lungs. No acid rain."

A sharp laugh.

"People are kind," Evelyn continued, knowing it wasn't exactly true, but telling herself it could be. "Welcoming."

"People are people."

"Well . . ." Evelyn closed the bin. "I think you'll love it there. I think—"

"Why didn't you let me make up my own mind about my grandfather?" Kareela leaned forward, her elbows on her knees. "Do I have other relatives? Cousins?"

"Second cousins." Evelyn reached for another bin. "They're older though. Older than—" She pushed the word out, trying it. "Antony would have been."

Kareela's eyes widened.

Evelyn focused on her breathing. "One cousin was nice, the others . . . were all right."

"Did . . ." Kareela hesitated. "Antony meet them?"

Evelyn's pulse raced, her throat dry. "No. So"—she kept her gaze away from Kareela—"we'll keep all these baby clothes."

Kareela sighed. Her hand reached out, pulling the box on the floor closer. "We keeping my baby toys, too?"

Evelyn looked in. Not just Kareela's, but Antony's. "If you want." She hesitated, a burning creeping its way through her lungs, up her throat. "Or pick some, donate the rest."

Kareela grabbed a ball, threw it in the air, then caught it. "Was this mine or his? It looks old."

Evelyn swallowed the fire-filled sting. "His. First."

Kareela threw the ball one more time, then held it between both hands. "This is where he lived. This house. This city. He's barely . . . anything to me now." She stopped. "I mean, I can't really see him. Hear him. There are just these flashes, you know? Moments. That I feel." Her gaze fell. She squeezed the ball. "I know I'm not supposed to talk about him."

No! Evelyn should say. *You can. It's okay.*

Kareela didn't look up. "And I get that. And so knowing he was here makes it easier. Not even just this house. But the street, the buses, the subway. I go to the Eaton Centre and think—Antony was here. Sit in the food court and know it's possible he sat in the same chair. I visit his grave and talk to him."

The burning flared, the pain a roar. Kareela visited his grave?

"I feel like by making us move, you're trying to make us forget. Maybe make Dad forget? And I get that, why you'd want to. Dad is . . ." She squeezed the ball again. "But I don't want to forget. I want to remember."

"That's not—" Evelyn shook her head. She reached out, her hand hesitating then falling upon her daughter's knee, her voice unsteady. "That's not what I'm trying to do. I could never forget. I think about your brother every day. Every moment."

Evelyn kept her hand on Kareela's knee, despite the way her body shook. "I imagine him, too. On the streets, the bus, the subway, when I visit some place I'd been with him or know he'd been. I see him. Sometimes so clearly I have to do a double take." Evelyn fought the urge to pull away, stop talking—the pain so raw—to never speak of Antony again. "I visit his grave, too. But leaving this place, it won't be leaving him. He's here." Evelyn gestured between them, her voice shaking. "He's in us. In you. Your smile. Your eyes. Just look in the mirror."

Kareela turned her face away.

Evelyn pulled back. "I'm not saying . . . you're your own person, obviously. I'm just saying he won't disappear. And I'm not trying to make him. But a new place, a new start, would be good for all of us. Maybe your father most of all. And outside of that, we simply can't afford to live here. Not on my salary alone."

Evelyn stared at her daughter, this person she hardly knew. Whom she'd hardly tried to know, so scared of living this pain over again. So scared that the closer she got to Kareela, the more she'd screw her up—her own grief, guilt, shame, wiping out any chance of her daughter finding joy. She'd provided for her needs—physically, financially—but failed in every other way. She didn't want to keep failing.

Evelyn shifted closer. She put an arm around Kareela's shoulder, despite the way her daughter stiffened, and pulled her close. "Moves are always hard. I know you don't want to go, and I hate that. I hate it for you. But I hope, in time, you'll see this as a positive thing. A new start." Evelyn squeezed tighter, her heart squeezing, too, to have her arms around her girl.

A new start. Starting now. With so many fears removed, she'd stop being absent in her daughter's life. She'd spend time with her, get to know her. Be a mother to her, the kind of mother she was sure her own mother had wanted to be.

Evelyn held Kareela tighter at the thought of her father—the ghosts of memory she'd pushed aside when deciding to move back to his house flooding in. But, as she'd just told Kareela, memories weren't attached to a place . . . or at least they didn't have to be. They would paint and redecorate. They would make their own memories. They'd, maybe, do more than survive.

Kareela

When I step into the clinic's waiting room, Thomas stands, hands in his pockets, an expression on his face I can't read. A small child plays in the corner. A man coughs into his elbow, making everyone tense in this post-pandemic world, which isn't really post at all.

Thomas's jaw twitches. Our eyes meet, a crevasse between us that seems too wide to cross. Silent, he turns toward the door, holds it for me.

Outside, we step to the side of the building. He turns his face to the sun. "You didn't feel anything? Seeing our child, hearing the—"

"Of course I did." My voice is quiet. Tight. Squeezing off all I felt, all I'm feeling still. "But I don't want to make this decision on feeling. I don't want to bring this baby into the world simply because it would be hard not to."

"I don't get—"

I turn to him, place a hand on his arm, and at last he looks at me. "I'm sorry for what this is putting you through, but I know what it is to have a parent who doesn't want you. Who wishes she hadn't had you. Who blames you for the life she's leading."

Confusion crosses his face.

"I could have this baby, sure. Take care of it. And resent it, because that's not what I wanted for my life. Not now, not—"

"Not with me."

I drop my hand. "We didn't plan this."

"But it was the plan, eventually, right? Marriage, a house, kids."

I shrug, knowing, at last, it's time I spoke the truth. "Your plan."

He steps back, and it's as if I can see the rapidly fraying edges of our relationship, hovering there between us.

"I never actually said it was mine."

His voice cracks. "You didn't say it wasn't."

He isn't wrong. I smiled and nodded, just like I had when it came to us moving in only six months after we met—his suggesting it quickly turning into deciding it, because I never said the opposite. Because it felt good to know I had someone—beyond Gran—who loved me, wanted me, thought I was enough. Because I was so silently broken up over Dad's death, and the idea of someone at home waiting for me, someone to curl up with during the continued isolation of social distancing, held some appeal. I lower my gaze to the ground. Cement blocks, a candy wrapper, at least five cigarette butts. "I should have."

I look up and his eyes are closed, his arms tensed. Seeing his pain, I want to say yes, we'll have the baby. We'll be a family. But I can't. I won't. Not this time.

"This is my choice," I say. "I'm the one who's going to make it."

"I know it's your choice." He wraps his hand around mine. "I get that. But I love this baby. I want this baby, even if you don't. And I know that's asking a lot—"

"It is." My pulse races as I pull my hand away, try to consider what the doctor said—going through the full forty weeks, the aches, the pain, my body so clearly not my own, never to be my own again in the way it was before this happened.

"It'd be a lot for you, too," I say, still mostly thinking of myself, of holding that baby, or even if I didn't, to know it exists, that the heart I heard today was beating somewhere, aware I didn't want it. "A single dad. As a paramedic? The hours you'd be working . . . they're not exactly conducive to daycare. To school. Not without someone to help you."

"I'd figure it out." He pauses. "I'd go back to accounting if I had to. Just like we would figure it out. Like we could."

Again, he's right. Of course we could. Though I've been saying it, thinking it at times, we're not kids. We could do this. "My gran needs me right now." I could put on a ring, tie myself to this man forever. "And she already exists."

"This baby exists."

"I could have another child one day."

"I spoke too quickly about your gran." He throws the words out—desperate, like a badly tossed lifeline. "We could take her in. It could be great. Wonderful. We'll move out of town a bit. Get a bigger place. She could sing to the baby . . . you said she's a singer, right? Be that connection to your past you're always looking for. I know how important that is to you. We could be a family. I agree to your gran, you agree to the baby. That makes sense"—he leans forward, grasps my arms— "doesn't it?"

"Stop it!" His hands fall from me, as if my flesh has burned him. I stand, shocked at the force of my words, at the realization that pulsed through me as I finally understood what he's doing, what he's done, whether he intended it or not, so many times before. "You're trying to manipulate me."

"I'm sorry, I—" Thomas hesitates, guilt and regret in his eyes. Hurt. "I didn't mean it like that." He lets out a shuddered breath. "I just feel desperate. I want this baby. And I want you, too."

We stare at each other, the fissure a chasm.

"Are you calling the clinic, then?" He bites his lip, not meeting my eye. "The abortion line? Or whatever it is?"

I nod, still shocked at my outburst. "To make an appointment. Just in case."

"So you've decided."

"No. I just need a little more time."

"There's no time left. You heard the doctor." He extends an arm toward the clinic, his voice shaking. "If that didn't make up your mind, seeing your child, *our* child, alive inside you. Hearing that heart. What would?"

What would? What would? What would?

I think of doing nothing, letting nature take its course, and it terrifies me. I think of showing up for an appointment, lying down, then spreading my legs to have this all over . . . and it terrifies me. I open my mouth but can't speak. And then, like a tendril of fog slowly making itself visible, until it's all I can see, something occurs to me—in choosing the baby, regardless of whether I want it or not, Thomas is not choosing me.

"You want this baby," I say, as betrayal seeps in, abandonment. "And if I don't, but I have it for you, you're choosing it over me. We're finished, right? Because how can we be together if you're raising our child but I'm not?"

"That's not what I want."

"But it is. That's what would happen."

He looks at me in a way he never has before, like I'm the stranger I've realized myself to be for months now. "If you wanted it to, yes. But not because I wouldn't want you, because you don't want me. Us." He gestures to my stomach.

"That's not fair!"

"None of this is."

We stare at each other until he shakes his head, sadness distorting his features. "You say you don't know if you want our child, but more and more, it seems tied with not knowing if you want me."

"I didn't say that."

"Kareela, you don't have to. I love you. I want you. But I don't want to be with a woman who doesn't love me."

Sweat breaks out along my spine, under my arms. "I didn't say that!"

"Exactly." Moisture fills his eyes, his voice tight. "*Love ya. You too.*" The way you'd say it to a friend. But no, you haven't actually said you love me. Not for months now." He looks away from me. "Maybe we both need time to think. About us, if nothing else. I can pack a bag, head out for a few days."

"What?" I step toward him, my hand lifted, but it stops, rather than reaching out.

"I can stay with friends. Or my mom."

He's silent. Waiting for me to tell him to stay? Tell him I've changed my mind? That I want him and the baby? The words are on my lips—because I know I may never again find someone as kind and thoughtful and solid as this man. But this man, also, has just chosen this child I'm growing over me, over our relationship, and I'm not even sure if I can blame him.

He turns. The sun beats down, cars weave in and out of the strip mall, birds crow, and my baby, presumably, flips and twirls along with my thoughts as I watch him leave.

Thomas reaches the bus stop. I wait, the sweat pouring, as part of me tells me to run after him, and another part is saying maybe this is just what I need. A bus whisks him away, and a question arises: *Not for months?* I thought I'd said it. I know I said it in the past. Meant it.

But . . . as I walk toward the bus stop, my mind travels through the moments, like one of those movie montages, and I realize he's right. *Love ya. You too.* A hug or kiss. The last time I said it, straight out, was the first night I'd started to question, uncertainty tinging my voice as I waved goodbye, which made me, unconsciously I suppose, hold back from saying it again.

It was after that party with my colleagues. Seeing the look in their eyes at seeing him, the look in his at the way my body had stiffened—the first fissure popping up along a fault line we'd never allowed our-selves to see. We said good night—me staying downtown to dance with the girls, him heading home due to an early morning shift. He'd laughed, though there was no true humour in the sound, as he said I talked differently around my work friends. Moved and stood differ-ently, too.

I'd laughed. Though I saw he was right. That with him, I was one woman, with them another, altering my language, my interests, myself, to be most pleasing to those around me—be it my mother, my father, friends, or the man I claimed to love. That I'd been doing it for years . . . that, ever since the day I was surrounded, it had become a compulsion.

But with that realization—my colleagues' looks, Thomas's words—came the question of whether this woman I created, that *he* wanted, may not be the one I wanted, too. That maybe the person I wanted to be was someone who'd find it hard to live her life tethered to him.

THE BUS COMES and I step back, wave it on, then sink to the bench, head in my hands as I see the baby, that definitive forehead and nose. Those puckering lips and that whooshing heart. I imagine keeping that child, and Gran, whether bringing her to live with me—especially without Thomas there to help—is more insane than I imagine. It's too much to think of. All too much. Needing a distraction, I pull out my phone, remembering the text from Jasmine I'd swiped away before the ultrasound. *Hey girl, you coming today or what? Carson says it'll be a fiery one!*

Fire. To sit in a crowd. Have their energy become mine. Focus on something, anything, other than this life I'm failing.

The bus that'll take me two blocks from the BLM headquarters comes around the corner. I stand. As the city passes in a haze, I stare, trying to banish the baby and Thomas from my mind, focusing only on the smiling faces about to greet me, faces who will make me feel—for a few moments, at least—as if I belong.

Evelyn

L ay low. That's all I'm saying."

Kareela stared at Evelyn. Disbelief. Disappointment. Disgust. All whirling in her eyes. "How do you suppose I do that? Paint my skin? Shave my head?"

"Don't be ridiculous."

"*I'm* being ridiculous?" Kareela paced the kitchen Evelyn's mother once had. Evelyn never noticed before—the slant of her daughter's shoulders, the curve of her forehead, the way she walked, on her forefoot rather than heel, how much it was like Helen. Here, in her mother's space, her mother's house, the similarities flew at Evelyn, hitting her with a gale force.

"No, I'm saying stay away from things that make you stand out. You can do a project on any topic, so don't choose civil rights."

"It's what Antony would have done."

Evelyn stiffened.

"Antony was out there changing things. Antony—"

"And it killed him!"

Kareela stepped back as Evelyn inhaled, fighting to lower the intensity that had just shot out of her voice. "I'm sorry, I . . . I know it's not the same thing. That it's just a school project. But that's how it can start. And since we've been here, it's like you're trying not to fit in."

Kareela crossed her arms as she slumped against the counter, her voice and look hesitant. "That's not—"

"The music. The clothes. The . . ." Evelyn hesitated. "Ebonics."

"Ebonics!"

"You didn't use to talk like that."

"So?" Disdain, with a touch of uncertainty, poured from Kareela's voice.

"People can see you have Black in you. It's not like—"

"Like what?"

"Like you have to rub it in their faces."

"Rub it in their faces?" Kareela closed her eyes with a caustic laugh that shifted to border on a sob. She lifted her gaze to the ceiling. "Maybe I'm just trying to keep hold of who I am."

Evelyn kept her voice soft, hoping it came out inquisitive rather than accusatory. "Is this who you are?"

Kareela's lower lip quivered. "I'm not them. That's for sure. And this is what they expect, anyway. Isn't that the thing to do—live up to people's expectations?"

"So that's why you're suddenly morphing into this whole new person?"

"I don't know!" Kareela spun. She let out a moan. "What if this is who I am? Who I've always been? Just because that happened to—" Kareela drew a breath, then released it. She pressed her hands against her face.

Evelyn swallowed, searching for the right thing to say, coming up with nothing.

"It's just." Kareela dropped her hands, her eyes moist. "They look at me like I'm an alien. Their jaws fall. Their heads literally turn to stare at me as I walk by."

"Your classmates?"

"It's happened." Kareela looked away. "In the first few days. Now it's mostly in stores. At community events. People touch my hair without asking. They giggle and laugh."

"To your face?"

"No." Kareela's bottom lip stuck out. "But I'm sure they're laughing about me."

Evelyn stepped closer. "People did that to me, too. In Jamaica. They stared. They touched my hair, my skin. Some laughed. But it wasn't meant to be hurtful. They'd just never seen someone who looked like me. They were curious. Interested."

"I'm not an animal in a zoo."

"I know. But it's possible some people in this town have never seen a Black person in real life. I hadn't until I moved to Jamaica."

Kareela rolled her eyes. "Mom. It's 2011, not 1950."

"I did not move to Jamaica in 1950. I wasn't even born in 1950."

"Whatever." Kareela stepped from the counter and stared out the window, arms still folded, as Helen so often had. "Maybe it's not about that, anyway. Maybe it's just about understanding who I am. Wanting to find somewhere to belong."

"You're Kareela Jackson. You're my daughter."

"I'm more than that. Not that anyone here even believes I'm yours. They don't think it's possible."

Confusion filtered through Evelyn. "What do you mean?"

Kareela scoffed. "You know that girl you and Dad met last weekend. Stella? Who's nice enough and whatever. Fine. But ignorant. She asked me this week what it was like being adopted."

Evelyn stared at her, not understanding.

"And when I said I wasn't, she goes, oh, so is that your stepmom? She, like, literally couldn't comprehend that I could have come from you. That a Black man and a white woman would make a Brown child."

"You're right," said Evelyn. "It's ignorance. Not malice."

"Too ignorant." Kareela sighed. "And I don't like the way they look at Dad. All suspicious. Even frightened. You said it was nice here. You said, small town, people will be friendly. Welcoming."

Evelyn stiffened, caught in the half-truth she'd spewed out of hope. It hadn't been her experience. Not really. People were kind, sure. Welcoming, in a way. If you were one of their own. Her mother hadn't been, coming from somewhere in Central Canada, and so when Helen was on the outs with Evelyn's father, she was on the outs with the town. Their allegiance with Joseph Godfrey, with the Godfrey name, they'd kept silent, turned their eyes from her suffering, her bruises.

Officers let off his drinking and driving with warning after warning. The few barkeeps in town occasionally took his keys but continued to serve him, even though half the town must have known what those drinks would mean. And when the babies came too early, her mother's face and arms and belly bruised, the doctors had, presumably, written no reports, contacted no authorities.

The memory made her shiver, made her shrink to the girl she once was, peeking into her parents' room, seeing her mother's once near-ivory face purple and green against the pillowcase, her arm an inkblot of colour upon the sheet. Later, she'd seen her mother's belly, loose and floppy, like a limp balloon, discoloured, too.

The doctors, the town, Evelyn's aunt and grandparents, had done nothing.

In coming back, Evelyn told herself their turned-away eyes were the result of the time, not the people. That the world had shifted. Domestic violence was simply violence now, as criminal as any other kind. Alcoholism, drinking and driving, were no longer whispered about and dismissed. It was dealt with. And so she hoped only the goodness of the town would remain. Casseroles that turned up on your doorstep during hard times. Neighbours watching out for each other's children. And not a hint of racism, beyond the occasional joke.

"If it bothers you so much that people look at your hair and want to touch it," said Evelyn, not knowing what else to say, "straighten it."

Kareela's shoulders fell. The disappointment, disgust, and disbelief even stronger now.

And Evelyn could see why, but . . . "It's what your father did. To get to where he is now. He didn't stop being Black. That's impossible. But he dressed like the people around him. He kept his hair short and tidy. He—"

"Mom. Argh!" Kareela paced again.

Evelyn winced at Kareela's tone; she was doing this all wrong.

"It's like you can't even hear yourself. And to get to where Dad is now?"

"I mean where he was. Before." She hesitated, wanting to get it right, say the thing that would help Kareela understand. "A position at a prestigious university. A good salary. A house in—"

"Mom!"

"All I'm saying is he tried to make himself fit in, to make himself more approachable. To help people feel comfortable, so they're not . . . put off. Or nervous. Or—"

"Put off? Nervous?" Kareela shook her head. "You think being Black puts people off. So Black people should, what? Just do all they can to be as un-Black as possible?"

"That's not what I'm saying." Now Evelyn's voice ratcheted, and she worked to bring it down, to calm not only her own flaring emotions, but Kareela's. "And in your situation . . . I'm sure I used the wrong words. But you said how people stare at you, your hair. That's because they're not used to it. It's different to them. So if you don't want them to stare—"

"That's not my job. It's not my job to make white people comfortable."

Evelyn's chest tightened. Her throat, too. Nausea rolled through her. She was doing this all wrong, but she didn't know how to do it right. She just wanted Kareela to be happy and safe. Or happier, at least. Rather than this sullen, quick to anger, obstinate person she was turning into. It scared Evelyn that, maybe, this was who her daughter had always been. It scared her how much Kareela reminded her of Antony. After spending so many years of her life trying to make things easier for those around her, the girl was suddenly sick of it.

"Just promise me you'll choose a different project," said Evelyn, suddenly desperate. Terrified Kareela would turn into Antony. End up like Antony. "Promise you'll leave all that to other people. No marches. No standing in the street. I can't—" Evelyn's voice cracked, the tears threatening. She looked away, unable to bear how much of him stared out through Kareela's eyes, how easily it could happen to her, too.

"I . . ." Kareela swallowed, her lips pinched, her body as stiff as Evelyn's. "Okay, Mom." She rested a hand on Evelyn's shoulder. "I promise."

Evelyn nodded. She inhaled, then blew the air out slowly, tension trickling through her body. "What about Beyoncé?"

"What?" Kareela dropped her hand and looked at Evelyn as if she had two heads.

"Her hair is straight." Evelyn's voice shook. She fought to regain her composure. "It doesn't mean she's trying not to be Black. No one would ever say that."

Kareela stared, then offered an unconvincing smile. "That's true, Mom. I'll think about it." She stood for a moment, then turned and walked out of the room.

Evelyn slumped in her chair, exhaustion like a cloak, Antony's presence looming over her—with disappointment, chastisement. Three months. Three months they'd been in Juniper Cove, and each day seemed harder than the last, the ghosts of her past, more powerful than she'd realized, colliding with the ghosts of her present—with Antony, whose absence still haunted them all.

Kingsley's drinking had lessened, at first—as he sent out resumés, interviewed at the closest university, then applied to the ones in and around Halifax, not even receiving a callback. He now worked at a medical supply manufacturing plant. On his feet all day, performing repetitive tasks, wasting that brilliant mind. He wouldn't give her many details on the job, but he was bringing in a salary barely more than a third of what he'd made as a professor.

She'd told him he could wait. Keep looking for something better, that the money they'd made on the Toronto house would tide them over, especially with the income she'd be bringing in with her secretarial job at the local elementary school. But he'd insisted, shame in his eyes. "It has potential," he said, his voice so much hollower than it'd been when they met, so less refined. "One of their product assessment specialists is near retirement. That role requires a master's as a minimum, doctorate preferred. They promised they'll consider me."

And so he worked, mostly nights, then came home and drank to make it through the day. He cried, too. Though the walls here were so much thinner, so maybe he'd been crying all along.

Evelyn cried, too, in a way she'd rarely let herself in Toronto. But only when the house was empty, or in the privacy of her car. She was bone tired. But determined. This would be the change they needed. Their fresh start. Their way to keep their one remaining child safe. Evelyn rubbed a hand across her face. She'd try again with Kareela, figure out the right way to say what she meant, to help her daughter through this.

She rose and stepped into the hall in search of Kareela, then Evelyn stopped. Listened.

"Yuh mama been through hard times. It make her scared. It make her t'ink the way to safety be blendin in. But dat de way to lose yuhself, and it not likely to make yuh any more safe. Yuh got to just be you. Look at me. Yuh t'ink me can't speak like dem? I can speak. Me just don't like dem words, de sound a dem coming out ah me mouth. Like me wearin someone else's body, using someone else's tongue. I can speak dem words, pickney, just as good as yuh. Yuh fatha could speak mine, once, but den yuh grandpappy, he stole dem out he mouth, stole de movements out he body, all to be like dem. To fit in with people who never even wanted he to fit." Violet paused as Evelyn kept still and silent.

"De way me see it, we had we lives, we heritage stolen once. Why we gonna let it be stolen again, just to make dem more comfortable? Me can understand dem, and dem, if dey take de time to listen, sure can understand me. That what matter. All that should matter. Being who yuh is, not changin yuhself for no one else. Not walkin every day in fear. So wear yuh curls. Wear what clothes yuh wanna wear. Talk how yuh wanna talk, and don't let no one, not even yuh mama, tell yuh different."

Evelyn stepped away, back to the kitchen, shame and uncertainty passing through her in equal measure. She knew something was missing in Kingsley, something that had been trained out of him by his father, his private school teachers, that, decades later, was part of the reason he couldn't stand straight anymore, was why he seemed to think what happened to Antony was largely his fault—that if he had given Antony what he was looking for, that connection to his past, he wouldn't have looked so desperately for it elsewhere.

And maybe he was right.

Yet when it came down to it, if the blame for Antony's death should fall on one of them, it was Evelyn. She hadn't backed up Kingsley, hadn't put her foot down against Antony's political activities. She'd tried to support her son—going to the rally, leaving that voicemail. When she'd finally figured out how to make the phone work, how to access the messages, the one she'd left was saved, which meant he'd heard. And if he hadn't, if she'd never gone to the rally, never called— her words bolstering him up—maybe he would have lain down with the others. Maybe he'd be here still.

Evelyn poured a glass of water and drank it whole. In that way and a million others, she'd failed Antony. She wouldn't allow the same fate for daughter.

She closed her eyes, breathed, desperate to do better. She would have to guide Kareela through this crisis of self. She racked her brain, searching for some spark of connection, some activity or interest not about appearance or background, then remembered a conversation in the break room—a colleague with children in the high school. Children who thrived.

She made her way to the living room and breathed a sigh of relief to find Kareela sitting alone. "Maybe I was wrong," she said. "Maybe the trick isn't to make them more comfortable, but to show them who you are. Get involved." She hesitated, then pressed on. "What about Model UN? It could be perfect for you. Show them you're not just the Black girl. The new girl. Show them how smart you are. Make them excited to call you one of their own."

Kareela raised her eyebrow, skepticism in her eyes, but curiosity, too.

"If not that," said Evelyn, "drama. Or the school newspaper. Something to take their focus off your newness, to make them see you, for all you are."

Evelyn waited for a response. Some flicker. Hoping this was the right suggestion and not simply what she'd said before, dressed up in different clothing.

"I'll think about it." Kareela's voice was hesitant. "Model UN actually sounded pretty cool. But there's a qualification process. I don't know if I—"

Evelyn's shoulders relaxed. She released the tensed hands she hadn't realized she'd been clenching. "Kareela"—she held her smile firm—"you can."

Kareela

The BLM meeting room is full. Jasmine waves me into the middle of a row, toward an empty chair beside her. I excuse myself, then sit, as a woman with long braids, lean and muscled arms, and eyes so large they make her face seem that of a child's, speaks. The energy in the room, thick and pulsating, presses against me as I take in her words. Not just the story, but everything behind it, the collective memories of hate, of pain that goes back generations: being sent to the back of the bus or theatre; having homes bulldozed, belongings carted away in garbage trucks by order of the city.

She stops, and the crowd is hushed, their attentiveness palpable, those memories—of being beaten, chased, feared and suspected and surrounded for doing nothing but daring to be born Black—like a heavy fog, rising in the room.

She continues, her expression incredulous at the injustice she speaks of, because no matter how much we expect it, when it happens to us—these injustices, these atrocities—it's disorienting. A surprise.

The thrum vibrates through us, through me. Anger. Conviction. Pain. And that's what Carson wants. Why this woman is telling her story. With a sigh and a slump to her shoulders, a sad little smile, she stops.

Carson joins her onstage and locks his fingers with hers—half handshake, half handhold—before turning to the crowd. "I imagine every person in this room has a story like that one," he says as the woman returns to her seat. "Our stories, our experiences, are what brought us here. What brings us together." He looks to the crowd, his gaze sliding from person to person, meeting as many eyes as he can, meeting mine. "Every person's story matters. Every voice matters. It is our voices, our collective voices, that will effect change." A murmur of acknowledgement crests around me and I squirm in my seat, that conviction, that call, rising in me, too. This is not what I came for.

"A lack of safety, a sense of terror," says Carson, "we're not born with these things, but we learn them quickly. I've already given my seven-year-old boy the talk." Carson gives a little grin. "Not *that* talk." A few chuckles sound. "You know the one, the more important one, if we want to see our sons turn into men. The one that teaches them the opposite of what little white boys are taught. That tells them to make themselves small, to be pleasing and obedient, if they want to stay alive." Heads nod, the murmur of assent grows, and the words in Antony's file seem to rise up, swirl around me. How he wasn't pleasing. How he didn't obey.

"Because they don't see my boy as a boy, my daughter or wife as any other girl or woman." Carson leans forward. "They see us as inherently dangerous, violent, criminal. They see us as a threat. Something to be stomped down, restrained, taught to bow to authority. And every time one of our boys or girls is beaten, is harassed, is street-checked, pulled over, taken down to the station, or taken from this world for the simple crime of living, every time that happens and an officer is acquitted or not even charged, it tells all of us, again, we're not safe here. We're not wanted." Carson pauses. "But this is our home. This is our one life. These are our children. And they shouldn't have to be afraid."

Carson's face blurs, and I see Antony, his face as it was, as it would have been. Standing in front of a crowd like this one, speaking words like these. It's hard to look, but there's no point in averting my gaze. Since opening that file, I've seen my brother everywhere: a Black man corralling his children into the car; a professor riding his bike to Dalhousie; a homeless man standing on the street corner, despondent and downtrodden. I see all the people he could have been and isn't. All the lives he could have lived.

I only half listen as Carson talks about the upcoming rally, in two months' time, which will end onstage at Grand Parade, with media there to broadcast our voices across Atlantic Canada and beyond.

"Our stories!" he says, his voice growing in urgency. "That's what will make people listen. That's what will stop making us a meaningless statistic people can turn their faces from, pretend doesn't exist, doesn't matter. That's why our sister was up here today. That's why we need you. Each of you."

His gaze passes over the room, meets mine, and I hear his call, what he wants: My voice. My story. Antony's. At his dinner table, Rania told him it wasn't time, but now . . .

"We're in this together," he says. "We have to be. We need people to tell their stories. We need people to spread the word. Flyers, posters, social media."

It all rushes in: his chest, his shoulder, his hip, his head.

"We want as many signatures on that petition as we can get. We want people the city will recognize—"

The witnesses who tried to tell their stories but were silenced, threatened.

"Doctors, lawyers, teachers, professors, mechanics."

My father, sinking into himself until he was a shell, until I couldn't even remember what had once filled him.

"We're not powerless."

My mother, not wanting me to listen to Black music. For a time I gave in to her urgings—straightening my hair, modifying my speech, becoming as culturally white as possible—because of the fear of those boys who'd surrounded me, of others like them.

Carson says it again. "We are not powerless!"

But aren't we?

"We never have been, and we never will be. But we have to work that power."

Antony, despite all his bravado, all his passion, was torn from this world.

"There is a club." Carson's hands lift, a preacher on a stand, his voice commanding. "Not a club you'd ever ask to be a part of, made up of people who've been beaten, broken."

Who bleed.

"Generation after generation." His congregation is on the edge of their seats. "But are we beaten?"

"No!" Voices rise—several bodies, too, energy thumping like an angry bass beat.

"Are we broken?"

"No!"

Something in me wants to shout, too, and I writhe, because this is *not* what I came for.

"We've lost our loved ones—and not just from the killings. From the fear. Because fear, that shit will eat you alive!"

I came for distraction. To feel as if I belonged, with no intention of standing up for that belonging.

"All our Black and Brown faces, they see those faces. But they don't see us. They see something to be erased. They see inferiority." A breath. "But are we inferior?"

"NO!"

"No. And we're here. Here to stay."

My legs twitch.

"We're not going anywhere."

"NO!"

"So hand out those petitions."

Shouts and claps fill the space. An ache rises in the back of my throat—fear, but also a yearning. For change. For Antony's death to have not been in vain.

"And not just to your Black friends. All your friends. Tell them your story."

A memory surfaces.

"Pass out those flyers. Bring your mama, your grandmother, your next-door neighbour. Bring everyone. Of every colour, every race. Because we've had enough."

Antony. Twirling me in the air, laughing.

"We've had enough!"

Joy.

"It has to stop!"

Love.

Carson's face glistens. His arms shake, and I can almost see Antony up there on the podium, calling out. Calling to me. "No more beatings!"

"NO!"

Energizing the crowd.

"No more killings!"

"NO!"

Carson's voice lifts, filling the space, as Antony's would have. "No more being afraid to run through the park. To drive your car. To live!"

But Antony's not here. He never made it to Carson's age. Never made it to mine.

"It may not happen today. It may not happen tomorrow. But we need to defund the police!"

"YES!"

His chest, his shoulder, his hip, his head: and all that love, that passion, that joy, was gone, just like that. My parents gone, too. Never to return—not in the way they once were.

"Disarm them!"

"YES!"

And we need to. But do I? Resistance, fear, like a vise, clamps down as people around me rise—hands in the air. Shouts, too.

"So hand out those flyers. Print those petitions—take them to your work, your church, your great-aunt Petunia's nursing home." Chuckles erupt. "We need as many names as possible, no matter the hue. And seriously, pen and paper. Don't trust people to go home and visit the website themselves. Netflix will make them forget."

More laughter. But I can't appreciate the humour. Not when I'm expected to tell my story. Stand up the way Antony did. Risk myself.

"Blow up social media. Take the information packets on what defunding the police actually means, because you know people will have questions. And those questions need answers."

Possibly lose my life, when I've already lost so much.

Carson steps down and those who hadn't already stood, do. Desperate to leave, I jump up, weave my way through these Black and Brown bodies, ignoring Jasmine's questions, the hands on my shoulders, the smiling faces.

A chant of song rises around me, Rania's voice leading the flock in this church of the movement. I'm five feet from the door when Carson steps in front of me, like a mirage taking human form. "Kareela, I was hoping to catch you before—"

"No." My limbs tingle, my mother's, father's, brother's face in front of my own.

I won't be his spokesperson. I won't bring this baby into this awful world. I'll stay with Thomas, who is safe and kind and stable. And if he leaves me because of the baby, or because he finally sees how damaged I really am, so be it. He wanted the baby more than me, anyway.

I'll take in Gran. And, somehow, figure out a way to make it work.

"Kareela?"

I dash past him toward the door, not looking back, the word erupting from my throat more for me than for him. "No!"

Evelyn

Blue sky filled the horizon; cottontail clouds popped across the expanse. The air was warm, the promise of summer not too far away. And Evelyn, for the first time in a long time, felt hope. Felt as if she'd made the right choice. She crossed the lot to her car. Almost nine months now, she'd been in this job, in this town—that was at once so different and so similar to the one she grew up in. Almost nine months since she'd torn her daughter from the only life she knew and thrust her into this unfamiliar and alarming one. But last weekend, Kareela had spent the night at a friend's house, one of ten girls invited for a sweet sixteen sleepover party. And this morning, she smiled, her eyes lit with excitement as she told Evelyn and Violet about the upcoming Model UN trip, how out of the twelve people on the team, she was one of two to be chosen to take the trip to Halifax next month.

Evelyn shifted the car into drive and pulled out of the lot. She rolled the windows down, the air increasingly chilly as she picked up speed. She bore the cold, for the freshness it brought, the feeling that so much of what had held her down, made her feel like she was struggling through the mire, was finally, slowly, drifting away.

At the high school, she drove past the nearly empty lot to the small walkway at the back of the school. Normally, parents weren't supposed to wait there, but this late, it wouldn't matter. Evelyn hoped the meeting had gone well, that the teacher had approved Kareela's speech for the Model UN, that her girl would be glowing.

Evelyn looked at the dash before turning off the engine, then angled her gaze down the long path, which curved behind a copse of trees before leading to the school doors. She was ten minutes late, her boss delaying her with final notes for tomorrow's assembly. Kareela should be here by now, and Evelyn wanted to step out of the car and check, thoughts of Antony, of how quickly a life could be derailed, flooding her mind. But Kareela had made it clear, parents coming to the door looking for their children, entering the school and roaming the halls, was not cool.

Evelyn took a long, slow breath, leaned her head back, and focused on the cleansing breeze. She glanced up. Kareela stood just past the tree line, arms tight against her side, head down. Evelyn straightened in her seat. Kareela lifted one foot, then the other, and the other, faster, until she ran. Evelyn thrust open the car door and rushed around just in time to catch her daughter in her arms. "What? What is it?" She pushed Kareela away enough to scan her face, her shoulders, her arms for injury. Kareela threw herself against Evelyn again. Silent but clinging. Evelyn held on, her heart racing, her mind whipping through all the possibilities.

Kareela stepped back. She wiped her sleeve under her eyes.

"They . . ."

"What?"

Kareela closed her eyes, shook her head. "A bunch of them. Seven. Ten. They saw me. One yelled. Then another. They told me to go back where I came from. They called me a—" She stopped. Lowered her

gaze, clenched her jaw. "You know." She raised her head—fire and fear
and raw terror in her eyes. "Over and over. They kept saying it, saying,
go back where you came from. They called me an African flea. They
said, *go back to Africa you*—" Her lip trembled as she clearly fought
with whether to repeat the word. "You know what." Confusion mixed
with the emotions in her eyes. "But I come from here, Mom. I come
from here."

Kareela looked to the side, as if staring at something Evelyn couldn't
see. "I wanted to tell them, but I couldn't speak. Couldn't move. One
spit at me. He missed, but . . ."

Evelyn gripped Kareela once more, pressing her body against her
own, wishing she could take her back inside of her. Protect her. Always.
She let go. "Stay here."

"What?"

"Get in the car and lock the door."

"Mom!"

"Now."

Kareela opened the door and Evelyn strode, each footfall propelled
by the image of her daughter surrounded by a bunch of brainless
yokels, by the thought of her son, at the same age, shoved by officers,
witnessing his friend being assaulted for walking in their own neighbourhood. Propelled, by the officers who raised their guns because her
boy refused to cower. Propelled, by anger with her own ignorance. For
thinking they'd be safe here.

She turned the corner and took in the boys. Nine of them. All their
heads shaved or closely buzzed. The ones who weren't looking her
way turned when they noticed the silence, the stiffened postures, the
dropped cigarettes of the others. Evelyn's lip curled. Her chin lifted.
"You."

The boys watched her, silent, on edge. A tingle of fear sprung up her spine, but rage dampened it. "You. Spineless. Pathetic. Ignorant children."

One boy shifted. He took his hand out of his pocket.

"You think you're better than her?" Evelyn shook her head, looked at them like the swine they were. She quelled her shaking as she sensed their disgust, their hate, the tense energy that she knew could snap at any moment—send them hurtling toward her. But she also sensed their fear. She laughed, to throw them off, to remind herself she was a grown woman, and they were pitiful boys. "You're nothing. A pack of losers who were born in this town and will probably die in this town." She was sure she recognized at least three of the boys, not specifically, but the features of their parents living on in their offspring. She cast her gaze on one whose father must be the same boy who'd called her trash—the daughter of a drunk—when his own parents were second cousins. The words coming out of her mouth were vile, but she said them anyway. "You. I know you, or your father, at least. Your inbred father." Her lip curled. "And you think you're better than her?"

They all stood, unmoving, except for the clenched fists of that tow-headed prick, his eyes burning with hate.

"My daughter was born in this country. She belongs in this country. Just as much as any of you. And she'll go further than you could dream. She'll leave you in the dust, like the sad half-wits you are." She stepped forward, no longer speaking only to these red-necked hicks, but to the officers who'd shoved Antony and beaten Malik, who'd killed her son, to the one who'd showed up at her door—all of them thinking they were better, that their lives were worth more than her children's. "And if you ever accost her again, if you so much as look at her in a way that makes her uncomfortable, you will pay."

Evelyn turned on her heel, fear making her breath come quick, disbelief at the words that had come out of her mouth catapulting her back down the path toward Kareela. Terror rushed through her, terror that she'd made it worse, that she'd been just as stupid and rash as they had, and that her daughter would pay for her foolhardiness.

She wrenched open the car door, fell into the seat, secured the buckle.

"Mom?"

She gripped the wheel, turned the ignition.

"Mom?"

Evelyn turned to Kareela. "They won't bother you again." She prayed her words were true. "It's over now."

She pulled away from the curb, the glare of the sun amidst that bright blue sky making her cringe, and reminded herself to breathe.

Kareela

I step out of the BLM headquarters and into the sun. Sweat beads on my brow, and despite the oppressive heat, I decide to walk the thirty minutes to our apartment. As I stride along Gottingen, an elderly man tilts his head, taking the time, despite my obvious rush, to give the nod. I return it with a small smile, my shoulders releasing ever so slightly, my pace slowing.

As I cross streets, moving closer and closer to home, farther away from the North End, the Black and Brown faces fade and that part of myself fades, too. I'm less likely to nod or wave or smile at the people I pass—whether I recognize them or not. A buzz in my pocket makes me jump and I pull out the phone, see the words from Thomas.

There. It's all yours. I'm gone.

His message stops me mid-stride. And just like that, all my decisiveness from just moments ago swirls away like dirty dishwater. If I still want him, I should type:

I'm sorry.

Don't go.

We'll figure it out.

I should call him, tell him I can't have this baby, but I can have him, want him. That we'll have another baby when we're ready. We'll get the house and the dog. We'll exchange rings. But I stifle a sob and slide the phone back in my pocket, almost certain too much damage has been done.

By the time I arrive home, I'm drenched. I drop my bag beside our dining table, peel off my T-shirt, and let the air hit my moist skin.

I walk through a quiet that has never seemed so loud, surveying the empty spots in our apartment—my apartment, for the time being— and grab a tank top from our too-bare closet.

I've never lived alone. Never taken the time to decide for myself how I like things done. Never considered who I am outside of others' expectations of me.

Not wanting to unpack these thoughts, I sink to the chair beside my bag, reach for my laptop, and open up my case files. The light shifts as I read and make notes, stretch my neck, rub the small of my back, continue on. I rise for tea and some breakfast cookies Thomas must have made—my favourite. When the doorbell sounds, I tap my phone, see that almost three hours have passed. Pain slices at the thought of Thomas returning for something he forgot—ringing the doorbell instead of coming right in.

The chime sounds again, and I rise from my seat, step through our door, down the shared stairwell, and then pull open the outer door to see Carson. "Wha— what are you—?" I stutter and step back. "How do you know where I live?"

He shrugs, looking sheepish. "Jasmine. Can I come in?"

I step aside to let him in. Upstairs, our cozy apartment seems smaller with him in it. "Nice place." He smiles, and the sheepishness is gone. "Reminds me of our first apartment, Rania and me. Though this is bigger." He shakes his head, his smile one of tender reminiscence. "Twenty-one, a baby on the way, just dropped out of uni—disappointing everyone who thought I'd be the first to get a degree. To get that money. That respect."

My brows furrow. "You dropped out?"

He nods.

"Well, anyway, I guess you didn't need it." I step back, wishing I hadn't let him in. Wishing he would leave. Or that I could. "Don't you have your own construction company?"

He nods. "That learning didn't come from school. My dad is a carpenter. He wanted something more for me. So did I. He knew history was my love."

"History?" I direct him to the table. My body tenses as I imagine why he is here, what he's about to ask.

"Yep. I was going to be Professor Downey. Dr. Downey. Would have had a nice ring to it."

"What happened?"

"A pregnant girlfriend, then wife. A need to pay the bills. To make sure at least one of us got to follow our dreams. It made more sense it was her." He shakes his head, the smile still there, but slighter. "It was a constant fight, anyway, a constant struggle. The history I wanted to tell wasn't the history enough people wanted to learn. Once Rania got her degree, started working, she wanted me to go back. But I decided I could make more of a difference as I was, at a job that would allow me the time and freedom to enact change, rather than merely teach the past."

"BLM?"

"You got it." He taps his fist on the table. "The past is important. I'm actually writing a book of Black history in Atlantic Canada, but the future—"

"Wait, what?" I interrupt him. "With all you've got going on, you're writing a history book?"

He laughs. "It's slow going. But as I was saying, the future—that's my core focus. That's what's going to make the difference for my kids. For yours—" He gestures.

I lean back, my body instantly tensing. "You know?"

"I have three of my own, could see the signs."

I nod, hating that he knows rather than suspects, hating that this secret isn't one any longer.

"So whether you keep this child or have ones in your future, they're who I'm fighting for, who I hope we're all fighting for."

"Which is why you're here." The pressure I feel, the frustration and betrayal—that this is why he's been so kind to me—leaks into my voice. "To make me the face of the movement."

He frowns. "I don't know that I'd say it like that."

I straighten, shoulders back, ready, at last, to listen to Gran, to stop being the person others want me to be.

"Rania told me not to come. She said if you wanted to speak, you would. And if you didn't, we should leave you be." He taps his fist again. "And maybe she's right. But you showed up tonight."

"Then left."

"Which is why I'm here."

"To convince me?"

"To talk." He leans forward. "It's your choice, Kareela. And I understand if you're tired of this being your life. I'm tired. We're all tired."

I raise a brow at him, waiting.

"I understand if you're afraid. Is that it?"

I cross my arms and look to the ceiling.

"How could you not be? Of course you're afraid."

"It's more than that." I bring my gaze back to him, thinking of the promise. "It's more complicated than you could imagine. My mother, for one."

"It would bring things up?"

"To say the least." The promise I've already broken. But this . . . "She's white."

"I know."

"How do you—?" Right. The file. "Anyway, she's not like the white people who come to meetings. She's not an ally. Not in that way. She . . . she wants nothing to do with any of it. Rallying. Protests. Which makes sense, given—" I stop. "But even before, I don't think she wanted Antony to have anything to do with it. My father certainly didn't, which is even crazier. And now that—"

"Not really."

I hesitate. "Not really, what?"

"They came from Jamaica in 1980, right? At the height of political unrest, urban warfare, people dying in the streets, the people who did get out having to start anew with nothing."

I stare at him, unnerved he knows more about my parents' apparent history than I do.

He leans in, his tone softening. "It was rough there, Kareela. Your parents never talked about it? What they went through . . . saw? They were living in Kingston, right?"

"Do you have a PI on me or something?"

"No!" He laughs. "The year they immigrated, it was in the full report. That they were from Kingston, that your mom was a white woman from Nova Scotia before that. I didn't ask for it. It was just there. And the rest . . . I'm a Black history enthusiast, remember? I know what it was probably like for them. Over eight hundred people were murdered. The city was terrorized. Almost everyone affected. Afraid to walk out their front doors, losing friends, neighbours, family."

A wave of dizziness overtakes me. Had they lost more than Antony? Heat floods my cheeks.

"So I get why she'd be afraid," continues Carson. "Especially now. But even before. I get why you would be. Just remember, this isn't Toronto. This isn't the US. It's not perfect here. I'm not saying that. There'd be risk, but the rally will be televised. We won't be breaking any laws. We won't be rioting. It'll be peaceful. It'll—"

"And what about after?" My voice squeezes. Aunt Ella. I've heard little about her—from Mom, from Gran—but enough that Carson's words have knitted what little I know together, that, like Antony, she must have died standing up for what she believed in or been killed in the crossfires. "What about the people who aren't peaceful?" Anger and fear builds to a crescendo as I see those boys around me, their eyes. The officers' eyes. "The people who'll see me and know. See me and hate—"

Carson lays his hand on mine. "Those people hate you, anyway. What about the people who see you, hear you, and are convinced? What about the possibility for change?"

I yank my hand away as blood rushes through my ears. "They hate in general. You're asking me to become the face they hate. To have them see me as not just another Black woman, but the Black woman who's trying to disarm and defund the police. To become the focus of their hatred."

He leans back. "You have a point. That's possible. Though it's not likely they'd do anything physical about it. Not here. Not now. But it is possible."

"Yes." I push back from the table, thinking of how I didn't stand over two years ago, when it could have made a difference to my father, how, now that he's gone, now that I've lost the chance to do this with him, it makes even less sense to speak. "It's possible. And you brought that possibility on yourself, on your family. But my family has had enough." My voice shakes as I see my dad on that couch, empty bottles around him, limbs contorted, lifeless. "I've had enough. I'm not Antony. And I don't want to be." I stand, my breath heavy, the fear heavy, weighted with the grief of that image, which will forever live in my mind. I wait for Carson to say something. But he's doing that trick again. Waiting. Listening. "I won't be your spokesperson," I spew, my hands shaking, now, too. "I'll work with you, for you—"

"For all of us."

I turn from him, my gut twisting. I know he's right, that my story, Antony's, would be the most powerful story they have, the strongest example of how broken and inherently racist the system is.

My face—my light-skinned face—will make people more apt to listen than if Carson were to tell this story, with his dark skin, his broad shoulders and muscled arms. The Black man—whose kindness, intelligence, they don't open their eyes to see.

I shake my head, pacing. "I don't want people stopping me in the street, the grocery store, knowing I'm Antony Jackson's sister."

The Black man—who epitomizes their fears, embodies their ideas of danger, demon, who is safest behind bars, or not breathing at all.

"I don't want his death to become my identity." To end up like him . . . or like Aunt Ella.

Carson's face softens, and I see something—pity?—in his eyes. "But it is your identity."

I stop pacing. "It's not."

"It is." His smile, his voice, is gentle. "A part of it, anyway, a big part. Everything in your life, every pain, every major event, it all connects to Antony's murder. I saw it the first time I saw you, standing in the crowd at the rally. That hurt, that scar—it's a part of you, Kareela."

My brows tense, my eyes hot and wet, but I don't blink, don't let a tear fall. Who is this man who thinks he knows me? My fists clench. Thinks he can tell me my own life? I open my mouth to tell him he's wrong, that Antony doesn't define me, except—my mouth closes, my chest rises, then falls—he does.

"Even the career you chose. Where you chose it. Working in a province whose history is more rife with anti-Black racism, with tense Black/white relations, than any in the entire country. In a neighbour-hood that epitomizes it. That wasn't an accident, Kareela."

My fists unfurl.

"The best way to heal," says Carson, standing, "to make meaning out of this kind of loss, is to not let his death be for nothing. Yes, I'm asking you to do this for the movement. But that's not why I'm here, invading your privacy. I'm here for you. Because this is how you can take this tragedy, which has defined you, and turn it around, define yourself. You came to the rally, the meetings. You've been giving of your time, your energy. You're the one who's shown you wanted to take this tragedy and turn it into something else, in the hope, I imag-ine, that others won't have to face the same pain."

"You're wrong," I spout. "It didn't have anything to do with that. I just wanted . . . wanted . . ." I look to the floor, my shoulders heav-ing, determined that my life can be about more than Antony without doing what he says. "Somewhere to belong. For once in my life, some-where to belong." That was why I broke the promise, took the risk that brought me to this moment. "It wasn't about Antony. It wasn't even about helping. It was about having a community. Not always feeling so split, so on the outside. It was about . . ." I breathe and look up. "It was about me. Only me."

He nods and lifts his hands, palms out. "All right. You know you. And if that's your why, fine. I'll take it." He stands and steps toward me, places his hands on my shoulders. "And you belong, Kareela." My chest fills. "You are one of us." My lungs a balloon too big for this small cavity.

The door handle clicks. Our heads snap toward it and the balloon deflates, taking that brief feeling of hope and fear and joy with it.

Eyes wide with hurt and the anger of betrayal, Thomas looks from Carson to me. Me to Carson. His shoulders square as Carson's hands fall from my exposed skin. Thomas is not short. But next to Carson's height and broad frame, he looks it. His gaze meets mine. "Is this why?"

My brain seems to short-circuit as it switches from these last minutes with Carson to Thomas's question, to what he could mean, and then suddenly, it clicks. "No! No, that's not . . . no."

"Who are you?" Thomas turns to Carson. "What are you doing here?"

Carson extends his hand. "Carson Downey. I know Kareela from the Black Lives Matter meetings." Thomas looks at the hand but doesn't take it. Carson draws it back. "I just stopped by to talk to Kareela about an upcoming rally, but I'll be leaving now." He turns to me, probably thinking Thomas is some jealous monster, no way of knowing why Thomas is thinking what he's thinking. "Kareela, there is no one in this city whose words would mean more than yours, would have more power, but with all you've been through, I understand if you don't want to share that power. Because you're right, it is a risk." He smiles. "You're doing good work. Whether it's with us or not, and on whatever level you'd like it to be, I'm sure you always will." He steps back, one foot, two, approaching the door. "Just think on it. The rally's not for a couple of months. If you change your mind, great. If you don't, great. Just don't stay away because of what I've asked. Most of all, we want you, not your story. You have a community with us. A family." He stops, his smile deepening. "I mean that, Kareela. You belong. Always."

I nod, but don't speak, my throat tight. Uncertainty pounding. Because I'm no longer sure how true my words are, what the full reason was that kept me going back.

"Nice to meet you, brother." Carson steps forward to clamp Thomas's shoulder, and Thomas's entire body tenses as he shrugs off the touch. After a sidelong glance at Thomas, Carson looks at me. "Are you okay? Should I stay?"

I shake my head, but that doesn't seem enough to make him move. "Go," I say. "I'm fine. And thank you." With another wary look toward Thomas, Carson nods, then steps to the door.

Once he's gone, Thomas turns to me. "What the hell was that?"

"Nothing." Exhaustion floods me.

"It was not nothing. What was he asking you? What did he want?"

I hesitate, unsure how to explain. "To talk at a rally, about Antony, about . . ." I shake my head, weighted by all the reasons I can't share my story, but all the reasons I should, why I want to. "You wouldn't understand."

Thomas steps back, the emotions crossing his face even more pained than the ones when he walked through the door. "Maybe I could," he says, "if you'd open up. Give me a chance. Hurt, betrayal, fear, they don't just belong to you, Kareela. You're not the only one."

Regret slaps me. "Thomas, I—"

"Nah." He scrunches his face, anger brimming behind the moisture in his eyes. "Forgot my laptop." He crosses the room, then reaches for the drawer under the coffee table. He's just about to pass me when he stops. "Figure out your shit, Kareela. Figure out what you want." He pauses, his Adam's apple working, his body so tense he reminds me of a jack-in-the-box just before it pops. "Or those choices will be made for you."

&

THE DOOR CLOSES gently, and I almost wish Thomas had slammed it. Wish I had a reason to feel anger toward him: for his unreasonableness, for demanding that I make a decision I feel unready to make. But he's right. I need to make it. Have the baby, or don't. Each is a choice I don't know how I'll live with, each is one that will define my life going forward.

The way Carson's request would define it. And if I decide to go ahead with one of these choices before me, how could I possibly go ahead with the other? If I have this baby, I could go to the rallies, help behind the scenes. But it's hard enough to be a mother in this world, let alone a Black mother—or at least visibly so. To be BLM's spokesperson as well, to add any more reason to fear, would be beyond foolish. Self-harm at its finest.

I sink to the chair, look to my open laptop—all those files representing all those lives, each with their own trauma—and feel ill-equipped to help anyone right now. I slouch, the load of all these decisions depleting me.

Carson was right. Whether I like it or not, whether I want to admit it or not, Antony's death has determined my identity, influencing almost every choice I've ever made. Gran told me not to change any part of myself to make others comfortable—the way my father obviously had, with his speech, his clothing, his refusal, until those last days, to try to stand up to the way people treated us. But after those boys made me realize how easily Antony's fate could become mine, I understood my father's actions. I became a chameleon: being accepted, finding places to belong, seemed pivotal to my survival.

I think to the flat iron and how it took two years of living in

Halifax before I had the courage to stop using it, to the clothes my mother purchased at the local department store that never felt like me, but made me more like them—the girls in my class who became my friends, who welcomed me in when I stopped caring about who I was but moulded myself to who I thought they wanted me to be, who my mother wanted me to become before she stopped bothering to care: a person who seemed less at risk.

I think of Thomas, of how I observed him in those early days, moulded my preferences to his: dancing along to electronica, pretending it was something I could enjoy; keeping track of upcoming superhero movies and seeing them all in the theatre, a tub of popcorn between us; following tennis, and true-crime shows—acting interested and involved, while baffled that people wanted to expose themselves to such sadness and depravity when life has more than enough.

Even the BLM volunteering, as I just revealed to Carson, was more about wanting a community and acceptance than about passion for the cause—about making them believe I was interested, so they'd be interested in me. Yet somewhere along the way . . .

I'm pacing again, desperate for some outlet to all this coiled energy, needing to make at least one decision—one choice—for me. And from that choice, hopefully, others will come—like falling dominoes, forcing me to figure out my life: Who I am. Who I want to be. I pull out the pamphlet on abortion the doctor gave me, stare at the number. This is it. I'll make this decision, and then I won't falter. It's like Thomas said, if seeing that image on the screen, hearing that heartbeat didn't make up my mind, what will? I continue to stare at the number, my own heart beating almost as fast as the baby's did. One true decision. A choice based entirely on what I want for my life.

I stuff the pamphlet in my purse and dial.

Violet

Then there be Chevelle. Sweet, sweet Chevelle. Me last baby, me change-o'-life baby, whose father thought me past all that—who such a wretch, I'd never speak his name except to spit it in the dirt. But Chevelle not like him. She never hurt a fly in she whole life. She take every spider, every roach even, outside the house to live they life. She so happy, just the sight of her make others happy. She a little simple. Not so good at taking care of herself—forgetting things she should remember. And it take her a long time to find a man. But then she do, she near have she own change-o'-life baby, and she so happy and trusting, she don't even see her man a dog. Don't even believe he give her the clap, that he, more than her advanced age, the reason the baby come early. He the reason her insides like they 'bout to come out. He the reason neither she nor that baby survive. The reason the last of me baby girls under the ground before me.

And me, who shoulda been at home on my island, a host of grand-babies around me, only visiting this cold country a few times a year, living here instead, watching me boy kill heself slow. Trying to stop it, but never quite figuring out how.

Me boy, who I thought be the one to outlast me, who stolen away from me, then had so much of heself stolen, too, so that me one remaining grandbaby got no song to the way she talk, the way she walk. She go to my island, she be a stranger.

But she is who she is.

I is who I is.

That just life. Things get stolen. People get stolen. Along with the parts of us that never should.

And we all make mistakes, cause hurts. I got a lot wrong, despite trying to do right, to protect me babies—the ones I birthed and the ones I didn't.

But there no point dwelling on the shoulda woulda couldas.

That life.

And now I gotta do what I can to protect these ones I have left. The daughters not born through me, but still of me.

Do what I can to help them heal.

Kareela

Phone in hand, the abortion pamphlet stuffed back in my purse, I hear my mother's uncertain hello. "Mom." I take a deep breath. "I'll take in Gran. Sell the house if you're leaving."

"What?"

My voice wavers, the thought of what I may be taking on—the cost, the consequences—pulsing through me. "That'll help, right? Some of the money should be due to me, because of Dad?"

"No, that's not—" She sighs. "It's late, Kareela. Call in the morning, we'll talk about this then."

"I want to talk about this now, and this is what I want." Gran, who loved me, never expecting anything in return. Gran, who was there when my mother wasn't. "I'll use my share to help pay for whatever extra assistance she needs. I'll take care of her."

"Kareela, you do not need to spend your life taking care of an old woman, that's not what—"

"But it's fine that she upended her life? Left her home, her friends, to come take care of your daughter and husband, because you were too . . ." I hesitate, unable to find the words for what my mother was . . . is . . . weak? pathetic? broken? "Too much of a wreck to do it."

"Kareela."

"No, it's true." The anger I've pushed down so many times bubbles up, propelled by my determination to make this one decision, casting aside the concern that's only recently started to grow. "You checked out on life." Forgetting she had a daughter. Making Antony matter more than anything. More than me. "You gave up, and if it wasn't for Gran, wasn't . . . You stopped being my mom. Antony died and—"

"I tried, Kareela."

"Tried!" A laugh breaks out of me. My mother, doing the bare minimum. Acting like I was a chore. A burden. After we moved, it seemed like maybe things were changing, but then— "You didn't try." I'm yelling now. "Not for me. Not for Dad." Crying. Hating the tears, hating how much she means to me, when, clearly, I mean so little to her.

"Dat enough now." Gran's voice on the line shocks me into silence. "Dat not how it was. Yuh ma did her best, did what she could."

"She didn't."

"She did, baby girl." Gran's voice is firm. "And yuh ma is right. No need of her spending she life taking care of an old woman. And no need of yuh doing dat neither. Me will go in de home. It what best."

"No! Mom! You *should* want to take care of Gran, after all she's done. But I know you're too selfish, too—" I stop, not wanting it to seem like I'm trying to push Gran off on Mom. "It doesn't even matter. I love you, Gran. I'm taking care of you. It's decided."

"Me gonna go to de home," says Gran. "It de best—"

"It's not." Hate filters through the anger. I stand there, shaking, wishing I were staring at my mother, that she could see my eyes as I tell her, at last, how monumentally she's failed. That, when it comes down to it, she's a huge part of why I haven't been able to decide about this baby, because as much as I'm afraid of this shitty world, I'm afraid of myself, that with her as my example, I'd be as awful a mother as she is.

"This is . . ." My hand cramps as I grip the phone. "This isn't only about you, Gran. It's about me. It's about her." My voice shakes. "She lost a child. I get that. But then she was doing better." I stop. "Mom. You were doing better. We were. Then suddenly I didn't matter anymore. Suddenly you could hardly look at me." Yet again, Gran became the one to ask me about classes, friends, arrange the cake and presents for my sweet sixteen, wrap her arms around me the first time a boy broke my heart.

"If Gran hadn't been there—" Doing the cooking, the cleaning, Mom letting her be something between a nanny and a maid. "And now that she needs you, you just . . . Just—"

"KeeKee," says Gran. "Me shouldn't have made such a fuss. Me gonna go somewhere in de city. Near yuh."

"No!" I shout, my frustration about Mom not caring for Gran mixing with my anger about all the years she didn't care for me. "What happened?" I spew, at last asking the question that has lurked on the periphery of my thoughts for years. "When you were doing so good? Why can't you look at me? Touch me. Was it something I did?"

"Kareela." Mom's crying now. Something I haven't seen her do in years. Haven't heard. "It's not—"

The thoughts that, after all these years, had fallen into place just weeks earlier rise again. The accident. Mom's face: swollen and bruised, layers of makeup failing to cover the blotch of colours underneath. Her shoulder dislocated and arm broken. And yet the car . . . nothing but a few scratches and one large dent.

Moving out of Dad's room—and out of his life, in a way she hadn't before.

Avoiding Violet.

Avoiding us all.

Becoming a shell when it came to any emotionality, even worse than Dad had. Even after he started to crawl out of it, tried to pry her out, too.

And all those little signs I'm trained to see of abused women, victimized women, women suffering from PTSD—the tremor of a hand, the slant of a gaze, the unreasonable startle of fear from commonplace noises. All those signs that with my own mother, I've never taken the time to really consider, slam into me.

"The accident."

"What?" Her voice is high, surprised—but unable to hide all she's never said.

"What happened? I never . . . But the car. And you . . ." I can't figure out how to put into words the things I'm finally starting to see. "Something happened, didn't it? Something more than your car swerving off the road." And, cruelly, I almost need this to be true, because then it would mean it wasn't me. Wasn't just that I wasn't enough to assuage her grief. "Something bad." I breathe. "Something that's made you . . . made you . . ."

"It doesn't matter." Her voice is full of such pain, such defeat, that all thoughts of my own pain, my own need for answers, disappear. I know I'm right, that I need to go to her. Now.

Evelyn

Evelyn stood in the back of the auditorium, grinning. The students had pulled it off; the eighth-grader playing Alice was precocious and delightful, not missing a single line despite the near panic attack she'd had before going onstage, saying "Ms. Jackson, I can't do it. I can't!" as Evelyn rubbed her back and assured her she could.

Tweedledee and Tweedledum had performed to uproarious laughter from the crowd, and the cards, a mix of first- to third-graders with the occasional fifth- or sixth-grader to keep them in line, had charmed everyone.

As the curtain fell on the final scene of the end-of-year play, the audience stood with hoots, whistles, and applause. The curtain drew again and the children, smiles so wide it made Evelyn's heart ache, lined up to bow. Evelyn paused in her clapping to wipe stray tears from under her eyes, thankful for these kids, this school, this town that felt like her town for the first time since early childhood.

The only thing that could have made it better would have been if Kingsley and Kareela weren't out of town on opening night. If they'd been there to see what the children had accomplished, what she'd helped them accomplish when the drama teacher's appendix had burst, putting him out of commission for the final few weeks before the show.

She wished Antony had been here, too.

Evelyn collected herself, knowing she needed to get backstage to tell the children how well they'd all done. First, though, she squeezed her way up the aisle to Violet.

"What a riot!" Violet laughed loudly, her teeth on display. "Dem chil'ren. Dey know how to work a crowd!"

"You enjoyed it, then."

"Was a hoot!"

"I'm glad." Evelyn squeezed Violet's upper arm, affection flowing through her. *The sun still rises,* Violet had said all those years ago, and it seemed like maybe, at last, it was. "You remember our neighbour is driving you? I need to help with the pull-down."

"Yes, yes." Violet waved a hand in front of Evelyn. "Be off with yuh, nuh."

Evelyn smiled her farewell, then hurried backstage, a cluster of children rushing toward her, laughing, smiling, hugging, their rouged cheeks and defined brows looking darling instead of ridiculous.

ALMOST AN HOUR later, Evelyn waved farewell to the principal and ran across the parking lot to her car. The rain had come from nowhere, the afternoon's warm blue skies shifting to a ceiling of grey that had turned what should have been the last hour of twilight into artificial night. Thunder erupted as Evelyn turned on the ignition. Sheet lightning lit up the sky. Evelyn eased onto the lonely highway leading to their road. She swallowed, the muscles in her back tightening. She'd always loved thunder and the sudden, skin-tingling bursts of light in the sky just before it. But not while she was driving. After each flash, the unlit road seemed darker than before. The wipers were on full speed, but still she struggled to see the faded dividing line, barely visible beneath the coat of water glinting on the asphalt.

She tried to think of good things to distract herself—she'd read about this in some magazine. *To combat stress and fear, think of the good things in your life. The things that give you peace and joy.* She'd scoffed at first, but then she tried it, and it helped. She thought of Kareela these past months, the way she'd stopped dressing like she'd stepped out of a hip-hop video and actually wore the clothing Evelyn had bought her at the beginning of the year. How she'd given in to a flat iron and, every few days, let Evelyn spend hours straightening her hair. How she'd started walking, talking, laughing like the other girls. Evelyn couldn't say she liked the upward lilt that made every sentence sound like a question, but she liked that Kareela was making an effort, that as a result, she was making friends. The incident with those boys had been awful, but—

Evelyn screamed and swerved as a deer appeared in her headlights. She struggled to correct her course as the car hydroplaned, then soared across the thin highway, her breath taken in those few seconds of weightlessness. The car landed with a thud in the shallow ditch as Evelyn was thrown forward, then back, the airbag exploding in her face, trapping her. All she could see was white, and then black.

When Evelyn woke, her body seemed one large pulsing ache. Her head throbbed. Her left arm felt numb—she wasn't sure she could move it. With her other arm, Evelyn shoved the deflated airbag to the side and struggled to reach down to release her belt. She blinked, her clouded vision coming into focus. The rain had ceased, a short summer storm that, if it'd come twenty minutes earlier, would have saved her from this. She grasped the door handle and heaved her injured shoulder against it, holding on as it finally opened, almost catapulting her to the forest floor. She yelled in pain, then pushed herself to a high crouch, surveying the vehicle. There'd be no reversing out of this mess. She looked into the car, saw her purse on the floor of the passenger's seat. She limped around the front of the vehicle, her legs like jelly, and wrenched open the door. She scrounged for her mobile, grasped and opened it. Dead. She still used Antony's old flip phone. The reception was atrocious, the battery worse, and she was forever forgetting to charge it, but she liked it. Liked holding something in her hand that Antony had held. Knowing the last words he heard on it were likely hers—even if it was possible they'd done more harm than good.

She dropped the phone back in her bag and slung it over her shoulder. She was at least six kilometres from home. A not impossible feat. But like this? With her whole body a bruise, her head the victim of a jackhammer?

Not seeing another option, she made her way to the road and crossed, hoping before long she'd flag down a helpful soul. It had to have been at least twenty minutes of trudging, her limp arm propped by the other one, before she heard the distant whir, then saw the lights. She stopped on the gravel shoulder and turned, releasing her damaged arm so the other one could wave. A truck slowed, then stopped, the lights shining on her for one breath, three, five, before a door finally opened.

"Thank you. Thank—"

Evelyn's words died in her throat as four men and a teenaged boy stepped out of the vehicle.

"What do we have here?" The years hadn't been kind, but Evelyn recognized him—the boy who, all those decades ago, had called her trash. His son, whom Evelyn had called out, beside him. "Little Evelyn Godfrey. Scrawny little Evelyn Godfrey, who still looks good."

"I just need some help," said Evelyn. "My car." She cradled her arm. "But if you're too busy, I'll keep walking. Flag someone else."

The man, Ashley or Taylor, some name the other school kids had mocked for being feminine, laughed. "Are we too busy, boys?"

Two of the men shook their heads. The teen stared.

"Just like you weren't too busy to talk down to my son. You." He shook his head, spit to the side, a brown watery sludge soaring through the headlight's beam and landing on the asphalt. "I heard you were back in town. With a Black man, and your dirty little half-breed." He turned his head to the men. "Pretty, though, isn't she, for a nigg—" He paused. "Oh, wait." He looked back at Evelyn, mock alarm in his voice. "Better make sure we're politically correct. Wouldn't want to offend, like the boys did. Get you all in a tizzy."

Evelyn's heart raced, hot fear flaring.

"So what's the right term . . ." He scratched his chin as though contemplating, playing it up for the others. Then, his features stretched, as if a light bulb had gone off in his head. "Ah." He grinned. "Pretty, for a Black Canadian."

"It's 'cause she's half." One of the men laughed.

"Oh, a nigg—" Ashley or Taylor or . . . Courtney?—it was Courtney, she was sure of it now—stopped. "Black Canadian's a Black Canadian." He leaned forward, the scent of booze heavy on his breath. "And you know all about them, don't you, Evelyn?" Courtney stepped closer. "All about them." He raised his hand to her chin, grasped it between his thumb and forefinger. Evelyn imagined wrenching her head away, scratching him, kicking, running. But she was frozen. "Maybe what you don't know is what you're missing. Maybe I should teach you." He grabbed her shoulders as Evelyn screamed with the pain on her wrenched one. Her paralysis popped like a tense balloon, and she kicked at him, tried to wrench her good arm free.

"Hold her, boys." Courtney thrust her against the side of the cab, darkness suddenly surrounding her. The men stayed still. "Hold her!" Two of them burst into motion, their hands on her arms, against her thighs. She screamed again as Courtney's large, heavy hand landed on her mouth. With his free hand, he fumbled with her pants and underwear, worked his fingers between her legs and, with a burst of violent, violating pain, thrust them into her. "Wet and ready, boys." He laughed as tears ran down her face, spilled over his fingers. As he withdrew his hand and fumbled with his own zipper, a fresh burst of fear tore through Evelyn. She wrenched her head to the side and bit down hard, the metallic taste of his blood on her tongue. Courtney screamed and jerked his hand away, then sent it back, hitting her on the side of the head. He grabbed her injured arm, yanking her away from the men, and twisted it as she screamed, as her bone snapped, then flung her to the ditch, the gravel digging in as she rolled, then settled.

He stepped toward her, but a voice called out. "That's enough, Court. It isn't worth it."

Courtney stopped. She couldn't see his face, but the light from the truck behind illuminated the way his arms were clenched, his fists tightened.

"Let's get out of here," said another voice. "Anyone could drive by."

Courtney stepped back. "There." His voice was tight, as full of gravel as the arm she lay on. "Now you know what can happen. What *will* happen if you don't keep your mouth shut. To you, or maybe that sexy little half-breed. I bet her cunt is even sweeter and wetter than yours."

Evelyn gritted her teeth. Her lips trembled as she tried to read his eyes in the darkness, to determine if he was just fronting for those men or if he had it in him. If he could do this, or more, to a child.

He started to turn, then spun back, crouched, so his face was mere inches from hers, the scent of earthy-sweet chewing tobacco mixed with cheap beer on his breath. "Don't get any ideas. The sheriff is my brother-in-law. I've got four witnesses who'll say I was out with them all this time, doing whatever I tell them to say we've been doing." He stopped, and in the faint light she could see his eyes darting across her face, as if searching for the words. "Who'd even say you and me, we've been hooking up on the side for months, if that's what I decide to tell them. That you were scared your husband was about to find out, so you crafted another story. That these bruises are from him. That you went and did the same stupid thing as your mama, married a wife-beating drunk, and now you're trying to make someone else pay for it."

He spit to the side of her, his breathing heavy, his eyes glinting in the dim light. Evelyn bit off a groan as she used her good arm to prop herself higher, make it to her knee, level her gaze at his. He was insane if he thought he wouldn't pay for this, thought she'd stay silent. If he wasn't going to kill her, he'd pay. They all would.

"Time to head off, boys." Courtney stood and backed toward the vehicle.

"We can't just leave her."

Evelyn's heart leapt as the man who'd stood beside the boy spoke. Could they kill her? Dispose of her bo—

Courtney turned. "She can walk."

"And if she dies? And the cops check her over? Find bits of you on—"

"Fine!" Courtney threw his hands in the air, then bit his ugly lip.

"We'll drop her off at her house," the man said, and in the turn of his head, the roundness of his voice, she could almost hear a boy from her past. Someone who'd walked over with a Valentine's Day card, who'd smiled at her from across the schoolyard. He faced her square on, and behind the mounds of facial hair, she saw him, how young and sweet and shy he once was. "Then this will be over."

"I don't want her in my truck." Courtney spit again.

"We'll put her in the bed." The man strode past the men who had held her. He placed both hands on her shoulders and led her to the rear of the truck, then opened the back and hoisted her up. She groaned with the jolt. Once up, her whole body shaking, he wrapped his arms around her. The truck pulled onto the highway, and wind whipped around them. He placed his lips beside her ear as Evelyn stiffened. "Go home. Go to sleep." He paused, squeezing her tighter. "Forget about this. Forget all of it." Evelyn stared at the disappearing road, the darkness. "Pretend it never happened. Move on with your life. Lie low and stay safe."

The truck stopped at the turnoff to her road. Courtney appeared before them. "She can walk from here." The other man jumped down, helped her out. "Shower," he whispered. "Get a good night's sleep. In the morning, pretend it never happened."

He turned Evelyn toward her street, then climbed inside the cab. Evelyn didn't wait for the truck to drive off. She ran.

Kareela

Despite my best efforts, I couldn't access a CarShare until the morning, so after a near sleepless night I called in sick to work and journeyed the almost two-hour drive to Juniper Cove, hands gripping the wheel, my foot hard on the gas. When at last I arrived, shaky and fearful, I stepped into the house that never felt like a home, that, for us, was only a false escape.

I had to pull the story out of my mother, and now I sit across from her and Gran, slack-jawed, my eyes burning, my body pulsing. I replay what I've heard, trying to piece together how I got here. How we all did.

"Mom." I turn to her, the tears sliding down my face. "I just . . . all these years, to live with that." My voice quavers. "With what those men did." I hesitate. "Dad never knew?"

She shakes her head.

"You changed after. With him, too."

She looks to the window.

As the days stretched on after the accident, she seemed to want nothing to do with any of us. I thought she was fed up with Dad for settling for a low-paying job, for drinking too much, for being so obviously broken she'd had to pretend she wasn't. Fed up with me, for not being the type of daughter she wanted. For not being enough to make up for Antony. I didn't know what Gran could have done. Eventually, it seemed like hate. As the years went on, more and more like hate. For Dad, for Gran, for me.

"And this was why?"

At first, she'd pushed me away, while reining me in. Never allowing me out alone after dark. Refusing to let me get my own car—driving me everywhere, asking Dad to, or forcing me to rely on friends. Making sure I always had a phone on me. Making sure she knew where I was. No drinking. No parties.

Control. But not love. As if I were a piece of property and it were her responsibility to keep me in one piece. Not a daughter. Not someone to take an interest in, to love.

Eventually, though, the effort to control faded, and once I moved, it was if, being out of her house, I was out of her life. As if she couldn't muster up the energy to care at all anymore.

I thought it'd been about Antony. All that paranoia, about Antony. It had to be—at least in part—the terror of simply existing. The exhaustion of it. But . . .

"The boys from school," I say, needing to know I've gotten it right. Needing to be sure this isn't some bad dream.

"Just one of them." Her gaze is still toward the yard, where one squirrel chases another, their bushy tails zigzagging up a tree. "It wasn't the boy who did it."

But that was why. She doesn't say it, not in words—her silence saying it all. "He recognized you."

"That's not the point, Kareela."

Except it is. And I never saw it. Never tried to. I just hated her, and wanted her, and then hated her all the more for how much I loved her and wanted her to love me. To show it.

I think of what I've just learned, what Rania and Carson told me, too, the terror Mom lived through, again and again, and all at once, my whole life, our relationship, all the ways I've viewed her, seem transformed. "This happened because of me," I say, "because you defended me."

"That's not the point!" She looks toward Gran, and so many moments throughout the years flood back to me. Moments that made me think my mother hated me, the side of me that wasn't like her. Hated my father, for the colour of our skin. For what it had done to us. To Antony. Moments that made me believe she felt she'd made a mistake in marrying Dad, having his children.

And maybe she did. "Mom?" Maybe this was just one more reason.

Late afternoon light streams through the living room window, highlighting the dust particles' dance. Mom looks sidelong at Gran, then returns her gaze to the window. "Now you know, Kareela." Her hands slide across her middle, her chin high, her body slightly, so slightly I hardly see it, shaking. "Make of it what you will, and beyond that, let's just drop it."

"Mom." I cross the room and kneel beside her chair. "You have to report this."

She shakes her head, her lips tight, her back rigid, her body turned from mine. "Report what, Kareela? He didn't . . . He didn't actually . . . anyway, it's too late."

"He violated you. The other men helped, and they're still out there, they could do it to—"

Mom swivels, her gaze meeting mine. "That's not my responsibility. My life is my responsibility. And there's nothing to say he'll do it again. It was an isolated incident. He was angry. Probably drunk.

When I talked to those boys—to his son—I hurt their pride. I hurt their sense of how they believed the world should be."

A sick tremor surges through me. "Are you defending them?"

"I'm just saying—" Her voice rises. She shakes her head, inhales, as her speech returns to a level pitch. "The fact that he did . . . what he did . . . to me . . . it doesn't mean he'll do it to anyone else. They were trying to make a point."

"Mom." Emotion courses through me. Fear. Anger. Desperation. And understanding. So much understanding. First Jamaica, then Antony, then this. "Mom, you're wrong. You have no idea what else they've done, or what they'll do. And regardless, you matter. What they did to you has no justification. You have to report it."

"It's too late."

"No."

"It was too long ago."

I pause, not knowing how much to press, still trying to make sense of so much. "I don't . . ." I look between them, then lean forward. "Why didn't you tell us? Why didn't you go to the police then? Why didn't you try?"

"It was a different time!" She raises her hands in frustration, avoiding Gran's gaze. Avoiding mine. "Now you know why I fell apart again. Please, let's just leave it at that."

"You could get help. Justice."

She laughs. "Justice?" Then shakes her head. "They'll think I'm an old woman making up stories, trying to get attention for something that happened—"

"No. Listen." I grab Mom's arm. "It's not like that. People won't see it like that. They'll believe you. They'll understand how much harder it would have been back then. He forced his fingers inside you. That is rape. You have to—"

"Enough!" She stands, her body shaking. "I'm done talking about this."

"Tell her de rest." Gran's voice rises from the silence, her gaze on Mom. "Your ma, she wanted to go to de police, she would have—"

"I said enough!" Mom's fists clench. "It doesn't—"

"It all connects," says Gran. "How yuh become. De fact yuh done with me now."

"What?" I look between them.

Gran looks to the ceiling, her bottom lip shaking. "What me did to yuh, to all of yuh. How me split dis family." Now she looks to me. "Yuh mammy was tryin to put yuh all back togetha, comin here, and it was workin. Then me, with me plan, broke it all to pieces, thinkin I was keepin it togetha."

"So you admit it!" Mom stands. "After all these years. How you put Kareela and Kingsley ahead of me. Protecting them, always them, instead of me. Letting those men get away with it. Even after you saw how I was failing. How much I needed you—" She's shaking, arms rigid, eyes moist. "I needed you to give me permission to speak. To tell me I deserved protection, too. Help, too."

I look between them, a cauldron of hurt and confusion boiling. Gran's eyes widen. "No, that not—"

"You never brought it up again," continues Mom. "Never asked me how I was doing. You told me to forget it and acted like you did, too." She stops. Breath heavy. Jaw twitching. "Maybe if I could have talked to you about it, had someone to—" She casts the back of her hand below her cheeks, clearing the evidence of the tears she's let fall. "You left me all alone with it!" my mom half yells, half cries. "You deserted me. You were supposed to love me, too, be there for me, too. And now, what, you want me to explain why I kept silent? When you're the one who convinced me?"

Gran stands, shakily, her arms out, waving, as if she's trying to wave away Mom's words.

"Tell her," Mom continues, gesturing to me before turning back to Gran, "lay all my secrets bare. Protect her again, so she won't have the burden of hating her mother even more for being done with you, for not devoting the rest of my life to someone who cared so little about me." She takes a breath, her voice lowering. "Well, hate is hate. Should it matter how much? But still you push. Despite me saying enough is enough. Despite me saying the past could stay there, just like you wanted." Mom shakes her head. "It's always about them. About protecting them. And I get it—" Her breath hitches. "I decided to protect them, too. But I needed you, in at least some small way, to be there for me, to protect me, too."

Gran takes another step forward, her lips pressed in a quiver, an expression on her face that seems to indicate she's fighting not to see years of her life, their life, transformed as the scales drop from her eyes. Her outstretched arm grasps Mom's. "It about you." Her voice is strained, confused. "Me use Kareela and Kingsley to convince yuh, and yes, it about dem a bit, but mostly it be about you. For you. So yuh didn't have to go up against dat man. Dose men, who woulda called yuh a liar. So yuh didn't have to see dey faces, de face of yuh coworkers, once de whispers started, of yuh neighbours, as yuh stepped into suddenly silenced rooms, knowing de last name on dey lips was yours. I was silent, told yuh to be silent, to protect yuh."

Mom steps back, anger, and something else—disbelief?—emanating from her like waves.

Gran drops her arm and pulls it to her middle. "Me was here, takin care of yuh. Of yuh family. Me didn't bring it up because a wound isn't helped by cutting it open, but by leaving it to heal."

Mom laughs again. Dry and caustic. "Unless it's infected." She flings her hand forward, as if throwing the words. "Then leaving it lets it fester."

"Me thought—"

"I don't care anymore." Mom swallows, her shoulders straightening. "I told you I was done, and I am." She turns from us, crosses the hall, and disappears up the stairs.

"Me thought me was helping her heal."

"Gran?" I pivot, my stomach tight, my throat raw, the pain of this, of all of it, like an ocean above us.

Gran shifts her head, her gaze focused on something I can't pinpoint. "Me suppose after a time, me knew de healing wasn't happening. Not as it should. Dese t'ings. No one ever really heals. But we move on, and dey become a blip in de length of a life. A moment of bad amidst all de moments of good. Or dey can. Me thought dey should. Dey would. If we kept silent. But me shoulda known. She not like me." Gran pauses, her gaze still focused on something I can't see. "She never wanna talk with me again, 'bout anyt'ing, so me thought me what make it worse: me knowing. That she avoiding me because she afraid me gonna bring it up, to her, or maybe to yuh Daddy. Me thought she didn't want to talk about it. Just like she never want to talk about she boy—de good parts or de bad. So me give her space, and—"

"Gran." I step toward her. "What was Mom talking about? What did you have to do with all of this?"

Gran turns to me, her expression almost stunned, as if she just remembered I am in the room. "De most important t'ing," she says, "is nuh to be mad at her. It not yuh motha who created all this sadness. All this hurt. It me. Me and dose men. All dose men." She pauses. Looking older. Smaller. She reaches her hand out, gesturing for me to join her on the couch. "And me understand if dis not somethin yuh can forgive—stealing yuh mama from yuh like dat. Lettin her break." Another pause. "But me thought me was doing what would prevent worse breaking."

My chest sinks. Outside, the leaves sway, the clouds shift in their slow-motion journey across the sky. "Gran, what did—"

"I'll tell yuh de rest." She turns to the window, a sigh lifting then settling her thin shoulders. "Yuh motha, she be frantic when she come in. Plannin to call de police. But den . . ."

Evelyn

Blinded by tears, fear, pain, Evelyn ran, stumbling. When she reached the door, she fumbled at the lock, dropped her keys, cursed, struggled again. The door opened.

"Ev—"

Evelyn fell into Violet's arms, the sobs coming hard and heavy.

"Evelyn." Violet looked past her. "Where yuh car? What happen?"

Once she was seated on the couch, Evelyn recounted the story: from the rain, to the deer, to Courtney and the other men. The boy.

"From de high school," said Violet. "One a dem boys yuh tell me about, who surround we girl? Who said all a dem t'ings?"

Evelyn nodded and continued.

Violet held Evelyn's hand. She caressed her good shoulder. When she was done, Evelyn began to stand. "We need to go to the police." She hesitated, remembering she had no car. "Or call. I need to call the—" Violet's hand, still holding Evelyn's, tugged her to sit.

"No, sweet girl. Me don't t'ink—"

"What?"

"T'ink on de cross on dat yard up de Valley," said Violet, her gaze firm. "De burning."

"Near Windsor? What does that—"

"Dey a mixed family, too." Violet placed her other hand around Evelyn's, gripping it. "T'ink on what happen to Kareela. Dese times. Dese places. De man who whispered to yuh, maybe he right. Maybe it time to call this done."

Evelyn yanked her hand from Violet's as disbelief, fear, flooded her. "I need to report this. That's what will protect Kareela. To see these men in jail."

Violet leaned forward. "It like what yuh told me, when dat officer come to yuh door years ago. When yuh stopped trying to fight." She shook her head. "Four men's voices to yours. White men. With him threat."

"No." Evelyn turned to the kitchen again. "No, this is different. I was attacked. And he couldn't blame it on Kingsley. Kingsley's away! And there'd be evidence. DNA, maybe. The best thing to do is—"

"A trial?" interrupted Violet. "De town all knowing. Kingsley knowing. Kareela, too?"

Evelyn's chest thrummed. Her mouth went dry.

"Dey been through so much."

I've been through so much, Evelyn yelled silently, reliving his hands on her. His fingers inside her.

"Kingsley, he so fragile."

I'm so fragile, she shouted back. *What about me?*

"Dey hate we all so much, already," said Violet. "Some a dem. Too many a dem. Yuh don't wanna give dem reason to hate we more."

Evelyn stared at Violet with the hope that she couldn't mean what she was saying. But hope was frail, like a moth in the wind.

"Dese things, dey happen. Dey shouldn't happen. But dey do. And yuh lucky it wasn't worse. Yuh brave to stop him. Be a different kind of brave now. Put it behind yuh, like de other man said. Stand strong, like yuh have been. And maybe dat enough to show dese wicked men dey didn't break yuh. To show yuh have de power. Not dem."

Evelyn averted her gaze, the thrum in her chest making her sick.

"Clean yuhself up," said Violet. "Me gonna draw a bath. Then yuh get some sleep. And t'ink on it. T'ink of yuh man and dat sweet girl comin home tomorrow. Seeing yuh. T'ink on whether yuh want dem to see a wife and motha who been in an accident, or a wife and motha who been through this night, who about to take yuh all through de gates o' hell."

Evelyn opened her mouth to speak, but the air seemed pulled from her. She struggled to breathe, let alone talk, a deep wrench in her throat. *What about me?* like a track on repeat in her mind.

She eased against the back of the couch, the pain in her body finally taking over, making her feel faint. "I think my arm is broken."

"Okay." Violet pulled her up. "So we clean yuh up. Then we get to de hospital, not de police." She led Evelyn to the bathroom, put the stopper in the tub, pulled essential oils from the cabinet—Jamaican wild mint, cinnamon leaf, sweet orange peel—letting the drops mix with the water. She helped Evelyn undress, cautiously, then assisted as Evelyn stepped into the claw-foot tub. She wet a cloth and rubbed Evelyn's skin in a way Evelyn hadn't felt since early childhood, singing softly. Violet cleansed, as Evelyn shook.

Kareela

I sit and listen, imagine my mother in that moment, after all she'd been through. Knowing what she needed to do, should have done, being strong and brave enough to do it, and then being told—even if it was only a tactic on Gran's part—that she didn't matter, only Dad and I did. That she needed to forget, move on from what had happened.

For us.

I pull my hand from Gran's and shift away as she speaks, tells me the rest of the story. The police at the hospital, ready to help. The doctor suspecting. How Gran dismissed their concerns. Whether she meant to or not, dismissed my mother—her pain, her need for justice, for validation of this trauma.

When she finishes, Gran raises her gaze. "Me thought me was doin what was right. For yuh, yuh fatha. Yuh motha, too. Most of all, yuh motha. Me thought me needed to stress it be for yuh, 'cause she so determined. And she had no idea what woulda come. How bad it could be for a woman. De aftermath. Worse, maybe, than de actual assault, when everyone know. How it make yuh relive it, again and again. Make yuh question every choice yuh made to lead yuh to it, every choice during it." She wrings her hands. "Truly, me was tryin to protect her."

The pressure in my head is a thousand knives battling to force their way out. I stand, distancing myself from Gran, this woman who is more of a mother to me than I have any clear memory of my mother being. This woman I'm about to change my life for.

My eyes close. I want to yell, tell her this wasn't her choice to make. That it should have been my mother's, only my mother's. That she did wrong. That I didn't ask for this protection or want it, and neither did Dad. That it wasn't the type of protection my mother needed.

Instead, I choose my words carefully, make my voice as even and calm as I can. "I need to see Mom."

I stand, aware of all Gran's done, all she's been—for me—aware that nothing she's told me erases that. I caress her shoulder as I walk past and hope my barely there touch conveys the love I can't speak.

Evelyn

JUNIPER COVE

2022

Evelyn took the old creaking steps to the room she'd slept in as a child, the room she started sleeping in again after that night—the shame of Courtney's touch, the secret of it, making it impossible to lie beside her husband.

When she had gotten out of the bath that night, she called a cab, then went to the hospital, Violet beside her, patting her hand. She told the intake nurse about the deer. A cop was called, and she told him approximately where the car swerved.

He looked at his chart. At her address, she presumed. "And how did you get home? That's a long walk."

"I . . ." Her voice shook. Her stomach clenched. "I walked some. Then someone picked me up."

"Why didn't they take you to the hospital? Why didn't they call us?"

Violet squeezed her hand. Evelyn lowered her gaze.

"De woman shook up," said Violet. "De woman just want to get home."

"Is that true, Mrs. Jackson?"

Evelyn nodded.

The officer stood, silent. "Mrs. Jackson?"

Evelyn raised her gaze.

"Were you drinking this evening?"

She shook her head as Violet leaned forward, her finger wagging. "She not drinking! She scared. Yuh see dat bump on she head? She not t'inking straight. Or straight as she should. She t'inking home. She need to get on home."

After several more questions, the officer left, saying he'd send someone out to find her car, tow it to the town's mechanic. She was led to an X-ray machine, then returned to the room, where a light shone in her eyes once, twice. Fingers were raised in front of her face, reminding her of other fingers. Cold tingles poured over Evelyn. Her stomach turned at the thought of Courtney's smirk, the sweaty nicotine taste of his hand on her mouth. His fingers as—

The doctor hesitated, his hands lingering on her exposed arm.

"Mrs. Jackson, these bruises?"

Her breath. She needed to focus on her breath. Not the blur of the room, or the doctor's words. Focus on what Courtney had threatened, what Violet had cautioned: if she told what happened, the pain would go on for months, years, not just for her but for her husband, her daughter, who had been doing so well.

"Mrs. Jackson."

The whole town against them, Violet had said. Standing with their own, the way they had when Evelyn's mother lay beaten and bruised.

The words squeezed through her throat, burning. "They're from the accident."

"These look like handprints, Mrs. Jackson. Fingers. And the break in your arm. It's a spiral fracture. I don't see how—"

The whole town doing nothing. Letting it go on, year after year. Until her mother, broken and bruised, took the ultimate escape.

"If you're in trouble, Mrs. Jackson—"

And they'd likely do the same thing now, with not only Kingsley as collateral damage, but Kareela, too, knowing about it all. Dragged through all that would come.

"Mrs. Jack—"

"The accident! It's all from the accident!"

The doctor stared, silent. He set Evelyn's shoulder, which burst with pain. Set her arm. Cold wrapped around her, pulsing through her veins as he placed the cast.

That night, Evelyn crossed the hall to her childhood bedroom— set up and ready for all the guests they never had, never would. She crawled into the bed, then curled her knees up to her chest, the way she had so many years before.

When Kingsley and Kareela arrived home from the Model UN the next morning, full of concern, looking at her like a cracked vase, she brushed off her bruises, the cast, her sling. She forced a joke, determined to brush off their worries, too. "You think I look bad? You should see the car!" She forced a smile, congratulating Kareela on her second-place win at the conference. She asked about their visit to the harbour, the Citadel. She continued to smile as Kareela told her about the Black people there, that there'd been at least five others just in the Model UN. And in the streets, at the restaurant.

"People didn't stare." Kareela laughed, as Evelyn fought not to cry. "At first I couldn't figure out what felt different, weird, and then I realized that all day, not a single person had stared."

Evelyn looked to Kingsley, who was smiling as he clapped his hand on Kareela's shoulder, and wondered if maybe Violet was right. If her pretending it didn't happen was the right thing: for them, at least.

"It was a good trip," said Kingsley, wearing a more genuine smile than Evelyn had seen in years. "A nice place. We should go there again, as a family."

Evelyn nodded, imagining Courtney. His threat. His eyes. She held her smile.

After lunch, Evelyn took to her bed, saying she was tired, that the accident had taken more out of her than she'd realized. She stayed there, missing three days of work, and then four, missing the final performance of *Alice in Wonderland*, the chance to sit beside her husband and child as they witnessed her accomplishment. When Kingsley wasn't at work, he brought her food and drinks. He propped up her pillows and kissed her forehead, telling her how glad he was she was okay, that nothing worse had happened. Evelyn nodded as tears slid down her face, as unsaid words pulsed in her throat.

She determined she'd made the right choice. And that should be enough to help her through this. After a week and a half in bed, she forced herself to get up and out the door for the final week of school. Her bruises had faded from pink to purple to green, and makeup hid them. Mostly. After entering the kitchen for the first time in ten days, she flinched at Kingsley's touch as he placed his hand on the small of her back. She'd wanted this for so long—his attention, his concern, his ability to step out of his own grief to see theirs, to see his family again—but now . . .

"It good to see yuh up." Violet turned to her, smiling, as if all Evelyn had been through was an accident—something that injured her body, shook her up. Something she could overcome with a few days' rest.

Her head throbbing, her limbs still tense from the way Kingsley's touch had felt like a violation, Evelyn looked away from Violet, the break she felt between them too painful for words. The hurt too vivid.

In the weeks to come, her confidence that she was doing the right thing—for her—faltered time and time again. She didn't know how many times she picked up the phone. Once, she dialed the first six numbers—to report those men, seek justice for what they had done.

To not be this woman, trapped inside herself, made weaker than she ever was, broken, at almost the exact moment she'd finally believed becoming whole again was possible.

But Kareela had a handful of close friends now and was actually looking forward to school next year. Kingsley had been switched to the day shift. Instead of spending his evenings in front of the TV, a drink in hand, he was updating his book, determined to try again, to sell it as a textbook on medical sciences, all his years of teaching now focused on sharing the methods his students had once thrived under. He drank, but less. He asked her about her day, asked when she was coming back to their room.

"When it hurts less," she'd said—her words implying she meant physically—"when I don't toss and turn from the ache."

He kissed her temple, smiling sympathetically, then asked the next week, and the next, until she'd snapped at him, told him she'd come back when she came back, anger at herself for treating him this way flaring more furiously than the anger with which she'd lashed out at him.

She never went back.

But still he tended to her, made small but noticeable efforts to show he cared for her. He was, at least a little, becoming the man she remembered, taking on the role in their family and in Kareela's life that he'd left for Evelyn, and then Violet, to fulfill. As if Evelyn giving in to debilitating grief had snapped him out of his. It's what she'd wanted all these years. Craved. Thought would be the thing that would help them heal, become *them* again.

But trapped in this prison of fear, living the assault over and over, the most she could do for him, for her family, was to set the phone back in its cradle, wondering if her mother had picked up this same phone only to set it back down, too. If she'd debated the way Evelyn did. If her father, like Courtney, had made threats. If Helen, too, had told herself the violation, the abuse, wasn't as bad as it could have been, so wasn't worth the pain reporting it would bring. If, as a result, Helen had felt so small, so weak and insignificant, so shamed by her own silence, she stopped thinking she even deserved to pick up the phone, deserved justice.

Eventually, Evelyn learned how to give the appearance of functioning, but she'd lost the desire to be who she'd been becoming. She became, instead, a person who tensed each time a car slowed near their drive, who saw danger everywhere, feared each step outside her own front door—for herself, Kareela, Kingsley. Who lay awake at night, reliving the way Courtney's hands had been on her, *in her*, and the hands of the other men, too, as they'd held her down. Who spent each breath waiting for the moment her attacker and his men, or some other danger, would finally come. Who sank into this endless cycle of terror, this pain, all the pains that had come her whole life long, until she was in too deep to feel much of anything. To care. To love, as she once had.

Because she knew, now, loving was dangerous.

Footsteps outside the door snapped Evelyn back to the present.

"Mom?"

Her throat tightened. At the window seat, Evelyn pulled her legs up to her chest and wrapped her arms tight around herself.

"Mom?"

She told her daughter to go, but the door opened.

Kareela

I take the stairs to my mother's room slowly, the weight of all that I've learned making my steps heavy. All the memories, the hurts, the frustrations, turn over in my mind and are rewritten with a new script, one that highlights the perspective of this woman whose side I haven't bothered to see.

I've been blind to her pain, thinking only of my loss, my father's—how the violence against Antony seemed a harbinger of the ever-present threat against us. That Mom's skin protected her from that. That, in some small way, her skin made her complicit in what happened. Yes, she lost her child, and I saw the pain of that, but my father lost not only his son, but his career, his respect, his sense of purpose in the world. I lost my brother, my home, my friends, her. And she was responsible for those final three. I hated her for bringing us to this place, hated her for checking out again, after teasing us into thinking things were about to get better.

So I didn't see the signs, even when I should have—after I'd been trained to. Even though, despite the hate, I loved her, too.

I stand outside her door, my throat tight. I lift my arm, then knock. "Mom?"

"Leave me be, Kareela. Please."

I turn the knob anyway, step through. My mother sits on the window seat.

"I'm sorry, Mom." I lean against the sill, not sure exactly what I'm apologizing for—that I didn't take the time to ask her what was wrong, ever? That, because of the hatred of the world, she became a victim of her choices: marrying my father, having us as children, everything that followed? That I thought of her, in some small way, as complicit, that the loss of Antony would have harmed her less, or should have.

Seeing her now, thinking these thoughts in a more concrete way than I ever have before, the foolishness in them is clear. If my mother were in any way complicit, then wouldn't I be, too? At least half as much. Wouldn't Antony?

I lean forward and rest a hand on her leg. I feel more than see her stiffen.

Here I've been victimizing myself, trapped in my decision of whether to be with Thomas, to have his child in a world that's so much better than the one my mother started that phase of her life in, never even considering the parallels and divergences.

Shame filters through me. I've been afraid that in having a child with Thomas, I'll miss out on the identity I think I crave. She feared for her life, her safety, her children's.

"Gran never should have done that."

She remains silent, face toward the window.

"She should have stood up for you. We would have stood up for you."

She pulls her knees to her chest, like a child.

"You loved us, right?" My bottom lip quivers. I bite to keep it steady. "And it wasn't the way we would have wanted you to show it, but that's why you did it?"

She's still, as if I'm a ghost, as if my words haven't passed the veil between two parallel universes.

"Do you love us now?" I ask, desperate. "Me?"

"Kareela." She shakes her head, looks at me at last. "To ask such a thing."

"Do you regret us?"

She continues to look, as if seeing me for the first time in years—angst in her eyes.

Every muscle in my face tightens. "Mom. Do you regret us? If you hadn't met Dad, if you hadn't had me, Antony, your life would have been so different. He died and then . . . it's like you hated me. The part of me that came from Dad. That was like Antony. It's like you wanted to rip it out, erase it, and when you learned you couldn't, you just—"

"I love you, Kareela," she says, yet doesn't deny the regret. And that lack is a scimitar, cutting open my deepest fears. "Your brother, you, your father, you brought me joy." She pauses, and I can't help but wonder if she's omitting the word *once*. "I would never change those memories."

But the others . . . "Mom?"

"Kareela." Her voice is a whisper, soft and tired. Like her grief is a tsunami. Like she's already drowned.

That tsunami swallowed my father and, my whole life, has been threatening to swallow me.

I stand, step away from her, realizing as I do, that yet again, I've made this about me. My pain. My fears.

In his final days, after being stuck in the house for months, my father sat on the couch, unshaven, watching that video over and over again. I yelled at him to put the tablet down, stop watching, let it go. With bloodshot eyes he stared at me, his voice slipping into the lilt of his childhood. *Let him go? My son?* Yanking back the tablet, he shook it at me. *They do this. And there nothing done to dem. Nothing, yuh hear! Let him go?* Slamming his chest. *He here always. He everywhere.*

Days later, when the rallies were happening in every major city, in ours—not two hours away—despite a part of me being thrilled to see some spark of energy in him, some passion after the weeks of keeping his eyes glued to the tablet, of drinking more and more each day, I told him to stay home. Told him the virus was too dangerous. That he couldn't drive, drunk like he was.

I should have bought masks and driven us there. I should have embraced him, telling him how much I missed Antony, too.

Instead, I directed him to the couch, disdain in my voice that was as much for me as him, for my fear of the riots, the beatings, the shootings that occurred in the wake of this tragedy, for the fact that he, who after all we'd been through, after years of seeming somewhat better, of at least remembering I was alive, was now willing to put himself at risk.

In telling him no, I—just like everyone and everything else— helped kill him.

My mother, at least, has survived. She, at least, is still here, despite it seeming the opposite. I shift closer, hesitate, then throw my arms around her, for being here. Maybe not in the way I've wanted. But here. For trying—in her own way, as much and as well as she could— to protect me.

She stiffens, freezes, for one second, two, before quickly, almost cautiously, hugging me back. But before I've barely registered the faint pressure of her arms, she pushes me away.

"Kareela." She straightens, her voice shaking. "It was long ago. All of it. I'm fine, now. And I love you, of course . . ." Her voice trails off. "But I'd really appreciate some time alone. So, please, can you give me that?"

I stare, wanting to pummel her for the way she's pushed me away, yet again. Wanting to scream. But also wanting to wrap my arms around her once more, forcing her to submit to my embrace—for what she's been through, for the fact that this is the first time I've taken the time to care.

Instead, I respect her wishes and step to the door, all the words I've never said, the words I wish I could, stuck in my throat.

Evelyn

JUNIPER COVE

2022

Evelyn's head pressed against the aged wood of the window frame. Her eyes closed. Shame flowed through her. Hate. For life. For the way it unfolded. For herself.

A woman who, after all that had happened, just pushed her daughter, her one remaining child, out of her arms. Who'd hesitated in telling her she loved her.

Before that night, she'd been doing so well, had started to truly embrace the fresh start she thought the move to Nova Scotia had given her, but the attack—that final thrust of the knife in what felt like a lifetime of injuries, the silencing afterward—had stripped it all away. Stripped her of the self she'd wanted to become, of her ability to love without fear, without anger, without a sliver of hate—for how much pain that love opened her up to as she tried to protect her daughter, her husband, at the cost of protecting herself.

Evelyn opened her eyes to see Kareela stepping onto the front walkway, turning toward the woods. How many times had she watched her child disappear down that path? Especially during the early lockdowns—when all four of them were trapped in the house. Safe, together, for the first time in years. But trapped, them and the ghosts, the ghosts and all the unspoken words.

Evelyn hadn't wanted Kareela to go. Just like she didn't now, the solitude of the woods the perfect venue for violence, especially when raised tensions had rippled through the town. Via a fake account, Evelyn had stalked Juniper Cove's Facebook group, saw the people who, for the first time it seemed, had become aware of this country's atrocities, claiming they were ready to learn. To be allies. But also the ones whose hatred flared, who proclaimed the sovereignty and inculpability of the white race.

The pandemic was barely two months in when the news came.

Kareela's training, which had at first been put on hold, was being conducted online. A good thing, since they were told not to leave their communities, not to embark on any but the most necessary travel. Kareela, who'd been home for a weekend visit when they'd been notified of the first lockdown, had wanted to go to her apartment, get her stuff, at least, water her plants, but Kingsley pleaded no. "That's the worst spot to be." Fear in his voice. "That's where this virus will get you."

Then, all those weeks later, weeks of enforced isolation, Kareela had been the first to hear about the murder. She'd been scrolling on her phone when a sound escaped her throat that whipped all their heads toward her.

"What?" asked Kingsley.

"Nothing." She stared at the screen, then lowered her phone, her eyes still looking down, as if whatever she'd seen was burned across her vision. Eventually, in the face of the silence, she blinked and wiped her sweatered arm across her lids.

"What is it, me luv?" asked Violet.

"Nothing."

Kingsley shifted over, gesturing to the phone. "Sweetheart, what . . ."

"Another murder." She looked up. "By the police." She stopped. "Trust me. You don't want to know about it. You don't want to see it."

She was right. Evelyn didn't. But Kingsley reached for his tablet. "Dad, don't."

He watched, silent. Evelyn moved over to him. Violet, too. Their breaths held, at first, but they couldn't hold them until the end. Not even close. No one could.

When it finished, Evelyn moved back to her seat in the armchair, her hands shaking with all the hatred. The bullets into her boy. Into Omar, a child in the wrong place at the wrong time. The blades into Ella. And then there was the hand over Evelyn's mouth . . . and elsewhere. The knee on that man's neck. And so many others. So many others.

Violet stayed beside Kingsley on the couch, her hand wrapping around his. Kareela looked out the window, jaw tight, quivering.

In the weeks following the news, following those eight minutes and forty-six seconds, all those allies on social media—not just in her town, but the world over—claimed that this, *this* was what had shocked them into acknowledging the horrors that had been going on for generations. This was the moment for change. As if all the previous deaths weren't enough. As if Antony's wasn't.

The TV stayed on through the day and into the night. Kingsley drinking it in, that all-consuming grief that had started to ease just when Evelyn had sunk so deeply into hers, taking over him again. When the news on TV was about something else, he watched those eight minutes and forty-six seconds on his tablet, as if he could decipher something from it, unravel the past, the hatred that, inadvertently, led to Kingsley losing his life. That led to Evelyn barely knowing her daughter, letting her grow up at arm's length, for fear of what that hatred would do to her girl, that one day it would take her, the same way it took her boy. Evelyn knew if she loved Kareela as she'd loved Antony, with abandon—

each accomplishment, each failure so intertwined with her sense of self they were like her own—she wouldn't survive.

Though that's all she'd been doing: surviving.

"It just like Antony," Kingsley half cried, half yelled when she'd brought him a drink, a few nights before his last, his eyes red-rimmed, his skin sallow and loose on his face, the tablet still in his hand all those weeks later. "The man didn't do nothing. But dey talk about him like he did. Like he nothing but some criminal. Like he deserve it. And that officer, he going to go free. You just watch. He going to go free. Live he life. Like dey all do. Like dey all always do."

Evelyn leaned down, in a way she hadn't in years. She placed a hand against his chin and cheek. She kissed his forehead, handed him a whisky, knowing she shouldn't, and walked away—feeling his pain, his anger, but unable to express it, unable to find a way through this agony, together.

The autopsy said the drink killed Kingsley. Poisoned him. But it was only a symptom, the physical expression of a death that'd been years in the making, then happened all at once. The grief was what really killed him. The lack of power he felt to change anything about his life. Their lives. The anger and pain with no outlet. She knew that ache, felt it daily, but had never had the taste for alcohol.

Today, Evelyn stared at the gap in the trees through which Kareela had vanished. She shifted her head, looking at the opposite window frame, the scratches she'd made in it as a child as she sat listening to the shouts, the sound of flesh on flesh, the silence that followed.

Loving was dangerous. But she loved Kareela. She felt it when she'd heard her yelling on the phone, heard the hurt and pain in her voice— that outburst awakening emotion that had sat dormant in Evelyn for years. She loved her, but was no good for her.

Evelyn turned her gaze back to the woods. She was tired—the slow inhale and exhale of breath a constant effort—a tiredness she imagined her mother felt. A tiredness that made her empathize with why Kingsley had given in, drank till it killed him—given up on the effort, the burden of love. She'd thought about it, so many times. Had tried once: a bottle of pills that she'd thrown up minutes later, her fingers in her throat, though she couldn't have explained why.

Kareela, maybe.

Evelyn stood. She kept her gaze on the trail, hoping to see her daughter's face, to tell her . . . she didn't know what. That she was sorry? That she'd wasted her life because of all that fear and hatred and pain? That she was weak and wished she'd been stronger, wished she'd been the mother Kareela deserved? That the best thing, now that Kingsley was gone and Violet would be taken care of—whether in a home or by Kareela—was for Evelyn to go?

To stop bringing her girl down with all her damage.

To find a place to live out her days, distanced from her fear, like in those early days in Jamaica. Somewhere no one would know her or her family—the one she'd been given or the one she'd chosen. Some place where maybe, just maybe, she could feel safe and hope that, somehow, her daughter would be safe, too—from her, at least.

And then Kareela appeared, running out of the trailhead and onto the road, morphing before Evelyn's vision, flashes of her at fourteen, at ten, at six. Then back again, a twenty-four-year-old woman—strong and beautiful—who, despite every reason why she shouldn't, was thriving.

Evelyn opened her door and travelled down the stairs, ready to tell Kareela she was sorry, that she wished she'd done better, that she made mistakes.

Leaving wouldn't be a mistake. Leaving would be the first right thing she'd done in years.

Kareela

I reach the bottom step after leaving my mother's room, my feet warm from where the sun hits the wood. I look to the living room where Gran still sits, her gaze on the yard. If I were to sit beside her, settle my hand on hers, the skin would be soft, smooth, like fine paper. But I don't. I can't.

I step through the side door, the sun bright and full, as if it's trying to offer comfort. My steps take me down the long gravel drive and onto the rail trail up the road.

It's just as I pass into the woods that I run, pushing my body until I can't anymore, until my scream reverberates through the trees, sending a flurry of activity from the birds and squirrels. I stop, breath heavy, heart pounding, then pick up a fist-sized rock and launch it, the impact against a nearby stump not nearly a satisfying-enough thunk. I throw another and another, then collapse to my knees, everything I've learned in the past hour crashing upon me.

My hands on my head, I sink, wishing Gran hadn't told me her part in it. Gran—my salvation, my comfort, my only source of uncompli-cated love—to have done this.

I breathe. In. Out. In. The memories flashing like bursts of light in a darkened room. Gran. Her touch, her smile, her listening ear. Gran, who loved me when my parents forgot how.

When she told my mom to keep silent, washed away the evidence of the attack, she couldn't have known what she was doing. How it would wash away my mother, who had come here hopeful, trying to create a second chance for all of us.

If not for this festering secret, if she'd had help to work through the attack and all it brought, if she'd had the resolution of knowing the man was, at last, behind bars, maybe that second chance would have happened.

Maybe my father's love, his desire to help his wife, if he'd known the reason she needed help, would have snapped him out of his own catatonic grief for good.

Maybe he would be here now.

Another yell erupts, shattering through me—for how broken we all became. My father. My mother. Me. So broken and lost in our pain, our grief, our history, that we lost each other—the one thing that may have saved us.

I lift my head to the sky, then sink to let it fall to my knees, thinking of my family. Not just my grandmother, my father, mother, brother, me, but all the people who came before, who shaped us.

Trying and failing. Trying, and then no longer being able to.

Cotton candy clouds drift across the expanse above me, guiding my breath to slow, my shoulders to fall. All of these ancestors, doing the best they could with what they knew and had—what strength, what fear, what crippling pain.

The way my Gran did. Because she couldn't have meant for any of this to happen.

I stand, brush off my pants, place my hand on my abdomen, see again that small form on the ultrasound screen—so innocent, so fresh.

So real. Hear, again, that frantic beat, declaring life, fighting for it with every multiplying cell, despite my uncertainty, my inability to commit.

Blood rushes through that life. The blood of my mother, my father, Gran—all the ones before and now gone, who, in their own ways, have tried to protect me. Who, in their own ways, have loved me.

And suddenly, it's clear: that's what matters. That's what life is about. Love. Not hiding from pain, anger, grief. Not trying to protect yourself from all the shit this world has to offer. But love.

In so many ways, my parents, my gran, have done life wrong. Succumbing to the pain, letting fear be their guide, keep them silent. I've done it wrong. But I won't anymore. Not like those two women back at the house, who made mistakes, passing on a love that's fractured, battered, and bruised. Those women I came from—through—the way my child will come through me.

I turn back, the revelation so clear, despite my fear; I am having this baby. Thomas was right. It doesn't matter if this wasn't the plan. It doesn't matter if I'm not ready, if this child will tie me to a man I'm not sure I want to be tied to: If I truly didn't want this baby, I would have ended the pregnancy weeks ago.

So, I'll hold her . . . or him. And, unlike my parents before me, I'll tell our stories. Let this child make sense of them as best she can. I'll lay it all out—the good, the messy, the horrible, my whole damn life, and theirs—as much as I know of it. Everything we've been trying so hard to forget when, most likely, what we needed was to remember.

My feet fall, one in front of the other, faster, faster, down the path, the driveway, until I burst through the door, breathless.

My mother and Gran sit across from each other, my gran's eyes wet, my mother's hands clasped in her lap, working nervously. Their heads turn as I open my mouth. "Gran, I'm taking you in. You're not going to some home." Gran's eyes crinkle, the moisture making them glisten. "And Mom . . . leave this town, this house. But why not come to Halifax? Find a job. An apartment."

My mother's features tighten, just slightly, but she makes no other movement.

"It would be nice"—a smile builds in me, starting deep down and rising—"if you were near your grandchild. Got to know her . . . or him." I place a hand on my abdomen. "Let her"—*us*, I think—"get to know you."

Gran pushes to standing with more energy than I've seen in years. "Oh, KeeKee? For truth?" She crosses the distance between us, cups my face in her hands. "This is wonderful." She pulls me close, and I sink into her arms, realizing how much I've missed her touch, how incredible it will be to see her every day rather than a few times a year.

As Gran releases me, I glance over her shoulder at my mother, still sitting, a hand over her mouth. She rises slowly and stands about six feet from me—as if it's a habit she's been unable to break from the years it was required. "A baby?"

I step from Gran, so we make an isosceles triangle in the room, Gran and I still close enough to touch, my mother the far point. I nod.

"It's Thomas's?"

My chest constricts. "Of course."

She smiles, and a glimmer of that essential thing that's seemed missing for so many years—had been stolen, perhaps—seems back.

"It's Thomas's, but . . ."

"But you don't know if you want him. Kareela." She steps forward. "Hold on to him with all you've got. He'll give you a good life. Safe. Sta—"

"I'll give myself a good life, Mom. Don't worry about that." The realization from the woods still coursing through me, I step closer and she stiffens. "But it'd be nice if you were around. If we could get to know each other better. Make up for lost time. Even if you don't report the . . . what happened, I'd love to see you get help. Support. And I could be part of that." I pause, meet her gaze. "I want you in our life."

Mom's lips quiver. She shakes her head, crosses the space between us, and takes my hand in both of hers. "Congratulations, Kareela. I hope everything works out for you." She pulls her hands away and looks at her watch, her arm trembling. "I have a board meeting. I haven't given my notice yet, but I will tonight. And I'll list the house soon. You'll need to find a new place—more room. I'll do my best to help. Financially. But you should get started on that. On looking."

She nods, then backs out of the room, gripping her hand to still the trembling.

"Your ma been through a lot." Gran steps to me. "So, nuh let her dampen yuh." She places her palm on my belly. "Dis is gud, baby girl. Dis is gud news!"

I nod, smile, a genuine smile, despite the hurt from my mother's apathy, which maybe isn't apathy after all, and meet Gran's gaze. There's a lot to figure out. A lot of hard to come. But she's right. This *is* good.

Evelyn

Evelyn released Kareela's hand. At hearing her daughter's news, she'd wanted to wrap her arms around her, the way Violet had. To hold on tight, instead of pushing her away. But for years now, it felt as if she were being held together by nothing stronger than faint wisps of a spider's thread. That if she let herself truly connect to her daughter, when it was time to step away, she'd fall completely apart.

So she backed away, the news hitting her like a mallet to the chest. A baby. A new life.

Her daughter was thinking of becoming a single mother, with an elderly woman in her care. And Evelyn, who after all these years had thought she was finally free, thought she could leave without guilt—no one to care for but herself—was planning to abandon her.

A baby. Evelyn couldn't process what this meant. Not now. "I have a board meeting," she said. "I'll do my best to help financially."

She walked toward the side door, where her purse hung on one of the old wooden hooks her father had made. She stared at it. She was about to leave this house, this town, this life, but Kareela had asked her to stay. Evelyn slung the bag over her shoulder and stepped out the door, onto the gravel drive.

"Mom?"

She turned. Kareela stood, hands crossed in front of her, face so wide and open and expectant.

"Mom, are you happy for me?"

Evelyn bit her inner lip—happy, yes, but terrified. For Kareela. For herself. "You want this baby? Knowing the way it will change your life? Knowing what the world is like, and . . . doing it on your own?"

Kareela stood, her face still as a statue. "I won't be on my own," she said at last. "Thomas will help. Probably more than I want." She chuckled. "He wanted this baby all along."

"But you didn't."

Evelyn saw the slight convulsion of her daughter's throat as she swallowed. "I wasn't sure."

Evelyn registered surprise at the smile she felt spread across her face as she stared at her girl—the six-year-old version, ten, fourteen, today. The way Kareela's expression said, *I am now.*

"I'm happy for you." Despite the fear.

Kareela's face lit.

"And all of Gran's costs," said Evelyn, "if you're sure that's what you want, will be covered. Help with a bigger place, too. With some home care, if she ever needs it. You won't have to worry about that." Evelyn hesitated, her hands against her middle—uncertain, now, if she should leave. If she wanted to, after her daughter's request, after the news of this child. "Well. . ." She gestured to the car, fighting the urge to cross the distance between them, take Kareela in her arms the way she should have upstairs. To stay, even though she'd convinced herself that if she wanted to be any good to her daughter, the best thing to do was leave. "I better . . ."

"Go." Kareela waved her off.

Evelyn sat behind the wheel. She turned the ignition. Her baby, a mother. She looked back at her daughter, tempted still, to get out of the car, run, take her in her arms the way she used to. But she wasn't ready yet. She was too raw. Too broken. Too ashamed. She hoped she would be ready. One day. She slowed the car over the gravel drive.

The night that had haunted and sullied every moment was out in the open. Her daughter knew, and that knowing, surprisingly, was a relief. It reminded Evelyn she'd been someone different once. Someone who laughed and hoped and planned for the future. Who had relationships that meant something.

For the first time in years, she wanted to become that person again. Or someone close to it. Evelyn put her foot on the brake, thinking of Antony as a baby, of Kareela, of the joy she was certain she would feel if she held her grandbaby in her arms. She had been broken. But for a baby—for her baby—maybe she could put herself back together again.

She put the car into reverse, eased it back up the drive, then stepped out to see Kareela still standing at the door, watching her. "That night. . ." Evelyn swallowed. She blew out a long stream of air, then continued. "It broke me. I was trying so hard. Had been trying so hard my whole life. Despite my father. My mother. Ella. Antony. Those boys in the schoolyard and all the years of so much hate. Of trying to ignore it, be above it . . ." She shook her head. "I don't know, live, despite it. Then after that night, it was just too much. It was too terrifying to love. I mean, I did. I do love you. But . . . it broke me, Kareela. They broke me." A shiver of revulsion ran through her as she recalled all the times she'd seen the men in town, seen Courtney, and the small smile and nod he always gave—as if he owned her. As if he'd won. "And keeping silent about it, just letting it all fester inside with no way out, I couldn't see a way to put myself back together again. After a time, I couldn't even care enough to want to."

Evelyn stopped, her fists clenched to dull the shaking. "So, I don't know what more to say, except that I don't regret you. I regret the hate, the fact that I brought you into a world that can be as awful as this one. But not you. You, I love. Even though I've not known how to show it, been too afraid of letting myself feel it the way I used to."

Kareela stood, brow furrowed, biting her lower lip. She gave a slight nod, as something like a whisper escaped her closed lips.

Evelyn nodded back. "You, I love."

She stepped into the car, eased down the driveway, and pulled onto the road. Not five minutes away from the house, she pulled over and closed her eyes, thinking of the last time she'd been truly happy. Of the people who brought her that joy. Her mother. Kingsley. Her children. And her one real friend, who she'd pushed out of her life—pride and anger and fear making her do it.

Evelyn pulled out her phone, not Antony's, which she'd had to retire years ago. And the act of reaching for it—expecting Antony's and being reminded that this last piece of him was gone—sent a tremor of pain so intense, so fresh, it was like she was back in that moment the officer stood at the door, speaking the words that would alter all their lives forever.

She took several breaths, not letting the shock of emotion steal her resolve, and dialed a number she still remembered after all these years, hoping as it rang.

"Hello."

"Hi, uh . . ."

"Hello?" The voice so much the same, yet different.

"Dani? It's Evelyn."

"Ev . . . Jackson?"

"Yes. I . . . well . . . I heard about Charles. I'm sorry."

"I heard about Kingsley."

Silence.

"I just . . ." Evelyn closed her eyes, regret at all the lost years rushing through her. "I miss you. I miss who I was when you were my friend."

"Oh, Evie." That laugh, the one Evelyn didn't know until this moment just how much she'd yearned for. "I miss you, too. I miss us, and was hoping you'd call."

Evelyn stared at the field, stretching as far as the eye could see, wishing she'd made this call years ago: the night that second officer showed up at her door, the night she realized for herself the true reason Charles, and Dani, had refused to stand beside her. "I'm going to do some travelling."

"Oh?"

"I thought maybe I could come see you. Or that we could go somewhere together?"

"Oh!"

Evelyn hesitated. "I have Kingsley's ashes. I didn't know what to do with them. But he always wanted to go home." Evelyn straightened as the idea came to her. She'd thought she could never return without Antony, but, she realized, he would have wanted her to. Thoughts of the good times—hot sun, cool breezes, and friends—filled her mind, and she knew that's what she'd do, whether or not Dani joined. Not find some place to wait to die, as she'd thought weeks ago, when formulating the decision to put Violet in a home and flee somewhere, but go back to the last place she'd felt truly safe. See their old house, their old friends—the ones who were still left—and, hopefully, remind herself how to live.

"If you wanted to come," said Evelyn, "I could show you where he's from. Where we were from."

"I always said I wanted to go to Jamaica. That one day, you had to show me around."

Evelyn laughed, the sound and feeling so foreign it startled her. "You did say that. And I promised I would." Evelyn's smile grew as a flock of starlings rose out of the field, hundreds of them soaring across the sky. "Also, I'm going to be a grandmother."

"You don't say." Evelyn could almost see Dani shaking her head, the way she did. "You'll love it. I have two."

"Two!"

"Twins. They're better than your own kids. You get to send them home." Another laugh. "It's good to hear from you." Dani's voice sounded wistful, yet full of joy. "So many times I picked up the phone to call, but I wasn't sure . . ."

"Me too." Evelyn paused. "It's in the past." For the first time, she believed it, hoped that not just that, but so many hurts she'd held on to, let weaken her, cripple her, steal the things in life she most wanted, would one day be in the past, too. "I haven't done well," she said. "In life. But I want to do better. I think I need help."

"Travel and therapy," said Dani. "Not just friendship therapy. I have an incredible psychologist I can get you in touch with."

"A psychologist?"

"Of course. You know how nutty I am."

"I tried that once." Evelyn shook her head, despite Dani not being able to see. "Well, not a psychologist, exactly. A support group. Talk therapy. Not for me."

Dani gave a half laugh. "What? So you tried something kind of like counselling once, and you're going to write off every psychologist on the planet?" She paused. "It was hard, losing Charles just after losing both of my parents. And those sessions . . ." Evelyn imagined Dani was shaking her head, even though Evelyn couldn't see it. "Don't knock it till you try it."

"Huh . . ." Evelyn looked to her hands. She'd always wondered if maybe she should go back to a group—especially after taking that bottle of pills. Or something different. Something like what Dani was talking about.

"The best thing," said Dani, "is she does virtual care. The pandemic did bring some good changes—no more sitting awkwardly on a couch."

Evelyn glanced at the car's dash. Maybe she'd try; call up the woman who'd helped Dani, see if she could help her, too. She couldn't make things worse.

Evelyn would do it. She would call the therapist. Travel to Jamaica. Maybe other places, too, and then, hopefully, come back—for Kareela. For her grandchild. And for Antony. For who he would have wanted her to be. How he'd want her to continue on, embrace this reason to live: new life. And embrace the life that had been there all along, but that Evelyn had failed to see.

"I should get going." Evelyn kept her gaze on the field, seemingly empty again, but holding so much possibility. "I'm on my way to a work meeting. About to give my notice, actually."

"You don't say."

Evelyn could almost see Dani's smile, the crease at the side of each eye. Would her hair be grey? Or dyed the same red that had always matched her firecracker spirit.

"I'm glad you called, Mrs. Jackson."

A warmth flowed over Evelyn. "Me too."

Kareela

HALIFAX

The following weeks pass in a blur. By the time my pregnancy is nearing the end of the second trimester, the old family house has been sold, I've found a two-bedroom apartment in a house less than a ten-minute walk from my old place, where Thomas still lives, and Gran is settled in the room next to mine.

I overcame my fears and spoke at the rally, talking about how Antony's death shaped and altered our family, defined us. How it still does. Most importantly, I told the story of that day. Not the one in the officers' reports, or what the news relayed. But the true story. From the people who were there. Who saw. I told them who my brother was, who he could have been. Who our family was, too.

It's hard not to sink into wondering what would have happened if I'd taken this path sooner: if I'd aligned with my father's burst of passion, would it have brought him out of his despair? Brought us together? Would he be here still, speaking beside me?

But wondering won't help. So I told that story, too, how my father was also a victim of those officers' crimes, of the media's heartless and inaccurate reporting, how our whole family was, and how it scarred us in ways that will never fully heal.

A few days after, I received a call from Deja, who told me her part of the story: what I already knew from the file and intimacies she hadn't shared there. Memories of a day I didn't recall until her words brought back flashes: the three of us taking the ferry to Centre Island, riding all the rides I was tall enough for, eating cotton candy and funnel cakes, and how Antony had seemed so happy. So proud to be my brother.

She still thinks of him regularly, all these years later. Like me, she imagines who he would have been, the life he could have lived.

I've turned down all requests for further interviews. Antony's story is out there. Our story. It exists. And that's enough. I'll continue to work with the movement—because it's work someone needs to do—but I don't want to be their spokesperson, the contact the media call every time another Black person is beaten or killed. Our story exists. And it's time for me to exist now, outside of that history.

I called my mom before the rally. She asked me not to do it, not to endanger myself. When I told her I had to, despite my promise, that it was the right thing for me: to make some sense of all that had happened, to try, at least, for some semblance of good to come out of it—she stopped. She didn't want me to. She thought I shouldn't, but, "It's your life," she said, "so do what you have to do."

I tried to keep her on the line, to figure out where she was, what she was doing. "Living," was all she would say, "trying to remember where I came from. Who I was. And trying to get better."

She ended the call by reminding me of her love. And this time, with words, I reminded her of mine, too.

A delivery arrived from her today: two large bins. As I open the first one, a scent I haven't smelled in over a decade drifts out, along with a memory that had all but been forgotten—sitting in our Toronto home, my rage at having to move momentarily tempered by a whisper of Antony.

I hold the small sleeper in my arms, my own child somersaulting within me, and the tenderness in my mother's voice as she folded my baby clothes, her hands delicate and slow and full of a love that I'd barely taken the time to register, comes back to me. The depth of it hits me in a way I've never been able to appreciate before—what she lost, how it would have wrecked her. This little life inside of me, who, at first, I wasn't even sure I wanted, now means so much I'd rip the world apart to keep her safe. And I haven't even met her yet. To have held her, raised her, loved her for twenty-three years, and then . . .

Holding back tears, I open the second box to see a small notecard sitting atop a bright swathe of neatly folded fabric. I lift the notecard, instantly recognizing my mother's small and distinct script.

I used this wrap to carry both of my babies and thought you should have it. I'm sure Violet could show you how to use it, but wait for me? I'll be back in time to teach you. If you'll let me.

The doorbell sounds and I wipe my eyes, then rise from my seat at the kitchen table. Thomas stands on the stoop, a toolbox in one hand, a bag, which I'm sure is full of food, in the other. His smile is tight. But he's smiling, which is progress from those first tense interactions after the five-hour conversation we had when I returned to tell him I was keeping the baby but letting go of us: romantically, at least.

He sets the food on the counter, then heads to my bedroom where the disassembled crib we'd gotten from one of his cousins lies in a pile against the wall. He tried to convince me to stay together—at least for the baby—get a three-bedroom apartment, so he could be there to help me through the nights, through those initial months of sleeplessness and trying to adjust. And then, he said, once the baby was older, he'd leave if I wanted, give his room to her. It made sense. It would be the practical thing to do—but life can't be about practicality. And I love him too much to give him false hope—that the hurts we've caused would disappear, that we could ever be more than co-parents again.

I follow him down the hall, watch as he assembles the crib. If we'd met at another time—a year from now, three, maybe we could have worked. But Thomas doesn't even know who I am, only the person I falsely showed myself to be. I don't quite know who I am, but am certain I need to figure that out on my own.

In the first news report, and in the ones following, I saw my name and the descriptor beside it: Kareela Jackson, a mixed-race woman. The first time I'd ever seen those words written in black and white—that compound—describing me.

For the last decade, I've been defined as Black, or Black . . . but not quite, as if the white in me was an absence of what should have been but wasn't, as if I held on my shoulders the weighted responsibility of trying to make sense of it all.

I stared at those words, smoothing my finger over the letters—*mixed-race*—and saw the freedom to let go of the need to define myself by one identity over another, one race.

I'm not a Black woman, exactly, not a white one, certainly. Both and neither. Like a bridge, one foot planted on each side. Able to exist in both worlds—in some capacity, at least—cross lines that have no need of even being there. Be who I am, regardless. And my daughter, if I raise her that way, will be able to do the same thing.

"Oh, look at dis!" Gran's voice sounds from the kitchen. "What a baker dis man is!"

She strides—as much as she still can—down the hall and into the room. "Gud to know dis girl chile won't be eatin only food off de shelf."

"Definitely not, Mrs. Jackson!" Thomas stands, smiling at me, at Gran, doing his best to mask the pain behind his eyes. "We'll take good care of her."

"Violet, I tell yuh. Violet."

Thomas nods, then meets my gaze, and a part of me does wish I had met him a year from now. Two. That I could introduce him to the self I'm starting to discover, see if he loves her.

But who knows, that person may not have loved him.

Thomas returns to the crib, adjusting a few final lug nuts, then closes and lifts his toolbox. "Well, I guess I should take off. See you at the ultrasound."

We've had discussions about boundaries. About giving each other distance, and when the baby comes, how we'll split time, share holidays. That things may have to change when each of us finds other people to share our lives with—a topic he doesn't like to talk about, not wanting this family to be what he sees as a broken one.

And that, I tell him, is what he's got all wrong. Not broken, but multi-faceted—with more histories to learn and understand, more cultures and ways of being to embrace.

"No." I shake my head. "Stay and eat."

He grins, and doesn't say no.

After we've eaten and cleaned up, Thomas washing and me drying, I shut the door behind him and sit with Gran. In the past weeks, she's told me about Femi and Ella and Chevelle. About my father—how he was taken, how, although she wasn't able to help him as much as she hoped, she's so thankful she had those extra years with him, could care for him again. Care for me when he couldn't.

"If there be one thing me got right," she says now, "it be to carry on. Because life, no matter what form it in, no matter de pains tacked onto it, means something." She places her paper-frail hand on my cheek, cups it. "We here for a reason, baby girl. We here until we not. And with de life me got left, me gonna hold dat great-grandbaby, and if me can't see her, me gonna smell her, and feel her. Smooth me fingers over her cheeks, her lips, her palm.

"Me gonna get up in de morning and keep on getting up, just like me always have, even if me no longer see the sun, 'cause the sun still rises."

She stops, and in her eyes I see the memories, the losses: her children, and all the people who came before.

"As long as yuh alive," she says, "in every bad, if yuh wait, if yuh look, eventually yuh see a good. A good that wouldn't have happened if not for the bad. Some lesson, some joy, some somet'ing. It doesn't mean yuh happy de bad t'ing happened, but yuh happy for de good t'ing. Yuh hold on to dat. Yuh be thankful. Holding de good."

It's what my mother never realized, but, I hope, is starting to discover. It's what Gran, clearly, has done, what she had to do, after what she lost: her babies, and other things, too. Things she's barely brushed the surface of, but that I sense, lingering in her pauses, the way she skips through certain aspects of her personal history, what she alluded to the day the secrets started unravelling, and in the advice she gave my mother that long-ago night.

She lowers her hand to mine, squeezes, smiling. "This be de good I have now. You. Dat baby to come. And you, Kareela. Yuh a good t'ing. Yuh enough."

Moisture builds behind my eyes as I exhale, raise her hand back to the side of my face, and lean against our joined flesh.

I continue to ask her questions about the past. Not that the past on its own can give us answers. We've got to carve those out for ourselves, or at least that's what I think . . . what I hope. What I'm trying to do.

Author's Note

Dear reader,

As referenced in the dedication, the initial inklings of this story came from wondering how my family's story may have been different with a matriarch to guide them through their lives in Jamaica, and then after moving to Toronto and eventually Atlantic Canada. For the most part, the similarities end there. This is a work of fiction, and although here and there events or emotional experiences are pulled from the real world, each character is a complete work of fiction.

However, the pain that they experience, the struggle, the expectations, the pressure to fit into a society that too often doesn't want them, and sometimes attacks them, is real, and experienced by millions, as is the lack of belonging, confusion, and pulling of loyalties experienced by many biracial people. To learn more about the Black and biracial experience, please see the selected list (on page 383) of some of the resources I used to research this novel.

If you've enjoyed this novel, if it made you think, or see aspects of the world in ways you hadn't before, please take the time to leave a rating and review on your favourite retailer's website and on

Goodreads. Ratings and reviews are key to an author's success and, even more importantly, help potential readers decide whether a book may be for them!

I love building relationships with my readers, so if you'd like to keep in touch, please sign up for my newsletter at charlenecarr.com. When you do, you'll receive a free e-novella about a woman determined to make her most precious dream come true.

If social media is more your thing, you can find me on Facebook and Instagram, but Instagram is where I spend most of my time.

Thank you, and keep reading!

All my best,
Charlene

Acknowledgements

There are so many people to thank, and I'm sure I'll miss some, but here goes!

A huge thank-you to my wonderful agent, Hayley Steed. This would have been an incredibly different book without her: in my first imaginings of the story, Kareela didn't even exist, and it was Hayley who suggested I find a way to bring the story to the present day, which resulted in the birth of Kareela! Thanks, also, to her assistant Elinor Davies and the team at Madeleine Milburn Literacy Agency. To my Canadian editor, Iris Tupholme, who, from the outlining stage, helped to bring out the best in this story, and to my editors Julia McDowell, Jennifer Edgecombe, and Kate Roddy, whose insight and wisdom, along with Iris's, helped to make this story what it is. To the production, design, publicity, and sales and marketing teams at HarperCollins Canada, Mountain Leopard Press, and Sourcebooks Landmark, there are so many names I could list, but if I did, I'm sure there'd be even more I missed, so instead a huge thank-you to everyone for all of your wonderful work in getting this story into readers' hands!

To all of the booksellers and librarians who helped get *Hold My Girl* into readers' hands and who I'm sure will champion *We Rip the World Apart* in the same way, thank you. Your support means so much. And to the readers and Bookstagrammers who've posted about my books on social media, left reviews, shared them with your friends, and provided so much encouragement, I can't say thank you enough. You're who I do this for.

To Enrique Ferreol, program officer for Arts Nova Scotia, thank you for your support, guidance, and encouragement. And to Arts Nova Scotia and Canada Council for the Arts, I am so grateful for not only the financial support to write and revise this story, but for your belief that this was a story worth telling.

To the kind police officer who took time out of her day to research what violation could have brought Antony into a station without actually having him arrested, I'm leaving you nameless, but so appreciate your help.

To my mother, who sent me pages and pages of answers to questions about my family's time in Jamaica and their early years in Toronto (before I came on the scene), to my father, who answered many questions, too, and to my brother, Sheldon, who allowed me to interview him about what it was like growing up biracial and visibly Black in Toronto in the eighties and early nineties, I am so grateful. Thanks, also, to my Nesbitt cousins, for their insights on Jamaican dialect and the different ways it presents itself depending on age, location, and time away from the island.

To the Black writers who came before me, providing insight, encouragement, and a place to stand from—words aren't enough to express my gratitude. And to Jeff Cooper, creator of the Mixd Project, whose interviews with biracial people helped me realize that I hadn't missed the mark with Kareela's struggles with her biracial identity, and that the experiences, emotions, and confusion I've lived with but never discussed until recent years were not unique. Tears flowed as I listened to those interviews and felt a connection I didn't know how much I needed. It is my hope that Kareela provides that same experience for my biracial readers, and Jeff, your project makes me think it will.

Finally, thank you to my daughter, for being so understanding of the time this book took away from my ability to play, and to my husband, who is so supportive of my work and, when I'm in the zone or need to take days away to focus, does far more than his fair share of running our household.

The author gratefully acknowledges the support of Arts Nova Scotia and the Canada Council for the Arts.

Additional Resources

Chariandy, David. *I've Been Meaning to Tell You: A Letter to My Daughter.* McClelland & Stewart, 2018.

Cooper, Jeff. The Mixd Project: A Collection of Photographs and Narratives of Black Folks of Mixed Race. themixdproject.com.

Diverlus, Rodney, Sandy Hudson, and Syrus Marcus Ware (eds). *Until We Are Free: Reflections on Black Lives Matter in Canada.* University of Regina Press, 2020.

Hill, Lawrence. *Black Berry, Sweet Juice: On Being Black and White in Canada.* HarperCollins Canada, 2002.

Martis, Eternity. *They Said This Would Be Fun: Race, Campus Life, and Growing Up.* McClelland & Stewart, 2020.

Maynard, Robin. *Policing Black Lives: State Violence in Canada from Slavery to the Present.* Fernwood Publishing, 2017.

McWatt, Tessa. *Shame On Me: An Anatomy of Race and Belonging.* Penguin Random House Canada, 2019.

Walcott, Rinaldo, and Idil Abdillahi. *BlackLife: Post-BLM and the Struggle for Freedom.* ARP Books (Arbeiter Ring Publishing), 2019.

Williams, Ian. *Disorientation: Being Black in the World.* Penguin Random House Canada, 2021.

We Rip the World Apart
DISCUSSION QUESTIONS

Some are serious, some are lighter; pick and choose the ones you feel best suit your group. If you're interested in having Charlene drop by for a virtual (or possibly in-person) visit to your book club, send her a message at contact@charlenecarr.com and she'll do her best to arrange a visit.

** SPOILER ALERT **

Do not read through these questions until
AFTER you've read the book!

1. Did this novel make you think differently about the world in any way? If so, how?

2. Do you feel there should have been a public investigation into Antony's shooting? If you were on the jury for a similar case, do you think you would find the police officers guilty? Why or why not?

3. How could Kingsley have been more supportive in the aftermath of Antony's death? Do you agree with his view that Evelyn shouldn't try to fight the police force/city for justice? Why or why not?

4. Why do you think it was Evelyn and not Kingsley who wanted to fight for justice regarding Antony's death?

5. Following Antony's murder, Kareela is very passive about her emotions and seems hesitant to express her feelings to her parents. How do you feel this behaviour affects (or doesn't affect) her relationships and life choices over time?

6. What do you think of Kareela's hesitancy about "tying" herself to a white man while she is trying to become a part of the Black community? Did her fears make sense to you? How do you think her life would (or wouldn't) change if she'd stayed with Thomas?

7. Did you think it was appropriate for Carson to ask Kareela to share her family's personal story at the rally? Why or why not?

8. What did you think of Violet's decision to convince Evelyn not to report the attack to the police? If you think that decision made sense for the family, would you have liked to see Violet handle things between herself and Evelyn any differently?

9. Why do you think it took Kareela so long to realize that something else was behind Evelyn's sudden pulling away from her in her teen years? When Kareela started to realize it, why do you think she didn't really want to know the reason?

10. For you, what were the biggest factors in Kareela's decision to keep the baby? Why or how do you feel the revelations from her mother and grandmother led to this decision?

11. What did you think of Evelyn's decision to return to Jamaica with Dani and Kingsley's ashes instead of offering to take Kareela and Violet? Do you think this was selfish, or was it necessary for Evelyn's personal healing process?

12. When you think back on the novel, which scene stands out the most in your mind? Why?

13. If the novel were made into a TV show or movie, who would you like to see cast as the main characters?

14. How do you interpret the title *We Rip the World Apart*? What does it mean to you? What do you think it means to the author?

15. As you read the final lines of the book, what struck you most about the story and how did you feel?

CHARLENE CARR spent much of her childhood creating elaborate, multi-faceted storylines for her dolls and reading under the blankets with a flashlight when she was supposed to be asleep. A bit of a nomad, she's lived in four countries and seven Canadian provinces. After working an array of mostly writing related jobs, she decided the time had come to focus exclusively on her true love – novel writing. She lives in Nova Scotia with her husband and daughter. *We Rip the World Apart* is her eleventh novel.